SPOTSWOOD

Bruce I. Brodkin

Disclaimer

"This book is a work of fiction. Names, characters, businesses, organizations, places, events, and incidences either are the product of the author's imagination or are used fictitiously. Any resemblance to actual persons, living or deceased, events, or locales are totally coincidental. The author did grow up in Millburn, N.J. and went to summer camp in Northwestern N.J., but the plot of the book is completely fictional and was not intended to offend anyone. "I have only fond memories of my town, my friends, my family, and my camp."

Copyright © 2014 Bruce I. Brodkin
All rights reserved.

ISBN: 1499309414
ISBN 13: 9781499309416
Library of Congress Control Number: 2014908224
CreateSpace Independent Publishing Platform
North Charleston, South Carolina

Acknowledgments

I would like to thank my family, in particular my wife, Kathleen, who offered encouragement, proof-reading, and the motivation to follow my dream of writing a novel and having it published. To my step-daughters, Kendra George, who helped to finalize my manuscript for publishing, and Karen Tatro, who graciously typed my manuscript, and to my son, David, who patiently read and edited the material, I give my whole-hearted thanks. To the nurses and staff members at Capital Health System in Trenton N.J., I give thanks for their support and opinions. To the Fairview Lake YMCA Camps, celebrating their 100 year anniversary in 2015, I offer my gratitude for the many wonderful summers I spent there; they helped shape my future.

Lastly, I want to thank my friend and colleague, Sivan Veksler, for the hours he spent in an effort to make this book a success. He developed strategies to get the book published and marketed through www.createspace.com and taught me computer skills along the way. For this I will always be grateful.

Prologue

Summer 1920

The rain was coming down in torrents. It had been raining off and on for several days, and now the ground was so soggy that his boots sank almost a foot into the mud. It was a Herculean task that required all his strength just to lift his feet, much less drag the body.

He had readied the shallow grave days before, and now his efforts would be rewarded. The body was covered with mud, yet the wet earth could not conceal the horror of her death. Her face had been mutilated and her skull crushed. The eye socket on the left side had been shattered, with the eye protruding, creating a macabre mask. The right side of the skull had been severely fractured and was covered with mud, matted hair, and blood.

Tugging at her, he remembered the mocking way she had made fun of him, calling him "fat boy." Of course most of what he remembered was just his perverted imagination, but it made it easier for him to kill her, crushing her skull with a shovel like stepping on a bug.

At the end of the lake in the Kittatinny Mountains in northwestern New Jersey, he buried ten-year-old Lilly Miller, hopefully never to be found.

***

The rain had stopped hours before, but Lilly had not come home and it was time for dinner. Worried, her father and older brother went out looking for her. After searching for an hour with no results, Sam Miller and his son George started to become concerned. It would be dark in a few hours, and this was not like Lilly. Their overwhelming fear was the lake, although Lilly was a good swimmer for her age.

Sam and George went back to their lakeside house, hoping that Rose Miller would have news that her daughter had returned. Unfortunately Lilly had not returned and the mood of the family turned to fear. Sam grabbed his hat and ran to his motorcar in the gravel drive.

"I have to get the police. It's not like Lilly to just disappear. I'm going to Stillwater for help."

Rose and her two other children, George and Ruth, were fearful that sweet Lilly might have drowned.

"Why did I let her go out alone in the rain?" wailed Rose.

"Mom, Lilly went near the lake all the time. No one worried about her," said George.

"I know something bad has happened. I can feel it," said Rose.

The police arrived in less than an hour, but by then it was almost dark. They did what they could by candlelight and torches, but turned up nothing.

By the morning, they had dozens of local and state police, search dogs, and volunteer divers. They combed the woods and searched the lake while Rose and Sam Miller, out of their minds with fear, clutched to the faint flicker of hope that Lilly may still be alive.

After five days, the search was called to a halt. She had simply disappeared and was assumed drowned. There were some who feared the worst and thought that she had been abducted and probably murdered. The authorities had a different theory and declared on day six that Lilly Miller had most likely drowned and that her body was caught in submerged trees and brush so prevalent at this end of the lake. The lake was muddy and deep, and there was a limit to what divers could see. Besides, her rowboat and rain slicker were found by the shore.

Rose and Sam Miller were in a state of shock and could barely function. A doctor was called, and he gave Rose a sedative and then sat with Sam and the two children.

"Mr. Miller, what can we do to help you and your family get through this tragedy?"

"Doctor, there is nothing you or anyone can do or say that will lift this heaviness from my heart or stop the tears from flowing. I will take my wife and family back home and we will make arrangements for a service for Lilly. My rabbi will give me guidance."

"Isn't there something, anything that will help? I'm a healer, sir, and I wish to be of some use."

"You're a kind man, and I'm sure an excellent and caring physician, but what our family needs can only come from God."

In the morning what remained of the Miller family boarded up their summerhouse and loaded the car with suitcases readying for the long trip to Brooklyn. Sam, a successful haberdasher, had purchased the property as a summer retreat in 1918. It was a two-day trip by motorcar from New York City, but the family spent the entire summer there away from the heat of the city. They had enjoyed the warm days by the lake and the cool nights on the porch. Now it had all changed.

The boarded-up house would be put up for sale by a local realtor, and the Millers would never return to Lake Spotswood. Life would go on, but healing would take time and would never be complete.

Of course, all this despair could not have mattered to the gawky, obese teen who had watched the frantic search for Lilly Miller. He even had a faint smile on his face.

PART ONE

The Camp

Summer of 1959

CHAPTER ONE

It was truly an exciting time for me. I had graduated from high school a week before and would be off to college in Pennsylvania in the fall, but now I was preparing for my new role, camp counselor. I had been a camper for eight weeks almost every summer since age nine, and now I would be a full-fledged counselor, the first at Camp Spenser who was not a college student or college graduate.

I was busy packing when my dad came into my room.

"Do you need any help, Bob? I'm in for the evening, and my expertise is getting twenty pounds of clothes in a ten-pound suitcase."

"Thanks, Dad, but I'm almost done and I don't have much to take. I will need some help later when we load the car."

"You got it. We'll have dinner in about an hour; something special mom whipped up for your last night."

I finished packing and took a quick shower before the evening meal. I couldn't wait for the morning to meet the staff, some old friends, and my campers. I loved camp life, and now I would have responsibility and play a part in the growth of young boys. I just had a special fondness for Camp Spenser. Set on a hill overlooking Lake Spotswood, it was a series of rustic cabins, ball fields, swim-areas, and a boathouse, all dominated by a huge lodge. I remembered summers of swimming, boating, softball, archery, hiking, canoe trips, arts and crafts, and, most importantly, wonderful friendships. Many of my bunkmates in those days were from my hometown. We had gone to school together, and now we spent our summers at Camp Spenser. We were the crème-de-la-crème, the all-American boys when it was popular to be so.

During those years in the early 1950s, our parents wanted us at camp for the summer for two reasons: the polio epidemics of the late forties and to have peace and quiet for two months. This was OK with me, as polio was scary. I had a friend who got it and had to live in a metal container called an "iron lung" in order to breathe. Imagine living in a metal tube, not being able to walk or breathe on your own. He was paralyzed from the neck down, although his mind was perfect. As far as I was concerned, that was the pits. I'd rather be dead. We didn't know how someone got polio, some kind of virus, I think—but no one contracted it in the country. It was a city disease for the most part, spread in swimming pools, amusement parks, and confined spaces, or so my parents said. At camp, my folks assured me that I couldn't get it. I felt invincible.

I did remember one argument with my mother in 1950. School was out and my older sister and her friends wanted to take me to Olympic Park, an amusement place in nearby Irvington. We would take a bus and go on rides all day, maybe even swim in the Olympic-sized pool.

"No way, Bob. You and Ginny have no chance of going. Between polio and perverts, you and your sister must be out of your minds. Don't even try to argue. The answer is no. I don't know what your sister is thinking."

"But Mom, all the kids go there. I'm the only one who hasn't. Please, please. I promise I won't get sick, and I'll stay with Ginny like glue."

"Forget it, Bob. The answer is no, and that's final."

And so it was. There was no arguing with Mom when she had made up her mind.

***

After toweling off, I finished packing, and Dad helped me load the car. We would leave late Friday morning, and the kids would be arriving on Sunday.

Mom was bustling about with my sister, home from college, putting the finishing touches on dinner. It smelled wonderful. She had set the table in the dining room, which was rarely used except for company and on holidays. We usually ate in the kitchen. She even had candles, although it was not Friday night.

Once seated, Dad gave the blessing, and Mom then disappeared into the kitchen and returned with a beautiful rib roast surrounded by oven-roasted potatoes. My sister followed with a bowl of peas with tiny pearl onions and a basket filled with warm dinner rolls. This was incredible, a real feast.

I was flattered when Mom said, "Bob, this special dinner is for you. We'll miss you and we wish you success in your new job and your upcoming freshman year in college."

Dad followed with a toast to his lovely wife and his accomplished children and commented on how blessed he was.

As we ate and chatted, I thought about how fortunate our family was. My folks had worked hard, lived through tough times, and provided my sister and me with security, love, and good values.

My mother came from a wealthy Brooklyn family and had married my father during the depression years. They struggled during the early days of my dad's medical practice, and when they finally saw the light at the end of the tunnel, Mom got pregnant with my sister and then had me just before Pearl Harbor. We moved from relative to relative while Dad spent two years in the Pacific. Mom never complained, although we knew she was worried sick about her husband. Dad made it home after the Japanese surrendered, and several years later we moved to Millburn.

My sister, Virginia, is almost four years my senior and perfect: pretty, popular, and smart. A hard act to follow through grade school, junior high, and high school; not that we were competitive.

The roast was perfect, tender and succulent, and I outdid myself with two big slabs, to the delight of my mother, who got great joy out of feeding people. After the dishes were cleared, the piece de resistance was served: strawberry shortcake. Mom had gone all out.

That night I slept like a baby without a care in the world and awoke to the smell of fresh brewed coffee. I got out of bed, put on a pair of shorts and a Millburn High School t-shirt, and walked into the kitchen.

"Coffee smells great, Mom."

"I'll pour you a cup. Dad is shaving and will be here in a sec. I'm letting Ginny sleep late."

I glanced at the kitchen clock and could not believe it was nine.

"I can't believe I slept this late. I guess I needed time to digest that incredible meal. You are the best."

I leaned over and gave my mother an affectionate hug and a kiss on the cheek. She beamed.

CHAPTER TWO

At ten-thirty we left for the two and one -half hour drive to Camp Spenser, near Stillwater in Sussex County, New Jersey. My sister had staggered out of bed in time to give me a kiss good-bye, but passed on the invitation to join us for the drive to camp.

It was a crystal clear, warm mid June morning, not a cloud in the sky, and I prayed silently that the fine weather would continue. Rainy weather put a damper on camp activities. We arrived at the lodge at twelve forty-five, and my folks were about to help me down the hill to my cabin when I was spotted by a friend from the previous year, Jim Butler.

"Hey, Bobby boy, how are you? And, by the way, how's that good-looking sister of yours?"

"We're just fine, both of us. It's great to see you."

"Dr. and Mrs. Berman, it's good to see you both again. I'll take good care of Bob; you have nothing to worry about."

Dad started to pick up a piece of luggage, but Jim stopped him.

"No Doctor. I'll carry the bags with Bob. We're going to cabin five."

"In that case, we might as well say our good-byes here. No need to navigate the hill."

Mom did not look happy, as I think she wanted to make up my bed and make sure I was settled, but she acquiesced to Dad, and they prepared to leave. Dad shook my hand, patted me on the shoulder, and told me he was proud of me. Mom, on the other hand, embarrassingly kissed me and gave me a huge hug in front of Jim and several members of the staff.

As Jim and I walked down the hill toward the cabins, he updated me on the plans for the day. Lunch was at 1:30, giving me time to unpack and make up my bed.

I unpacked my two suitcases and made the bed. I chose the upper bunk on the front left side.

"What are your plans for the fall?" Jim asked.

"Going to Lafayette, a real sin in our family of Lehigh alums." Lafayette and Lehigh had an intense rivalry for sixty years, almost as intense as Army and Navy. My going to Lafayette was akin to marrying out of my religion.

Jim laughed, perhaps remembering his choice of Cornell when his whole blue-blood family went to Harvard. Although Cornell was Ivy League, Harvard was Harvard.

"At lunch we'll meet everyone and schmooze. Then we'll do a little jog if you're up to it, maybe shoot some hoops, whatever. At dinner we get the list of the campers with short bios, listen to speeches, and get oriented."

Jim was a real fitness nut, and a jog with him would work up a sweat. He was tall, almost 6'2", and muscular. As a freshman he made a name for himself in a pretty tough sport, lacrosse.

"Yeah, I could use a little work. A jog would do me good." At 5'11", I was hopefully still growing. I'd barely started shaving, and at eighteen, I looked sixteen, a source of constant embarrassment. But my sister's friends thought I was good looking, and I never had trouble getting a date. I had brown hair, brown eyes, a good complexion, and broad shoulders. I was fairly athletic, although not a star by any stretch of the imagination. I had a pretty good academic record in high school and would go premed in college. God forbid if anyone in our family wasn't a doctor.

I changed into running shorts, and Jim and I headed out for a quick (and exhausting) three miles. Luckily, it was not humid.

"So tell me about your fine sister."

"Jim, she already finished college. You're going to be a junior. She dates guys who are pushing thirty."

"I can still hope."

"Don't waste your time. She finished Syracuse with straight A's and is off to medical school in Philadelphia in the fall."

"She's a tough act to follow, Bobby boy."

Jim had a thing for my sister after seeing her last year at Visitors' Day. Unfortunately my sister didn't really notice.

I made it through the run, winded, but feeling a sense of accomplishment. We shot hoops with a several other counselors for about an hour, and then took a refreshing swim in the cold lake. After a long shower and change of clothes, we walked up the hill to the lodge for dinner.

It was a beautiful, balmy evening with a light breeze, causing Old Glory to billow on the flagpole. The lodge was imposing, a huge structure overlooking the cabins and the lake below. The building was made of weathered logs and had a huge wraparound porch. It housed the kitchen, mess hall, infirmary, laundry, arts and crafts and nature rooms, and the mailroom. The canteen was in an adjacent small building and was the most popular spot at camp. The kids had accounts set up by their parents and could purchase candy, pens and pencils, postcards, playing cards, toilet articles, paperbacks, arts and crafts supplies, and numerous other items.

From what I heard, a house had been abandoned on the lake and back taxes were owed. The town of Stillwater repossessed the house, which happened to have two thousand feet of lake frontage, a huge boathouse, and two hundred acres. It sold for a song at auction, back taxes were paid, and Camp Spenser had been born. Over the years cabins were added, docks built, ball fields laid out, and the lodge constructed. Now, thirty-five years later, it would be home to ninety-six campers, six junior counselors, twelve counselors, administrative staff, a nurse, a cook, instructors, maintenance staff, and counselors-in-training for eight weeks.

The rest of the property around the lake was largely undeveloped, with just a handful of private summer homes. Only one house was winterized, and as far as I knew, it belonged to a widower named Lester Cartright who worked for the state highway department. I found him to be kind of an odd duck who helped with occasional maintenance work and was hired to drive us to neighboring camps for ball games or swim meets or to bring our canoes to the Delaware Water Gap for trips down the river. He had a good-sized truck, and I guess the extra bucks came in handy.

The lake was about a mile and a half in length, half a mile wide, deep and cold. There were a lot of reeds at both ends, supposedly making it good for bass fishing. As a camper I had met the challenge of my peers, successfully swimming the length of the lake, followed by two rowboats filled with the swimming instructor, a lifeguard, and my counselor; sort of overkill on the safety end. I remember my greeting and short-lived adulation when the feat was announced at evening mess. I was a star, at least for one evening.

My other claim to fame during my camp years came in the horseshoe pit, of all places. During the finals of an intense competition, I stepped up against the defending champ from the year before. After splitting the first two games in the best of three, it came down to the last two throws for both of us, the score tied. My opponent went first and heaved the shoe directly at the metal stake. It landed with a clunk, slid down the pole and stayed precariously as a leaner. He smirked. It was now my turn, and my only thought was to dislodge his leaner. I carefully took aim, threw, and watched in disbelief as my shoe hit his leaner and bounced harmlessly away. We each had one throw left, and it was do or die. Alas, my opponent's aim was true, and with his last throw he made a ringer but dislodged his leaner. It was now up to me. Only a ringer would help. If not, I was an also-ran, a has-been at age twelve. I let fly, and the "crowd" around the pit gasped as my shoe landed just short of the stake, flipped over, and slid forward.

As the dust settled, the referee ran toward the stake to make a ruling. He knelt and then took a ruler out of his pocket. Could it be that close? Time stood still as he measured and re-measured to see if the prongs of the shoe had cleared the stake. Finally, after what seemed hours, he declared my shot a ringer. Incredibly, I had won by covering his ringer with one of my own. I became an icon, a legend in my own mind.

***

Standing on the porch of the lodge, I could see cabin 5-my cabin. Like the lodge, it was made out of rustic logs, with wooden steps leading up to doors, which slid into recessed grooves when opened. There were four bunk beds around the periphery, two to each side, with windows to the side of each bed. Of course, there were no screens. There were cubbies at the far wall to store clothes. There was one single bed in the middle of the cabin. Trunks were kept under the lower bunks to get them out of the way and store extra clothes. The boy in the middle bunk would keep his truck at the foot of his bed as a common sitting area.

There was a central washroom near the cabins with shower stalls and a huge round sink with foot pedals to turn water on or off for washing hands and faces and brushing teeth. It could accommodate about twelve boys at a time, which turned out to be ample, as the water was lukewarm at best. There would be no dilly-dallying. The bathroom, called the latrine, was a separate building at the edge of the woods. It was not an outhouse but had flush toilets and urinals. Unfortunately, there were no partitions between the toilets, so privacy did not exist. Hey, this was camp, not a hotel. Because the latrine was away from the cabins, it would be scary for a boy to go to the bathroom at one in the morning with only a flashlight in hand. I had memories of hoping that someone in my cabin had to also go when I woke up to pee. Going alone was frightening, but waking your counselor to accompany you was out of the question.

Jim tapped me on the shoulder and said, "it's time for dinner, buddy."

***

I recognized many of the staff, especially the counselors from years past. With each handshake and backslap, memories of good times resurfaced. We chit-chatted for several minutes before the bell sounded for us to be seated. We haphazardly sat at tables set up around the head table and awaited introductions.

In the middle of the head table sat Al Simmons, the camp director. Al was a former athletic director at a large high school in Central New Jersey and was now semiretired. He still had the body of a jock, though he was probably close to sixty. He was still powerfully built and looked like he could do a hundred-yard dash in ten-flat, followed by fifty push-ups. He had been quite an athlete in high school and college. He could run, pass, catch, swim, shoot. You name it, and he could play it.

With him at the head table were his wife, Kathy, and his daughter, whom he introduced as Jean. Kathy was blonde, pretty, and athletic-looking, the perfect match for All-American Al. However, she appeared to be much younger than Al, and Jean I guessed to be about sixteen or seventeen. I presumed that either he had married late in life or it was a second marriage and Jean was his step-daughter. Jean could be a problem, especially with my newly raging hormones. She was adorable; a real beauty, with long, lean legs, breasts just starting to develop, and a smile that could knock your socks off. Since my love life was nonexistent and Jean was too young for most of the counselors, I started to plan my introductions and strategize a way to ingratiate myself.

Al had taken over as the camp's director with the retirement of the beloved Cap Hanson. Cap would be a hard act to follow, although Al seemed quite capable of holding his own. Cap had made the camp into a success with a long waiting list. He had made boys into young men with a program filled with activities, sports, and camaraderie, and had instilled self-reliance and spirituality in the campers. He had taught them life skills in a fun atmosphere. Aside from the usual swimming, boating, softball, archery, and arts and crafts, Cap had also built a chapel- by- the- lake for evening vespers and Sunday services.

Al now introduced his staff: Betty Sloan, the nurse; Bernie Allen, the assistant director; Bob Beebe, the athletic and swim director; Nellie Flanders, the cook; and Bob Williams, arts and crafts and nature lore. Several I had already known from years past, and I liked what I saw in the new staff.

After short speeches and dinner, we adjourned and received our campers' lists, short bios, and special needs. I would have eight boys for eight weeks, and I knew that most would be apprehensive, but after a few days, the ice and fear would be broken, and camp life would become something special.

CHAPTER THREE

Back in my cabin, as I looked down the list, I couldn't help but think of my first days as a camper, nervous but eager, anticipating the best and the worst. Being away from home for an entire summer was scary, and I must admit that I was homesick at first, but the thought of freedom and being with buddies my age was appealing and exciting.

I turned my attention to the list.

Danny Golden: age eleven and never away from home before. Shy, introspective, nonathletic, but smart. His parents were concerned about his frail build and asthma. They included numerous notes about his medications. His dad was a doctor, and I could already see that the family was nervous about their little boy being away from home. Danny's next eight weeks would be beneficial for his self-reliance and self-worth if I could get him through the first week.

Bob Moore: age twelve, big for his age and very athletic. He was able to hold his own with older and bigger kids. I pegged him for a leader, but he had to be watched to make sure he didn't try to dominate the smaller and younger campers.

Tony La Rocca: age twelve, from an Italian working-class family in the Vailsburg section of Newark. Unlike Danny and Bob, he was not from a fancy suburb like Short Hills or Millburn. I figured that he was probably streetwise beyond his years.

Mike Kennedy: age twelve. An Irish kid from Orange, New Jersey, the home of Monte Irvin, my hero from the New York Giants of the fifties. I figured that he was a tough little kid, as he filled out the entire application for camp as well as the descriptive material. He just had his parents sign the forms.

Jeffrey Lebowitz: age eleven. From his application I knew he was overweight. I also knew that the others would probably pick on him. This would be a potential problem, and I would have to keep an eye on things. He was also the youngest, as he had just turned eleven in May.

Kenny Sawyer: age twelve. His name and picture on the application made me think of Mark Twain's Tom Sawyer. He had red hair and that mischievous look of a real devil, probably a lovable troublemaker and a practical joker.

Paul O'Neill: age eleven. A nice-looking kid with blond hair and blue eyes. His parents stated in confidence that he had been a bed wetter until recently.

Steve Wilder: age twelve. Camp experience at Boy Scout and YMCA facilities. He fit in well and was reliable and well- liked. He could be counted on during those early days when the other kids were getting acclimated to camp life.

There you have it – my charges for eight weeks.

***

I spent Saturday going over activities lists and plans for the first week, with breaks to shoot baskets with Jim and play a pick-up softball game with other counselors. After lunch I took a short swim. Jim had asked me to join him and a couple of buddies for a movie and pizza in Newton, the closest "big town" and the county seat of Sussex County. We would leave early enough to catch a seven o'clock show. I felt honored to be included but knew that I was probably considered as a younger brother.

It was a beautiful mid-June night, and we all piled into Jim's old '52 Chevy—Arnie Flowers, Bill Chambers, Jim, and me. Arnie had just finished his freshman year at Colgate, so we were pretty close in age, although I did not know him well. I would make it a point to try to strike up a friendship. Bill was a guy I had known from last year. What I remembered was that he was a real intellectual, not a drip or a loner, but someone who was really smart. He was the only person I had ever met who had been accepted and then turned down Harvard. You just didn't turn down Harvard, but he did. He was now going into his junior year at Swarthmore and thriving at the small, elite liberal arts college, writing for the school paper and performing in the drama club.

As we drove, I just sat and listened to the chatter with ample kidding, corny jokes, and comments about girls. Although just a high school kid, I really felt that I was a part of it. These guys treated me like an equal, a peer, and I ate it up.

After the movie we shared two pepperoni pizzas and got back to camp at about eleven. Tomorrow was the big day, the arrival. "Oh, this is going to be a great summer," I thought.

CHAPTER FOUR

By ten on Sunday morning, cars had started up the dusty camp road. I could hear the motors whining, see the dust, and faintly make out the sounds of excited voices. Moms, dads, sisters, brothers, grandparents, friends, and dogs accompanied the campers to help with trunks, suitcases, knapsacks, sleeping bags, fishing rods, bats, balls, and mitts. I stood in front of my cabin, greeting each boy and his family, introducing myself and helping with his belongings. By noon all had arrived except Jeffrey Lebowitz. I watched as mothers made up beds, dads helped load cubbies with clothes, and kids greeted one another and made decisions about taking an upper or lower bunk.

Danny had looked apprehensive, and his mother had immediately taken over and made up his bed so tightly and neatly that I could have bounced a quarter off it. His dad, the doctor, had arranged all his medications and insisted on going over the dosage schedule with me. He stressed that timing and dosage were of utmost importance and seemed unconvinced that I could handle it. I hated him immediately.

"You look pretty young for a counselor." Dr. Golden said.

I had already pegged him as pompous as I replied, "I just finished high school and will be starting college in the fall. I'll be OK. I've been a camper here for years as well as a counselor-in-training and junior counselor. I assure you that you needn't worry about Danny." Why did every kid with asthma have pain-in-the-ass parents?

He leaned closer to me and whispered, "Danny has a problem, and I need you to give him special attention. He lets bigger boys bully him, and he has no self-confidence."

I assured Dr. Golden that I understood and would keep an eye on Danny. As he turned toward his wife and son, I could not help concluding why Danny was so shy and such a potential target for ridicule. In just a short period of time I'd observed his parents to be stifling and overbearing. I decided that Danny Golden would spread his wings and blossom if I could get him through the first day or two.

I met Bob Moore, Tony La Rocca, Ken Sawyer, Paul O'Neil, and Steve Wilder and their families. No real problems on first impressions as we made small talk. Mike Kennedy, however, made my heart sink. He had arrived alone with a large battered suitcase. No parents, no siblings, no dog. He had been dropped off by a neighbor and left here for eight weeks. The kid looked tough, but I could tell he was hurt and feeling a little lost under the wise-ass façade. I didn't know who had paid for his summer, but I was sure that his folks were not involved.

My concerns with Mike were small potatoes when I met the last camper to arrive, Jeffrey Lebowitz. He was more than obese, he was Pickwickian. He was short of breath just carrying his suitcase. He was disheveled with his shirt hanging out of his pants, his pants pockets bulging from the strain of his tight zipper, and his hair uncombed. His whole appearance was slovenly and unkempt, a complete contrast to his family. His parents were slim and attractive, and his older sister was a knockout. Jeffrey would definitely be a problem, a target of jokes and ridicule.

Over the next hour or so, I mingled with the boys and their families, trying to be helpful and hoping that someone would decide to leave. I convinced all present that their sons would enjoy their eight weeks and return home happy, healthy, and more self-reliant. They would also come home with a trunk full of dirty clothes. That got a few laughs.

Finally, thank God, the Moores said their good-byes to Bob, shook my hand, and left. That opened the floodgates, and all the other families followed suit. I walked them to their cars and again reassured them that my charges were in for a great summer and were not going to prison. Separation anxiety was rampant, but eventually the cars exited one by one, and the summer began.

CHAPTER FIVE

"**O**K, guys, gather 'round. I want to give you a little briefing on the next few days. The bugle will sound in a few minutes, and we'll all climb the hill together and meet at the flagpole for a greeting from the camp director and then lunch. We all sit together at the same table, and it will be marked with our cabin number on the wall, number 5. I'll sit at the head, the waiter will sit at the foot of the table, and the rest of you will sit on benches on each side. Since Steve has been to camp before, he will be our waiter this week." I gave Steve a quick wink. "Each of you will have a turn to be a waiter for one week. The waiter has to get to the mess hall fifteen minutes ahead of meals to set the table and put out plates of bread and pitchers of milk or "bug juice" (Kool Aid). When everyone is seated and grace is said, he has to go up to the kitchen counter to bring back plates and bowls of food. It may take several trips. After the meal he has to take the dirty dishes, cups, and silverware to the dishwasher and then clean the table. It really isn't all that bad. Get together, arrange your order, and give me the list. Steve, you're in charge." The boys seemed a bit overwhelmed and I gave them a few moments to digest the instructions and then continued. "**Now** after lunch we'll check the bulletin board for the activities list. You will all be assigned to activities for the afternoon, and each day things will rotate so you'll all get a chance to participate in everything from softball to swimming to arts and crafts. We all rest after lunch for about an hour. You may want to talk, play cards or checkers, listen to the radio, or just relax. You may want to write postcards or just take a nap. Activities begin at 2 pm and end at 5:30 pm to get ready for dinner."

"Tonight we are having a huge welcoming bonfire and then evening vespers by the lake. I guarantee that you'll all be tired by the end of the festivities, so we'll get a good night's sleep and be fresh on Monday. Oh, I almost forgot.

You're expected to make your beds each morning and help clean the cabin for daily inspection. Your moms will be thrilled to hear that you learned how to make a bed and clean."

As I was talking, the bugle sounded; it was time for lunch. We headed up the hill as a group and gathered by the flagpole, other cabins joining us. We lined up by cabin number, and each boy's name was read off as he was acknowledged. Al Simmons welcomed us all and then led us to the mess hall to the sounds of the bugler. Steve had set the table and was ready for us. Not bad. Plates, silverware, cups, napkins, bug juice, milk, and a plate of bread all accounted for. I didn't think that anyone would notice that the knives and spoons were on the left and the fork on the right, but I was wrong. As we sat, Danny saw the mistake right away and unfortunately brought it to everyone's attention. Steve just glared at him, and Danny cowered. One point against Golden and counting.

Lunch was uneventful after this rocky start. The boys cautiously conversed as they ate bologna sandwiches with chips and pickles. Dessert was Jell-O and cookies. As I ate my Jell-O, I thought back to a family vacation in the Catskills when I was in junior high. I was at the age where I didn't mind going away with my parents, although my folks knew it would be short-lived. Around age fourteen you wouldn't want to be caught dead on a family vacation, much less share a hotel room and meals with your parents. But what I remembered about the resort hotel was that they always served Jell-O for dessert. Of course there were other choices, but they always had Jell-O. Not a fruit mold with sour cream or a fancy job with layers of different colors, but just plain lumps of the stuff scooped into small sundae dishes like what was now in front of me.

After lunch we went back to the cabin for rest period before the afternoon's activities. All had started reasonably well, but Danny had a kind of worried, maybe even lonesome look on his face, and Jeffrey seemed distracted and withdrawn. At least Danny wasn't wheezing. After an hour we would split up for the various activities and then reassemble for dinner and the much-anticipated bonfire.

CHAPTER SIX

As the sky started darkening we assembled at the flagpole with flashlights, sweatshirts, blankets, and bug spray in hand. The excitement was electric. You could feel the anticipation as we made our way down the narrow trail to a secluded clearing ringed with large boulders. A huge stack of logs was in the center of the ring, and as we entered, an unseen archer shot a blazing arrow into the gasoline-soaked woodpile. The conflagration was spectacular with flames shooting at least ten feet in the air. As we watched the dazzling fire, "warriors" appeared seemingly from out of nowhere, dressed in loincloth, war paint, and war bonnets.

As the warriors danced in a circle and whooped their war cries, a figure appeared in the darkness, at first a shadow, and then an ethereal-looking presence. He was tall and muscular and was wearing buckskin trousers to the waist, a beaded breastplate, two armbands, war paint, and an incredible war bonnet of eagle feathers. He was impressive and at the same time frightening, with a hawk-like countenance and the air of a chief. As he stood in the shadows, the warriors stopped their dancing, and the air became still for a few moments. Then we heard it, the distant sounds of a drum beating rhythmically and slowly. The intensity of the sound increased—thump, thump, thump. The tension among the boys was almost palpable. The beat got louder and louder. The boys looked more apprehensive. As I reached over to reassure them, there was a blinding flash of light as someone threw something into the fire. The campers were startled and before they could react, the chief spoke in a deep, resonant voice:

"I am Yellow Bird, chief of the Lenni Lenape. You are on the sacred land of my people. If I allow you to stay, you must follow my rules. You must respect the land, the trees, the animals of the forest, and the water in the streams and rivers. The white man disobeys often, and he has paid the price of not caring for nature's wonders. He ignores the earth and its bounties. Where he walks, the earth cries."

As I watched I noted that my boys were spellbound by this foreboding figure's words. He was a man, but with a mystical appearance—a spirit.

As quickly as he materialized, he was gone in a large puff of smoke. The fire crackled, but there was no other sound. The stillness was intense as we all sat in awe and silence. Suddenly Al Simmons appeared and restated the chief's words of caution: that we were on Native American land as visitors and that we must respect the privilege. He then settled down on a large rock and began to tell the legend of Lake Spotswood:

"There was a great warrior who won many battles for the Lenni Lenape. He was strong and brave and a great hunter. One day he was stalking a large buck. As he carefully approached the deer, the wind shifted and the buck picked up his scent and bolted. The warrior did not give up and followed the buck's tracks for miles to the side of a large lake that he had never seen before. As the deer drank from the lake water the warrior took his bow, strung an arrow, took aim, and let the missile fly. His aim was true and the stag fell in place. The brave bent over the animal and blessed it, asking the spirits to retrieve its soul. He thanked Mother Earth for her bounty. He unsheathed his knife, and as he was about to cut the animal and remove its heart, he thought he saw its eye open. Yes, he did. The deer was still alive. Not wanting the animal to suffer, he plunged his large hunting knife into its heart. As he did, he felt the power drain from his body."

"He hunted out of necessity and only killed what he and his tribe needed, but this encounter had changed him. He could not kill from that day on, and he was disgraced as a warrior. One night, as moonlight shimmered over the surface of the lake, the once-great warrior walked into the cold, murky water and disappeared, never to be seen again. Legend has it that on certain moonlit nights the warrior can be seen rising from the muddy depths of Lake Spotswood, scanning the shore in hopes of regaining his power to hunt."

All fell silent again as we left the ring of fire and went up the trail to the chapel for vespers. Fifteen minutes later we were washing our faces and brushing our teeth, and once back in the cabin, the boys fell onto their bunks, physically and emotionally exhausted.

***

Later that night Danny Golden had to go to the bathroom. He got out of bed, took his flashlight, and although he was scared, went out of the cabin into the darkness. I was jarred awake, moments later, by a blood-curdling scream, almost hitting my head on the beam above my bed. Instinctively I shot out of bed and dashed toward the latrine, where the screaming was coming from. As I almost ripped the screen door off its hinges, I charged in to find Danny cowering in the corner between the toilet and the wall. In front of him was a timber rattler, coiled and menacing, ready to strike.

"Danny, don't move, and don't scream or talk. Stay as still as you can."

Danny was trembling, near hysteria, and starting to wheeze. Quickly I took off my t-shirt and pajama bottoms, hoping the snake would not strike before I was ready.

"Danny, I'm here. Keep calm and we'll get out of this."

In one swift movement that even surprised me, I threw my clothes on the snake and almost at the same time grabbed Danny. By this time, help had arrived to handle the snake. I carried Danny to the cabin, trying to comfort him, but he was wheezing badly. I grabbed his inhaler and made him take two deep puffs. He was shaking, perspiring heavily, and his lips were blue. Now all the campers were awake, as well as most of the counselors. Jim Butler arrived and helped me with Danny while others ran up the hill to get Al Simmons and Betty Sloan, the camp nurse.

"Danny, please talk to me. Tell me you're able to breathe."

Danny gasped but didn't answer. He squirmed in my arms and then vomited all over Jim and me. He looked terrible, and at that moment I thought he might die.

"Jim, get your car. We have to get him to the hospital in Newton. I don't think he's going to make it."

Betty and Al arrived with an oxygen tank and mask. They slapped the mask on Danny's face as he hungrily took deep breaths. His color improved slightly, but he was still wheezing badly.

"We have to get him to Newton as soon as possible," said Betty in a troubled tone. "He needs inhalation treatments, IV fluids, and steroids, and we have to call his parents."

Just thinking of Dr. Golden's reaction to his son's condition sent a shiver up my spine. "He is going to go crazy and he will definitely blame me," I thought. With time of the essence, we loaded Danny and the oxygen tank into Jim's car rather than wait for an ambulance. Betty and Al would follow in the camp car while Bernie Allen, the assistant director, called the police to arrange a meet in Stillwater and a high-speed escort to Newton.

The cops picked us up when we hit the sleepy burg, and with sirens blaring, we high-tailed it to the hospital. They were waiting for us at the entrance to the ER, a small, quiet unit by city standards, and I prayed that they knew how to treat asthma.

As we rushed into the triage area the doctor on duty said, "How old is he? Does he have any medication allergies? Did you give him any medications?"

We told him about the inhaler and the oxygen as they whipped Danny onto a gurney. I remembered from his father's profile of meds that he was allergic to sulfa and I stated so to the doctor, who was now busy starting an intravenous while a nurse gave the boy oxygen bubbled through water. Once the IV was started, I think they gave him a sedative because he began to settle down. The doctor said he would be giving Danny bronchodilators and steroids and that he should improve. Regardless, once stable, he would be moved to the three-bedded ICU until he was completely out of the woods.

After several hours Danny seemed much improved. His breathing was no longer labored, there was no audible wheeze, and his lips were not blue. I was feeling better about the situation; that is until Dr. Golden, MD-SOB, arrived to give us all a setback. I prayed that Danny would stay sedated, convinced that if he saw Daddy he would start to wheeze again. Dr. Golden created the expected brouhaha, antagonizing everyone and threatening to move his son to one of the "biggies" in New York City. After blowing off steam and glowering at me, he led his wife to the lounge for coffee and the all-night vigil in the ICU.

When we were convinced that Danny was stable, Jim and I began the ride back to camp as the sun was rising. Hopefully the kids would be calm and coping with the crisis. I would fill them in on his condition, being honest but optimistic.

Once back at camp I checked the cabin, and surprisingly, all the boys were still asleep. I took the opportunity to hit the latrine, as my bladder was about to burst. I went through the screen door, which automatically snapped closed after I entered, and as I stood at the urinal, I looked down the line of toilets. They were in a row with no partitions. The floor was solid wood and the walls and joints were flush and well sealed. There were no holes, gaps, or cracks where the walls met the floor, and the screen door was tight. An uncomfortable thought now hit me; how did this usually shy snake get into the bathroom at one in the morning? Did someone put the snake there? Nah, couldn't be. Yet I couldn't dismiss the idea, and I had to discuss it with Jim.

"Jimbo, tell me I'm crazy. Tell me I'm sick."

"What are you talking about?"

"I think someone planted the rattler."

"You must be kidding."

"No, I'm not. I checked the latrine, and there is no way a snake could get in on its own."

"But who would do that and why? It doesn't make any sense."

"I know, I know. There must be a reasonable explanation for what happened, but I have an uncomfortable feeling that someone planned this."

CHAPTER SEVEN

I was absolutely exhausted, both physically and emotionally, by the events of the past night. After I'd talked to Jim, the boys had awakened, and we went as a group to the washroom where I showered, submerging my aching head in cold water. Five minutes later I felt a little more refreshed, and after toweling off and putting on fresh clothes, I led my charges to the flagpole to watch the stars and stripes being raised to sounds of the bugler. Breakfast followed: cold cereal, fruit, and pancakes with butter and warm syrup. We were ravenous and ate like there was no tomorrow, probably nervous energy.

Jeffrey was the first to talk.

"Do you think Danny will come back?"

I could tell that Jeffrey was concerned about Danny's welfare, but he also needed a "foil" to keep the rest of the kids from riding him.

"I don't know, Jeffrey. His dad was pretty upset and probably feels that his son is not safe here. For Danny's sake I hope that he returns. I think camp life would be good for him."

Steve, our waiter, returned with a new platter of pancakes, and we took a short break to eat.

"I thought that we would call the hospital today to get an update," I said. I was surprised to hear streetwise Tony La Rocca and tough Mike Kennedy say, "Great idea."

"First things first. After breakfast we have a cabin to clean and beds to make, and then it's off to the waterfront for your swim tests."

It was kind of a chilly morning, but that would not be a deterrent to the boys, already changing into swimsuits and charging down the hill to the cold lake water.

The waterfront consisted of a large dock, which looked like an upside-side U structure with the shallow water between the arms of the U. The deeper swim area extended out to a good-sized raft, and the entire area was roped off. There was a diving board on the left side of the dock and a ten-foot high tower on the right. Ten to twenty yards down from the dock was a boat launch and boathouse. There were canoes, rowboats, and small sunfish sailboats moored in the shallow water. To the side of the boathouse were racks of wooden and aluminum war canoes capable of holding ten campers and a counselor. In the shallow swim area the bottom was sandy, probably poured by the owners. The deeper areas were muddy or rocky, and to the extreme sides, the shoreline had many reeds and marshy spots. The water was cold as the lake was spring fed, but this did not seem to bother the boys, who were already getting wet.

A whistle blew and all eyes turned to Bob Beebe, the swim director, who was standing on the dock with a clipboard in hand. Tall and lean, with an athletic build, he had already started on a summer tan. I guessed him to be in his late twenties.

"Boys, I want you to line up according to your cabin number. We'll take each cabin in order starting with number one. I want you to tell your counselor if you know how to swim. If you don't know how, we'll teach you. If you do, we'll make you better. But we have to start somewhere, so I'll give each of you a trial run to see what group you belong in. Don't panic. If you start in a beginner group, you have all summer to work your way up."

I thought back to my days as a camper and remembered the disappointment of being put into an intermediate group rather than advanced. It meant that I couldn't swim to the raft and had to stay in the shallower water. It was a low time for me, even painful now that I thought about it. But over several summers, I became a good swimmer and even got my junior lifesaving certificate.

The boys looked nervous, especially cocky La Rocca and tough Mike Kennedy. Jeffrey, however, looked embarrassed in his swim trunks. He had rolls of baby fat and had breasts like a young girl. The teasing would start soon enough. Childhood could be so painful for some.

I soon found out why Tony and Mike looked so nervous. They confided in me that they didn't know how to swim. Being from tough neighborhoods and not the suburbs, they'd never had access to a pool or lake to learn. When they took their tests, they struggled in the shallow water, gasping and spitting, and Tony even got sick to his stomach and vomited. I watched and felt their pain. They were just young boys who were out of their element and felt humiliated. As they climbed onto the dock, I whispered much needed words of encouragement. Aloud, I said, "That took guts, and I'm proud of you both."

That did little to mollify the boys, and they took their places with the other beginners to start lessons at the shallow end.

I now took a deep breath as Bob Beebe ordered Jeffrey Lebowitz, along with athletic Bob Moore and all-around camper Steve Wilder, into the cold lake. Jeffrey was already shivering while holding onto the side of the dock, a bad sign. As expected, Bob and Steve swam well and were put into the advanced group. Now it was Jeff's turn, and I did not look confident. He was shaking, and his lips were blue. I feared the worst. To my utter amazement, Jeffrey pushed away from the dock with a powerful, graceful stroke and my heart soared. This non-athletic, obese boy, the target of ridicule, was gliding like Johnny Weissmuller. His beautiful crawl would receive the accolades of his peers, and he would wallow in the limelight, be in the advanced group, and eventually be king of the waterfront. This was very, very good indeed.

***

That night we ate like pigs and slept like logs, and we got good news about Danny. Life was good, and we were excited about our next adventure, a hike along the Appalachian Trail through the Kittatinny Mountains. The trail ran from Maine to Florida and was the most hiked area in the country. We would pick a campsite, pitch tents, gather wood for a fire, cook dinner in the outdoors, and then tell scary stores while roasting marshmallows and drinking hot chocolate. There was nothing like sleeping in the woods in a warm sleeping bag by a crackling fire.

The Native Americans had blazed this trail and knew it well. The mountains were hills by western standards, but the inclines were still challenging. The foliage was dense and wildlife abundant: deer, groundhogs, porcupine, skunks, squirrels, chipmunks, gophers, and the like. Dangerous animals like mountain lions, bear, and poisonous snakes were rare, thank God. The hike would be pleasurable, weather permitting, with the only hazard being mosquitoes and gnats. The trail was well marked and easy to follow, and there would be endless streams, small lakes, and ponds with clear, clean water to soothe our parched throats and cool our sweaty bodies.

CHAPTER EIGHT

At the crack of dawn we awoke to pack our knapsacks, fill our canteens, dress for the hike, and go to the mess hall to pack supplies and food. We were in jeans and lightweight, long-sleeved shirts and swathed in bug repellent. As per my instructions, the boys wore hiking shoes or sneakers with good socks, so important to avoid blisters, which could spoil the day.

We made our beds and headed to the lodge for breakfast. At nine on the dot, we headed to pick up the Appalachian Trial.

I was in the lead, with Steve Wilder and Bobby Moore picking up the rear. I tried to keep a steady pace that would not overtire the kids and would make it easy to keep tabs on everyone. As we walked farther into the woods, the foliage became denser and more bug-infested, and we all started to sweat. It was not a very warm day and the woods afforded shade, but the pace of the walk made us perspire, and we replaced the long-sleeved shirts with cotton t-shirts in spite of the mosquitoes. By noon the sun was directly overhead, and we stopped at a clearing for a snack, rest, and water. Nellie Flanders had prepared sandwiches, packs of cookies and chips, which I unloaded from my pack. The boys were ravenous.

After eating, we gathered papers and litter in a garbage bag, relieved our bladders, and restarted our trek. About an hour into the second stage of the hike, I turned to check things out and found Jeffrey huffing and puffing and sweating profusely.

"Jeffrey, are you OK? Do you want to stop?"

"Nah, I'm fine. I can keep going."

In spite of his denials, I felt it wise to stop for another break. Luckily there was a brook running through this part of the forest and we stopped to rest. The boys dropped and took off their knapsacks and then went knee-deep into the brook to wade and fill empty canteens. It was at that moment that I noticed Bobby but not Steve.

"Bobby, where's Steve?"

"He stopped a few hundred yards back to pee and said he would catch up," Bobby said calmly and matter-of-factly.

This temporarily relieved my fears, but I was really jumpy after the Danny Golden incident. I almost hugged Steve as he suddenly appeared from the woods. I was becoming a wreck.

After the short break, I decided to let Steve and Bobby lead, and I picked up the rear. I figured that I could watch things better from that vantage point. We hiked another two to three hours, covering about five miles, and then stopped at a clearing to look at maps and check compass readings. We were close to our goal, the banks of a small tributary of the Delaware River, where we would pitch camp for the night.

By four-thirty we had arrived at the spot. We were on a small knoll above the stream, an ideal place for our camp. We helped one another, pitching five pup tents in a circle around where we would build our campfire. After the tents were up, we unrolled the sleeping bags, stowed our gear, and then headed into the woods to collect logs and kindling and larger rocks for the campfire. We used small spades and axes for the job, and with eight boys we finished the work in no time. We put the large rocks in a circle within the tent area and built the fire within the ring of stones, starting with small kindling on top of dry birch bark. Once the small twigs caught and we had a good blaze going, we added dry pieces of wood and eventually large logs. God we were good! The remaining larger pieces of wood and logs were stacked for use throughout the night and to cook breakfast in the morning. Next we dug a deep hole about fifty feet from camp, next to a flexible sapling, to use as a latrine. With the campsite ready, we headed down to the stream to wash off all the grime and sweat. The water was bone -chillingly cold, but we all waded in and flopped down, eventually submerging ourselves completely with our clothes on. It felt great. We all undressed in the water and rinsed out our clothes, rung them out, and tossed them onto the bank. We took out soap and washed our tanned skin and tangled hair and then submerged again to wash off the soap. We then swam, splashed, and horsed around as young boys do.

Once our skin started to shrivel from the water, we emerged, stark naked, to climb the hill to the campsite, not the least bit self-conscious. After toweling off, we all dressed in clean and dry clothes and hung our wet stuff on a makeshift clothesline near the fire. We would spend the next hour preparing the dinner of the summer.

Half the boys went to fill canteens and get buckets of water for washing hands and utensils and for cooking. The other boys gathered more wood and green sticks for roasting hot dogs and marshmallow, whittling the ends to sharp points or what we referred to as "campfire skewers."

I unloaded my pack, which was heavy and on a frame and contained two pots, nine mess kits, and the food. Nellie had packed dry ice to keep the hot dogs cold. I also had three cans of beans and two large cans of bread, which I opened and put on the coals near the main fire. The boys had made a makeshift table by dragging a large log from the riverbank and putting it near the fire.

The beans started to boil, and the smell was pure ambrosia. Imagine Campbell's baked beans, the kind you hated at home, cooking over an open fire. They became a gourmet delight, and I could see everyone salivating. When the beans and bread were done, we wrapped towels around our hands and lifted the cans onto our log "table." I cut the bread, and we all skewered the hot dogs on our green sticks and roasted them over the open flames until they were charred, cracked, and oozing juices.

"Boys, I'm proud of all of you. You will never feel better, eat better, or enjoy each other's company more than you will today."

After eating three hot dogs each, and plates of beans and bread, all washed down with grape Kool-Aid, we were ready for the finale, marshmallows. To the delight of all the boys, I produced a large bag of the fluffy balls. We were stuffed, but how do you turn down marshmallows.

I watched as each boy stuck one on a green stick and held it over the open fire. First there was a light browning, and then charring, and then the ultimate; the marshmallow caught fire. The inside would be gooey and delicious, but you had to know when to blow out the flame. Too long and you had gooey ashes; too short and you had no goo at all. The kids seemed to have an innate sense of timing and usually produced perfect results. We emptied the bag in no time and then sat by the fire digesting. The air had cooled and the fire felt good, all helping to keep the insect population at bay. Except for a few mosquito bites, I felt comfortable, but some of the boys got jackets and sweatshirts.

By the time we cleaned up, it was starting to get dark.

"Tell us a scary story?" Steve asked and the rest of the kids seconded the request. "Make it something really scary."

All kids want to hear scary stories, watch monster movies, and surprise people by yelling boo in the dark. Yet under this façade, not one boy would go into the woods alone to pee without second thoughts. So I knew that I would temper my tale somewhat. There was a fine line between utter fright and telling a cool story. With this in mind, I started an old New England tale:

"It was a hot, humid night in July," I began. "The humidity created a foggy mist that hung like a rug over the small coastal town in Massachusetts. The "Laura *Mae*," a small fishing vessel, was overdue. She should have returned with her load of cod by mid-afternoon. It was now nine o'clock and no word. No mayday, no radio call. Nothing. Most of the people in the town were waiting on the pier or were in Ernie's Place, the local watering hole, and the rest were in church praying. At about nine-thirty, someone on the pier thought he saw a light near the harbor entrance. The townsfolk all strained to see, and someone yelled, "I see it, a light." Slowly, the bow of the boat became visible through the mist. Oddly, there was no sound of a motor, and as the entire craft came into view, there was no sign of the crew. The vessel inched toward the dock, so slowly. A tragic outcome was probable, and they all feared the worst. As the boat touched the wooden planks of the dock, several men jumped on board, while others secured the fishing craft with a rope, fore and aft."

I could see some uneasiness among the boys; they were a tad scared. I paused for a moment and Kenny Sawyer took the opportunity to tell us that he had to go "take a leak." This elicited some snickers, but no takers to accompany him.

"We'll wait until you come back; you won't miss a thing."

After about five minutes, the kids were getting restless, and Kenny had not returned.

"Come on, finish the story. The heck with Kenny," they all bellowed.

"Let's give him a few more minutes," I countered.

So after a few more minutes and no Kenny, I continued my tale.

"The men who jumped on the deck, four in number, scoured the entire boat, finding no one. No signs of damage to the vessel, no signs of foul play, just a missing crew. There were no reports of recent storms along the fishing banks. The gas tanks were half full, and when the men checked the motors, they sprang to life as soon as the ignition key was turned. What had happened here? Where was the crew? While pondering the mystery, someone in the hold opened one of the refrigerated compartments used for the catch. There, lying on heaps of cod, was the captain; stiff, cold, and very dead with a knife between his fourth and fifth rib to the left of his breastbone, presumably in his heart. The man who had made the gruesome discovery started to scream. The other men ran down the ship's ladder and saw the contents of the refrigerator. They, too, stepped back in horror. They recovered enough to check the other cold lockers, but found none of the crew. Where were they? How did the boat make it home with the motor off and without a pilot and crew to guide her?"

I looked up. The boys seemed mesmerized but scared. I was about to continue when I realized that Kenny had not returned.

"Boys, I don't want to go any further or Kenny will miss everything. Bobby and Steve, take your flashlights and go look for him. He's been gone too long; maybe he's sick."

CHAPTER NINE

The two boys headed into the woods and within seconds were yelling for help. I sprang to my feet, as did all the kids, and we headed at full speed toward the screams. As we approached a small clearing, we saw Bobby and Steve kneeling over Kenny. He was face down in a pool of blood, barely breathing and barely responsive. We rolled him over, protecting his neck and the back of his head. His face was covered with dirt and blood.

"Bobby, Steve, go back and get a canteen of water."

In seconds they returned, and I soaked several shirts and started wiping his face and scalp. I found a deep laceration above his left eyebrow just below his hairline, about two to three inches long and actively bleeding. I applied pressure to the wound, but the blood just soaked through the balled-up shirts.

"How do we stop the bleeding?" yelled Mike, almost hysterical.

"I don't know, but we have to," I responded with some hesitation. I had an idea, but I was so nervous, almost on the verge of panic. I had to try something. I told Tony and Paul to put two of the marshmallow sticks in the fire. They ran back and did what I told them, getting the ends red-hot. With great fear and trepidation, under the glow of an almost full moon, I grabbed the skewers from the boys with my hands shaking.

"Hold Kenny down! He'll probably move and even scream."

The boys complied, holding Kenny's arms, legs, and head while I leaned over him with a red-hot poker in my right hand. Sweating profusely, scared to death, I thrust the hot stick into the deep gash. There was a sickening, sizzling sound and the odor of burning flesh, but the bleeding slowed. More importantly, Kenny moved. He felt the pain. I almost cried, but I was too keyed up. I took the second poker and placed it more carefully into the wound with even better results. I then took a t-shirt and ripped it into strips, the boys doing the same with the help of pocket knives. We bunched up some and pressed them against the wound and then tied the strips around his head, covering his forehead and brow, to keep the pressure dressing in place. For now the bleeding seemed staunched, but Kenny looked bad, and he had lost a lot of blood.

I had to think clearly. We were ten miles from camp over rough terrain, and it was the middle of the night and I didn't know what to do.

"Is Kenny going to die?" asked Jeffrey. "No, I won't let him die, and I need your help. I think we should make him comfortable and hope that he comes around now that the bleeding has stopped. He probably has a concussion and could have a skull fracture, but I won't risk trying to move him at night."

So we moved Kenny into one of the tents near the fire, placing him in a sleeping bag. We placed wet pieces of t-shirts on his face and neck and listened to make sure he was breathing normally.

"What do you think happened?" asked Paul.

"I think he tripped in the dark and hit his head on a sharp rock." As I was finishing my explanation, I glanced over my shoulder and thought I saw Kenny move. It was imperceptible at first but then I noticed a subtle blink of the eye and a slight twitch of the hand. Yes he had moved. I was sure of it and I ran to him. He responded and opened his eyes. He started to cry and I held him tightly, my tears intermingling with his.

"God, you scared the shit out of us."

"I feel sick," he said and promptly became the second camper to vomit all over me. I was so relieved that I could have cared less. I was so happy that he was lucid and talking.

"Kenny, lie down and sleep. We'll wake you every so often just to make sure you're OK. We'll move out early in the morning to get you back to camp. I want the nurse to look at that cut. It needs to be cleaned and properly bandaged. If we don't get back soon it will get infected." I cleaned the vomit off his face, gave him a drink from the canteen, and lay down beside him.

Once Kenny was fast asleep, I descended the slope to the stream, and with Paul, Mike, and Tony holding flashlights, I stripped off my vomit-covered clothes and immersed myself to my shoulders in the cold, dark water. I rinsed my hair and smelly clothes and eventually felt clean. I toweled off and dressed by the warmth of the fire. Enough excitement for one night; we had a long hike home.

As I lay in the tent next to Kenny I could hear the boys dozing, often tossing and turning. We all had a lot on our minds, and it was going to be difficult in the morning. Although I was restless and worried, I knew one thing for sure. I would not leave Kenny to get help and I would not split up the group.

I must have worried myself to sleep, for the next thing I knew I was awakened by the sound of the boys stoking the fire and collecting firewood. It was early, as there was a chill in the air and a perfect moon was still visible in the sky. The fire was blazing, which was good, as everything was damp from the morning dew.

As I emerged from the tent, I almost tripped over Jeffrey, who was huffing and puffing from carrying wood.

"How do we get Kenny back if he can't walk?" Jeffrey asked.

I reassured Jeffrey that I would find a solution and that Kenny would be safe.

My instincts had told me to keep everyone together; I could not risk Kenny going sour while I was miles away getting help. Besides, if carrying him proved fool-hearty, I could always reconsider and go on ahead on my own later.

"You just reinforced my decision. Win or lose, we will stay together."

This met with cheers, and my spirits heightened. Now I had to figure how we would carry him.

***

Breakfast was grilled toast with peanut butter, packets of cold cereal with powdered milk, and hot cocoa. We let Kenny sleep while we broke camp.

CHAPTER TEN

All non-essentials were left to lighten our load. We would pick up the stuff the following day, so we left the tents, cooking utensils, sleeping bags, and most of the knapsacks. After the unenviable task of filling the latrine hole, we scattered the fire and poured water on the hot coals, followed by wet sand from the stream. We didn't need a forest fire.

We broke camp as the sun was coming up. The bugs were intolerable, and we practically bathed in insect repellent and wore long-sleeved shirts. The boys helped put Kenny on my back. He wasn't a big boy, but was probably about ninety to one- hundred pounds of dead- weight. If this didn't work out, we could try to construct a makeshift stretcher, but it would be unwieldy on the narrow trail. The boys draped his limp arms around my neck, tied his forearms together with t-shirts, and rigged a sling-type apparatus with jackets to keep him from sliding off my back. Surprisingly, he didn't feel that heavy, and we started down the trail retracing out steps. We were able to go for over an hour before I announced our first break.

Kenny did not look good, ashen and sweaty, but his breathing was not labored, and he was able to take sips of water. The boys lifted him from my back, and we washed his hands, face, neck, and wrists with cold water from the canteen and gave him more to drink. It had become appreciably warmer, but less buggy as the dampness burned off.

"Let's try for two hours before we stop. Are you up to it?"

Everyone said yes, but I had doubts about Jeffrey.

The next two hours were tough. With Kenny repositioned on my back, I stayed in the middle, with Bobby and Mike leading and Steve picking up the rear. The trail was rocky and steep in spots, but was well marked. The trees offered some shade, but it was getting hotter by the minute, and my mouth was getting dry. I looked up and the sun was almost overhead, suggesting it was close to noon.

"Let's take another break, guys." My muscles were aching and twitching and I needed water. The boys did not object.

"How much longer, would you guess?" asked Bobby almost pleadingly.

"I'd say about four or five hours. We have to be close to halfway."

I passed out the remains of the marshmallows and packs of raisins. We refilled our canteens at a nearby brook, and I encouraged the boys to drink.

Back on the trail the next hour went by quickly, aided by, of all things, singing. Without any prompting, my charges suddenly burst out in song after song. They even started to giggle and joke as if they knew we had turned the corner and would make it.

In spite of my recently uplifted spirits, I was starting to become concerned. I had an uneasy feeling that nothing looked familiar. Trees, rock formations, the width of the path, and the angle of the sun all seemed wrong.

"Bobby, Mike, hold up a second," I yelled. Both boys stopped, turned, and waited for the others to catch up and close ranks.

"What's the matter?" Mike whined.

I could tell he was tired and just wanted to be back at camp. I moved close to Bobby and Mike so that the others wouldn't hear.

"I think we're on the wrong trail. Nothing looks familiar and I don't think we're going in a northeastern direction. I want to check my compass and map, so let's take five."

"How could we be lost? We've been following all the trail markers to a T," cried Mike.

"I know, Mike, but I have this gut feeling, and I have to check."

Our campsite was approximately ten miles southwest of Lake Spotswood, so we would have to return on a northeasterly course. My compass reading showed that we were going due north, almost northwesterly. We would have to adjust and go due east to pick up the trail. I turned to Bobby and Mike.

"Guys, we have to go east to try to pick up the main trail. I don't think we went too far out of our way, but hiking cross-country will be tougher and take longer. Can I count on you two, or should I go alone and bring back help?"

"I think we should stay together. You can count on us. We'll make it," said Bobby.

It was not pleasant, but in less than an hour, we picked up the main trail, recognizing the white arrows and dots painted on the trees and rocks. Things looked familiar and within a half- hour, we reached a lean-to on a small knoll that we had passed on our way out. I knew we were about two hours from camp.

"Boys, it's rest time, and we're almost back. About two hours or less should do it." This met with rousing cheers.

I checked Kenny. His pulse was full and regular, and he was alert enough to ask for water. I didn't know if he had a fever, as we were all hot and sweaty. After fifteen minutes we optimistically rose for the last stage of our journey, energized by the fact that we were close.

We covered the remaining few miles in what seemed like record time and headed straight to the camp infirmary. We attracted little attention, that is, until everyone noticed the bloodstained bandage on Kenny's head. Betty Sloan, followed by a pale-looking Al Simmons, ushered Kenny into the treatment room.

I asked the boys to go stow their gear, shower, and get ready for dinner while I stayed with Kenny. I could tell by the grumblings that they wanted to stay with their pal.

"You'll just be in Nurse Sloan's way. I'll fill you in on his condition as often as possible." Reluctantly, they all left, sulking.

CHAPTER ELEVEN

Betty had started to remove the makeshift dressing while Al directed the surgical light and rolled over a table filled with dressings, swabs, cotton balls, alcohol, tape, various clamps, and scissors. In the harsh light of the surgical area, I could see the extent of the injury; a deep, ugly gash over his eyebrow that by now had become swollen and bruised. His eye was nearly closed, and his nose looked to be broken, the left side of his face and forehead a purple-blue color.

Betty stopped her ministrations when she found no further bleeding and checked his blood pressure, pulse, and general condition. She put a thermometer under his tongue while listening to his heart and lungs with a stethoscope. She then asked Al to turn off the light, and she checked Kenny's eyes with a flashlight. She seemed pleased with what she saw.

"What does that tell you?" I asked.

"His pupils reacted to the light by contracting, and that's a good sign," Betty replied.

I felt somewhat relieved as she continued her examination by checking his reflexes and what she called "his level of consciousness." In the end she seemed satisfied, and I was fascinated by her skill. Finally, she thoroughly cleaned his laceration with soap and water, hydrogen peroxide, and merthiolate, which made Kenny really squirm. She bandaged the area and then drew up two syringes of medicine and gave him a shot in each butt cheek.

"What's that for?" I asked, starting to become engrossed.

"Penicillin and a tetanus shot," said Betty.

Betty and Al moved Kenny to an infirmary bed and covered him with a blanket while I ran out for a second to let the boys know that he was all right.

When I returned, Betty and Al were talking and looked concerned. My spirits started to deflate.

"What's the matter? Is there a problem?"

Al spoke up first.

"We want to move Kenny to Newton for observation and to be on the safe side. He needs x-rays of his forehead, nose, and eye socket and IV antibiotics. For all we know he could have a skull or facial fracture, and Betty feels that he should be seen by a neurologist," Al continued. "I'm going to call his parents, and then I want you to tell me what happened, every detail."

I sensed that Al had questions about my performance and my fitness to be a counselor. My pulse rose and I could feel sweat on the back of my neck. I was being called to task, which was a given. After less than a week, a quarter of my campers would be in the Newton Hospital. I could sense that the shit was about to hit the fan, and Al did not look happy.

While he called the Sawyers and Betty started arrangements to transport Kenny to Newton, I asked if I could check on the boys. They had showered and changed and were ready for dinner. I asked them to go to the lodge and play ping-pong and cards until dinner. I took a quick lukewarm shower, shaved, brushed my teeth, and put on fresh clothes, all in ten minutes. Then I returned to the infirmary to face the music.

***

By now Al was in a snit and was pissed that I'd left to shower and change.

"Berman, what the hell happened out there?"

The fact that he called me Berman and not Bob was not a good sign, but I spewed out my account of the incident in minute detail, and I thought he believed that I was not negligent. Stupid or unlucky, but not negligent.

He agreed with my decision to keep everyone together and not leave Kenny with a group of twelve-year-olds while I went for help, but he did question my failure to follow the trail.

"Sir, I don't know how that happened because the trail was clearly marked on the trip out."

"Be that as it may, I am impressed with the way you stopped the bleeding and the way you got him back."

Thank God, I did something right.

"Go now and gather your troops for dinner. I'll wait for the ambulance and go with Betty to Newton. I have to talk with the Sawyers when they arrive at the hospital; they will have questions. You can imagine how upset they are, and I want to defuse the situation."

CHAPTER TWELVE

Dinner was a blessing. We had meatloaf and mashed potatoes with gravy. Who cared that they were powdered? We were starved. I ate like a horse in spite of being worried and upset. After two portions I scarfed down apple crisp for dessert with three glasses of cold milk.

"What's going to happen to Kenny?" A concerned Jeffrey asked.

"He's on his way to the hospital to be on the safe side. Nurse Sloan feels he'll be OK, but she wants a doctor to check him out."

After dinner we stayed together in the lodge to play board games and just talk and joke around to let out pent-up emotions. We seemed to need each other's company and sort of gained strength from each other, a mental osmosis. We were all physically fatigued, but mentally wired. Eventually fatigue won out, and we went back to the cabin. Tomorrow was another day with a lot planned, and we would hope for good news from Newton about both Kenny and Danny.

Before going to bed we got out our laundry bags for pickup in the morning. We labeled the bags with our names and made a list of items. Exhausted, the boys fell into their bunks, and I turned on the radio, keeping the volume low.

The Yankees were playing the Indians and the boys, although tired, asked me to turn it up. Mel Allen was describing Whitey Ford's delivery and his mastery of the heart of Cleveland's batting order. As the announcer droned on about baseball and Ballantine beer, the Yankee sponsor, my mind started to wander and I couldn't help but wonder how I had lost the trail and where we might have ended up. We would have gone miles northwest of our destination, and Kenny might have been in real trouble. I shivered at the thought.

My mind wandering was interrupted by the screams of Mel Allen. Hank Bauer, the Yankees' reliable right fielder and a former tough marine, had just

42

robbed Rocky Colavito of an opposite-field homerun by diving into the stands by the right field foul pole and making a sensational catch.

I heard some of the boys snoring, so I turned off the game and read for a while with illumination from my flashlight. After a few pages of *"Catcher in the Rye,"* I started to doze, only to be startled awoke by Jim Butler shaking me.

"Bob, I heard what happened. How the hell are you?"

"I'm fine, maybe a little achy and tired, but OK. Kenny's another story. He's in the hospital in Newton along with Danny. "Two out of my eight kids are in trouble. How's that for a morbidity rate? Pretty bad, huh?"

"I heard that bullshit. None of this was your fault. Matter of fact, the rumor is circulating that you saved Kenny's life."

"I didn't do anything but get him back."

"Stop the crap. I heard you kept your wits about you and stopped the bleeding. And for that matter, you also saved Danny Golden a lot of aggravation."

"I guess so, but it was more instinct and fear than clear, rational thought." I felt good about Jim's support, but I also needed his opinion on two unsettling events; how did the snake get into the latrine, and how did I lose the trail markers?

"Jim, when we have a few hours off, I'd like you to humor me and take a jog along the trail where I hiked with the boys. I don't know how I lost the trail, and I have to satisfy my curiosity. I have a very uncomfortable feeling about it."

"Anytime, buddy. Get some sleep. I'll see you in the morning."

***

That night I had a very disturbing dream. I was in the woods, blindfolded and disoriented, frightened to the point of panic. I walked in small steps before tripping and falling. I started to crawl, scraping my arms and legs. A moment later I was falling off the side of a hill and into what I thought was mud. It wasn't mud, it was quicksand. As I started to sink, my blindfold loosened and I could see. There in front of me, laughing, was Lester Cartright, the guy who drove us to ballgames in his truck. I began to sink further in the warm ooze, and he made no effort to help me. He just continued to laugh. My mouth and nose were covered and I was suffocating.

I awoke in a profuse sweat.

"I'm going nuts," I thought. "I'm sure I am." In less than one week my cabin was decimated and I was having paranoid thoughts about a plot to get my boys. "Stop it now," I said to myself. My breathing slowed and I began to calm down, eventually falling back to sleep.

CHAPTER THIRTEEN

In the morning I awoke to reveille and a full bladder. Inexplicitly I felt calm and refreshed and ready for the day. The most pressing issues were checking on Kenny's progress and Danny's asthma. My prayers were answered at breakfast, when an exhausted-looking Al Simmons arose at the head table to announce that Kenny Sawyer was stable.

"There were no fractures, but his deep cut had become infected, and he needed what they called "debridement" in the operating room. This meant that they had to clean the wound and cut away the dead tissue. The doctors are optimistic and think he will have an uneventful recovery." He added, "Danny was out of the ICU and would be discharged today or tomorrow."

The announcement met with raucous applause. Life was getting better.

Al caught up with me after breakfast and asked for a moment of my time to speak with him and the assistant director, Bernie Allen. I took a deep breath and followed him into his office, fearing the worst. I could feel my pulse quicken and sense the sweat on the back of my neck. I knew this would be bad.

"Bob, I'm concerned about what's going on. We've been in camp for a very short time, and there have already been two major accidents." At least he called me Bob and not Berman.

"Sir," I countered, "you can hardly blame Danny Golden's asthmatic attack on me. I do, however, feel a sense of responsibility for Kenny. The accident happened on my watch, so to speak, but I don't see how I could have prevented it. I can't be with the boys twenty-four hours a day, and I'm not sure that they would want me to accompany them to the bathroom."

"I know that, Bob, but we have to be more careful and diligent. We are responsible and liable for all the campers. Their welfare depends on us, and their parents left us in charge."

"Sir, I've been a camper here for years, a CIT, and a junior counselor. I think that I'm experienced and careful, and I will do everything in my power to minimize any exposure to trouble. I don't want to put my boys or the camp at risk, but I don't want to keep second-guessing myself. I don't want to feel like I'm under a microscope, walking on eggshells."

At this point I felt like I was almost shouting, proclaiming my innocence, when Bernie Allen piped in like a referee.

"That seems reasonable. Just keep your eyes and ears open and your wits about you. That's all that Al and I ask."

"I'll do that. Trust me."

Al seemed satisfied, and I got the idea that I was dismissed. I headed back to the cabin feeling somewhat betrayed and depressed. Was I really negligent? Al had sure implied it.

As I entered the cabin, slumped and with my head lowered, I didn't notice anything or anyone ahead of me and almost walked right over one of the boys. I looked up, and my mood soared. In front of me stood Danny Golden, of all people. I couldn't believe my eyes.

"Danny, what are you doing here?"

"I feel great, and I convinced my dad that I had to come back to camp. I want to be here."

"You're a sight for sore eyes, and you don't know how much I needed to have you back. Things have really gone downhill for me and cabin five. Kenny is now in the hospital with a bad cut over his eye from a fall. His parents are coming up to be with him, and I don't expect him back."

"Do you think he'll be all right? I mean, he isn't critical or anything, is he?"

"The doctor said he has no skull fracture, and he was awake the last time I saw him. These are all good signs."

"Geez, I'm sorry. It looks like I started a run on Newton Hospital."

"It's good to have you back, Danny. I mean that. Let's catch up with the guys, they'll be thrilled to see you."

CHAPTER FOURTEEN

Things went well over the next week with good weather and no incidents. To my utter surprise, I received a call from the Sawyers thanking me for my efforts and quick thinking on Kenny's behalf. Even better, they spoke with Al Simmons and Bernie Allen, convincing them that my actions were life-saving and that I should be commended. Al didn't go that far, but he did ease off, and I stopped looking over my shoulder.

Danny was fitting in. He was even becoming popular. He was happy and blossoming, and more importantly, he was not wheezing. Reports on Kenny were optimistic, and life was looking better.

Happy days were here again, and I felt elated as I headed toward the ball field with the boys. A softball game had been planned for the afternoon, campers versus counselors. So that the counselors would not have an advantage, they would have to bat left-handed if they were naturally righty and vice versa. The kids were excited and anxious to knock off the staff. Bob Beebe, the athletic director, had picked two boys from each cabin to play against the counselors while Al organized the staff team. By four o'clock, the entire camp was there, either to play or cheer. Nellie Flanders and her crew had set up barbeque grills and tables ahead of time and were now bringing supplies and food from the mess hall. The game would be followed by a cookout: hot dogs, hamburgers, potato salad, baked beans, Kool Aid, and gobs of ice cream.

The campers took the field first for their warm-ups. While Bob Beebe was busily organizing positions and the batting orders, Al was hitting ground balls to the infielders and Bernie was hitting fly balls to the outfield. Our cabin was ably represented by Bobby Moore and Tony LaRocca, and the boys cheered loudly when they were introduced.

Now the counselors took the field, warming up stiff throwing arms, judging the low sun, and checking the field for rocks and ruts, which could cause bad bounces. At four-thirty, Al blew the whistle and announced that "the game" would begin.

Jim Butler was our designated captain and Bobby represented the campers for the all-important coin toss to determine the home team. As Al flipped the half-dollar in the air, Bobby yelled "heads." The coin landed in the dirt, flipped a few times, and settled with heads showing. The campers were the home team and would have last licks. As the boys ran onto the field, the crowd went wild.

I was the leadoff man, and being a natural righty, I had to bat left-handed. Tony was the pitcher, and with a smile on his face, he fed me slow, looping stuff that begged me to swing. My first effort was a powerful whiff, and I could feel my face redden with embarrassment. As I repositioned myself for the next pitch, I glanced over to the third base line and saw her- Jean, Al's lovely daughter. God she was cute, tanned, and in a t-shirt that said "Camp Spenser." She was eying me and I knew at that moment that I had to do something big. I had to get a major hit, even a home run.

The next pitch, a big, fat, juicy tomato arched toward me, so easy to hit. It began its downward path, and I started my swing when it was at eye level. I didn't feel or hear any contact, all I felt was air. I had missed the ball by a foot as it landed on home plate. Things looked bleak, with an o and two count, and I thought I saw a smirk on Tony's face.

I said to myself, "Wait for the ball, and don't be over anxious. Just make contact, and don't try to kill it. Bat to ball, a short, compact swing."

With a grin Tony unleashed a slow backward spinner. I waited, and waited, and waited. It looked like a pumpkin and I swung, abandoning all my strategy. I swung with all my might, unfortunately taking my eye off the ball, which I had been told by my father never to do. Alas, like mighty Casey, I had struck out. To the roar and then the jeers of the campers, I slinked back to the bench to sulk. I had struck out on three straight pitches in front of the entire camp and Jean. She didn't seem very upset or disappointed in me and just giggled, seeming to enjoy my shame and discomfort. Lucky for me, the next two batters singled, and Arnie Flowers cleared the bases with a home run. At the end of the top of the first, we were up three to zip. I shouldn't have gloated over our lead against a bunch of kids, but I couldn't help myself.

In the bottom of the stanza, the boys mounted a rally. The first two batters walked, and Tony came up. The cocky son of a gun laid down a perfect bunt and the bags were loaded for Bobby Moore. I had a bad feeling as he came to the plate. The kid was a great athlete and looked like he was fourteen or fifteen. He fouled the first pitch down the left field line about twenty to thirty feet beyond the outfielder and only about two feet outside the foul line marked in lime. The next pitch was a ball that almost hit him. This was followed by a fat blooper, which he promptly stroked between the left and centerfielder. The line drive kept rolling, as there were no outfield fences, and the bases cleared. Bobby got the green light as he rounded third and slid into home just ahead of the throw for an inside-the-park homer. The crowd went wild, with everyone slapping his back as he returned to the bench. Once order was restored the inning was finished with no further damage, and the score stood, four to three for the campers.

The second inning was a wash except for a solo, tape–measure homer by Len Aarons, a massive guy who played football at West Virginia. Batting lefty, he put the ball over a cabin that was a hundred feet beyond the right field grass. No one even tried to find the ball. It was four to four after two.

The third and fourth innings were marked by error after error, especially by the campers. We scored five unearned runs, and it might have been eight if not for a great catch by a kid from cabin six named Jimmy Sullivan. He caught a deep drive over his shoulder in right center with the bases loaded and two out.

Going into the fifth, we were up nine to four, and like "big kids," we started to gloat. It was a mistake. We went down 1-2-3. In the bottom of the inning, the boys began bunting, running, and spraying base hits instead of trying for the long ball. The result was three runs and the gap tightened to nine to seven. Matters were getting serious.

You know how it is when you play a kid in chess or checkers. You kind of let him win, but after awhile something inside, your competitiveness, takes over and you try a little harder. Soon you try to win. You're tired of letting the little prick win; you want to teach him a lesson. Well, that's how it was in the sixth inning. To a man, we all came to the same conclusion. We knew we needed a bigger cushion than two runs, and we knew we had to win. The boys were getting cocky. Not a very mature approach or one that I'm proud of, but there you have it.

I led off the inning with a scorching liner that almost hit the first baseman, who ducked in time. I looked up after sliding safely into second for a double and thought I saw a smile on Jean's face. At any rate, the hit restored my confidence and erased some of the embarrassment of my early failures and generally poor play. Two more hits followed, and then Jim Butler lofted a huge high fly to left-center, which was dropped by the outfielder, who looked like he was going to cry. When the dust settled and the inning ended, four runs were in and we were up thirteen to seven. An inning and a half to go, and the boys started to look worried. They came up with one run, and going into the last stanza, we had them thirteen to eight.

In our half of the seventh, we again started to overswing and popped up often. We did have a leadoff single, but the runner was stranded when the next three batters flied out. The stage was set for the bottom of the inning, the campers' last hurrah.

The frame began benignly enough with the first batter grounding out. However, our diminutive foe was not done, as two singles followed. Bobby Moore came up and again delivered with an opposite-field double that cleared the bases, 13-10. Another single, an error, and a walk and we were in serious trouble with the potential winning run coming to the plate. The next batter stroked a fly to left field that Bill Chambers lost in the sun, but recovered in time to make a shaky catch. The runner on third tagged up and scored.

So, it all came down to this. 2 outs, 2 runners on, and the score 13-11. Tony La Rocca stepped to the plate and I had another bad feeling. He lined the first pitch over the shortstop and into the gap between left and center. Two runs were in as Tony turned toward third base. As he was reaching the bag, the throw from the outfield went over the cutoff man's head, and Tony was able to walk home. The crowd went berserk as the makeshift stands and blankets cleared, the kids screaming and jumping up and down. They had beaten the unbeatable, fourteen to thirteen. David had slain Goliath. They carried Tony on their shoulders, or at least they tried to. It was a great moment for the underdog, and we tried to be gracious losers. We all shook hands and patted each other on the back. Al Simmons was beaming. This was Camp Spenser at its best.

No one noticed the lone figure on the hill who was watching with hate in his eyes.

CHAPTER FIFTEEN

By now Nellie and her staff had burgers and franks on the grill, and the smell was incredible. On a picnic table were large bowls of baked beans and potato salad, plates of sliced onions, tomatoes, cheese, bowls of pickles, and pitchers of Kool Aid. On another table were stacks of paper plates and napkins held down by rocks to keep the wind from blowing them away, buckets of plastic utensils, paper cups, baskets of hot dog and hamburger buns, and open cans of ketchup and mustard. We all lined up to get our plates and then we filled them with franks and hamburgers, hot and juicy on the buns, and all the other goodies. This was heaven on earth.

We all sat on the grass alongside the playing field, and as we ate, I felt an incredible sense of pride. Pride in what camp meant to a boy and what a maturing boy did for a camp. These kids were everything good and healthy, and as corny as it sounds, everything that was good about the youth in our country.

"Who said youth is wasted on the young?" I thought. Nothing was wasted on these boys.

I felt a light touch on my hand. I looked up and saw Jean above me, the sun behind her forming a soft yellow corolla of light.

"Hi. Mind if I join you?"

Before I could respond, she had settled down next to me with her plate on her lap. What a smile. What a beauty. Perfect teeth, perfect eyes, slim arms, long legs, and a summer tan like you saw on girls down the shore. At sixteen, she was developing into a young woman with a great body that I couldn't help but notice. As I looked at her, my hormones started to stir. This girl was going to be a problem, a pleasant one, but a problem. She looked and smelled wonderful.

"You didn't do so well today but you have great potential."

"I'm not much of a switch hitter, but righty, I'm fine," I said defensively.

"Well I think it was sweet, even noble, letting the boys win."

"I assure you that we didn't let them win, but I like being considered noble and generous."

"Win or lose, I enjoyed watching you. Not you as in a group of counselors, but you as in you."

I stared at her in disbelief. Was I hearing things, or did this adorable creature just come on to me?

I was cautiously optimistic as I said, "I have to admit that I was staring at you as well."

"I know."

With the ice broken, I started to relax and we just ate and talked. She was going to be a senior at West Orange High School, turning seventeen in December. I would be eighteen in October, or did I already mention that? As I had guessed, Al Simmons was her stepfather, having married Jean's mother seven years earlier. Jean had little contact with her biological father and Al had taken on the role of surrogate dad, which he apparently filled well. She felt a great fondness for him, although he was a strict disciplinarian. This meant no phone calls after eight on weeknights, no going out at night with friends during the school week except for school functions, and limited dating on weekends. In 1959 these were not unreasonable rules. Jean, however, seemed a tad annoyed by what she considered "old-fashioned" standards. She seemed to have a rebellious streak, a wild side that could spell trouble ahead for Al.

She just talked, laughed, and oozed personality, even sensuality, without realizing it. She told me about her family, friends, interests, and future plans. I just listened and nodded.

Abruptly she stood up and announced, "Let's take a walk."

The kids were eating and talking, excited and busy, so we would not be missed for the next hour or two. " "Let's go down by the lake," I said

"That sounds good to me," she responded.

It was warm, and it would be light out for another hour or more, so we headed toward the waterfront. Jean took my hand, and her touch caused an incredible sensation. Anticipation and excitement would be the best way to describe it. When we reached the water's edge, we took off our shoes, I rolled up my jeans to the knees, and we waded in. The water was cold, but refreshing rather than numbing. As if reading each other's minds, we both dove in at the same time with reckless abandon.

We emerged laughing and shivering and fell against each other. Jean's t-shirt was plastered against her chest, and I could feel her breasts and taut nipples as our bodies came together. She looked up at me coyly, and I bent to kiss her, at first tentatively and then more assuredly. She responded by pressing closer, and I could feel her leg between my thighs. She opened her lips, and I slid my tongue into her mouth. We were both out of control, panting and hot as hell. We moved out of the water and laid on the grass near the boathouse. She let me put my hands under her shirt, and I gently stroked her firm breasts, feeling her hot breath on my face. I began to move my hand downward when she stopped me.

This was 1959, and we were both virgins. I only knew of one girl in high school who "had gone all the way," and that was only unsubstantiated rumor. We were two horny kids groping and rubbing, but going much further was, God forbid, a real taboo. So we just lay there for minutes, holding one another and feeling warm and content. After a while we got to our feet and went back in the water to "cool off." Incredible thoughts and sensations went through my mind and body. I couldn't believe what had just happened. We hardly knew each other.

As we hugged and lightly kissed each other in knee-deep water, I had the uneasy feeling that someone was watching us. There were no campers or staff in the area. A voyeur, perhaps? No. It was more the uncomfortable feeling that someone was observing with malice or evil intent. I looked over Jean's shoulder and scanned the woods by the boathouse. I saw nothing but heard the rustle of trees above and to the left of where we were standing. Was someone there, or was it the wind or my imagination?

"Let's go, Jean," I said. "It's getting dark and we'll be missed."

"Will I see you tomorrow?"

"Are you serious? I'll find a way to see you every day."

She smiled.

We walked up the hill, hand in hand, toward the ball field. The festivities were winding down, and everyone was sauntering back toward the lodge and cabins. Unfortunately we were noticed because we were absolutely soaked and shivering. We made up some cock-and-bull story that we had capsized a canoe and hoped that no one questioned it. The boys were no problem; it was Al that I was worried about.

CHAPTER SIXTEEN

The next day was rainy and hot, and all activities had to be moved indoors. The arts and crafts area was packed, and Bob Williams had to move back and forth between supervising there and giving talks on nature lore in the main lodge. The boys were excited about the opportunity to do crafts while it was raining, as Visitors' Day was coming up in a week or so, and they wanted to make presents for their families. They got busy carving, sanding, and painting small totem poles, making key chains by braiding leather strips, and making bracelets by stringing beads. I really didn't feel in the mood for arts and crafts, so when the rain slowed, I asked if anyone wanted to go fishing. I got an immediate yes from Danny and Jeffrey, my only takers.

So we grabbed our rain slickers and fishing gear, including a jar of dirt filled with worms, and headed for the boathouse.

"Danny, grab the front with Jeff and I'll push the rear," as we launched a good-sized rowboat into the water.

The boys donned life jackets and then sat side by side at the oars. I sat in the stern while "my crew" rowed. We hugged the shoreline, reaching a good reedy, boggy area. This would be a good place to catch bass, but also to snag hooks and line.

"This looks like a good spot," I yelled, and the boys ran the boat into the reeds. We were about a quarter mile from camp, and we began to bait our hooks.

Danny was the least squeamish when it came to that task and adeptly threaded the barbed hook through the worm and threw his line overboard.

"Man, you're a real pro. Where'd you learn to do that?"

"My grandpa took me fishing a lot of times before he died. Dad never seemed very interested."

I figured old man Golden probably wouldn't want to get his hands dirty.

Since Danny was so skilled, Jeffrey and I let him do the honors, and he gladly baited our hooks. Within minutes Danny got a bite, gave a yank, and started to reel in his fish. The pole bent and the kid became really excited. He reeled, and reeled, and reeled. His arms and shoulders ached and his forearms burned, but he got his catch to the side of the boat, where Jeffrey and I were able to snag the fish with a net.

"Wow, it's huge," said Jeffrey, excited but with a note of envy in his voice.

I was able to lift the slippery son of a gun out of the tangled net and drop him into the middle of the boat.

Danny was absolutely beside himself. The fish was at least two to three pounds, and he couldn't wait to lift it and remove the hook.

Grabbing it deftly by the gills, the kid expertly removed the barb and dropped his catch into a bucket of lake water in the stern of the boat.

Jeffrey and I just gawked in disbelief. Danny was like a pro. He was so excited, getting up and down, to recheck his prize.

As Danny was basking in his glory, Jeffrey felt a pull and felt his rod bend. He really didn't feel a bite, but he was sure he had something, so he started reeling in his line. He worked at the spool, slowly at first, and then more rapidly, and then in a frenzied pace as he felt the resistance increase.

"I got something. I'm sure."

"Slow down, Jeff, or you'll lose him."

But Jeffrey wasn't listening. He was working like a madman, sweating, huffing and puffing, determined to land his catch.

The resistance in his line lessened as his "catch" reached the surface. Disappointingly it looked like some kind of object covered with mud, sticks, and pieces of reed; it was definitely not a fish. Once on board, we washed off all the mud and debris, leaving what looked like an old shoe. It was old and rotted, almost falling apart when touched, but it was definitely a small shoe, a little girl's shoe. We all burst out laughing, Jeffrey the loudest, as he threw his "catch" back in the lake.

Another hour of no bites, and we decided to pack it in and row back to camp. The sun was trying to break through the clouds; the sky was definitely lightening. It had been a glorious afternoon.

When we got back to the cabin there was a note waiting for me on my bunk. It was from Betty Sloan, who was happy to report that Kenny was much improved, fully alert, and out of danger. He was in a regular room and hopefully would be discharged within twenty-four to forty-eight hours. This was a major relief.

Danny wanted to take his bass to Bob Williams, the nature expert, to have it stuffed and mounted. I convinced him to let us photograph him holding the fish and then get an official weight to announce at dinner. This was OK with him, as he really didn't want to kill the fish and he certainly didn't want to eat it. Once done, we carried the bucket to the side of the lake and let the fish go.

In the mess hall that night, I announced that Danny Golden had set a new camp record by landing a two pound and nine ounce large-mouth bass. Everyone clapped and whistled, and Danny just smiled, the most genuine, glowing smile I had ever seen.

As we ate dinner, I sneaked a few peeks at Jean, and she in turn gazed back at me. God she was gorgeous. I just couldn't stop thinking about the day before and when I would sneak off with her again.

CHAPTER SEVENTEEN

Over the next few days, the boys seemed to be gearing up for Visitors' Day. Parents, brothers and sisters, and assorted dogs would make their appearances for the afternoon. It would be a zoo, with cars and people and pets all over the place. We had to pray for good weather, as rain would be a disaster, forcing hundreds into the lodge and causing the cancellation of outdoor activities. It would be havoc trying to feed and entertain the masses in a crowded, stuffy lodge. With good weather, plans were for all kinds of activities for parents, sibs, and campers followed by a barbeque lunch. There would be canoe and swimming races, archery contests, horseshoes, tag-team races, a softball game, and numerous other amusements.

Nellie would barbeque hundreds of pounds of chicken on huge outdoor grills made from oil drums, to be served with baked beans made with bacon and corn on the cob, really good New Jersey corn, sweet and tender. The parents were told beforehand that they could bring desserts, so there would be plenty of chocolate cakes, apple, blueberry, strawberry, and rhubarb pies, strawberry shortcake, and peach cobbler. The boys would be able to show off their new-found skills and craft projects and just enjoy a day with their families.

The afternoon would be fun, but there would be a letdown at the end of the day when it was time for family and friends to leave. You always felt it no matter how old you were or how long you had been a camper. When your folks departed, it was like being left behind. They were going home, and you weren't. Luckily it was a fleeting feeling, and by nighttime you were back into the swing of things.

Families, friends, and pets started to arrive by ten-thirty. They were excited to see their sons and proud as well. I'm sure they all felt that their kids had grown at least four inches and were healthy and happy. Jeffrey's parents and sister were delighted to hear about his exploits at the waterfront. Mr. Lebowitz pulled me aside to ask about his son's weight and stamina and if he was being picked on. I assured him that his son was making friends and fitting in, and was not the object of ridicule. He smiled and shook my hand, slipping me a five-dollar bill. Visitors' Day was great for tips, and who was I to argue? It seemed crude to tip your son's counselor, but it was done at every camp in the United States.

Soon the Wilders, O'Neills, and Moores arrived, all chattering, kissing, hugging, and extolling the virtues of camp life. Mike and Tony hung together while this was going on, as they did not expect any visitors.

As I was feeling sorry for them, I caught a glimpse of Dr. Golden walking toward the cabin, ten paces ahead of his wife, as if she were a servant or second-class citizen. The blowhard immediately came up to me, shook my hand, and asked about Danny's progress.

"I bet he's not taking his medications regularly. I bet he's wheezing," he rambled on. "I bet he has trouble keeping up."

"No, Dr. Golden. Quite the contrary," I said biting my lip. "Danny is very excited about being back, and he has participated in everything. The other day he set a new camp record by landing a good-sized bass. We took pictures of the event, which he'll have developed when he gets home. He has had absolutely no wheezing, and I think the fresh air is good for him."

Dr. Golden could only agree. He looked disappointed that he couldn't argue or even make a point. He almost seemed deflated by his son's success.

While we were talking, Mrs. Golden started checking Danny's clothes, bed, and dirty laundry bag.

"Please leave the kid alone," I thought.

I held back the urge to tell her to get lost. Her son didn't need her doting, especially in front of the other boys and their parents. There would be plenty of opportunity for her to obsess over him when the summer was over. Fortunately after a few minutes she stopped her prying and returned, like a lap dog, to her husband's side. Danny, luckily, took it all in stride and paid little attention to his folks.

As the morning progressed into afternoon, I couldn't wait for things to end. Visitors' Day was always disruptive. Just as everything was in order and running smoothly, along came the parents to fuck up the works. But on the plus side, the tips were great and were welcome for the upcoming college year. Also, the activities were fun, and it turned out to be a beautiful summer day. Another plus was that Jean showed up off and on, giving me what I interpreted as seductive looks. Where did a girl that age learn these things?

After the fun and games, the bugle sounded for the highlight of the day, Nellie's barbeque.

CHAPTER EIGHTEEN

The festivities continued until four-thirty, when everyone was uncomfortable and about to burst from overeating. The Gelusil and Tums were being passed around as the stuffed families began to gravitate toward their cars for the final farewells and the drives home.

I said my good-byes, shook hands, and noticed that none of the boys seemed reluctant or upset to have their parents leave. As I waved my last farewell and smiled as if my face would crack, I turned to find Jean by my side. She reached over and took my hand. I felt the hairs on my back of my neck stand up and my pulse quicken.

"Can we take a little walk?" she said somewhat longingly.

"Sure, but I have to get the kids settled first. I'll let them go to the lodge with Jim's cabin for cards and games."

"I just want to stop by our cabin to pick up a sweatshirt, and we'll need a flashlight in case it gets dark. You don't mind if we take my dog?" Jean asked.

"I've heard about your dog, but I've never seen her. What is it, a poodle or a cocker spaniel?" I joked.

"No, it's not a her, it's a him. It's a German Shepherd, a real dog. I think I'll order him to keep you in line."

"What's his name, this scary guard dog of yours?"

"It's Max. He's a real gentle giant, about one-hundred-thirty pounds and just a baby. He's very laid-back and lovable, but I warn you that he is very protective of me."

"Is this some kind of threat? If my hands or lips wander, good old Max will attack?"

"No. I'm sure he'll like you. Just let him sniff you, and it wouldn't hurt if you petted him before we leave."

With trusty Max by our side, we walked the path through the chapel to the waterfront and boathouse. Once there we sat on the steps, tossing stones into the water while making small talk. Then we gently kissed. She opened her mouth and I slid my tongue in. So far so good. Max had not yet ripped me to pieces.

My hands slipped down to her breasts and then inside her sweatshirt and t-shirt. She did not have on a bra and her breasts were firm and warm, her nipples taut and erect. We were starting to lose it again when Max began to bark and bolted into the woods.

Within seconds we heard rustling sounds in the foliage and then a whimpering sound. Max emerged with blood streaming from his mouth and ears and collapsed onto the grass next to where we were sitting. Jean ran to his side and began stroking his huge head. He seemed more stunned than hurt, but Jean was beside herself.

I ran to the water and took off my shirt, soaked it in the lake and rung it out. I used it to wash the blood from Max's mouth, face, and ears. He had been hit with something and happened to get a piece of whoever did the hitting, for in his mouth were shreds of fabric, possibly from pants or a shirt.

I removed the small pieces of cloth from his mouth and put them in my pocket so that I could take a better look in the daylight. Once Max recovered we decided to get him back to the Simmons's cabin. He was able to walk but was a little unsteady and had some trouble negotiating the hill from the chapel to the main camp.

We got him settled in for the night, and I think he enjoyed the extra attention. Within minutes he was snoring away, and Jean and I sneaked out to the porch to talk.

I told her about the strange happenings surrounding Danny Golden's asthmatic attack, Kenny Sawyer's injury, the lost trail on our hike, and my uncomfortable feeling of being watched.

"Someone has been purposely doing these things. I'm sure of it. He has been watching us, and I don't know why, but I intend to find out."

CHAPTER NINETEEN

After leaving Jean, I went back to the cabin, where I took out the shreds of fabric and laid them on my bed. With illumination from my flashlight I was able to make out most of the colors, mainly red, green, and yellow on a background of white in a plaid pattern. It was probably cotton, but heavier than t-shirt material and could have been light wool. Had I ever seen this cloth before? I really couldn't say, but I didn't think so. I wished that I had a larger piece, but this would have to do.

In the morning, while the boys were at the swim area, I would search the woods near the boathouse for clues. Maybe I would find more evidence like a footprint, a torn shirt, or the weapon that injured Max.

After breakfast and cabin cleanup, the boys went to assigned activities, and I snuck off to investigate the woods near the boathouse.

To the left of the building and deep in the brush, I found broken twigs and trampled grass. Clinging to the branch of a small tree was a piece of fabric similar to the one I had, but definitely bloody. Below it was a large chunk of wood covered in blood, which could have been wielded like a club, probably to clunk the charging Max. That incredible, fearless animal must have been a scary sight for the perp, and he had obviously lashed out at the dog. "But who and why? What threat could we possibly pose?"

I searched further, but found little more, and as I made my way up the hill to camp, I pondered on the situation. Were all these happenings connected or was it a bunch of unrelated incidents that fed my paranoia?

At any rate, I decided to run everything by Jim and Jean to get their take on the situation. I was too freaked to offer a sensible, logical explanation.

***

"Let's say you're right, Bob, and I'm not convinced. What would anyone gain by terrorizing you or a bunch of camp kids?"

"The only thing that comes to mind is that with each incident, Camp Spenser and Al Simmons come under fire. It becomes a financial and a liability issue that could close the camp."

"Think of it this way. Each boy who gets hurt has two caring, worried parents. Soon they start to think. "Why are there so many incidents? Is the counselor negligent? Is the camp poorly run? Should I send my boy back next year?" This could add up to a lot of negative publicity that could affect the enrollment for the next year. It could even raise questions for a lawyer."

"So you think someone is doing this to create a negative image of the camp and possibly threaten its future existence," Jim said.

"I'm just saying that it's a theory, but I think a pretty good one."

"If I accept your premise, Bob, then why? What would the closing of Camp Spenser do for anyone except to cause some eleven to fifteen year olds to find another camp or another summer activity?"

"That's what you and I have to find out."

CHAPTER TWENTY

That night I lay on my bunk going over all the possibilities. As fatigue was setting in and I started to doze off, a thought began to take form in the back of my brain. If someone created enough fear to cause the camp to close, eventually the property would have to be sold. Could this be the motive? Could the land be that valuable? Probably to a developer or a wheeler-dealer type.

Could there be something of value in the land, like gold or oil or uranium? What if a person knew there was some asset here? Wouldn't it make sense to get rid of the camp, maybe even cause a foreclosure? It would then be possible to buy back the property at a bargain-basement price.

The land and the beautiful lake had always been there, and land values had changed little in the past fifty years, mainly because northwestern New Jersey was still fairly rural. What if someone knew that this was about to change? What if the bad guy knew that there would be a chance of major development in Sussex County: houses, shops, schools, whole communities? For this to happen, there had to be access to the area. That would mean a major highway or highways. Northeastern New Jersey was heavily populated and becoming more crowded and expensive due to its proximity to New York City. Bergen, Passaic, and Essex Counties were growing by leaps and bounds, but not Sussex County. Further growth could potentially be there, and maybe the bad guy knew it.

I fell asleep and did not dream, and in the morning I awoke with fresh ideas and a focus. I would start delving into my theory, ask around, and maybe even make some calls on the pay-phone to friends and relatives with political connections. But first things first. Today we had a major outing. We had a swim meet and softball game at a neighboring Boy Scout camp in Andover. The entire cabin was going, and we would leave right after lunch.

CHAPTER TWENTY ONE

An excited group of boys assembled at the flagpole. In the driveway by the lodge sat Lester Cartright's truck, a large, dark green, open model with slotted sides to about shoulder height. The boys crowded around the perimeter of the vehicle's bay ready to load. There were no restraints, but who cared? This was summer fun, riding in an open truck along a dirt road with dust flying and the wind in your hair.

Lester pulled out a slotted panel from the back of the truck and wedged it against the back bumper as a ladder. He loaded the boys one at a time, along with the equipment bags. I rode in the back with the boys while another counselor, a guy named Bill Rutherford, joined Lester in the cab after he closed the back panels and tied the sides and back with rope. Lester was silent and humorless, and the look on his face said "no horsing around or climbing up the side panels or you'll walk home."

With a lurch the truck began to back up and turn. Lester jammed the gear-shift into first, the motor coughed, and the truck eased forward. After a series of shifts we were on our way down the dirt road leading to the camp entrance. Once we passed through the two large, decoratively painted totem poles we made a turn onto the paved rural road to Andover. As we gained speed the boys started to sing. When we passed a car going the other way, they whistled, yelled, and waved.

After about twenty minutes Lester turned onto a dirt road and decreased his speed. The road was bumpy and dusty and filled with potholes. As we descended a small hill, we saw the entrance to Camp Shawnee. A large wooden sign said, "Boy Scouts of America." We passed under the sign and turned right up an incline lined by huge pines. At the crest of the small hill, we came to a clearing that seemed to be a parking area, and Lester stopped the truck, put it in gear, and put on the brake. He came around to the rear, untied the ropes, and lifted out the back panel to unload the boys onto the gravel parking lot. We took a path to our left and descended the hill until we saw the roof of the lodge, several cabins, and a slate-blue lake below.

We were greeted by the camp director, who was in a scout uniform, complete with a sash of merit badges. Several boys, in similar attire, said hello and escorted us to the lodge for cool drinks and introductions. While we were walking toward the rustic lodge, I glanced over my shoulder and noticed that Lester had lit up a smoke, probably a Lucky or a Camel. He was leaning against the cab of the truck and seemed bored and disinterested. He would wait for us to return and would not make an effort to watch the ballgame or swim meet. I guess he was getting paid by the hour and it was strictly business.

Earl Cooper, the camp director, turned out to be a master of organization, directing half our group to the softball field and half to the waterfront. The softball field was a joke with scruffy grass, plenty of rocks to cause bad hops, and little dirt. There was no backstop and the bases weren't secured to the ground, so they would have to be repositioned after each runner passed. The good thing was that there was a fence extending from left field to the right field line, and the distance for a home run was short, I'd say about one-hundred-twenty-five to one-hundred-fifty feet. Danny, who was in charge of the softball equipment and was the official scorer, arranged everything. The bats, balls, and mitts were neatly aligned, and he was busy setting up a makeshift scorer's table and helping Bill Rutherford with the starting line-up and batting order. He was quite knowledgeable about baseball and knew all the stats, memorizing the starting line-ups of all the major league teams and most of the leaders in RBIs, homeruns, slugging percentage, and runs scored for both the American and National leagues. Furthermore, he knew how to keep score, how to substitute players to maximize the batting order, and how to position fielders for certain hitters. In short, he was a walking baseball encyclopedia and a coach's best friend.

At the waterfront, Jeffrey would be our ace in the hole. He would swim the crawl, breaststroke, and backstroke and anchor the relay teams. Earl Cooper had organized all the events, but Shawnee's swim director, whistle in hand, would officiate.

As Jeffrey took off his t-shirt and baggy shorts, the giggles started. He had lost some weight over the weeks, but he still had rolls of baby fat and "breasts." His embarrassment was obvious, but this was about to change!

The first event was the hundred-yard medley: twenty-five yards out in the crawl, twenty-five yards back in the breaststroke, twenty-five yards in the back-stroke, and then the last twenty-five yards in the crawl. Earl had had the swim area roped off well with six lanes. Jeffrey would be in lane one, Steve Wilder in lane three, and a kid from cabin 4, named Alex Cross, in lane five. The three scouts were in lanes two, four, and six. Jeffrey seemed anxious, but as the swim director yelled "swimmers to their marks," he seemed to focus.

Ready, set, and then the whistle blew. Jeffrey hit the water like a whale, almost drowning the kid next to him. With the grace of a leviathan, he cut through the water and hit the twenty-five yard mark a clear leader. Coming back in the breaststroke, he widened the gap to at least ten yards over his clos-est competitor, Steve Wilder. Going into the backstroke he seemed to tire, but fortunately, this stroke allowed for more glide, and he hit the seventy-five yard mark with the same margin or more. He blew through the water in the crawl and touched the dock twenty yards ahead of Steve and twenty-five yards ahead of the rest.

As he climbed awkwardly onto the dock to towel off, everyone was stunned, mouths agape.

How could this clumsy boy, this oaf, be so graceful and swift in the water ? It just couldn't be, but it had happened right before their eyes.

As the initial shock and disbelief wore off, they started to clap, at first just a few claps, but eventually building into an enthusiastic applause. Jeffrey just smiled, an infectious, broad grin. He went on to win five events and probably would have won eight except he was really tired.

Meanwhile, at the softball field, we were getting our asses kicked. The "scouts" were out-hitting, out-fielding, and out-running us to the tune of fif-teen to six. With two innings to go, I asked Bill Rutherford if Danny might pinch-hit, pinch run, or play the field. Bill agreed, as the game was lost, and sent Danny up to bat in the top of the sixth. On the first pitch, he rifled a shot between short and third that was bobbled by the leftfielder, and he ended up on second base. He went to third on a ground out and scored our seventh run on a sacrifice fly to shallow center, sliding into home plate just ahead of the throw.

He was absolutely mobbed by his teammates, and the backslapping lasted for more than a minute.

I gave a little nod and a wink in Danny's direction and he smiled. That was our last run, and we lost nineteen to seven. We ate some humble pie that day, but we also found our little "Pee Wee Reese."

The ride back to camp seemed to take no time at all, and we showered, changed clothes, and went to dinner. Between dinner and dessert, Bob Beebe announced Jeffrey's exploits to foot stomping and hand clapping. Jeffrey stood and took a bow and then hammed it up, a bit too much.

PART TWO

The Body

CHAPTER TWENTY TWO

The following day we awoke to cloudy skies and a misty rain. The air was thick and heavy, a good day to stay in bed and read, but unfortunately not an option. It was the kind of day you dreaded at summer camp, but on a good note, the kind of weather that provided a chance to fish, do arts and crafts, or play cards or board games. After breakfast, Danny made a beeline for the table with a chessboard and pieces. As I walked by, he motioned to me.

"How about a game?" he said almost in a mocking tone.

"I'm not a pushover," I warned. "I used to play this game at a decent level."

He seemed unafraid and motioned for me to sit. He then took the black and white kings, putting one in each hand behind his back, and then brought his hands forward and asked me to choose. I touched his left fist and when he opened it, the black king fell to the board. It meant Danny had the white pieces and the important first move, a warning of things to come.

We matched pawn moves, and he quickly and adeptly mobilized his queen after a minute or two. In short order he pinned my knight, and then took the piece and threatened one of my bishops. As the game progressed, a crowd started to develop, probably sensing the kill.

Making an effort to gain some control, I dug myself into a deeper hole, and things did not look good. I became fascinated by Danny's seemingly effortless play, which caused me to be even more tentative. He seemed to anticipate my every move and had a counter. In addition he played rapidly and methodically and obviously had talent and smarts.

The end came suddenly. As I was beginning to see some daylight and a chance to recoup, he moved his bishop for check and then his queen for mate.

I was stunned. I'm not a bad player, but the kid demolished me and in less than a half hour.

I always loved chess, crossword puzzles, word games, and bridge. I also thought I had a reasonable IQ, but this kid absolutely dismantled me. Talk about being put in your place! I congratulated Danny and slinked away from the table, praying that no one would challenge me to ping-pong or checkers.

***

That night we all gathered after dinner for movies. It was pouring out, and since there was nothing to do, the show was a welcome relief.

While the kids mulled around, chattering with anticipation, two counselors hung a large white sheet at one end of the mess hall. The projector, a noisy eight-millimeter job, was put on a table at the other end of the room with benches arranged in rows between. A large reel of film was attached to one arm of the projector, and threaded through to a take-up reel. When all was ready the lights dimmed, and the excited boys hurried to the benches.

Grainy black-and-white images appeared on the sheet - The Three Stooges. The boys went wild, laughing and hooting at the slapstick craziness. Abbott and Costello and a Buster Keaton silent segment followed, and they were rolling in the aisles, although they had all probably seen this stuff many times before. Finally, the main attraction - John Wayne in *"The Sands of Iwo Jima."* After watching about three thousand Japanese die, we trudged back to our cabin and, in spite of umbrellas, arrived soaked but exhausted and ready for bed.

CHAPTER TWENTY THREE

D ay broke with a misty rain, but the sun was trying, with some success, to break through the clouds. The humidity was oppressive and everything was damp. My sheets and blanket were almost wet, and I couldn't wait to shower and get into dry clothes. The water was tepid at best, but after bathing and shaving, I put on clean shorts, a t-shirt, and docksiders and felt almost human. Today would be my first day off in nearly three weeks, and I left one of the six junior counselors in charge. Jean and I had planned a hike to the end of the lake, weather permitting, and then a picnic.

Even if the sun came out, everything would be wet and buggy, and I thought of cancelling. This was not an option, however, when I met Jean, who had already packed a picnic lunch and was in jeans and hiking shoes. So, along with trusty Max, we headed off down the lakeside path.

It was damp and the path was muddy, but who cared? I was with Jean. Walking along the soggy ground, picking and eating blueberries, we could have cared less about the weather. Max was even more excited than us, sniffing everything in sight, barking at birds, chasing chipmunks, and putting his head in every hole he saw.

"I pray he doesn't get skunked," Jean said.

"Would serve him right," I responded. "He's a pretty intimidating dog and would scare the hell out of any skunk or porcupine."

As I was stating the obvious, Max bolted into the woods in hot pursuit of something. Within seconds we heard a loud yelp, and out of the trees and brush came a "hurting puppy" with two porcupine quills in his nose. We just couldn't help but laugh; this huge shepherd brought to his knees by a ten-pound porcupine.

He carried on, whining and moaning, as we pulled out the quills. He played the suffering dog to the hilt, but calmed down when we washed his muzzle with cold lake water. We would treat his wounds with hot compresses and an antibiotic cream when we got back to camp, but for now it would have to do. After carrying on for a few minutes more, he returned to sniffing and barking at any sound in the woods. He seemed not to have learned his lesson.

"Am I going to hear from you after camp?" Jean abruptly asked.

"Why not?" I answered, not quite getting her drift.

"You know how they are, these summer flings."

"Is that what it is, a summer fling?" I answered.

"You know what I mean, Bob. You'll be off to college, meeting new people, especially girls, and I'll be in high school."

"Why don't we enjoy the summer and let the pieces fall where they may. I don't think that either of us is ready for a long-term relationship or commitment, but if things are right they will blossom."

Believe it or not, she seemed satisfied with this.

We reached the end of the lake by noon and spread an almost dry blanket on the damp ground. The sun had made its appearance, the air warmed, and a beautiful rainbow formed in the sky above us. Jean opened her knapsack and spread her cache of sandwiches, chips, and soda while Max foraged in the woods. He would be back once he smelled the ham and cheese sandwiches.

We lounged, snacked, and enjoyed the incredible setting. The grass smelled sweet and the yellow, pink, and blue wildflowers burst with color. Jean put her head on my shoulder, I put my arm around her, and we just rocked lightly in the warm sunshine. Her hair smelled of flowers and glistened as I kissed the back of her neck, eliciting the desired response.

Unfortunately at this moment, my buddy Max decided to return with dirt all over his injured muzzle and something in his mouth. He seemed excited as he dropped the object on our blanket.

"What's that?" queried Jean.

"Looks like an old bracelet. It's all rusted and tarnished, but definitely a bracelet."

"Let me see," said Jean as she pulled on my arm. She was able to wrench the small piece of jewelry from my hand and seemed fascinated by it. As Max intently watched, Jean tried to clean it with paper napkins, which failed, so she got up and grabbed a handful of sandy soil from the side of the lake and started to rub off the rust. The abrasive sand seemed to work, and the patina of silver became visible. It seemed to be engraved and I strained to see more.

"Looks like initials," she said matter-of-factly. "I think it's italics. Can you make it out?"

I strained to see the writing on the inside of the bracelet.

"Looks like the first initial is L. What do you think?"

"I agree. It's definitely an L. I think the second initial may be an M."

A small silver bracelet with the initials L.M., which looked to be years old. We gave it back to Max, who seemed delighted to have his "toy." He used it like a teething ring, but soon lost interest, dropped it on the blanket and ran back into the woods.

Jean and I hunkered in and started to make out, but again Max returned from the woods covered with dirt and seemed agitated. This dog was becoming annoying. He started nudging us, whining, and acting like he wanted to show us something. Finally, we gave in to his prodding and followed him through the foliage to a clearing not far from the shoreline.

"What's he up to, that big moose?"

"I don't know, but he sure is intent on finding it," said Jean.

There in front of us was Max, digging and sniffing like crazy. There was either something under the dirt that he wanted, or he was trying to bury something.

I looked at Jean, and she looked back at me and giggled.

"Let's help the mad dog."

We dug and dug, removing handfuls of dirt and Max became more excited. He started to dig furiously with his front paws. He was a machine, and within minutes he had dug a hole at least a foot and a half deep. We backed off, but he continued, intent on getting his whole, large body into the excavation. The soil flew backwards and the hole became so deep that he almost disappeared from view. We both stood and giggled, watching Max's frantic exercise. He was tireless.

Finally, he stopped digging. He stayed in the hole and began to cry, a disconcerting wail, and we had no choice but to get him out.

We walked over to the deep hole and looked down. Below us, deep in the ditch, was a small skeletal hand protruding from the earth. On the middle finger was a small gold ring. It was a human hand, that was for sure.

"Jean, we have to go. We have to get back to camp to tell your father."

"I think I'm going to be sick." She proceeded to vomit.

Max was getting upset, and Jean looked pale and shaky. We had to get back. "C'mon, Maxie. Let's go."

With great effort, the huge dog arose from the depths. I gathered our stuff and loaded the knapsack on my back. No idle chatter or handholding, just a rapid walk back.

***

As soon as we hit camp we made a beeline to Al, who seemed concerned with his daughter's health, as she was white as a sheet and looked like she might pass out at any minute.

"What's going on here, Berman?" Al almost screamed.

"Jean and I took a walk to the end of the lake with Max. We found a body, a human body. All we saw was the hand, but it was human, probably a child's because it was small. We have to call the police."

"Let's go to my cabin," said Al, a bit more calmly. I followed him inside, where he called the Stillwater police while Kathy Simmons ministered to her daughter. She seemed in a state of shock, and her mom had her lie down with a wet washcloth on her forehead. We waited for the police.

What more could happen this summer? I knew how I felt, but I could only imagine Al's thoughts, as he was the man in charge. Asthmatic attack, severe laceration, Dr. Golden's rantings - all small potatoes next to this. A body had been found near the camp, and this would be bad PR no matter how you looked at it. Al appeared to be on the verge of a stroke.

Twenty minutes later, the police arrived in force, unfortunately with sirens blaring, which called more attention to us. The kids gawked and chattered, and the rumors stated to fly. Everyone, it seemed, had already heard about the discovery and had his own theory about the body. Was it an Indian child buried many years ago? After all, we were on Native American land. Possibly it was a murder with the body hidden for years. Who was it?

With little explanation, the staff herded the campers back to their activities amid groans. They wanted to see what was going on and hear the gory details.

The police were briefed, and I led them to the internment site, where they quickly cordoned off the area with police tape, took snapshots with an old Brownie camera, and called the coroner. I didn't know shit about cop work, but I had read enough detective novels to know that they were out of their element. I guess they knew that they had bitten off more than they could chew because they quickly called the state boys. It wasn't that they were incompetent, but how many dead bodies could they have investigated? The state police were used to dead people, certainly homicides and motor vehicle accident victims.

I jogged back to check on Jean, who seemed to have recovered and was resting next to an exhausted Max. We did not talk about the skeletal remains.

CHAPTER TWENTY FOUR

I got back to the gravesite in time to see the coroner, a local funeral director, directing the removal of the skeleton, to be sent to his office, not a county morgue.

The state boys, who had arrived from the Newton barracks dressed in green and beige, over-saw the proceedings, looking seven feet tall in their uniforms. Why did state troopers always appear huge, rugged, and handsome?

From the look of things, the skeleton was small, definitely a child. Since Max had found a bracelet and the hand had a gold finger ring, I presumed that the deceased was a female. I wondered if this was obvious to the "coroner." What I found disconcerting was that one side of the skull had been crushed. Had this been a traumatic accident, or had it been foul play?

Surprisingly the police seemed to be doing a fairly professional job: gathering soil samples, searching the gravesite for hair, cloth, teeth, or even a weapon, scouring for any clues that would help in identification, time of death, and causation.

***

When I returned to the cabin, the boys wanted to know everything. They had heard all the rumors and seen all the police cars, state and local. God, what excitement! The theory being circulated was that the skeleton in the grave had been murdered by a "monster." Rumor, but enough to cause uneasiness throughout the camp, and it had to be dispelled. I assured the boys that no one knew when the body was buried or that a murder had even been committed. I pooh-poohed the crime theory and told the boys that the body was in a grave that was probably part of an old Native American burial ground. This seemed plausible and helped allay fears.

CHAPTER TWENTY FIVE

The next few days were uneventful, as the police investigation had moved away from the lake and the camp. While I welcomed the peace and quiet, it was short-lived, as on day three post-discovery, the local and state police arrived to officially question Jean and me. The press, fortunately, had not yet been notified, and there were no apparent leaks, but it was only a matter of time before reporters and TV and radio crews made their way to Camp Spenser.

"What were you and Miss Simmons doing at that end of the lake?"

"We went on a picnic, as I took the day off and the weather cooperated after a day of rain."

"How did you find the skeleton?"

"Jean's dog, Max, must have sensed or smelled the remains because he started digging until he unearthed the hand."

"Did you discover anything else near or in the grave?"

"Yes. We found a small bracelet."

"Please describe it as best you can."

"It was old and tarnished, but when we cleaned it off with some soil and water, it appeared to be silver or silver-plated, and it had the initials L.M. engraved. We gave it to the state police officer in charge."

The local police officer and the state trooper seemed to want me to continue so I obliged.

""I think that the remains are those of a young girl because of the bracelet and gold ring and the size of the skeleton. An engraved bracelet seems improbable for a Native American child, so my bet is that we are not dealing with a burial ground discovery. Also, the crushed skull seems to suggest severe trauma, either an accident or murder."

Jean chimed in, as if on cue, by telling them, "there was no flesh or clothing, so we think that the remains were there for quite a while."

Another ten minutes and they were through with us. Either they didn't want to hear what we had to say or they found us cocky and obnoxious and of no help, probably the latter.

While we were talking to one group of police, another group was taking statements from locals in the area and the few summer residents on the lake. Little was gained, as few were home, and no one had any information to offer.

CHAPTER TWENTY SIX

It was another story at the coroner's office. Common sense told him to call the county coroner, who was not a funeral director, for help. He, in turn, called the state medical examiner's office to analyze the skeletal remains, as he smelled foul play, possibly an unsolved murder from years ago.

The remains were examined over a two day period by the state authorities who had determined, unbeknownst to us, that the skeleton was that of a prepubescent female, probably around ten to twelve years old, who had died from severe head trauma, or at least these injuries contributed to her death. The child's age was ascertained by noting that the growth plates of the long bones, called the epiphyses, were open and not fused, which would occur at puberty. The shape of the pelvis was definitely female, and the density of the bone showed that the child was Caucasian and probably not Native American.

The state medical examiner found numerous crush injuries to the cranium, five fractures in all. The shape of the depressions made it probable that the blows were inflicted with a shovel or something like it. If death was accidental or purposeful, the damage was inflicted by someone of bulk, most likely a large male. The state coroner also found a broken left wrist, probably a defensive injury. With this preliminary knowledge the forensic work now centered on determining the length of time that the remains had been in the ground. This was not an easy task, as the burial site was a problem. Dampness, soil type, drainage, average rainfall and snowfall, and many other factors would skew the results.

After almost a week, the initial conclusion was that the body had been in the ground for at least thirty years and quite possibly forty, based on spectrophotometry, a chemical assay with boron, and carbon 16 testing. If the child had been murdered, which was the consensus, then the crime had been committed between 1919 and 1929 or there about. If correct, a thorough search of police records, newspaper articles for disappearances, kidnappings, and unsolved murders of children during those years would be a must. Unfortunately this would be a tedious, frustrating job, as records would be spotty or nonexistent, newspaper articles would be lost or discarded, and there would be only so much manpower that could be expended on a thirty to forty-year-old case. If only there were a network center in the state or country that would track these crimes-no such luck. If that weren't enough, it was very possible that the young girl may not have been from the area, having been killed elsewhere and buried in rural northwestern New Jersey.

CHAPTER TWENTY SEVEN

During that unforgettable week, I was questioned by numerous local and state police and a new guy, supposedly from New York City. I learned over time that he was an expert in forensics, "on loan" from the NYPD, with a national reputation in unraveling forensic evidence in violent crimes. He was pretty impressive and I guessed very good at his job because his questions were much more methodical and probing. His name was Lawrence Geller, and he had quite a reputation in NYC. He was a legend for solving the unsolvable, the motiveless crime, and had become a guru in the area of serial murders. He was a rare combination-cop and psychologist. I guessed him to be in his late thirties to early forties or older, just starting to gray at the temples, with piercing, intelligent dark eyes. Ruggedly handsome and with a quick mind, he conveyed an air of confidence, and quietly commanded respect from the men. You could see instantly that he was in charge.

"Mr. Berman, you've been a camper at Spenser for years." It was more of a statement than a question.

"Yes, sir, about nine or ten years."

"Do you remember ever hearing idle talk, gossip, or rumor about a young girl's disappearance, years ago, in these parts?" he probed.

"No, sir. I've thought about it a lot since I was first questioned and I can't remember any talk or rumor."

"Do you know any people who live in private homes around the lake?"

"The only person I know is a guy named Lester Cartright who does odd jobs around the camp and drives us to ballgames and overnight trips. He has a big open truck and lives in the next house down from the camp. He has a brother who may or may not live with him."

"Tell me what you know about Lester."

"He's a little strange, gives me an uneasy feeling when I'm around him. It's nothing he's done, just my take. I don't like him."

"How old do you think he is, Bob?"

"I'm not real good at estimating age, but I'd guess him to be in his early to mid-fifties."

"How about his brother? What's he like?"

"I don't know him. Only saw him once. A big fat guy with thick, "coke-bottle" glasses. I don't even know if he lives with Lester or what he does for work. I know he has been around Lake Spotswood."

"Well Bob, if you think of anything else, please call me." "Here's my card and you can call collect."

I gathered that I was dismissed, and I left the makeshift office that the police had established in the infirmary. Aside from the investigation and all the rumors, innuendo, and macabre tall tales being told, camp life went on fairly normally. Al was intent on making the camp experience a positive one and would not let the gruesome discovery at the end of the lake ruin the summer for the boys and the staff.

In spite of this major distraction, I still wanted to check out my suspicions about the snake attack on Danny, the incident with Kenny, the attack on Max, and my feelings of being stalked. I couldn't shake the mental image that these events were planned and carried out for some reason. I spoke with Jim, and we plotted our "investigation" for the weekend, although Jim seemed a bit skeptical. Both our cabins were going on a weekend canoe trip organized by Bernie Allen and Bob Beebe. Our services would not be needed, and we had Saturday and Sunday off. We figured that we would check things out on Saturday morning and have the rest of the weekend to ourselves. I wanted to spend time with Jean as well as the guys.

CHAPTER TWENTY EIGHT

I t was overcast on Saturday morning, but the sun peaked through at times. The boys had left after breakfast, and Jim and I began with the latrine, checking the floorboards, wall joints, junctions of walls and floors, seals around the toilets and urinals, and the screen door. There were no cracks or holes. The screens on the windows and door were intact and the door closed automatically and tightly.

"What did I tell you? No way a snake could get in unless it was put there." Jim had to admit it. " "It's very suspicious." He scratched his head.

Next, we grabbed the knapsack that we had earlier filled with long-sleeved shirts, bug spray, and canteens, and headed for the trail that I had taken on our camping trip. We followed the markers painted on rocks and trees, an easy trek with just the two of us. By this time the sun had emerged, and the forest came to life with the sounds of birds chirping, a nearby babbling brook, and the scurrying noise made by squirrels and chipmunks. Rays of light cut through the trees and the smell of pine and wildflowers was intoxicating, but my only thoughts were of a conspiracy. I was becoming obsessed, but I was sure that I was right. Continuing our walk, we finally reached the area where I thought I had become sidetracked. There Jim went north and I continued in a westerly direction. We had agreed to go about a mile on our paths and then return.

"This should take about forty-five minutes to go out and back given the terrain. We'll meet back here," I said and Jim agreed.

"I followed the marked trail for twenty minutes and then returned. The markers were in order and clearly displayed. I arrived at the rendezvous about a minute or two before Jim, and I anxiously awaited his comments.

"What did you find?" I asked with some trepidation, as Jim appeared from the woods.

"I found what you suspected," Jim said. "The trail going north was clearly marked with the same symbols as the east-west route. So if you went from west to east as you did with Kenny on your back, it would be easy to turn north at this spot and not even know it. The trail would take you away from camp, as it did."

"Well it's clear to me that someone painted trail markers to confuse us, and I'm willing to bet that this someone planted the snake and beat Max."

"I must admit that it looks that way. A number of the markers, where the trails meet, looked freshly painted," added Jim.

"Goddamn. I knew it!"

Back at Spenser, I showed Jim the piece of fabric from the woods near the boathouse, which we took to the arts and crafts room to observe under better light.

"I have an idea. Let's bring it to the infirmary and ask Betty Sloan if we may use her microscope."

I had spent many hours at home looking through my microscope at feathers, blood, cloth, urine, hair, pond water, and many other things. The scope was a gift from my folks for my sixteenth birthday, and I was fascinated by the microscopic world. It was a pretty good binocular with German optics. I thought it was an extravagant gift, but I put it to good use, and I guess my folks thought it was an excellent investment in my future. When they gave me the scope, they added that I could take it with me to medical school, thereby justifying the expense. Mind you, I was only a sophomore in high school at the time.

I gazed at the piece of cloth. The fiber was definitely spun cotton with red, green, and yellow dyed strands in a grid-like pattern. I also noticed a small hair embedded in the cross-fibers. It was black and course and could have been human, but it could also have been from Max. There were also particles of dirt and what looked like blood. Had Max drawn blood from his attacker or was it his own? A lab could be able to tell me if it was animal or human blood, but there was not enough to tell type and Rh.

To confirm that it was blood, I immersed the cloth in water, drew up a few cc's with a nose dropper, put a drop on a slide, and put on a cover slip. Under the power of the scope, I could see small, round, red corpuscles floating in the water. They looked like small donuts with dimples where the hole would be-definitely blood.

***

After leaving Betty's office, Jim and I reviewed the evidence and began to theorize on the motive and the perpetrator. We were like characters in a Dashiell Hammett novel, not professional sleuths, but rather amateurs creating a plot with minimal tangible evidence. I even went a step further by telling Jim that I suspected Lester and his brother, Peter.

"Who else could be a suspect?" I explained to Jim.

"They live in the area, know their way around the camp, and had opportunity."

"But did they have motive?" Jim countered.

CHAPTER TWENTY NINE

While Jim and I were playing detective, the real inspector, Lawrence Geller, was busy at work trying to determine the identity of the exhumed skeletal remains. He had enlisted the services of several of his investigators, who volunteered to work on the case in their off time. Science aside, the case would be solved by painstaking attention to detail and a slow, plodding investigation into the past. Newspaper articles, unsolved crimes against children, missing person reports, obituaries of children, real estate records of the area including sales and summer rentals, and many other leads would have to be checked out. Many people who summered in rural northwestern New Jersey were from the heavily populated counties of northern Jersey or even New York City, so Geller would start with the *"New York Times"* and the *"Newark Evening News."* The latter was a leading newspaper in the Newark area with a circulation that included many communities in Essex, Union, and Morris Counties. Needless to say it had wide distribution and a large reading public. Articles from *"The New York Times,"* if older than ten years, would be on microfilm, and finding them would not be easy. The Newton paper, the *"Daily Chronicle,"* which serviced the county seat of Newton and surrounding Sussex County, was only seventeen years old. The records of its predecessor were nowhere to be found. The Newark newspaper seemed to be the best bet for rapid results, and Geller had spoken to the editor. In addition, he had left messages at the town hall in Newton to review tax records and property sales around Spotswood.

CHAPTER THIRTY

With all that had been going on, I had spent little time with my campers. They had returned from the canoe trip and were anxious to do something with their "leader."

"How about a trip to Newton for a movie and pizza if I can arrange it with Al Simmons? No promises!"

This met with an enthusiastic response. Now there was no saying no. I had to arrange the trip, and I needed Al to say yes. Thank God Al felt we needed some R&R and OKed it as a tension release.

"I'll call Lester to make sure he's free. By the way, Bob, would you mind if I tagged along with my wife and Jean?"

"Fine with me, sir," I said magnanimously.

We would be picked up by Lester at five, plenty of time for a six o'clock show, *"Ben Hur."* It would be a long movie, about three hours, and we had to be done in time to grab a pizza. The kids were really excited, as the movie promised to be filled with plenty of action and gore. It was rare to have a first-run flick in Newton; usually we saw movies that were a year or two old. I couldn't wait to see old Charlton Heston take on the Roman Empire.

It was a balmy night with no threat of rain, and a ride in the open truck would require no more than a light jacket. When Lester pulled up, the kids were more than ready. They boarded rapidly and noisily and took their places at the sides of the slated bay. The sides were strong and shoulder high, and Lester again secured everything with heavy ropes. There were no restrictions on riding in an open truck and little concern about being thrown out of the vehicle in the event of an accident. It never entered our minds. Jim Butler, who accompanied us, climbed in the back with the boys and I rode in the cab with Lester.

About halfway to Newton the sky darkened and the wind picked up. Lester had been driving with his window open and his left arm, bent at the elbow, protruding. It was beginning to get chilly, and I could see goose -bumps on his forearm. He partially closed the window. A few seconds later, as I was putting on my jacket, Lester said, "Hey, kid, would you mind grabbing my shirt from behind the seat?"

"No problem." I replied as I reached over and pulled out a plaid, long-sleeved shirt. I was stunned, and my hand was shaking, as I handed the shirt over to him.

"What's the matter, boy? You look like you've seen a ghost."

"Nothing, sir. I just felt a chill. Made me kind of shake."

The shirt was a white cotton or light wool with a yellow, red, and green design. Well, maybe red and yellow, I wasn't too sure about the green. It looked to be the same pattern as the piece of fabric I had in my cabin. I had to get that shirt, no matter what.

Upon our arrival in Newton, we pulled into a public lot rather than park on the street with this boisterous crowd. As we unloaded the boys, I glanced over in time to wave at Jean, who had arrived with her parents in Al's beat-up Ford station wagon. She looked lovely, dressed in slacks and a sweatshirt that said "West Orange High Wrestling!" She whispered something to her mother, got a nod, and within seconds was at my side.

"It's OK for you to sit with us?" I asked.

"Why not, pray tell? You and Jim are upstanding citizens: responsible, honest, and honorable. My mother thinks you can be trusted. Besides, we will be surrounded by eight adolescent boys."

"I know your mother thinks we can be trusted, but what about your dad?"

She just laughed.

We attacked the theatre. Eight rowdy boys getting popcorn, candy, and soda. The manager looked green!

Jim got the tickets while I organized the boys and their refreshments. The popcorn machine gave you a bag for ten cents, and I had brought a whole roll of dimes from the canteen.

They took white bags from the holder, and one at a time opened their bag and put it under the dispenser, waiting for me to deposit the coin. After getting the popcorn, we moved to the soda machine, which dispensed a cup of your choice for a nickel. I had also brought a roll of buffalo beads. The choices were Coke, orange, and root beer. Once the coin was inserted, each boy pressed his choice, causing a cup to fall from somewhere in the machine, sliding down a shoot onto a grill to be filled by a stream of syrup and then soda water. With the tickets at twenty-five cents a pop, Jim and I were out $4.40 counting Jean. So I informed everyone that they were limited to one candy each, another fifty-five cents in the hole.

With soda and popcorn in hand, they ran to the candy machine, a large device with a partial glass front that displayed the choices. Next to the display was a coin slot.

Each boy put down his popcorn and soda on the carpet in the lobby and looked over the possibilities: Black Crows, Dots, chocolate-covered raisins, red dots, sugarcoated peanuts, and Jujubes. I deposited a nickel for each boy, turned the knob as each made his choice, and watched as the candy dropped into the receptacle at the base of the machine.

With their stash they ran into the auditorium and headed for the front row, much too close for us, so we took our seats in the tenth row. Jean sat between Jim and me, with me on the aisle. I inadvertently noticed Lester two rows back. He was not wearing his plaid shirt, as the theatre was relatively warm and would get warmer. Was his shirt on his lap or back in the truck? I had to find out.

The room started to darken and the boys started to cheer in anticipation of the movie. The curtain parted and the projector sprung to life. Previews of coming attractions came on the screen: a John Wayne western, *"Rio Bravo,"* and *"Splendor in the Grass,"* with Natalie Wood and a newcomer, Warren Beatty due out in the late fall. One look at Natalie Wood and I was in love. This was followed by several cartoons, Tom and Jerry, Bugs Bunny, and Sylvester the Cat and Tweety Bird. Boy you sure got your money's worth. Finally the main attraction.

There on the screen in all his glory, was Charlton Heston, bigger than life. I must say that things became pretty exciting, although I'm not into epics, especially three hour ones. But the kids were eating it up and seemed to like the action.

In spite of the entertainment on the screen, I was preoccupied with the thought of the shirt being in Lester's truck. I was planning my strategy when Jean reached over to hold my hand. It took all my strength and self-control to remove her hand and announce, "I have to use the restroom. I'll be back in a sec. Let me know what happens."

I walked to the back of the theatre and went through the swinging doors and into the lobby.

"I just have to go outside for a few minutes," I told the woman at the ticket booth.

"Make sure you have your ticket stub and I'll let you back in," she replied.

I had the stub in my right pants pocket.

Once outside I made a beeline for the truck. I had to work fast. Luckily the door to the cab was unlocked.

There on Lester's seat was the shirt, just sitting there for me to find. I couldn't believe my incredibly good fortune. I quickly checked the garment with the help of the overhead cab light, and to my surprise there was no tear in the material. The fabric was intact and moreover, the plaid seemed different, with a lot of red strands and no green. I couldn't believe it; it wasn't the right shirt. As I replaced it on the seat, I was startled by someone behind me.

"What're you looking for, son?"

I whirled around, after almost urinating in my pants. I was face-to-face with Lester Cartright. He must have followed me out. "But why? If he had nothing to hide or worry about, why did he follow me?" I thought.

Stuttering, I said. "I was just looking for my roll of dimes that I thought fell out of my jacket pocket, but it's not here."

Lester had a doubtful expression on his face. He obviously knew I was lying. He also was not leaving until I closed the cab door and returned to the theatre.

"I don't know where I could have dropped it, but I'm out two-fifty."

"Too bad, kid, but close the door. I'll lock it."

This I did, and Lester followed me back like a warden walking behind the condemned on the way to his execution.

I settled down in my seat, took Jean's hand, and smiled like a Cheshire cat.

"You missed a great scene." Jean whispered a quick synopsis.

The movie was a classic, and the chariot race was incredible. Everyone cheered when the film ended and the lights came on. It was late, almost nine-forty-five, and we had to hustle to get to the pizza parlor before closing time.

Kathy and Al Simmons elected to go home, but Jean convinced them that she should stay with us for pizza and ride back in the truck.

"We'll take good care of her, and we could use the help with eight hungry kids," I said.

They agreed, and we headed on foot for "King of Pizza."

Fortunately the lights were still on and several cars were in the parking lot, so we knew we were in luck. A good thing as I was starved.

As we entered the pizzeria, the smell of melting cheese, garlic, and baking dough hit us. I was drooling.

"We need two large pies, one with extra cheese and one with pepperoni and sausage." I yelled to the counter guy, who looked like he was ready to go home and was pissed that we came in so near closing time.

He was dressed in an undershirt with chest hair showing just below his Adam's apple and a Lucky Strike behind his left ear. He pulled the cigarette, lit it and took a long drag before calling our order to the dough guy.

"Do you want soda?"

"Sure. We'll take a few big bottles from the glass case. How about some paper cups?"

"You got it, buddy." He handed over a dozen and a half Dixie cups and napkins. There were containers of garlic powder, red pepper flakes, and grated cheese on the tables.

Ten minutes later, two steamy-hot pizzas arrived, smelling great and with cheese bubbling. We all grabbed at once, and I was able to get a slice of extra cheese, which I sprinkled with pepper flakes and grated cheese, folded New York style (you never used a knife and fork), and stuffed in my mouth, practically burning my palate. But it was worth it. The crust and sauce were delicious, and the soft mozzarella just stretched and stretched as I pulled on the slice with my teeth clenched.

"God this is heaven on earth," chimed in Jim. "Who'd a thunk it? New York style pizza in Newton, New Jersey. Thin crust, black on the bottom, I don't believe it."

We finished and Jim and I split the bill. Jean, who had packed away two large slices, offered no cash. I gave her a dirty look, which she ignored.

Lester was waiting, leaning against the truck's cab, smoking a cigarette and looking annoyed, probably because of the late hour.

He loaded the boys quickly, taking no bullshit. The night had cooled and the kids put on sweatshirts and jackets, sat in the truck's bay, and covered themselves with blankets. Jean and I climbed into the cab for the interminable ride home. Lester was totally silent, and I was happy not to have to converse with him or look at him, but he still made me feel uncomfortable.

As there were few cars on the road, we made it back in record time. Exhausted, the boys went to the cabin and fell into bed while I walked Jean home and kissed her good night.

CHAPTER THIRTY ONE

As the week progressed, I tried to put things in perspective and also spend quality time with the boys. I forced myself not to be preoccupied with the two on-going investigations, mine and the police's. I spent time at the waterfront, ball field, archery and rifle ranges, and craft shop, trying not to let my thoughts interfere with my effectiveness as a counselor.

Danny was blossoming and not wheezing, Jeffrey was at home in the water and fitting in on land, Kenny was out of the hospital and at home recuperating, and Bobby, Mike, Paul, Tony, and Steve were their normal selves. Still when I let my guard down, my thoughts would wander to Lester Cartright. I was sure he was the culprit, but the shirt incident had thrown a monkey-wrench into my perfect scenario and I was stymied.

Right then and there, I decided that I had to get into his house to check his room, his closet, and his chest of drawers to find the shirt that I was convinced belonged to him. I needed evidence of his wrongdoing. It would be risky. After all if I were caught, I could be charged with breaking and entering, or even burglary. College would be out the window, and I could not even fathom my parents' response. But I was obsessed, I had to know.

CHAPTER THIRTY TWO

While his men, the few he could spare, were working the newspaper angle, Lawrence Geller was attempting to obtain a list of families that had summer homes on the lake or lived there year-round. This did not even include renters, who hopefully were few. Unfortunately, the oldest realty company in the area was not established until 1929 and had no records that went back any farther. So fortunes lay with the town halls and tax offices for the Stillwater-Andover and Newton areas.

The forensic team was making progress. They had postulated that the injuries to the head had been inflicted by a large shovel, as small flecks of steel were found in the cranial bones and the depression in the left parietal bone fit this theory. The positioning of the body in the grave was ritualistic, face up with the arms crossed over the chest and the hands extended upward. The multiple blows and the defensive injuries to the wrists convinced even doubters that this was a murder and not an accident.

The police were checking jewelry stores from New York City to Sussex County. There was a small jeweler's seal on the back of the bracelet that said P and S. This was a long-shot, but it had to be checked out to some degree. The problem was a lack of manpower and the fact that the bracelet could have been purchased from anywhere out of the area or given as a gift from a relative or friend from anywhere in the U.S.

CHAPTER THIRTY THREE

While Geller, the cops, and the forensic team were at work, I had a talk with Jean and Jim, asking their opinions about my plans to check-out Lester's place, or as they put it," break-in."

"You're crazy. You're more than crazy, you're a moron," said Jean with a warning tone.

"This is out of hand, Bob. You're willing to commit a burglary and risk arrest and your future because of this obsession? Who gives a shit?" It's not worth it," said Jim.

Still, I was determined to get to the bottom of things.

"I know I'm not being rational, but the thought of someone putting children in danger or trying to close the camp makes me angry, and I just have to do something."

"Breaking and entering is not doing something, it's committing a crime," countered Jean.

So much for my friends' opinions. I was going to do this alone. My biggest problem, as I saw it, was Lester's brother. I didn't know whether he lived there or visited frequently, so his schedule was unpredictable. But Lester worked regular hours, Monday through Friday, eight until four or five, barring illness, and he was not the type to call in sick. So my plan was to "stake out" his place and wait for him to leave for work. Then I would call his home from the pay phone in the lodge (his number was posted under maintenance), and if there was no answer, I could be fairly certain that Peter was not around. I would try several times just in case he was at Lester's, but sleeping. At this point I would take Max, if Jean would allow him to be involved in a crime, to stand guard. Hopefully if anyone came by, Max would bark to warn me. I would jimmy the lock on the front door and make a quick search, twenty minutes was my max, and then I was gone. There was a good chance that the front door would be unlocked. After all this was rural America.

That night Jean warned me again that I would be committing a criminal act. I reminded her that I was not breaking in if the door was unlocked, and I was not stealing anything. I was just looking for evidence.

"That's bullshit, Bob, and you know it. I just don't understand where you're coming from."

"Trust me, Jean. I know what I need to do, and I won't be foolish," I rebutted.

"Well, count me out. I won't help, and forget about using Max."

After leaving Jean I gave a fair amount of thought to limiting my exposure. I could not even imagine life without college and med school. I had to figure out a reason for being in Lester's house if caught red-handed.

CHAPTER THIRTY FOUR

As morning broke I had an idea. The boys were scheduled for an away softball game and hopefully, Lester would be driving. I could easily feign illness, and Jim and Len Aarons would supervise and coach. Once Lester left the camp, I would simply walk into his house or break in if necessary. Jean, who had adamantly refused to help, had inadvertently abetted my crime. She had baked a plate of chocolate chip cookies for my boys that morning, and I now had my safety factor. I would take the cookies with me, and if caught in the house, I would simply say that I was dropping off the goodies in appreciation of Lester's driving us to Newton for the movie and pizza.

***

At two Lester's big green truck arrived at the parking area above the lodge. I walked up to Al's cabin, feigning illness, and asked Kathy Simmons for two aspirin. Jean had me wait while she packaged her cookies in a small basket, wrapped in napkins and still warm. I felt major guilt as I thanked her and told her how much the boys would enjoy them.

As soon as the truck left and I could hear it descending the hill leading to the camp entrance, I ran to the lodge to make my calls. Three calls spaced two minutes apart yielded no answers.

Grabbing the basket of cookies I made a beeline to the Cartright home, a rustic structure with a big screened-in porch in front, set back about two hundred feet from the lake and about a quarter mile from the camp flagpole.

Instead of being cautious, I ignored my game plan and approached the house openly with cookies in hand. As I neared the front steps to the porch, I called out to see if anyone would answer; no one did. I climbed the three steps and knocked on the wood frame of the screen door. Again no response. I knocked again and again to be safe, no answer. I tried the door and it was unlocked, so I entered the porch and walked to the front door. I again knocked and no one replied. I tried the door, but it was locked.

"Oh, shit," I muttered, but I wasn't giving up.

Knowing rural America as I did, I stared down at the welcome mat and bet dollars to donuts that a key was under it. I lifted the mat, and bingo! On the floor was the key to the front door, plain as day. At this point, I was about to cross the line.

I inserted the key, turned it, and heard the lock click. My hands were shaking as I turned the doorknob and pushed the heavy wood door open. So far, so good. I returned the key to its hiding place and relocked the door behind me as I entered the front hall. The house had a musty smell and was fairly dark for two in the afternoon. There were no womanly touches here. It was definitely the home of a bachelor or widower. I walked from the foyer toward the staircase to the second floor. To my left was a living room with a large fireplace, a Franklin stove in the opening. The furnishings were Montgomery Ward and bordering on worn and shabby. There were no drapes, only window shades. There were few mementos and no art work on the walls. There was, however, an end table that held an old telephone and a photograph of Lester and his brother on a fishing trip.

To the right of the hall was a small dining room with a maple table and four chairs. The table was old, but not in a charming way. It was unpolished and full of scratches. A swinging door on the far wall led into the kitchen at the back of the house. There was also another entrance to the kitchen from the hall, between the staircase and a small bathroom to the left.

The kitchen had knotty pine cabinets, and the floor was old, faded linoleum that had seen better days. There was an old Frigidaire refrigerator on one wall and a four-burner gas range against another. Next to the stove was a counter with a chopping block and next to that was a sink, the porcelain stained with iron deposits. Above the sink was a window, dirty with dust and grime, looking out onto the backyard. Against the wall on the left, next to a door leading out to the yard, was an old soapstone sink with a pump and spigot, probably used to clean fish or game because it only pumped cold water. There were no memorabilia, not even a framed hunting or fishing license. It was like looking at a summer rental rather than a year-round home.

I left the cookies on the kitchen counter.

As I turned to walk back to the staircase to the second floor, I noticed a door that I figured went to the basement. I decided to leave the cellar for last and explore the upstairs. The second floor was the usual, one bedroom on each side of the landing with a large bathroom between.

I quickly checked the bathroom and what I guessed to be the extra bedroom. Nothing of interest- no shirt that remotely fit the description that I was looking for. There was nothing in the bathroom, closet, or chest of drawers in the guest room.

Next, I entered what I guessed was Lester's bedroom. I checked my watch; I had been inside for seven minutes. On the dresser I saw several framed, faded photographs of him as a young man with his brother and another young man, handsome and athletic-looking. Another picture was of a man and woman I assumed were Lester's parents. The last picture showed Lester and his obese brother in a sailboat. He appeared to be around seventeen or eighteen, and in the lower right corner was a date, July 1920.

Next to the photos was an album. Thumbing through it rapidly, I found numerous snapshots of Lester, his brother, and his parents, probably taken with a Brownie camera and starting to darken with age. As I turned the pages, I came across newspaper articles, mainly about local fishing contests, hunting exploits, and trophies won.

An article, dated 1923, related the life and death of William Cartright, who had been found dead by his eldest son, Lester. Apparently he had taken his own life with a shotgun, after losing his job and self- respect. He was a life-long member of the community and was a member of the Congregational Church, the Elks, and taught Sunday school. He is survived by his wife, Hazel and his two sons, Lester and Peter, who will act as pallbearers. Internment will be at the town cemetery behind the church. Contributions may be made to the Congregational Church in lieu of flowers. The words "taken his own life" and "self-respect" were underlined in red.

Another article was dated 1925. It was an obituary for Hazel Cartright, which told of her suicide from carbon monoxide inhalation. She had been found in the garage where the family motor car had been left running. Apparently she had never gotten over the sudden death of her husband two years before and had been despondent, ending her life to escape the pain of living. Pallbearers included her two sons, Lester and Peter. The word "suicide" was doubly underlined in red. I closed the album and straightened the top of the dresser. I looked further checking the closet and a beat-up armoire, and found no signs of a plaid shirt.

I had been in the house for twelve minutes with no results. As I descended the stairs and headed for the cellar, I vowed that I would not stay longer than another eight minutes, ten at the most.

I flicked on the basement light and descended the rickety, open wooden stairs that creaked under my weight. In the dim light I entered a fairly large room. Against the far wall was a good-sized workbench with several vises and numerous tools arranged neatly on shelves above. On the back of the bench were many jars filled with nails, screws, nuts, and bolts of varying sizes. To the left were five large, deep shelves mounted on the wall and filled with hunting and fishing gear, neatly arranged. To the right was a smaller worktable loaded with equipment for tying flies. There were boxes and boxes of beautiful specimens for fishing; every color, texture, and design. Alongside this table, mounted on the cement wall, were glass cases filled with insects of every variety: beetles, grasshoppers, bees, wasps, locusts, crickets, moths, spiders, and flies, all meticulously mounted and labeled with their common name as well as their scientific genus and species. The most spectacular exhibit was a case filled with magnificent butterflies. I just stared at it in awe and admiration.

As I turned to reclimb the stairs, I noticed a small door in the far corner, probably leading to a bulkhead or root cellar. The door was locked, but I reached up and slid my hand along the top molding and found the key. I was surprisingly calm, my fingers were not even twitching. I inserted the key, turned the lock, and pulled the door open. It was tight, probably swollen from the slight basement dampness.

The room was dark, and I felt for a light switch. In the dim light of the overhead bulb, the small room appeared to be a treasure trove, filled with mounted rifles, cases of hunting knives, bows, and quivers of arrows. To one side was a metal cabinet with double doors that revealed shelves of ammunition, fishing reels and nets, rifle-cleaning equipment, collapsible fishing rods, and lubricating oils. Across from this was a taller, gray cabinet filled with rows of vests for fishing and hunting, wool hunting jackets, and numerous hats and gloves in orange and camouflage colors, all meticulously arranged and folded. On a shelf above were several plaid shirts, wool and cotton, neatly folded and arranged by color. Almost in a trance, I reached up for the cotton shirt that was plaid with a white background crossed by fibers of green, red, and yellow. I slowly unfolded it, more in control, and noticed a small tear in the sleeve, a piece of fabric missing. I shoved the shirt into my shorts and I carefully closed all the cabinets, leaving things in perfect order before shutting off the light and closing the door, which I relocked, replacing the key on the molding above. I glanced at my watch- twenty minutes inside. I had to move it.

I started up the stairs, and as I approached the door, I thought I heard a noise. I quickly flipped the light switch off and listened by the closed door, sweating and with my heart going a mile a minute. Hearing nothing further after ten seconds, I slowly opened the door, an inch at a time until I could just see into the kitchen. Someone was there. It was Lester's brother, a fat ugly guy, rummaging through the fridge. He found a beer, opened it with a church-key and took a long swig. He walked around the kitchen and there on the counter noticed the basket of cookies I had left. He unfolded the napkins, took a good whiff, and seemed pleased with his find. He took a big handful of the chocolate-chip morsels and started to munch over the sink.

I was feeling faint and starting to panic. If Peter decided to do some work in the basement, I was in trouble. I stood frozen in fear, not knowing what to do next, regretting that I had ever started this caper.

So far Peter had not moved from the sink and he didn't seem to wonder where the cookies came from. I nervously went over my options: Stay put and wait it out, hide in the basement, or make a mad run for it. I stayed put.

Soon Peter finished the goodies and beer, belched several times, and went back to the fridge for another brew. After opening the cap, he eyed the bottle and then took a deep gulp. He scratched his balding pate, belched again, and took another swallow. He then started to walk toward the cellar door.

I was paralyzed with fear. As Peter reached for the doorknob, I knew my life was about to end. I closed my eyes, waiting to be grabbed, beaten, and killed. Suddenly there was a loud ringing sound followed by "Who the fuck is calling?" Then I heard Peter trudge off to answer the phone.

I remembered that the phone was in the living room and not the kitchen. I had a chance, a slim one, but a chance. There was a faint glimmer of hope, but I had to move fast.

As I heard him lumber down the hall, I quietly and carefully escaped from the cellar and bolted for the back door, praying it would be unlocked. Peter could not see me, as there was no connection between the living room and kitchen. The door, thankfully, was unlocked, and within seconds I was out and had the presence of mind to close it quietly. I ran until I reached the woods behind the house. I was panting, sweating profusely from fear rather than exertion, wanting to die. I was a schmuck, a real putz, for even starting this caper.

CHAPTER THIRTY FIVE

The boys returned in the late afternoon, excited and victorious. Danny showed me the scorebook- 12-2, with Tony, Bobby, and Paul accounting for all the runs, either scoring them or batting them in. I owed the kids some time and attention. The shirt would wait. We were almost halfway through the summer and the boys wanted to know about the big mid-season event, the color war. It was a tradition, and over the next few days, all talk would center on the upcoming spectacle.

"Guys, you'll be divided by cabin into two groups, the green and the white, our camp colors. There will be contests in all sorts of sports and games. We'll have a tug-of-war, and it all ends with the treasure hunt."

"Tell us about the treasure hunt," chimed in Jeffrey.

"It takes a half day, and you have to follow a series of intricate clues, some very devious, until you find the prize, the director's cup," I responded.

"Doesn't sound so hard to me," said cocky Bobby Moore.

"You'd be surprised, Bobby. The clues are tough to decipher, and it's a stepwise process. One mistake early could throw off the whole search. There have been cases where neither team found the trophy."

"What do we get if we win?" Danny asked.

"Our team color, with the year 1959, is painted on the base of that tarnished, dented brass cup," I answered.

"That's all?" piped in Steve.

"It's a symbol of superiority, but you also get special privileges for one day."

"Like what?" asked Mike and Paul as one.

"Like, we get all three meals served by the losers the following day and they have to clean up. They also have to clean the latrine and washroom for one day," I told them.

"Sounds good to us," they all yelled.

The whole idea of the color war started well before Al Simmons and was always the highlight of the mid-season. It was designed to improve camp spirit that would carry through the rest of the summer. It made sense to me.

We would now have two days to prepare and practice. Even though we didn't know how the camp would be divided, we did know our own strengths and weaknesses. Strategies had to be discussed and planned, especially for the hunt. I was aware of how important planning was, as I had been involved in color wars for ten years. I would stress that every year was different, but the concept was a constant.

We talked for an hour before the bugle sounded for dinner.

CHAPTER THIRTY SIX

Lawrence Geller got a break. Someone from the town hall in Newton had called. A message had been left at department headquarters by Stella Williams, the town clerk and tax collector. It seemed that she was a jack of all trades at the town hall, handling dog licenses, fishing licenses, property taxes, deeds, current use properties, land transfers, and all gossip.

Geller returned her call and listened to three minutes of idle chatter before learning why she had called. Miss Williams, and she let Geller know it was miss, had come across records of real estate purchases, summer rentals, and owner-ship lists from the Andover-Stillwater area for the decade of 1920 to 1930. She had gone through the large tomes, concentrating on properties on Lake Spotswood. She had a list of ten homes on the lake, but some of the listings had several owners or lessees over the years, so the number of family names reached eighteen. Geller asked her to read the list, and the last known telephone numbers, permanent addresses, and what other information she had.

"I only have the list of names now. The rest I'll have to dig up."

"You don't have to do that," said Geller. "I'll send over a man to pick up the books."

This did not seem to please her, as it would end her involvement in "the case." I assure you, Mr. Geller, that I have ample time to peruse the records, and I know what to look for. These books are handwritten and difficult to decipher, and I'm sure the police have better things to do with their time."

"That would be a tremendous help, Miss Williams. We are quite short-handed, and the case is almost forty years old." Before hanging up he did make one last request.

"Miss Williams, were there any names on the list beginning with the letter M?" As the cop's pulse quickened, she slowly answered.

"Why, yes. There are two names, Mc-Millan and Miller, and you may call me Stella."

His grip on the phone tightened as he asked another question, the crucial one.

"Stella, did either of these families have young children?"

After what seemed to Geller to be an "hour," she came back on the line.

"Detective, are you still there?"

"Yes, I'm here," he replied.

"It seems the Mc-Millans had two married children who did not live with them at the lake, but the Millers had three children, two girls and a boy."

"Any names listed for the kids?"

"Nothing here, but I'll keep digging."

Geller thanked Stella and told her to call ASAP with any new information. He was sure he had hit pay dirt. He could feel it, and it felt right. The little girl was a Miller, and if she had lived, she would probably be in her mid-to-late forties.

***

Stella Williams stood by the phone for a few minutes gathering her thoughts. As town clerk for the last eight years she had had little excitement. The biggest thrill was dealing with the paperwork on a foreclosure involving property owned by one Thomas Prather, the town preacher.

He was the holier-than-thou pastor of the Congregational Church who had a yen for the choir director, a pretty young thing named Barbara Welles, ten years his junior. It seems that while preaching fidelity and righteousness from the pulpit on Sundays, he was busy committing adultery with the little choirmaster. Unfortunately for our preacher friend, he picked the wrong place and the wrong night. While going at it hot and heavy in the back seat of his car, parked at the edge of town, the brake accidentally released and the car rolled down the slight incline into the parking lot of the local bowling alley, hitting Sheriff Bob James's squad car. James happened to be off duty, bowling a few frames and having a few brews with the boys. In the well-lit lot, numerous observers noted the half-naked preacher and the undressed Mrs. Welles.

Needless to say, Mrs. Prather and Mr. Welles did not find the matter as amusing as the sheriff and the boys.

Mr. Welles threatened the clergyman with bodily harm and then proceeded to beat the shit out of his unfaithful wife, landing him in the county jail for three days pending trial. Mrs. Prather, the preacher's wife, was much more pragmatic and did not turn to violence. Instead, she consulted and retained a prominent attorney who summarily sued the padre for divorce and all his worldly possessions. Within months, poor, hapless Thomas Prather lost his house, car, and savings, and literally left town with only the shirt on his back. The bank took the property when Mrs. Prather could not meet her mortgage payments or pay her back taxes, and Stella handled the paperwork.

Now the possibility of being involved in an unsolved murder case had much more to offer Stella than the sordid affair of the small-town clergyman. This was big, New York City cop, media coverage, state troopers. Didn't Stella mean "star"? She sure hoped so.

CHAPTER THIRTY SEVEN

The color war was only a day away, and all our planning would be put to the test. At lunch the assistant director would announce which cabins were green and which ones were white. The boys were excited, and the electricity was infectious and spread through the camp. By noon the mess hall was buzzing with anticipation.

As we were eating our ice-cream, Bernie rose with a long list in hand. We listened as each cabin was named. Finally cabin #5 was announced- the green team.

"How good is that?" I whispered to the boys. We would be with Jim's cabin, a real plus. I could coordinate our strategy with him, and our kids got along great. We had less than a day to get together with the green team, pick boys for each event, and discuss the treasure hunt. Every camper would participate.

As a camper I'd loved the hunt. In 1956, the white team had lead by eighteen points going into the hunt, worth twenty-five. The title was up for grabs. The green team had to find the cup or suffer defeat for the third straight year. On their team was a crafty fourteen year-old from an upper cabin named Jessie Hyde, AKA Einstein. A better eponym would have been Willie Sutton, the famous bank robber and felon.

It was Hyde's idea to sucker the white team with false messages that he concocted while his teammates legitimately went after the prize. He carefully crafted clever, but vague clues on paper and sealed them in envelopes pilfered from the lodge office. The key was to get to the first clue before the white team and then start planting the false clues. This he accomplished, and the outcome was total disarray of the white team. While they searched and came up empty-handed, the green team calmly and methodically followed clue after clue and found the cup, winning the war by a mere seven points. The joy was short-lived, as Hyde could not keep from bragging about his exploits and the plot was uncovered, leading to forfeiture of the trophy and total disgrace for the green. The next year the rules were changed, and there were separate clues for each team.

Jim and I got together with our two cabins to plan rosters before meeting with the rest of the green team. We picked our best boys for archery, riflery, canoeing, sailing, softball, swimming and diving, and boating. In the tug of war, we were required to use all age groups and not just the older and bigger kids. We picked kids from all the cabins, including the upper camp, and we were now ready and eager.

CHAPTER THIRTY EIGHT

S tella Williams had called back with some information, including the last
known address of Sam and Rose Miller in the Prospect Park section of
Brooklyn. However he came up empty-handed when he found that the family no longer lived there and hadn't for more than ten years. Sam Miller, the
patriarch, had died in 1947, and Rose had passed away in 1953 at the age of
sixty-eight. Mr. Miller had had several heart attacks and died of complications
from diabetes. Mrs. Miller had died in a nursing home, where she had been for
five years with depression and dementia. The present owners knew that the
Millers had two children who had visited off and on, but they lived out of state
and were probably in their forties by now. Geller had to get their names and
addresses and dig further.

As he went over his notes, he had the uneasy feeling that he had missed
something. As was his routine, he decided to put the salient features on
a blackboard in his office so he could see what he had and what he didn't
have.

In one column he put the known:

1- The Miller family owned a summer home on Lake Spotswood around
1920.

2- They had young children, two girls and a boy.

In a second column he put the unknown:

1- Did they have a daughter who disappeared at around age ten?

2- Where were the children now, probably in their forties?

As he wrote and studied the columns, the missing piece that had troubled
him hit him like a ton of bricks. Stella had said that the Millers had three children, two girls and a boy. Yet neighbors and friends in Prospect Park told him
that only two adult children visited.

"Were they mistaken?" he said to himself. Maybe there was a third adult offspring who never visited, or maybe, there was a third child, a daughter who disappeared long ago and was never found. He sensed the answer. He had to find the two surviving siblings.

***

Geller had an idea. He called a Brooklyn exchange and asked to speak with one Nathan Feinstein, a retired pawnbroker and a former neighbor of the Millers. He was given Mr. Feinstein's name by the present owners of the Miller dwelling.

"Mr. Feinstein?"

"Yes, and who might I ask is calling?"

"Lawrence Geller from the NYPD."

"Oy vey, am I in trouble?"

"No, Mr. Feinstein, you are in no trouble. I just need some information."

"What would I know that you would find interesting?"

"I need some questions answered about a family you knew, the Millers, Sam and Rose and their children."

"Why?" said Feinstein, starting to become suspicious. "They never broke the law. Real nice people. Besides, how do I know that you are who you say you are?"

"I assure you that I am an inspector with the New York Police Department and I will give you a number to call to verify my credentials, or I could visit you in person and show you my ID."

"Nah, you sound honest," said a less cautious Nathan Feinstein. "Ask away."

"How well did you know the Millers?"

"They were neighbors, nice people. We talked occasionally, and we belonged to the same shul.

"Did they talk much about their children?"

"Not too much. They had a son who became a lawyer and practiced in Philadelphia and a daughter who married a doctor and lived in New Jersey."

"Did they ever mention a third child? I was under the impression that they had three children."

"Not that I remember, but it's funny you should mention it."

"Why do you say that, Mr. Feinstein?"

"Well one Friday night after services, Sam invited me and my wife, may she rest in peace, over for coffee and cake. I remember their home. In the living room was a beautiful piano with numerous photographs on top. I recall a family picture at a lake with Sam and Rose posing with three children, two girls and a boy. I recall how much the girls resembled Rose."

"Did you ever ask Sam about the picture and who the children were?"

"Never, I figured he didn't want to talk about it."

"One last question, Nate. I hope you don't mind that I called you Nate."

"Not at all, Larry," Nate countered.

Geller smiled and then asked, "Do you know where Sam and Rose are buried?"

"Sure. The Beth Israel Cemetery in the Jamaica Bay section of Brooklyn."

"Mr. Feinstein, you've been a great help. If you think of anything further that might aid in my investigation, please call at this number."

"Before you give me your number, may I ask what this is all about?

"I am not at liberty to give you any further information except that it is of utmost importance that we locate the Miller children."

After giving Nathan Feinstein his telephone number, Geller hung up and then immediately called information for the number of the Beth Israel Cemetery. He carefully dialed and after three rings, the phone was answered by a woman with a pleasant voice who said, "Beth Israel Cemetery. May I help you?"

"This is Lawrence Geller from the NYPD."

"Yes, Mr. Geller, what may I do for you?"

"I need some information about two people who are interred in your cemetery."

"I'm sorry, but that is confidential information and I am not in a position to give this out without authorization from the family in question or the director of Beth Israel, especially over the phone."

"If I stop by with proper ID, would that make a difference, miss? I'm sorry, what is your name?"

"It's Elizabeth Curry, and yes, that would make a difference. However I would still have to check with the director. Give me an hour or two to contact him and grab a quick lunch."

"Two hours will make it around one-thirty. Is that a good time?"

"Make it two. I'll give you directions."

Geller took down the route, hung up, and then made several more calls and cleared up some paperwork. He had brown-bagged it and took out a sandwich, ham and cheese on rye with mustard, which he washed down with stale coffee. After an hour and a half, he headed down to the carpool, where he picked up an unmarked, non-descript, dark blue sedan for the trip. He headed downtown toward Battery Park and followed signs to the Brooklyn Bridge, crossing the East River. He pulled out a roll of Tums, chewed two, and swore off black coffee for the umpteenth time. He followed Elizabeth Curry's directions, driving through some still lovely neighborhoods, private homes mixed with stately apartments, green lawns, and beds of flowers. Soon he saw signs for the cemetery.

He went through the ornate gate and continued down the narrow, circuitous road at the prescribed fifteen miles per hour until he saw an arrow pointing to information and the memorial chapel. He found the building, parked, and entered through a glass door. The room was comfortably cool compared to the outside temperature, and Geller approached the desk where an attractive brunette, probably in her early thirties, was seated.

She looked up, and Geller said, "Miss Curry?"

"Yes, I presume you are Mr. Geller."

"I am," he said, as he presented her with his NYPD badge and ID.

Miss Curry, looking up at Geller said, "How may I help you? You weren't very specific on the phone."

"I need information about the surviving children of a husband and wife buried here in the late forties and early fifties. The husband, Samuel Miller, was interred in 1947; his wife, Rose, in 1953."

"I have already touched base with Mr. Irving Stein, the director of Beth Israel, to make sure that I may release confidential material, even to the police. Mr. Stein wanted more specifics."

"I am investigating the death of a child who could have been a Miller and I need to find the siblings."

"I will relay your request to him, and if he approves, it will take time to go through the records for those years. We might not have current addresses or phone numbers for the surviving children. If the "children" are female and have married since the burials of their parents, we might not have their married names."

"I realize the stumbling blocks, and I am a very patient man."

He thought Elizabeth Curry had a beautiful mouth and incredible eyes, deep brown and expressive. Actually, he liked the whole package. She was a very attractive woman.

"I'll try to contact Mr. Stein this afternoon and if he gives me the OK, I'll start combing through the records today. Hopefully, it will not take long."

"I truly appreciate your help, Miss Curry. When you find something, please call me at my office." He handed her his card and said good-bye, noticing that she wore no wedding band.

***

The ride back to Manhattan was not pleasant. The light breeze had died away and the afternoon was hot, with temperatures approaching the mid-eighties. Traffic had started to build, increasing his mental and physical discomfort. By the time he got back to the office, he was in a foul mood and had sweaty armpits. He turned on the fan, sat at his desk in shirtsleeves with his feet up, and ruminated about Elizabeth Curry. She was lovely, and he would make it a point to revisit the cemetery with more questions.

There was a knock on the door.

"Enter," he yelled.

"Sorry to intrude, chief, but Sal and I have to go over some updates on a couple of cases," said Jack Vetti.

"Shoot. I've been preoccupied by this crazy case in North Jersey and I know you have plenty to go over."

***

Two hours later, he was back in the car going toward the Midtown Tunnel to his Queen's apartment. He stopped at a midtown deli after negotiating only a few blocks of traffic, double-parked, pulling down the NYPD visor to avoid a ticket. He entered and took a seat at the counter. He was getting a headache and couldn't face the bumper-to -bumper on an empty stomach.

He perused the menu briefly and ordered a turkey on rye with coleslaw and Russian dressing and a Dr. Brown's cream soda. It wasn't exactly cool in the deli, but at least there was a fan blowing. He glanced through a *"New York Daily News"* left by a departed customer and checked the headlines and baseball scores.

The sandwich arrived in minutes, and he ordered another soda. He ate slowly, although he was starved, savoring each bite. It was delicious, huge, and filling. He couldn't handle dessert, but had a black coffee and two Tums. He paid his bill, left a generous tip, and went outside to the heat and to continue the journey crosstown.

CHAPTER THIRTY NINE

After an early haze that followed an overnight shower the day emerged bright and sunny, a perfect start for the color war. The teams seemed to be well-matched, at least on paper. Al and Bernie wanted things to go down to the wire and make sure that nothing was a foregone conclusion.

We donned our green t-shirts and assembled at the flagpole to the bugler's call, joining a host of white shirts already there. Each counselor was given a list of activity times and the boys assigned to each. Some boys I didn't know well, but most were familiar. Each cabin would have two representatives for the tug-of-war, including the older boys from the upper cabins, but the individual sports were open to anywhere from one to three boys. All would compete in the treasure hunt.

When the whistle blew, all the boys ran to their assigned places: Danny to archery, Jeffrey to the waterfront for swimming, Bob and Tony to the softball field, Paul to riflery, and Mike and Steve to boating. After the initial competitions, which would last all morning, we would meet for the tug-of-war and then break for lunch. The hunt would take up the entire afternoon and could last up to four hours. Dinner would be late, around seven and awards would be presented. Let the games begin.

***

Danny held his own, especially at the shorter distances of ten and fifteen yards. He was very accurate, but he had trouble at the longer distance of twenty yards, having difficulty pulling the bow enough to reach the target without his arm and hand shaking from the effort. At any rate, he scored admirably and the green team trailed by a mere two points in this event.

Meanwhile at the waterfront, Jeffrey was blowing them away, although he was getting little help from his green-shirted teammates. Each team scored eight points, and at the end of two events, the white team was up eighteen to sixteen.

We made our move on the ball field. The competition included batting, throwing, and base running. The field had markers in left, center, and right at fifty, seventy-five, one-hundred, one-hundred-twenty-five, and one-hundred-fifty feet. Each boy had six swings and received points based on the distance that the ball traveled in the air: two points for fifty feet, four points for seventy-five, six for one-hundred, eight for one-hundred-twenty-five, and ten points for one-hundred-fifty feet and beyond. The same pattern of scoring was in place for the softball throw, but each boy only had three chances. The last event was a timed run of the base paths. Each had two shots at the circuit, the best time would stand. First place was worth five points, second was worth three, and third was worth one point. Bobby and Tony scored big. In batting they scored sixteen and fourteen, respectively. Bobby was the only lower cabin kid to score ten points with a drive that landed about twenty to twenty-five feet beyond the one-hundred-twenty-five foot marker. They did equally well in the throw, finishing with fourteen and sixteen points. They tore up the base paths for a second and third finish. This catapulted the green team to a ten to six win, and after three events, we were up twenty-six to twenty-four.

At the rifle range, Paul O'Neill was excelling. He was patient, exacting, and steady.

The competition involved shooting from three positions: prone, kneeling, and standing. Each boy would fire five rounds at each of two targets in all three positions, a total of six cards to be scored. Paul had the highest total and received ten points. The event, however, ended in a tie, as his green-shirted teammates couldn't hit the broad side of a barn.

The boating events included sailing small sunfish, canoeing, and rowboat races. Mike and Steve were out of their element, but their athleticism kept them in the hunt. What they lacked in technique they more than compensated for in strength and stamina. In the rowboat race, they finished fourth and fifth, just nosed out at the finish by a fifteen-year-old for third. The canoeing was easier, as the boats were sleeker and more fluid. However, they had more wobble and could capsize easily. They both scored in the two-man and war canoe races. But with all that effort, the team score was deadlocked after five events. Al Simmons was beaming.

***

The tug-of-war was the last event before the lunch break. The staff had prepared the area for the "big pull," as it was called, a rectangle measuring one-hundred by ten feet, marked with white lines of lime. In the middle was a ten by ten foot pit dug to a depth of a foot and a half and filled with water, creating a pool of mud. A large rope, sixty feet in length, with knots at both ends and a white handkerchief tied at the mid-point, was stretched across the pit of mud, thirty feet on each side. Each team would position the boys in a specific order that could not be changed. Once in position, that was it. The strategy was to put the biggest, heaviest, and hopefully, strongest boys at the ends as an anchor.

When all the preparations were in place and the kids were ready, Al raised a red flag, and the crowd murmured. All eyes were on him, and he waited several seconds for effect and then let the flag fall to his side while shouting, "pull."

The assembled crowd roared, and the boys started to pull with all their collective strength. They dug in their heels and pulled with little advantage to either side, and after two minutes the handkerchief had barely moved. It would now become a matter of stamina and will rather than brute strength.

Sweat was pouring down all their faces, and the strain was evident, yet there was little give. Finally, after six minutes in the baking sun, the white towel started to move, slowly and almost imperceptibly at first, but definitely toward the white team. With the ardent urging from the spectator-campers, the white team seemed more energized, gaining its second wind and pulling harder and more efficiently. The rope moved farther and the advantage seemed more apparent.

The first boy on the green team was within a foot or two of the mud pit, and all seemed lost. Almost miraculously and without any reasonable explanation, the towel stopped moving. The crowd gasped.

Slowly the tide began to turn and the white flag started to move the other way. The ebb and flow continued for several more minutes, and the sun was brutal. Suddenly the whites made their move. With a tremendous pull, accompanied by screams and grunts, they broke the backs of the greenies and pulled the first two boys into the quagmire, followed in short order by the rest of the team. The greenies who were watching, did so in stunned silence and disbelief. They were utterly shocked by the abrupt conclusion. With the victory came ten points and a sizable lead. All would be decided by the hunt, worth up to twenty-five points if finished. Covered in mud, the green team headed for the showers with heads bowed.

CHAPTER FORTY

L unch was a boisterous affair. We ate ravenously, keeping the waiters busy going back and forth for seconds and thirds. We were losing, but you would never know it by the way we ate. The treasure hunt would start at precisely two and end at six. If neither team completed the course, points would be awarded for each clue unraveled. Some clues would be worth two points, some one, depending on difficulty. Each team had a different set of clues to follow, but they all lead to the final prize, the cup.

After Al laid down the ground rules, we separated by color to the softball field on the west side and the infirmary on the east. At precisely two, he fired the camp "cannon," and with a roar the final event was underway.

Our first clue was handed to us in an envelope. It said,

"Follow your nose to the hose that washes the clothes on Wednesdays."

"What the hell does that mean?" I thought.

"I know we bring our laundry to the lodge on Wednesday," said Danny.

"Yeah, but we don't wash our own laundry, and I've never used a hose," said another boy.

"We send out the laundry and it comes back in a week," added Jeffrey. Then it hit me. There was a hose behind the washroom next to a clothes-line. I often rinsed out shorts and bathing suits there.

"I know what the clue means, guys. Let's hit it. Follow me," I yelled.

We ran to the washroom, and waiting for us was a large hose with a large brass nozzle. We uncoiled it- nothing. We unscrewed it from the spigot- nothing. Then we took off the nozzle- voila! Rolled up in the brass head was a note, the second clue, a little wet but legible. We documented clue one on our treasure hunt sheet and scanned clue two.

It said, "Take aim, the apple is waiting."

It had to be a reference to either archery or riflery, we all agreed. Almost as one we yelled, "William Tell," the guy who shot an apple off his son's head with a bow and arrow.

We all ran to the archery area, scouring hay bales, targets, and arrow holders with no success. In exasperation, we looked around the woods behind the targets and there in front of us, to our amazement, was a beautiful crabapple tree, laden with fruit.

Below the tree were numerous unripe apples that had fallen to the ground, shaken off by squirrels or the wind. We checked each one and finally found what we were looking for, a small green apple with a telltale slit in the peel and flesh. Stuffed into the opening was a small piece of paper, clue three.

***

Things progressed well throughout the afternoon, and we got to clue twelve with fifty minutes remaining. This was the last and probably most difficult clue leading to the cup. We were in good shape, but we had no idea how the white team was doing. Twelve turned out to be a crusher, although at first glance it seemed simple. It was our invitation to the trophy, but we all drew a blank when we tried to decipher it. The clue read, "Mickey and Willie Dillie roam."

"Willie who? Mickey who?"

"Could it have something to do with a cartoon?" someone offered. "Maybe it's Mickey Mouse."

"But who is Willie Dillie?" said another. Precious minutes elapsed with no solution. What was the connection between Mickey and Willie? Who were they?

"Oh, my God," Tony shouted, elated and jumping to his feet. "Mickey Mantle and Willie Mays. It's gotta be."

"He's right," screamed another boy.

With barely a second lost, we all ran to the ball field to begin the search. Luckily the white team was nowhere to be seen, a good sign. Everyone knew that Mantle and Mays both played centerfield, Mickey for the New York Yankees and Willie for the New York Giants. We scoured the outfield and found nothing. Searching the infield, we lifted bases and even pried up home plate with no luck.

"We're missing something," Jim Butler said.

"Let's get organized and think this through. If Mickey Mantle and Willie Mays are correct, then the connection is baseball and maybe even centerfield, but there must be something else because there is obviously no trophy here."

"Both those guys were power hitters and base stealers, who could run like the wind," Mike interjected.

"They were great team players and hit for average as well as power and scored and batted in many runs each season," I added.

"They did everything and always lead the league in slugging percentage," said Danny, our "baseball encyclopedia."

"What's slugging percentage?" asked Jeffrey.

"It has to do with hitting for extra bases. Like, if you got two hits in a game but they were singles, your slugging percentage would be much lower than a guy who also had two hits, but they were a homer and a triple," added Danny.

"That's it," shouted an excited Jim. "Extra bases- that might be the clue. Where do they keep the softball equipment, Bob?"

Before I could answer, Danny shouted out, "In the rec-room of the lodge."

With twelve minutes left we all ran to the lodge. Once in the rec-room, we saw the closet door, our last hope. If we were wrong, we would run out of time. It was do or die.

Almost ripping the door off its hinges, we tore into the storage area throwing out softballs, bats, gloves, bases, catcher's masks, and shin guards, but nothing that resembled a camp cup.

"How much time do we have?" I yelled.

"Nine minutes," responded Jim.

Dejected we were about to pack it in when one of the boys found a chest protector for the catcher. It had a funny lump in the padding. With our collective breaths held, Jim and I felt the lump. There was definitely something hard and roundish inside.

"Danny," I yelled. "Go to the mess hall and get a large knife from Nellie and move it."

Danny ran off. There were seven minutes left. Nellie did not give Danny the knife without the third degree. She was not about to give a dangerous weapon and her prized cutlery to a kid. A quick compromise was reached. Nellie would accompany Danny back to the softball equipment closet.

126

With five minutes to go, I plunged the blade into the stuffing. There was cotton everywhere, and when I reached in, I felt a metal object. Things looked good.

To the delighted screams of the boys, I lifted the camp trophy from the decimated remains of the chest protector.

"Let's move it, guys. We only have three minutes," yelled Jim.

With Danny in the lead, holding the cup above his head, we all ran to the flagpole, where we arrived with a minute to spare. We danced around, passing the cup for each boy to kiss, sort of like a Stanley Cup celebration in hockey. We gloated as the white team struggled up the hill empty-handed, hoping that we too had missed finding the prize. At that moment the bugle sounded. It was six o'clock. The color war of 1959 was history.

That night, dinner was a dream for the greenies. The white team waited tables and, true to tradition, filled the cup with Kool Aid so that each of us on the green team could drink from it. After dinner, awards were presented, and Jim Butler and one of his cabin boys, our team captain, Bill Sommers, accepted the winner's banner. Exhausted, elated, and filled with pride, we went back to our cabin to talk, joke, and tell stories. Sleep came before ten.

CHAPTER FORTY ONE

L awrence Geller had finally tracked down the Miller siblings. Both were in their late forties. George Miller was a lawyer in Philadelphia and Ruth Berman was married to a doctor and living in Essex County, in northern New Jersey. He got their last known addresses and telephone numbers from Elizabeth Curry and placed calls to both. George Miller was not home, but the maid was expecting him and his wife for dinner at about seven. He was in Washington, D.C. for a conference and could not be disturbed, but she promised to leave a message for her employer to call back at the number Geller gave her.

The call to Mrs. Berman proved to be much more fruitful. Her daughter, who sounded to be a young adult, told Geller that her parents were on vacation for another three days and would return his call at that time.

As an afterthought, just as he was about to hang up, he asked the Berman girl if she knew whether her mother had a sister who was deceased.

"Why, yes," stated the daughter, whose named was Virginia.

"What were the circumstances of her death?"

"I don't really know. Mom doesn't talk about it."

"Did you ever ask?" prodded Geller.

"Yes, I was curious. I got bits and pieces, but I think she disappeared during a summer vacation a long time ago."

"Did this happen in northwest New Jersey on a lake called Spotswood?"

"I don't know, Mr. Geller, but I think my mother said grandma told her that her sister had drowned. My mother was very young at the time. It happened almost forty years ago."

"Bingo," thought Geller. A young girl disappeared, presumed drowned, about forty years ago. It had to be.

"Last question," said Geller. "What was your mother's sister's first name?"

"Elizabeth."

Geller was crestfallen. Everything fit except this. The bracelet had the initials L.M.

But just after she gave this disappointing answer, Virginia added, "but they called her Lilly."

His hand was stuck to the phone receiver. He had a positive ID on the skeletal remains. Well, not quite a positive ID, but very, very good circumstantial evidence.

***

Over the next few hours, Geller documented his evidence in preparation for a meeting with the state police for Sussex County and the Andover-Stillwater police force. But his emotions were centered on the upcoming visits with the surviving siblings, Ruth and George.

He did not look forward to the long drive again, but he had to make the trip. He liked face-to-face.

In 1959, there were no Routes 80,78, or 287, so crossing northern New Jersey took time. He navigated the Lincoln Tunnel and took Route 3 to Route 46 heading west. Arriving in Newton he drove to the state police barracks, meeting Chief Bills from the locals and Troop Leader Parker from the state police. He quickly brought the two officers of the law up to speed.

"The skeletal remains are probably those of one Lilly (Elizabeth) Miller, daughter of Sam and Rose Miller, both deceased. She disappeared and was presumed drowned about forty years ago. Forensic tests on the remains were those of a prepubescent female, consistent with Lilly's age. The cause of death was multiple cranial fractures causing brain injury, inflicted by a heavy metal instrument, probably a shovel. The young girl had been murdered around 1920 by assailant or assailants unknown. The injuries were so extensive that the perpetrator (or perpetrators) was probably a large male. There are two surviving siblings, George Miller, an attorney in Philadelphia and Ruth Berman, a housewife married to a physician, living in Essex County, New Jersey. Both were unavailable for questioning at this time, but I will be contacting them individually over the next few days."

"Anything that we should be doing here?" asked Parker.

"I have to question the sister and brother first for details. They may not know much, as they were just children at the time of the killing, but they might remember someone who showed an interest in Lilly or someone who hung around a lot. The perp (or perps) may have been a local living near the lake. I also have to go to see Stella Williams to get a list of locals, renters, and summer residents from the 1920's."

"It's possible that the murderer may have been a transient, just passing through, or the bad guy may not even be alive," added Bills, the Andover-Stillwater chief of police.

The meeting broke up and Geller made his way to the second floor of the Newton town hall to visit Stella Williams. He had to go over the completed list of locals, renters, and summer people from the twenties that Stella had prepared. He realized that most of the data would be outdated or of no help, but he had to look.

When Stella saw Geller, she blushed, primped, and started to babble, a nervous habit of hers when confronted by a good-looking man, especially one without a wedding band.

"It's good to see you, Mr. Geller."

"Please call me Larry, and it's good to finally see you in person. Your help has been immeasurable."

"Well, I try my best." At that point she handed Geller a complete list of what he needed.

"You're an angel. I'll keep in touch," Geller said sincerely. She blushed.

CHAPTER FORTY TWO

I finally had time to look at the shirt that I had pilfered from Lester's house. The torn area matched the size and shape of my small piece of fabric and the plaid pattern, material, and colors were the same. Lifting the shirt, it seemed very large to me, much too large for Lester. I looked at the label, 100 percent cotton, XXXL. Lester couldn't be more than 175 to 180 pounds, a large or extra-large at best. Could this be Lester's shirt or maybe his obese brother's?

I pondered what I had. A torn shirt belonging to the Cartrights, probably worn during the attack on Max. It told me that either Lester or his brother Peter had stalked Jean and me and injured the dog. I couldn't prove it in a court of law, but I was convinced that it was a planned act of intimidation. I also extrapolated that it was a good bet that they were responsible for the other misdeeds. I had to find out why.

It seemed to me that the Cartrights wanted to terrorize the camp and cause upheaval and personal injury. But why injure young boys and how would that benefit them? The stakes must be high, perhaps a personal vendetta, money to be gained, or something to hide.

As I was mulling over the possibilities I heard someone behind me, and I whirled.

"I had to track you down. I haven't seen you in ages. I think you're avoiding me," Jean complained.

"No way. I wanted to see you alone, but I haven't had the time with the color war and all."

"What are you doing now?" she said, ignoring my excuse and looking at the plaid shirt. "I bet you're trying to prove your conspiracy theory that Lester Cartright is trying to chase everyone away and close the camp."

"Say what you want, but I know Cartright is up to no good. I just have to find out why."

CHAPTER FORTY THREE

They had just returned from vacation, and Dr. Berman had Saturday and Sunday off before returning to work. Geller made arrangements to visit at ten on Sunday, giving them time to unpack, unwind, and go through their mail. He didn't want to be overly pushy or intrusive, but he needed information.

On a Sunday, the drive from Queens to Millburn would not be a problem, with little traffic. There was always the shore crowd to contend with, as Jersey had some beautiful beaches, but the heavy flow of cars usually didn't start this far north. He stopped for a coffee and bagel at a diner after negotiating the Lincoln Tunnel and then headed for Routes 1 and 9. The Pulaski Skyway took him into Newark, where he picked up Route 22 west toward Springfield. He followed back roads from the Springfield exit to the neighboring town of Millburn, and finally located the Berman home on a quiet, tree-lined street. It was a pretty area where streets were named after trees: locust, myrtle, walnut. The home was modest considering the old man was a doctor, but it was well-maintained and nicely landscaped.

Geller rang the front doorbell at exactly ten, and it was answered by an attractive woman dressed in a pale blue skirt, white sleeveless blouse, and sandals. She was fair and blonde, tall and slim, a real looker. Geller said hello, showed her his ID, and was allowed past the front door.

"How do you do, inspector? I'm Ruth Berman. Please come in. My husband will join us in a minute."

Geller entered into a small vestibule that opened into an inviting living room.

"Might I get you something? A cup of coffee, perhaps?" asked Ruth Berman.

"Coffee would be great," Geller answered.

"I just made a fresh pot. How do you take it?"

"Black, no sugar, please."

"I'll be just a minute. Please make yourself at home."

As Ruth Berman excused herself and went to the kitchen, Geller perused the living room. It was tastefully furnished with a mixture of antiques and traditional pieces. The fireplace had a beautiful hand-carved mantel and marble facing. On each side were custom-made bookshelves filled with hardbound editions and bric-a-brac. On the other side of the room was a baby grand piano. It was highly polished and covered with numerous photographs, mainly family pictures in black and white. There were several nicely done oils on the walls and a gold gilt sunburst mirror over the fireplace.

Geller walked to the piano to look more closely at the photos. There were several of children, some of adults, and many of the family in various locales doing different activities: sailing, riding, having a cookout, enjoying the beach. There was one picture that caught his attention, a family by a lakeside: mother, father, a young boy, and two young girls. The mother looked like Ruth Berman and the youngest girl had to be Ruth. Next to her was a pretty girl, about ten or eleven, with blonde curls reminiscent of Shirley Temple. In the lower right-hand corner in small print was written "Summer-1920."

As Ruth Berman returned with the coffee, Geller noticed several other photos, less aged, of a teenage boy and an absolutely drop-dead beautiful girl in a Syracuse University sweatshirt. Ruth noticed Geller staring and said, "She's beautiful, isn't she?"

Geller said, "very pretty."

"She's our daughter, Virginia, a senior at Syracuse. As smart as she is pretty," she said proudly.

"And the young man?"

"Our son Bob. It's an old picture, but he just finished high school and will be starting college in the fall. He's away at summer camp."

Geller couldn't help but feel that he had seen the boy before. The face was familiar. A nice-looking, clean-cut kid.

As Ruth Berman offered Geller a chair, Dr. Berman entered the room, introducing himself as Andrew. They all sat and Geller began guardedly.

"Mrs. Berman, I need your help in solving a case, a crime that intimately involves you but that you probably have limited knowledge of or remember very little about."

Ruth Berman and her husband looked puzzled.

Geller continued. "Approximately two weeks ago we unearthed the skeletal remains of a young girl who had been murdered. Evidence showed her to be about ten years old."

He was unsure of how much detail of the killing to provide, but he reluctantly pressed on.

"She had been killed by repeated blows to the head and was buried in a rural area of northwestern New Jersey. Unfortunately, I have reason to believe that she might be your sister, Lilly, who was presumed drowned in Lake Spotswood in 1920."

Ruth was stunned and confused, but tears sprang to her eyes and she held her husband's hand, looking somewhat unsteady. After trying to compose herself, she mumbled in a barely audible, trembling voice, "I thought she drowned. Momma told me Lilly had drowned and that she was never found. I don't understand."

"Mrs. Berman, do you remember anything about that summer? I know you were just a young girl."

Dr. Berman held his wife and said, "This is an old wound you're opening, inspector. Obviously it's very painful for her."

"I know that, doctor, but I need answers to solve this crime and your wife might be able to help me and Lilly."

Ruth summoned up her courage and said, "My parents are both dead and my brother and I hardly remember our sister. But we remember the effect her death had on all of us. We stopped laughing as much and our parents were never the same. They lost their zest for life and just went through the motions. They never recovered from the tragedy."

"Maybe I will be able to bring you some long overdue peace. More importantly, I will try to bring the murderer to justice, the person who robbed you and your family of a full and happy life and ended your sister's life just as it was beginning."

"Mr. Geller, I don't know how much help I will be. I've spent the last thirty-nine years trying to forget."

"Let me be the judge. I just need bits and pieces. The little clues, when put together, could break a case. Do you have any recollections of other people at the lake, like summer residents, locals, or children?"

She was quiet, concentrating, her thoughts almost palpable.

Geller continued to prod, gently but leadingly. "Take your time. Let your thoughts take over. Mention anything that comes to mind."

"I do remember how I idolized Lilly and followed her everywhere. I remember her yellow rain slicker. I remember how my dad taught her to fish."

She started to weep, the tears slowly rolling down her cheeks like sad pearls. She was going back in time to that horrific summer, to the day that changed all their lives and took the breath from her beautiful, loving sister.

"Do you remember any adults who disliked your family or your sister?"

"No. We hardly knew anyone at the lake. My parents wanted it that way."

"How about other children or teenagers?"

"I remember another family with teenaged children, but they never came to our house and they showed no interest in Lilly or me."

Geller could see that Ruth was starting to become lost in her reveries and knew it was time to quit. He thanked the Bermans for their time and got up to leave. He shook hands with Andrew and turned to Ruth.

"I want to thank you for your help. I know this is a painful experience, but if you think of anything, no matter how seemingly insignificant, please call me."

He gave her his card and turned to leave. As he put his hand on the doorknob, he had one more thought.

"Pardon me for overstaying my welcome, but I have one more question. Did Lilly have a friend or someone she hung out with at the lake?"

Ruth Berman took her time, hesitating and then said,

"There was a boy, not really a friend, who liked Lilly. He was a few years older and kind of strange, but they seemed to like each other. I remember that he was really quite obese. It was kind of funny seeing him with Lilly. She was so tiny and thin and he was hulking. But he was always kind to her, even protective."

"How do you mean strange?" Geller pressed.

"I remember that he loved bugs and snakes and things like that."

"Was he ever mean to Lilly, or did he ever hit her?"

"Oh, no. Lilly liked him."

"I know it's been almost forty years, but do you remember his name?"

"No. All I recall is that he was very fat. That's all."

"I'm sorry, inspector," Dr. Berman interrupted, "but I think Ruth has had it. We'll call you if she remembers anything. Good day, Mr. Geller."

***

Geller had a million thoughts running through his brain. He was so rapt in thought that he missed the turn-off onto Route 22 East. He doubled back and decided to stop for a quick burger and coffee at a diner he had seen about a couple of hundred yards up the road.

Sitting at the counter, he had a cheeseburger with fried onions and coffee and then indulged himself with a slice of coconut cream pie, a decadence he normally denied himself for the sake of his waistline. He paid the bill, left a tip, and grabbed a toothpick on the way out.

After about fifteen minutes on the road, it started, a burning sensation beginning in his chest and radiating to his throat. He reached for a packet of Rolaids, took two, and swore off burgers and black coffee for the umpteenth time. "Perhaps it was the pie that put me over the edge," he mused, though finding no humor in it. "I'm killing myself. Fourteen-hour workdays, gulping food and black coffee. Thank God I don't smoke."

As he drove back to the city, he organized his thoughts. He had to interview Ruth Berman's brother, George. He was several years older and might remember more. This meant planning a trip to Philadelphia. Next, he had to revisit Stella Williams in Newton to review the list from the Lake Spotswood area in 1920, the year of the murder. Maybe a local family had a really fat son who was in his teens at the time.

In the back of his mind, something was nagging at Geller. What was it? What had bothered him at the Berman home? He almost sideswiped a Chevy Impala on the approach to the Lincoln Tunnel as he suddenly realized what it was. The kid in the photo on the piano, the nice-looking, clean-cut boy; he was the counselor at Camp Spenser who had discovered the remains. How ironic that Ruth Berman's son was spending the summer at a camp on the same lake where his aunt was murdered, and he had no idea.

CHAPTER FORTY FOUR

Peter Cartright was in the basement. He was alone in the room with the cases of mounted insects, snakes, and small rodents. He as breathing hard, almost wheezing, partly due to the effort of walking down the cellar steps and partly due to the anticipation of what he was about to do. He had two covered glass jars, one containing a huge moth with brown markings on its wings and the other, a small bat. The lids had air holes punched through with a nail so that the "specimens" would not asphyxiate. They would die, but only when he decided. Peter was sweating profusely and could hardly calm himself.

First he gingerly opened the jar containing the moth, slowly and carefully, lest the creature escape and his work be for naught, his obsession deferred. He was so excited that he became erect. He took the struggling insect and pinned it through the thorax to a corkboard with a large straight pin. As the moth desperately beat its wings Peter took a tweezers and pulled off first one wing and then the other, both with the nauseating slowness of one seeking to produce maximum pain. Not satisfied, he picked up a book of matches and struck one. He slowly and deliberately moved the flame close to the insect's body and held it there. He could smell the burning tissue. He blew out the match before it burned his fingers and proceeded to "the next phase." This required paper ripped into strips and stuffed under and around the dying bug. With another match he touched a corner of the paper and watched as the insect was slowly consumed by flames.

He had great plans for the bat. He poured denatured alcohol into the jar and covered the breathing holes. Within several minutes the animal was stuporous, causing Peter to become hard again with anticipation, an erection so rigid that it was almost painful. He unscrewed the lid, lifted the bat, and pinned its wings to the corkboard, much as he had done with the moth. He then took the board and mounted it on the far wall of the cellar. He walked back to the table and opened a case filled with large, sharp weighted darts. It took only three throws before the bat was dead, a new record.

He'd been hard throughout the entire procedure, and then there it was, the utter release and ultimate pleasure. He came in his pants without ever touching himself.

In his post orgasm musings he remembered the feeling of intense pleasure, even when he was a young boy and then a teen, when he was torturing insects and anything else he could catch in his hands: rodents, newts, frogs, toads, and even small animals like puppies, the ultimate find. He'd drowned a cat and strangled a dog before he was twelve. He didn't understand this compulsion to kill, but he felt urges that were too overwhelming to deny. He would often fly into rages if he couldn't satisfy his perversions. This behavior had shocked and worried his parents. He had been a scary child.

And then there were his parents, from whose hands he had suffered years of abuse. Now they were reaping the fruits of their labor. One day he would kill someone. He saw several doctors for his deviant behavior but got no help from that quarter. Of course, he had faked reform, as he'd done so many times before, but would always return to his "games." The doctors had told his parents that he was slow, antisocial, and had something they had called a "personality disorder."

Who cared? His parents were now dead, gone for many years and unmissed. He could do what he wanted. It was just him and Lester, and big brother would take care of him as he always did.

CHAPTER FORTY FIVE

I awoke with a splitting headache and the day matched my physical condition, gray and dreary. The summer had been mostly day after day of sunshine and warmth, but today it was damp and chilly, with rain forecast off and on all day. On an upbeat note, however, I had received word from Al Simmons that Kenny Sawyer was fully healed and rested and already asking to come by for a visit.

"That's great, Mr. Simmons. I'll tell the boys."

"I told the Sawyers that tomorrow would be fine, and they'll be up in time for lunch."

"Great. He'll sit with us and spend the day. Do you think there's any chance that he'll stay for the rest of the summer?"

"I doubt it, Bob. There are only two and a half weeks left in the season and his mother said the doctor wants him to avoid strenuous activity and sports until the start of the school year. But next summer is another story."

Excitedly I returned to the breakfast table and filled the kids in on Kenny's status and his visit the next day. It was as if I'd told them that a movie star or sports hero was coming. They couldn't wait to see him.

As I was leaving the mess hall Al called me over.

"Inspector Geller called," said Al. "He'd like you to return his call ASAP. He wants to get more information. You can use my private phone."

"Did he say exactly why he wants to talk to me? I think I told him everything I know."

"No, he didn't say anything more, but you did find the body and he probably has thought of more details that need clarification."

I went to Al's cabin to place the call. Jean was there looking lovely, in white shorts and a pink tank top that showed off her tan. For the first time I noticed that her hair had lightened from the days of sun. She looked wonderful.

"Mr. Simmons said I could use his phone to call New York City."

"Go right ahead, Bob," said Kathy Simmons. "Use the phone in his private office."

I dialed deliberately and after four rings, Geller answered.

"Mr. Geller, this is Bob Berman. You called earlier to set up an interview?"

"Yes. I have to ask you some questions relating to the body that you and Miss Simmons discovered."

"Anytime is OK with me except tomorrow afternoon."

"How about tomorrow morning?" responded Geller. "Say ten o'clock?"

"That's fine as long as I'm done in time for lunch. How much time do you need?"

"Fifteen minutes at the most as I have to get to Newton."

"OK, see you at ten," I answered and hung up. After returning the receiver to the cradle I shook my head and wondered what Geller could possibly want. Jean and I had told him everything we knew, or at least I thought so.

"Mrs. Simmons, I wonder if you have a couple of aspirins. I have a splitting headache and I really don't want to see Betty Sloan."

"I'm sure I have aspirin. Let me look." She briefly ducked into the bathroom and came back with two tablets and a glass of water.

"Here, Bob, take these. Do you have time to lie down for a while?"

"Yes ma'am. The weather is awful and the kids are just going to hang out in the cabin until the rain stops. They'll just play cards, write postcards, and listen to the radio." I thought about them arguing over a station and my head throbbed more.

"Good. You don't look well," she said.

Actually I felt even worse than I looked and Geller's phone call didn't help. What did he want from me?

***

At ten on the dot the next morning, Geller arrived at Camp Spenser. Al Simmons had arranged for the interview in a private office in the lodge. I had sent the boys to their activities, and now I sat with Geller, who was sipping a cup of black coffee. He took out his notepad.

"Bob, I know your mother told you that she had an older sister who died in childhood."

"She talked about her very little, but I did know that her sister drowned at age ten."

"Do you know where she drowned?"

"Mom said it was at a lake in New Jersey, but she's never been back there, not since she was eight."

"Did your mother ever recognize this area when she visited you when you were a camper or counselor?"

"Why would she?" I asked.

"Because Lake Spotswood, where this camp is located, was the site where her sister supposedly drowned thirty-nine years ago. Your mother and her family had a summer home a half mile to the east."

I was stunned, truly stunned by what Geller was saying, but I focused on the word "supposedly." Trying to stay calm, I responded, "Maybe my mother was suppressing her vague memories, or maybe she just didn't remember. She was only a child at the time."

I looked up at Geller, feeling a terrible foreboding as he started to speak.

"Bob, I don't know how to tell you this except to be professional and come right out with it. It seems that your mother's sister, your Aunt Lilly, did not drown. I believe she was murdered and buried beside Lake Spotswood in 1920. The skeleton that you unearthed several weeks ago was your mother's sister."

I was numb, sitting there just looking at Geller incredulously. The remains were my aunt, murdered less than a mile from where I spent so many summers as a camper and now a counselor, and my mother and I didn't have an inkling.

"Mr. Geller, if you know all this, why did you come to talk to me?"

He answered matter-of-factly. "Because you are going to help me find the killer or killers, if still alive and in the area,"

"How am I going to help you solve a crime that occurred more than twenty years before I was born?"

"You might start by telling me all that you know about the Cartrights, aside from what you related a few weeks ago. Start with a physical description of the brothers," said Geller.

"Well Lester is a real outdoorsman. Seems pretty physically fit with strong arms and hands. Peter, on the other hand, is a mess physically."

"What do you mean, a mess?"

"He's real fat and wears thick glasses. Really slovenly-type fat. You know, the kind of guy who has a belly that hangs over his belt and jowls, and is always sweating and out of breath. But I think I told you all this."

Geller thought, "Could this be the fat boy who hung out with Lilly?" He would call Stella to check the tax records for dates of birth of both brothers.

"Did either of them ever mention the Miller family or Lilly?"

"No, definitely not."

"One last question," Geller promised. "Did Lester or Peter ever display any cruelty toward animals or go on a tirade in your presence?"

"Personally I think that Lester, or more probably Peter, attacked Jean's dog with a stick, hitting him hard enough to cause a pretty deep cut. I can't prove it, but I have some pretty compelling evidence. I also think that Jean and I were stalked before the attack."

"Did this occur before you found the skeletal remains?"

"Yes, days before."

"Why do you think Peter or Lester, or both, stalked you and hurt Max?"

"I have my theories."

"Let me hear your thoughts, Bob."

"I think the Cartrights would like to see our camp close down and would probably like the summer residents to leave as well. Whether this is for some personal gain or a vendetta of some sort, I don't know."

"Could it be a matter of fear, the fear of something being discovered?"

"I really don't know, but I think they were somehow involved in two other happenings at the camp where two boys were injured."

I continued,

"As I told you before I have a theory about the "why." I have no actual proof, so what I am about to tell you is purely supposition. Lester, as you know, works for the county highway department and is privy to information about new roads and highways, roads being widened and repaired, and routes being changed. Let's say Lester found out that within the next few years the state was planning to upgrade its highway system, especially the northern and north-western tier to ease the population sprawl in Passaic, Bergen, Union, and Essex

Counties. It would affect properties values considerably, and in Sussex County, a fortune could be made if you had the right connections. If the Cartrights, probably Lester since I doubt Peter has the mental capacity for it, were to force people out of the Spotswood area, they could buy up property at bargain prices and watch them escalate in value. Taxes were low, and they could have probably socked away thousands in property over the years. They certainly don't spend money on themselves or their home."

"When you alluded to this before, I found it very interesting and plausible. I am in the process of looking into it," said Geller.

Geller got up to go and we shook hands. "Oh, just one more thing while I think of it."

"What's that, Mr. Geller?"

"Do Lester and Peter store any outdoor yard tools like shovels, hoes, or pick-axes?"

"I don't know, but I think they store stuff like rakes and shovels in a crawl space under their porch."

"Could you find out? And if you do, see if the equipment is old or new."

"Probably old. Like I said, the Cartrights don't have a lot of new stuff and don't spend a lot of money. I'll do my best to find out."

Geller thanked me and shook my hand again.

CHAPTER FORTY SEVEN

Kenny arrived with his mom in the early afternoon in time for lunch. The boys went crazy, hugging him, slapping him on the back, and jostling his mop of red hair. He looked great, rested and healthy, his wound healing with little scarring. The last time I had seen him, he'd looked to be at death's door.

"Mrs. Sawyer, unless you have made other plans, would you consider letting Kenny stay until camp is over?" I asked. "There are only a few weeks left, and you have already paid for the whole summer anyway."

"Well Bob, Kenny and I hadn't really discussed that possibility," she replied.

Kenny, overhearing the conversation, interrupted and asked, "Can I stay? Please, please, please. I really want to be here, and I promise I'll take it easy. It's only a few weeks."

"Well." She hesitated. "I suppose we could, but it depends on your father. I'll call him to see what he has to say about it. I can't make you any promises."

While Mrs. Sawyer went to the lodge to call her husband, Kenny and the boys caught up on "old times." It was great having them all together.

In a few minutes Mrs. Sawyer returned, her lips curled in a half-smile. "OK, your dad said he had no plans and it was up to me. I think it's a good idea."

The whooping from the boys interrupted her in mid-sentence, but she needed to make herself clear.

"Wait a second," she interjected, having to raise her voice above the din.

"You can stay, but there are conditions. You know what the doctor said and he wasn't kidding. You really have to keep the running around to a minimum, Ken."

"Yeah, Mom, I will," he said briskly. It was a bit hard to believe as he was already hopping around, clowning and laughing with his friends.

"Really, hon, this is important."

"I know Mom," he said with a little more conviction and self-control.

"I'll make sure he doesn't go wild or do anything dangerous, but he's a pretty active kid. We'll go over some restrictions this afternoon," I said with a bit of false confidence but with an air of responsibility.

"I'm leaving him in your able hands, Bob." She then gave me a look that said, "Don't fuck up."

She kissed Kenny and said, "Dad will get a bunch of stuff together for you and bring it up tomorrow. Tonight, you'll brush your teeth with your finger. How's that for roughing it?" She smiled. She turned and said good-bye to us and then walked up the hill toward the lodge, I assumed to make arrangements with Al.

After lunch we spent the afternoon learning about Kenny's recovery and at dinner he received a standing ovation. He was back.

***

Peter Cartright was getting agitated. He was loosing control. He was sweating, pacing, and talking to himself. Killing bugs and bats wasn't enough. He needed something bigger, something that would show its fright and pain, pleading for mercy with its eyes. A dog or a cat would be good, a little girl even better.

CHAPTER FORTY EIGHT

That night I went to see Jean. We had spent practically no time together over the past week, but tonight the boys had a game night at the lodge, so I was pretty much free. I borrowed Jim's car and got permission from Al and Kathy to take Jean to the movies.

"Just drive carefully," said Mrs. Simmons. "I worry about you driving on these dark back roads."

"We'll be careful, Mom," Jean said, rolling her eyes at me.

Jean and I didn't go to the movies. Instead we parked near a cornfield outside of Stillwater and made out, steaming up the windshield. Our hands were all over each other, groping and rubbing. I slipped my hands inside her T-shirt and felt her firm, perfect breasts. Our tongues were in each other's mouths and I gently took her hand and guided it to my erection. She started to rub up and down while I probed between the legs of her shorts in a slow, rhythmic motion. When we were both on the brink, I rolled between her legs, grinding up against her until I exploded in my pants.

My head was spinning and I couldn't wait to become aroused again. We made out until around eleven and then drove back to camp. I walked Jean to the door and kissed her goodnight, praying that Al was not around to see the wet stain on my shorts.

When I got back to the cabin, all the boys were asleep except Danny, who was reading by flashlight.

"Danny," I whispered, "what are you still doing up?"

"Can't sleep."

"Any particular reason why?" I asked, knowing he was probably a little spooked about being alone in the darkened cabin without a counselor around.

"Nope. Just couldn't fall asleep."

"All right," I said keeping the skepticism out of my voice. "I'm going to the john and then I'm going to grab a shower. If you have to go, I'll walk you there and back."

"OK, I think I can go. I don't want to get up later," he said, working to keep a brave face.

I admired his effort to seem unafraid.

"Danny, if you ever have to go to the bathroom in the middle of the night and you're scared, just wake me up and I'll go with you. It's not a problem. Believe me. That's part of why I'm here as your counselor, buddy." Danny seemed relieved.

After using the latrine, Danny waited and talked to me while I took a quick shower in the usual lukewarm water. We walked back to the cabin together and I fell into bed, exhausted. Despite my fatigue, I lay awake for hours thinking of Jean before falling asleep around two.

CHAPTER FORTY NINE

Geller left New York City and traveled south to Philadelphia via Route 1 to meet George Miller, Ruth Berman's brother. Being four years her senior, he would hopefully remember more details about the Spotswood neighbors.

Traffic on Route 1 was horrible, and when reaching Philadelphia the road became Roosevelt Boulevard and the congestion increased further. It was bumper-to-bumper all the way downtown and he was in ill-humor by the time he worked his way over to Rittenhouse Square, following George's directions. Once he found the office building, he parked in an illegal spot, pulling down his NYPD visor and walked the one block to the entrance. He took the elevator to the tenth floor and entered the offices of Miller, Parker, and Nesbitt. The receptionist had him take a seat while she buzzed her boss.

George Miller's office was very nice. The man had taste and the money to indulge it, and the décor oozed success. Image, it seemed, was very important to his clients and prospective clients.

As Geller entered, George Miller got up from his gorgeous antique mahogany desk, complete with leather blotter and mounted gold pen and pencil set, to shake his hand. Behind the desk was a large picture window with an incredible view of the square and historic Philadelphia. In front of the desk sat two captain's chairs in a lustrous beige fabric, and George motioned for Geller to sit. While the attorney made his way back behind his desk, Geller quickly assessed the office. On the wall to the left were custom-built bookcases filled with leather-bound law books, a very nice touch. To the right, along the full length of the wall painted in taupe, were a suede sofa, an elegantly carved end table, and a fluted chrome lamp. Above the couch was a magnificent circular mirror, beautifully framed.

George Miller did not have his sister's good looks, but he did have a commanding presence, with silvery hair and tortoise-shell glasses. He was of medium height and beginning to become portly. He wore a well-tailored summer-weight blue blazer and gray trousers. Removing his jacket he sat down opposite Geller and said.

"So, how may I help you, Mr. Geller? I know from your calls and from talking with Ruth that you strongly suspect that our sister, Lilly, was murdered and did not drown."

"That's correct. I have reason to believe that the remains that were recently found in a shallow grave near Lake Spotswood in New Jersey are those of your sister."

"We were all convinced that Lilly had drowned, but her body was never found," he said with a bit of exercised calmness.

"How much do you remember of that day or that summer?"

"Well I was a teenager. Thirteen, I believe, so I remember much more than Ruth. But after we left the lake, my parents rarely spoke about Lilly's death, at least not in our presence. To be honest we all wanted to remember Lilly, but it was too painful to think of her tragic death.

"What I'm interested in, Mr. Miller, is catching who killed her."

"How am I able to help with that?"

"Well, Lilly could have been killed by a vagrant just passing through, but that seems unlikely. More probably it was someone local, either a summer resident or maybe an acquaintance."

"I really don't remember anyone in particular."

"Your sister seemed to remember a very fat boy, maybe a young teen, who liked Lilly."

"Yes," he said reflectively. "Now that you mention it, there was a boy about my age who was around. He lived several houses down the road. I remember that he was a little slow, more like Lilly's age mentally, and he was obese. He was also a little strange, as I recall."

"How do you mean strange?" Geller asked.

"You know, playing with bugs and crap. A weird kid."

"Well lots of kids that age play with bugs."

"This was different. He got a little more worked up about them than most kids."

"Do you mean he had a temper or fits of rage, that sort of thing?"

"I can't say exactly. He was just really possessive about the animals and insects he caught. I suppose he might have gotten mad if someone took one away from him. I don't remember any temper tantrums or fits of rage. Nothing like that."

"Did he seem to like Lilly?"

"Yes, as I recall they were friends, tiny Lilly and this large, fat teen. They looked incongruous together, but if memory serves me, they were inseparable."

"Any other boys or adults that you remember?" asked Geller.

"I recall that Lilly's friend had an older brother, but I can't remember either boy's names. He would be in his mid-fifties by now.

"Do the names Peter or Lester ring a bell?" Geller queried with a tremulous voice.

"No. It was so long ago; I just can't be sure. I just remember that the boy was slow and fat and had a brother and that Lilly liked him."

After a few innocuous questions of little significance, Geller thanked George Miller for his help, gave him his card, and left.

As he drove back along Route 1 North, his thoughts ran wild. He had a probable ID on the victim and a definite lead on the possible perpetrator.

Suddenly out of the blue, he thought of Elizabeth Curry, the young woman from the Beth Israel Cemetery in Brooklyn. Strange, but there it was, that appealing face.

Geller had been working for thirteen straight days without a break. He had had a lot of paperwork, a lot of travel, a lot of emotional stress, and a lot of black coffee. He hadn't been out on a date in months. He decided, at that moment, to call Elizabeth. Maybe dinner at a small restaurant in Little Italy or a bistro in The Village. Something with good atmosphere and good food, but not too dark and intimate.

He drove on, crossed the Delaware into New Jersey, and headed for Newark where he continued on route 1/9 to the Lincoln Tunnel to Manhattan. It was ten o'clock by the time he reached the office, and he spent an hour updating notes on the case before heading to Queens and a good night's sleep. He was bushed, but as was his habit, he added new findings and theories to the blackboard. In the morning, he would call Stella Williams about the Cartright brothers and then Elizabeth Curry for a date.

Geller was in his early forties and not bad looking but starting to show some subtle signs of age and wear- and-tear. He'd been divorced for ten years with no children and no ties. He loved what he did and often did it for eighteen hours a day, seven days a week. His job took its toll on his marriage and was starting to age him.

He had been responsible for breaking several high-profile cases in the city, one involving a serial killer. With his background in criminal psychology and forensics, he was instrumental in developing psychological profiling for the NYPD, allowing investigators an early glimpse into the minds of psychopaths and sociopaths. His specialty became the serial killer, understanding his motivation and twisted thinking. He understood his need to kill, his choice of victim, his choice of weapon, and the ritualistic elements characteristic of the crimes. He had kept some bad company, but his countless interviews with some of the most ruthless killers had paid off. His insight into these patterns of behavior had culminated in the apprehensions of several notorious sickos. This is what motivated him and what was behind the countless hours spent on this forty-year-old cold case in northern Jersey.

CHAPTER FIFTY

It was a great lift to have Kenny back, and it was obvious that the boys had been worried about him and now felt relieved. We would do something special at dinner.

I spoke with Nellie Flanders and arranged a "welcome back" cake that she would personally bring to the center of the mess hall after dinner. Al approved of the plan and even prepared a short speech.

We ate, talked, and joked that evening, and after the tables had been cleared, Al Simmons rose at the head table and tapped his water glass with a fork to quiet the crowd. He then officially welcomed Kenny back to Camp Spenser to a standing ovation. In the midst of the bedlam, Nellie wheeled in an enormous cake covered in thick chocolate icing and studded with sparkles. The lights dimmed and it was quite dramatic. Kenny was glowing as brightly as the sparkles, his eyes staring at the brilliant flecks of light, his mouth agape. He was thrilled.

Next came the chant, "Speech, speech."

The lights came on and Kenny reluctantly walked over to the cake, looked around the room, and said in his usual manner: "Gee, this is really great. I'm so happy to be back. Thanks a lot, guys." He was beaming with pride.

***

We got to bed early as we had a long canoe trip down the Delaware planned for the next day. The river near Dingman's Ferry was a good place to start, and the trip down river would give us plenty of opportunity to shoot rapids, which was all that the kids cared about. We insisted that Kenny wear a helmet which he reluctantly agreed to. We were going with two other cabins and there would be nine canoes.

As morning broke the boys were up and eager to leave an hour before the bugler sounded reveille. They just couldn't wait to get going.

Canoes were loaded onto Lester's truck, along with paddles, life vests, and backpacks loaded with food, drinks, dry clothes, and first aid equipment. Another two trucks, driven by Bernie Allen and Jim Butler, would carry the boys and counselors. We would be dropped off below the Delaware Water Gap and would paddle downriver for about fifteen to sixteen miles to our predetermined pick-up point. The current was good, but the river was low as there had been little rain over the summer. The rapids would still be good.

***

We arrived at Dingman's Ferry at ten and would be picked up at six-thirty, which gave us the entire day on the river. We unloaded the canoes from the truck and got them into the water, tied down the supplies in the middle of each, and put on our life jackets. There would be a paddler in the bow and one in the stern of each canoe, with a boy in the middle with the knapsacks. Halfway down the boys and counselors would switch around, so all would have a chance to paddle and run the rapids.

When everything was readied, we shoved off into the "mighty" Delaware. In northwestern New Jersey, the river is much better for canoeing than it is around Bucks County, Pennsylvania, where it is often so shallow that the canoes have to be beached and carried further downstream.

We reached the middle of the river and turned south, catching the current and paddling for a couple of miles before we heard it in the distance, the faint rumble of rapids.

Hearts started to pound as we approached and I could see the white water. I yelled. "Keep the boat straight. Don't get caught broadside."

We were able to do this at the first set of cataracts, but by the time we reached the second, my warning went unheeded and we turned sideways. I was in the stern using my oar like a rudder while the bowman stroked furiously. The canoe righted itself and we didn't capsize, although I think the boys wanted to. We did get soaked, however, as spray and water came in from everywhere. The boys loved it.

Gaining speed, we hit the third and last cataract head on. We were feeling great until we saw it, a huge boulder straight ahead. We started to back paddle and turned ourselves slightly sideways, but the current kept pushing us toward the hazard. I could see we weren't going to avoid the rock and I yelled, "Hang on." We nearly made it, but the stern hit hard, and the canoe tipped. We were thrown into the water, and my immediate concern was the location of the canoe. It was a weapon that could easily hit one of the boys.

Luckily I saw that it was caught on some rocks and was not a factor. All the boys were accounted for as we swam to the near bank. The other canoes made it safely through and pulled up by the shore. We now had to make plans to retrieve the trapped canoe.

Jim Butler and Arnie Flowers looked over the situation with me. They then walked about five hundred feet along the banks, going upstream above the stranded canoe and formulating a plan. They then waded in with a long rope and swam to mid-river. They let the current pull them downstream and maneuvered skillfully to reach the rock where the capsized craft was caught. With Jim holding one end of the rope, Arnie was able to wade to the canoe and slip his end of the rope around the gunwale. Returning to the bank, he and Jim pulled the rope until the craft freed itself and dutifully came to shore. We inspected it while it bobbed gently in the calm water. Then we unloaded and lifted it, turning it upside down, releasing a small torrent of water. I was relieved to see that it had not suffered any structural damage and we reloaded our packs and paddles and shoved back into the river.

The current was not exactly swift, but it was forceful enough to propel us downriver at a reasonable clip. We paddled leisurely, enjoying the fine day, in no particular hurry. The sky was clear and the sun warm with little humidity and thankfully, few bugs. We saw deer on the far bank drinking, always alert and ready for flight, but unfazed by our soft, lazy strokes. The sun was now directly overhead and we started to look for a place to bank the canoes and have lunch. Remembering landmarks from past years, I knew we were near a slight bend in the river where there was a sandbar creating an inlet behind it. About a half hour later we reached the spot and beached our canoes.

The boys immediately went swimming in the natural cove, where the water was still and not as cold. We had packed bologna and cheese sandwiches, a little soggy, but edible. When the kids had toweled off they devoured the food in seconds, washing it down with neon yellow bug juice, made form packets of Kool Aid powder mixed with river water. You could really build up an appetite on the river.

After lunch we drifted in an informal formation. The meandering current took us at about three miles an hour, so even without paddling, we could easily cover the ten or eleven miles remaining in our journey and be at the rendezvous point by six or six-thirty barring any problems.

By the time we reached the next set of rapids, the boys reacted like confident pros, probably too confident. There was no fear or anxiety and their fluid strokes positioned the canoes perfectly. This was almost too easy and I got the feeling that the boys wanted more action. The sun was still bright and at a level that suggested that it was about three o'clock. We negotiated the white water unscathed and continued to move gracefully along the Delaware making great time. I knew, however, that the real challenge lay ahead; a series of cataracts that were bigger and faster than anything we had seen. We hit them at four-thirty.

These were, indeed, swift and more dangerous than anything we had already navigated, so we spaced the canoes and went through the shoot one at a time at two-minute intervals to decrease the chance of ramming and capsizing. We all made it through, soaked but still floating, until the last canoe that held Arnie Flowers, his junior counselor, and two boys. They unfortunately shifted a little sideways, started to tip, over-corrected, and landed in the drink. They bobbed roughly through the turbulent waters and over rocks, buoyed by their life jackets. One of the boys looked to be in trouble. He was floating on the surface, but he was coughing and flailing his arms in panic.

I was slow to react and by the time I was ready to dive in, there was Jeffrey swimming toward the youngster with powerful strokes. Within seconds he was there, calming the boy before putting him in a life-saving hold and pulling him to safety. The boy coughed up mouthfuls of water and his breathing slowed and he started to calm. His lips turned from blue to a pale pink, but we wrapped him in a blanket to warm him and eventually changed him into dry clothes. He was embarrassed, but he was alive.

We got to the meeting place a half-hour ahead of time, emptied the canoes, wrung out our wet things, and then finished off the rest of the snacks. When the trucks arrived, we loaded the canoes and gear and then piled in. We were tired, wet, hungry, and ready for a shower and dry clothes, but we were feeling great.

CHAPTER FIFTY ONE

Geller had three chores: call Stella Williams about the Cartrights, call the editor of the "Newton Chronicle," and call Elizabeth Curry for a date. He wanted to call the newspaper editor to have him check for articles about the disappearance of children over the last few decades. It was a long-shot, but he had a hunch.

He called Stella first and her voice brightened when she realized who was on the line.

"I wanted to touch base with you because I again need your help."

"Anything, anything at all, Mr. Geller. What can I do for you?"

"There are two brothers who live on Lake Spotswood and apparently may have known the Miller family in 1920. The name's Cartright, Lester and Peter. I need anything you're able to uncover: how long they've been in the area, any other family, their jobs, whether they pay their taxes, anything."

"I'll start on it right away. I can reach you at your office?" she said fingering his card.

"Sure. If I'm not there, leave a message. I'll speak with you soon."

"Stella, one more thing. Could you find out if either brother has had trouble with the law or has a prison record.

"I'll use all my resources," she said.

Geller hung up and next called the "*Newton Chronicle*" to speak with the editor, William Tracy.

"Mr. Tracy, it's nice of you to speak with me. I'm Lawrence Geller from the NYPD, investigating the unearthed remains at Lake Spotswood."

"Sure, I'm aware of the case. How can I help you?"

"I need some information that you may have or you may be able to point me in the right direction."

"Shoot' I'll tell you yes or no."

"I want to know if there were any disappearances of children or young adults around the Newton area from 1920 to the present."

"Where can I get in touch with you if I find anything or have any information? You do realize that the paper didn't exist in 1920."

Geller gave him his telephone number, thanked him, and hung up to call Elizabeth Curry. He went through his file and found the number for the Beth Israel Cemetery. As he dialed, he tried to think of his approach.

On the third ring, a woman's voice said, "Beth Israel Cemetery. How may I help you?"

"I would like to speak with Miss Curry," Geller was barely able to get out.

"Speaking."

"Miss Curry, this is Lawrence Geller from the NYPD. You may or may not remember me. I was the one who needed the addresses and phone numbers of the surviving children of Rose and Samuel Miller and you were kind enough to pull strings and supply me with that information."

"Yes, I remember you," said the lovely voice.

"I have a few questions and will be in your area today. I'm on a tight schedule with little time to eat, so I was wondering if I could get the information I need over dinner?"

"Unfortunately I have plans for tonight, but tomorrow would be great, if it's OK with you."

"Tomorrow it is. Let's say around six-thirty. I'll pick you up and we'll drive to the city."

"That would be fine, but could you pick me up at my apartment in Brooklyn Heights?"

"No problem. It's not out of my way." She gave him the address and directions.

"That's perfect. See you tomorrow."

Did he hear excitement in her voice? He thought so.

***

He spent the rest of the day catching up on paperwork and was about to leave the office when his phone rang.

"Bill Tracy here, from the *"Newton Chronicle*," came the voice on the other end of the phone line.

"Didn't expect to hear from you so soon," said a surprised Geller.

"I think I may have hit pay dirt. Four disappearances of young children, all girls, from Sussex County between 1935 and 1955. We have nothing before then, as we didn't exist until 1930. In 1956, we covered a disappearance in Warren County, due to its proximity to us, but I have nothing since then. All were reported as possible abductions, but no bodies were ever found and there were no apparent leads. If they were kidnappings, no ransom notes or calls were ever received. All the children were presumed dead."

"You say all were female? What were their ages?"

"All were between eight and twelve years old and from families with other children."

"Were there any clues, suspects, anything at all?"

"Nothing. Poof, the kids just disappeared into thin air with no clues or signs of violence. One minute here, the next gone."

"Were the names Lester or Peter Cartright ever mentioned in the articles?" Geller asked.

"I don't think so, but I'll have to check it out. You know what? I'll just mail you the articles. It'll be easier that way."

"I'd appreciate that and let me know if you uncover anything else."

"Will do."

"Thanks, Bill."

Geller left the office and headed crosstown to his apartment in Queens. On the way, he stopped for Chinese takeout, a combination plate with pepper steak, pork fried rice, and an egg roll. Once home he took off his shoes, poured a Pabst, and went through his mail, bills and a fairly nasty letter from his ex-wife. He turned on the radio and started to read the day-old *"New York Times."* At seven-thirty he began eating and turned on the Yankees game. The Bronx Bombers were taking on the White Sox at the stadium and Mel Allen and Red Barber were already doing the pre-game. Funny how New Yorkers just called it "the stadium," as though no other venue could possibly exist. He was half-listening, background noise, while he mulled over the particulars of his case and the possibility of a serial killer.

***

When the game was in the third inning with no score, he got up. In a methodical way, he put away the uneaten food, took another beer, turned up the fan, and went into the bathroom for a long-anticipated shower.

He was exhausted and the warm water felt good. After toweling off, he put on a cotton robe and went back into the living room to listen to the rest of the game. He had a perfectly good TV, but he liked the commentary on the radio better. Those guys could really tell you what was going on. By the sixth inning, he was asleep in his recliner.

At midnight, he suddenly awoke and decided to go to bed where he tossed and turned until seven. Despite his restless sleep and two beers, he felt surprisingly alert and ready to face the day. He was keyed up by the break in the Miller case and his upcoming date with the attractive Elizabeth Curry.

He showered again, shaved and put on a pair of jeans and an Izod tennis shirt. In a valet bag, he packed his clothes for the evening, along with shoes, dress socks, and a change of boxer shorts. Before leaving the apartment, he grabbed his wallet, badge, and holstered revolver.

He triple-locked the door and descended the stairs to the lobby and then out into the already warm day. Driving to Manhattan, the traffic was surprisingly light so he decided to stop for a bagel and coffee. By the time he arrived at the office, there were two messages, one from Stella Williams and the other from Elizabeth.

He returned Stella's call first. She had a lot of information on the Cartrights and Geller was all ears.

"Lester and Peter Cartright, not surprisingly, own the house on Spotswood," she began excitedly. "But get this. They also own two adjacent houses and more than one- hundred acres on each side of the lake. The land is in current use and they get maximum tax benefits. Yearly, it costs them next to nothing. Pretty saavy for a pair of hicks," she added. "The main house was left to them when their parents died. Lester works for the state highway department, a good job with good pay and benefits and he makes extra income by helping out at the summer camp, doing odd jobs and transporting campers in his truck. In the winter he plows snow and in the spring, he does some landscaping and tree-pruning." She paused letting Geller absorb the information. "Peter rarely works except for some menial jobs that Lester arranges for him. He's a bit slow, by all accounts, and apparently has a quick temper, as he's lost a number of jobs because of that. I asked around, and the consensus is that they keep pretty much to themselves."

"Stella, that's great stuff. I don't know how you find these things and I won't ask, but nice job."

At the other end of the line, Stella beamed.

"Do either of them have a police record, or have they ever been in trouble with the law?"

"I'll have to check on that and get back to you. I'm afraid I overlooked it. It may take a few days because I'll have to check with the local, county, and state police."

"No rush," said Geller. "Also while I remember, could you find out if Peter has a driver's license?"

"No problem."

His next call was to Elizabeth Curry. His heart was pounding, as he worried that she was going to cancel on him. He dialed the number and waited. Three rings, four. Finally, she answered the phone.

"Hi, Elizabeth. It's Larry Geller."

"Hi, Larry. I hope it isn't an inconvenience, but I have to work later than usual, so could you pick me up at seven instead of six-thirty? I hope that this won't ruin your restaurant plans.

His heart rate slowed and he responded. "Sure, no problem. I'll call the restaurant; I know they will be able to accommodate us. I figure that since you're in Brooklyn and have worked all day, a good steak at Peter Luger's would probably fit the bill."

"See you at seven then."

It was a weekday, but just to be safe, he called the restaurant and changed the reservations to eight. That would give them time to leisurely drive there and have a drink. Next he got the Cartrights' telephone number from information and called in hopes of setting up an interview. No luck. No one was home. He would try again later.

He spent the rest of the day reviewing the Miller case: the forensic reports, the evidence, the suppositions. He also checked in on two other homicide investigations he was covering in the city, the murders of a pawnbroker in the diamond district and a high-priced hooker in a midtown hotel.

At five-thirty he showered again, put on cologne (something he rarely did), and dressed for the evening: a pair of well-pressed khakis, penny loafers, a light blue button-down oxford shirt, yellow cotton tie, and a light-weight blue blazer. He checked himself in the mirror and liked what he saw. In general women found him good-looking, with his short brown hair with hints of gray, straight nose, and strong jaw. Some thought him sexy. He didn't reflect on his appeal to the opposite sex that much, but tonight he wanted to look good. At exactly six P.M he left for Brooklyn Heights.

CHAPTER FIFTY TWO

While Geller was driving, Peter Cartright was spinning out of control. He couldn't even answer the phone when it rang several hours ago. The urges were coming and he couldn't control them. Voices were telling him what to do and he couldn't block them out. They were becoming overpowering, as they had been in the past. He was coming apart and he had run out of his thorazine. He really didn't like taking it; it made him feel like a zombie, all drugged up. He had to get out of the house. The walls were closing in on him.

He ran up the basement steps and through the kitchen to the back door. He almost ripped the door off its hinges as he ran out into the back yard, tripping over a small downed tree and injuring his shoulder. His breathing was labored and he had a dull pain radiating down his side, as he dove deeper into the woods. He finally stopped in a small clearing to catch his breath. He was hyperventilating and on the verge of passing out, his strained lungs nearly bursting from the exertion. He had to slow things down, which he struggled to do, and after several minutes he was less short of breath. Then he started to cry, his entire body heaving from the barking sobs. He was a sad, lost soul, mentally ill and sinking, but he was still dangerous nonetheless.

CHAPTER FIFTY THREE

Geller arrived at Elizabeth's apartment fifteen minutes early. Rather than seem rude or overeager, he drove around the neighborhood for a few minutes before finally parking across from her building. He crossed the street and hopped up the four steps to the front door, which he entered. In the small lobby he pressed the buzzer next to her name and in a few seconds heard a click and then her voice through the speaker.

"I'll be down in a minute."

She came through the door into the foyer where Geller was waiting, trying not to fidget. She was wearing a navy skirt, white silk blouse, stylish silk scarf tied casually yet deliberately around her neck, low navy and white heels, and delicate pearl earrings. She was stunning and her scent was subtle and delicious.

They drove toward the Williamsburg Bridge and turned down the street that lead to Peter Luger's, New York's ultimate steakhouse. They decided to have a drink at the bar as their table was not quite ready and they were in no hurry. Geller tried to guess what she would drink and figured either a glass of white wine or a martini, straight up. He was close as she ordered a Manhattan, straight up and very chilled with two cherries. He ordered his signature drink, a dry Rob Roy on the rocks with a twist and they toasted to the evening.

As they sat at the bar, she did most of the talking. Her eyes sparked in the light as she talked and she seemed more energized with each sentence until she suddenly stopped and said, embarrassed and slightly reddened. "I'm sorry. I'm babbling like an idiot and completely monopolizing the conversation."

"No, it's perfectly fine. I'm enjoying just listening."

Just then the hostess came to get them at the bar.

"Your table is ready, Mr. Geller," she said smiling.

They were lead to a table in the noisy dining room filled with serious beef eaters and were seated and given menus, which were not really needed as the only thing to order was the porterhouse. Perusing the menu was superfluous.

They chatted over their drinks and ordered a second round. He enjoyed her company and idle conversation and did not want to order right away. The waiter brought a basket of bread and butter and filled their water glasses. He recited a few appetizer specials and one chicken dish and then disappeared as he realized they wanted to talk.

He guessed her to be in her mid-thirties and she was a looker, but he sensed she was much more than that. She was bright and articulate and he learned that she had finished a master's program in art history at NYU. Her work at the cemetery was a favor to her uncle, who was the general manager and seemed to always be short of help over the summer. She had applied for several jobs, but the plum was a position at the Metropolitan Museum of Art, for which she'd been called back for a second interview. An upstate New Yorker, she had obtained her BA in fine arts at Cornell. She came to the city and did graduate work, found a job, and in the process the excitement and the pace was too intoxicating to leave. This place had become her city.

Now she wanted to hear about him to get a brief glimpse of what it was like to be a New York City cop. Conversation was easy for him, not because he had the gift of gab, but because he was articulate and interesting. He told her about his family, education, police work, and his brief, failed marriage. But, mostly he talked about New York City. It was comfortable talking to her.

The waiter made a brief appearance and asked if they were ready to order. They decided on a porterhouse for two, medium-rare, a baked potato to share, and a platter of sliced tomatoes and onions with their famous house dressing.

"Very good, sir. Another cocktail?"

Instead they ordered glasses of a California merlot and went back to their chit-chat. They found talking easy and never seemed to run out of things to say. He wanted to know more about her personal life, her tastes in music and food, what she did in her spare time, and her family and friends. He really wanted to know about her love life, but he knew that was not yet a topic open to him for discussion.

They continued to talk as the wine arrived, losing track of time until they were interrupted by the aroma of superbly cooked beef. The steak was at least an inch to an inch and a half thick, cut in slabs away from the bone, perfectly grilled to medium-rare.

He thought Elizabeth would have a stroke as the waiter placed the platter between them, portioning several pieces to her first and then to him. He carefully spooned the natural juices over the meat.

Using a spoon and fork, he placed a large baked potato, cut in half, between them and placed dishes of butter and sour cream with chives on the table. Finally, he portioned slices of juicy beefsteak tomatoes and rings of Vidalia onions on both plates and poured dollops of the rich house dressing on top. Elizabeth looked beside herself and Geller wondered when she had last eaten.

"Pepper?" the waiter asked.

"Please," responded Elizabeth and he grated fresh black pepper on her steak and salad. He nodded toward Geller and repeated the ritual.

Satisfied that they had everything, the waiter turned and left. Geller turned to Elizabeth, raising his wine glass.

"It doesn't get any better than this."

Elizabeth took that as a cue to attack, and with reckless abandon she threw herself into the mouth-watering meal.

Geller just sat and marveled at this petite woman with her lovely figure enjoying this carnivore's delight.

After several mouthfuls, she self-consciously lifted her head and saw him staring at her incredulously.

"Oh God, I'm so embarrassed. I'm eating like a pig. I don't know what's come over me. I usually don't eat like this, especially on a date."

She started to giggle and put down her fork.

"Now that I've made a fool of myself, I won't eat another bite until you start and you'd better eat like a real man."

"Let's chow down," he said.

They ate like there was no tomorrow, with no inhibitions and a great deal of fun.

He gave up first, saying. "I can't eat another bite, I'm finished."

"You're a wuss. You barely touched your steak. And you call yourself a man," she quipped.

"How do you do it? That steak weighed almost as much as you."

"I knew you were springing for dinner, so I haven't eaten in almost twenty-four hours. That was a good decision."

She daintily wiped the sides of her mouth with her napkin and then excused herself to use the ladies' room.

He stood when she rose from the table, which she seemed to appreciate, and his eyes followed her as she left the room.

She was a lovely woman, he mused, and he thought this could develop into something. He was really having a wonderful evening.

After drinking, dining, and talking for over two hours, they decided against dessert but ordered coffee. She declined a cognac, and Geller decided to pass as well.

"This was truly a lovely evening, and the meal was just an added bonus," said Elizabeth.

"I wasn't sure about a steakhouse, it's such a man thing and it's always so noisy. But the company was great, so it really didn't matter where we ate. I hope we can do it again soon."

She nodded her assent.

Geller paid the steep tab in twenties and left a handsome tip. After leaving the restaurant, they strolled slowly to the car, noting the lovely span of the illuminated bridge above them. It was a gorgeous night, warm with no humidity and a light breeze.

They reached the car and Geller noted a parking citation on the windshield. He grandiosely tore the citation in half, then in half again, as Elizabeth giggled. He had noted the cop's name and station number and would make a call in the morning.

"I see you have a lot of pull in the department. How much will this cost you? I'm turning out to be an expensive date."

"Real funny. You're a riot," Geller responded.

They drove to her apartment in Brooklyn Heights, laughing and talking the entire time and then he walked her up the shrub-lined pathway to the front door. She turned and thanked him for a beautiful evening, asking if he would like to come in for some coffee. As it was getting rather late, with great self-restraint, he declined.

"May I please have a rain-check?"

"I'll hold you to it," she replied with a grin.

"Look, I had a really great evening. I enjoyed your company and I think you enjoyed mine, so let's do this again real soon," he said.

"It's safe to say that I'm already looking forward to it," she answered.

"I trust you like the theatre, one so refined as yourself," Geller said slyly, remembering this adorable woman with juice dribbling down her chin after attacking her steak.

"Yes, refined." She clearly got his reference. "It's a passion of mine. Comedy, drama, musical, it doesn't matter."

"I have a contact in the theatre district. I'll see what he has. Will you leave it up to me?"

"Anything that appeals to you should be fine. Even if I've seen it before, who cares? I'll enjoy the company."

"How about Saturday night? An eight o'clock performance and then dinner."

"Sounds great," She beamed.

"I'll pick you up at six and we'll drive back to midtown, have a drink, and hit the show."

She gave him a warm hug and thanked him for a lovely evening. Then she turned and went inside.

Geller felt like a teenager, pumped up so that he literally bounded down the stairs barely touching the ground. He drove back to his apartment with a million thoughts swirling in his head. He was on the verge of cracking a forty year old case, and he had just met a woman who could be the real thing. Life was good and he deserved it. At any rate, he felt stirrings that he hadn't felt in years.

He arrived home, tired, but elated. He showered and got into bed going over a mental to-do-list. He would send flowers in the morning. No, that would seem too pushy. He'd decide after sleeping off the cocktails and wine and that incredible steak.

PART THREE

The Romance

CHAPTER FIFTY FOUR

In the morning he showered again and dressed, called about his parking ticket, and decided that he would, indeed, send flowers to Elizabeth. Something simple, understated, but assuring the lady that he found her alluring. He called the florist, an informant friend of his, and ordered one perfect long-stemmed red rose with greens and baby's breath. It had to be perfect, boxed and delivered to the cemetery. No florist would deliver a single rose, but this guy owed Geller big time and would come through for him. It would be perfect. The note would simply say, "Looking forward to Saturday night. Fondly, Larry." Twenty bucks would ease the florist's pain.

The mail came at noon and among the bills and junk mail was a packet from the *"Newton Chronicle."* He rushed to open it and found numerous clipped articles about the missing children in the area. He checked the dates and made a note to cross-reference the stories with the files from the *"Newark Evening News"* and *"The New York Times"* to see if they'd carried any articles about the children.

The first article was from July 10, 1940. A nine year old girl had disappeared from a summer home near Branchville, New Jersey, the same scenario as the Lilly Miller case. The child had just vanished. Again dogs, state police, local sheriffs, and volunteers had combed the area with no results. The disappearance had occurred during three days of steady rain so any footprints or other clues would have been washed away. No ransom note had ever arrived, so the overriding opinion was that the child had been abducted, murdered, and probably buried somewhere in rural Sussex County. The parents pleaded on the radio for her return and offered a $1,000 reward for any information leading to her whereabouts. The child was never found.

The next disappearance was an eleven year old girl from Andover, who vanished in fall of 1943 after a two day rainstorm. She, however, was from a local family and failed to return home from grade school. No clues, no witnesses, no ransom note, no body.

The other two disappearances were young girls, ages eight and eleven, in June of 1945 and July of 1947, one near Blairstown and one near Hopatcong with the same circumstances and no bodies.

Bill Tracy also included an article that seemed curious to Geller, a drowning in Lake Mohawk, near Sparta, New Jersey, in 1950. This time the victim was a ten year old boy from Newark on vacation with his parents. He apparently had drowned while fishing. His rowboat was found capsized in a reedy area of the lake, the boy floating face down in the reeds with his rain slicker on. Again a rainy day, thought Geller. There were no signs of foul play, although the child had had a large bruise on his forehead, which the coroner had attributed to the fall from the boat. He theorized that the boy had hit his head on the gunwale or possibly struck something in the water. The cause of death was officially "freshwater drowning" and was considered an accident.

Geller put down the articles and grabbed a legal pad. Under the heading "Similarities," he wrote:

1. All the disappearances occurred in rainy weather or after a rainstorm during the summer or early fall.

"Good weather to bury a body and erase clues," he thought aloud.

2. All were children between the ages of eight and eleven.

"Easy to control, murder, and carry off to a grave," he theorized.

3. All disappeared within a twenty-five mile radius of Spotswood, suggesting a local perpetrator and not a vagrant.

Add the Lilly Miller case and there was a real pattern of serial abductions and probable murders over a twenty-seven to thirty year period.

As he ruminated the phone rang. It was Stella Williams.

"Thanks for calling, Stella. I hope you have some news for me."

"I have some really juicy stuff for you, so sit down. It seems that Peter Cartright has had numerous minor brushes with the law: petty theft, animal cruelty, and minor mischief, like breaking windows in neighbors' houses and dumping trash on lawns. He was given suspended sentences and sent to a psychiatrist, who diagnosed a personality disorder, low IQ, and antisocial behavior and also reported his fear that Peter had the potential for violence. His recommendations for in-patient care were ignored by the state on several occasions, and Peter was apparently not about to commit himself. So Lester guaranteed responsibility for Peter's actions- case closed."

Geller was licking his lips as he listened to Stella's account, furiously taking notes while she talked.

"It seems that things quieted down for a while until about two years after the psych evaluation, when a family on summer vacation made a formal complaint to the police and the ASPCA. They had found their golden retriever mutilated. The dog had been tortured and killed by a sadist, who they insisted was Peter Cartright. He had been chased away on several prior occasions for harassing and teasing the dog. The police investigated and Peter confessed. He was sent to a psychiatric facility at the request of the court and remained hospitalized for almost two years."

"What was the timeframe of all this?" Geller asked.

"Most of the incidents occurred in the forties."

"What happened after his two-year commitment?" Geller pursued.

"It seems that Peter was still a problem. Lester was able to get him odd jobs, although most never lasted very long. Most ended in his being fired due to absenteeism, suspicion of theft, or rude behavior toward management and fellow workers. In fact, after being fired from a factory job in the early fifties, he became incensed and smashed several windows on his way out. Two days later there was a fire at the factory, but no evidence of arson was ever discovered. It seems an old furnace overheated and ignited some stacks of rags that were stored nearby. The damage wasn't extensive and the matter was dropped due to a lack of any conclusive evidence, but most locals suspected that Peter had been responsible. From 1952 to the present, Peter Cartright has been fairly well out of sight and not in any trouble. He has been living at the lake with his brother, who seems able to control him."

"Tell me, Stella, in your search, did you come across any evidence that Peter, or for that matter Lester, was ever questioned about any disappearances of children from the area between 1920 and 1950?"

"I didn't see anything, but I'll check my sources again with that in mind."

Geller gave her the circumstances, locales, and dates of the disappearances and was about to hang up when he thought of something else.

"One question before you run, Stella. Did Peter have a driver's license in New Jersey?"

"He couldn't pass the written test, but he did get caught on one occasion driving without a license. He was fined and no further action was taken."

Almost as soon as he replaced the receiver, the phone rang. It was Elizabeth.

"The rose is perfect, but how on earth did you get someone to deliver a single flower all the way to Brooklyn?"

"The guy owed me a favor," replied Geller in a mock Mafioso voice.

"You have some great connections. Do any bankers owe you a favor?" she teased.

"No such luck. I only know informants and petty criminals, and, of course, ticket agents."

"Well, for a tough cop you're a pretty sensitive guy. Looking forward to Saturday night." She said good-bye and hung up.

Geller was elated.

✳✳✳

Back to work. He had to come down on Peter Cartright and make him sweat. He had to intimidate him, question him, harass him.

He called the Cartright home and after five rings the phone was answered, but all he heard was the sound of someone breathing heavily on the other end.

"Mr. Cartright, this is Inspector Lawrence Geller of the NYPD. I would like to arrange a time to talk to you about the remains found several weeks ago near Lake Spotswood."

"I do-do-don't know what you're talking about," Peter stammered.

"Oh, yes you do, Peter. You know perfectly well what I'm talking about."

"Fuck you!" he shouted and slammed down the receiver.

Geller figured he'd harass him for a few more days, then drive up to Sussex County to confront him in person. Low IQ and a short fuse. Geller knew he could be manipulated into incriminating himself.

CHAPTER FIFTY FIVE

After the canoe trip, I was in no mood for any dangerous activities during the last week and a half of camp. I was, however, anxious to see Jean and we would have a chance tonight.

The kids were scheduled to watch movies at the lodge after dinner, a double feature - "Hopalong Cassidy," some cartoons, and a Bing Crosby-Bob Hope "road movie."

Partway through the cowboy movie, Jean and I snuck out, avoiding the watchful eye of her stepfather. We walked with flashlights through the outdoor chapel to the boathouse. No one was around, so we climbed through a window as the door was padlocked. Figuring we had about an hour before we'd be missed, we found a place between two boats and spread a tarp on the floor. As usual, Jean looked great in white shorts and a University of Michigan sweatshirt.

We lay down side by side and talked. We kissed lightly at first, and then more passionately and started to pet.

We fondled each other. She was panting heavily and I was hard as a rock. I rubbed her breasts while kissing her abdomen, licking her navel, but she stopped me when I tried to put my hand down the front of her shorts. Rubbing her between her thighs was OK as long as there was material between my hand and her vagina. After several minutes of this, Jean spread her legs and I rolled over on top of her. We had our clothes on, but we simulated intercourse, doing what we called dry humping.

Jean climaxed within minutes, arching her back with multiple spasms. I was out of control and within seconds came. When the last spasm subsided, I opened my eyes. It was pitch black outside, but I thought I caught a glimpse of someone ducking away from the window above us. I looked down at Jean and then up at the window again – nothing.

I lay on Jean for several minutes and we just held each other.

"I wonder what the real thing feels like. It must be incredible."

"I can only imagine," I admitted.

"I've never gone all the way, but I'm sure it would be perfect with you," she said.

We got up and then rolled up the tarp.

Embarrassed, I said. "What do I do now? My shorts are soaked, and I can't go back to the lodge."

"We'll stop by the cabin, and you can change quickly before we go up the hill to the movies."

As we walked I had the uneasy feeling that someone was behind us. My mind raced, and I felt that familiar paranoia. Was I imagining things?

I changed, and we sneaked back into the mess hall and watched the end of the movie, holding hands and looking guilty.

CHAPTER FIFTY SIX

Geller called Peter Cartright again on Saturday. He answered on the sixth ring, a little out of breath. Geller hoped that he had gotten him off the pot.

"H-hello," said Cartright tentatively.

"Hello, Peter," Geller began in a taunting voice. "You know who this is? I'm coming for your ass."

Peter hung up immediately, leaving a satisfied Geller with only the droning buzz of the phone line in his ear.

Geller knew he had him. He must be sweating, on the verge of cracking. Another day or two and he'd pay the Cartright's a personal visit.

***

He brewed himself a pot of coffee and retrieved his Saturday "*New York Times*" from his doorstep. He read and drank cup after cup of black coffee. After checking the box score of the Yankees game and going through the front section, he picked up the phone to check on his show tickets. His contact got him fifth row orchestra for the hot new show in town, "*Gypsy.*" He had called on Friday night and made reservations for two for a late dinner after the show at the Four Seasons, one of his favorites. A heavy tariff, but well worth it.

Geller had money. Years of frugality had created a sizable nest egg and he had few expenses - no alimony, no children, a city car, and a modest apartment in Queens. He liked nice clothes and loved to dine out, but a Porsche and a penthouse apartment were not his style.

He had a good salary and benefits with the NYPD, but his real money came from royalties from his books and guest lecture appearances. His books on forensics and psychological profiling were bibles throughout the tri-state area and even nationwide and he had good sales to graduate schools. He commanded large fees for speaking engagements, although his time was limited.

***

He dressed and drove into midtown, double-parking in front of a nondescript storefront. He pulled down his police emergency visor and ran into the place to pick up his tickets- fifty bucks. Next, he drove over to Fifty-first and Fifth and sprung for a garage. He walked to Saks where he bought a beautiful Tattersall shirt and a summer linen tie to go with his blazer. With packages in hand, he worked his way to Tiffany's. He wanted to get something simple that showed his interest in her, but not too personal or intimate, as that might seem pushy. There definitely was chemistry there, but they had only gone out once. A ring or a necklace was much too extravagant and personal. Maybe a simple bracelet. He settled on a silver, delicate one that was beautifully crafted. The saleswoman boxed his purchase in Tiffany's signature robin's egg blue. An expensive gift, but worth every penny.

He was feeling good, so he crossed Fifth Avenue and headed toward Central Park and the Plaza Hotel. It was now after noon, so he walked into the Oak Room for a drink. He sat at the bar in this venerable establishment filled with dark, highly polished mahogany, good-looking chic woman, and cigarette smoke.

The bartender brought over a crystal dish filled with salted mixed nuts and put down a napkin inscribed with the Plaza's initials.

"May I get you something to drink and would you like to see the lunch menu?"

"A drink would be great, but I'll decline on the lunch."

"What can I get you?"

"A Chivas on the rocks with a twist would do the trick."

The drink was served in a heavy cut-crystal glass and the ice was shaved. The place had class.

He sat and sipped and thought of Elizabeth. She was lovely. I'm really falling, he mused.

He drained his drink and declined a refill. At one time he had been a fairly heavy drinker, not a problem drinker, but he knew it had to be tempered. Drinking at dinner with a lady was one thing, but drinking alone was something else.

He paid the tab and left. He strolled back to Fifty-first, passing Bergdorf's and Harry Winston, seeing how the other half lived.

***

Back in the office he did busywork and checked his messages. The duty officer had two notes from him, both from informants on other cases. He called both stoolies and then took off his jacket, turned on the fan, and started the unavoidable, interminable paperwork. He attacked two on-going cases, putting his files in order, and then updated the Lilly Miller file, which had consumed most of his time and interest. He compiled copious notes, arranged newspaper articles, and made lists of evidence and theories on the crime. At three he called it a day and drove back to his apartment to get ready for the evening.

He checked his mail and picked up the phone to call Elizabeth.

"Just called to let you know I'll be by around six. That'll give us plenty of time to get back into the city."

"Sounds great. What are we seeing?"

"*Gypsy*." "I figured you probably haven't seen it, as it just opened in May. The music is supposed to be great, and I heard Ethel Merman is a show-stopper."

She was ecstatic. "Well, you're right. I haven't seen it, but not for a lack of trying. I've made tons of calls, but it's the hottest ticket in town. Who owed you a favor?"

"I have my sources."

He hung up and had the feeling that tonight would be memorable. Incredible that a crime committed almost forty years ago had led him to Elizabeth Curry.

He showered and shaved again, then dressed in a pair of nicely tailored beige slacks, dress loafers, and his new Tattersall shirt and yellow linen tie, all topped off with a beautifully cut navy linen blazer. He looked and felt great.

He arrived at her apartment a few minutes late and rang the bell next to her mailbox. She buzzed him in, and he walked up to the second floor, arriving just as she was opening the door. She promptly took his breath away.

She was ravishing in a clingy, rose-colored dress that accentuated every curve of her beautiful body. Her hair was up, with wisps of curls falling in front of her ears. The dress was low cut and revealed her lovely, slender neck, around which was a single strand of pearls, and the curved V of her breast line. Her scent was subtle, clean, and probably expensive, possibly Chanel. She was truly magnificent, and Geller was virtually transfixed. How was this woman still available?

"Do we have time for a quick drink? I chilled a half-bottle of champagne."

Geller nodded. "We'll have to make it quick."

Her apartment was nice, spacious, and well-decorated. You can't get these high ceilings and wood floors in new buildings, he thought as he gazed around approvingly.

She brought out two chilled flutes and a half-bottle of Moet & Chandon. Good taste.

"I'll do the honors," said Elizabeth, and she uncorked the bubbly with a loud pop. She poured two effervescent glassfuls.

They lifted the flutes, touched them lightly, and in unison said: "To your health." What Geller was too embarrassed to say was, "To us."

He looked at her glowing eyes and radiant face, and he could barely stop from staring like a schoolboy with a crush. They sipped champagne until finally, realizing the hour, hurried down to the car to drive back to Manhattan.

***

After crossing the bridge, they hit the usual traffic on Canal Street, finally turning uptown with only fifty minutes before curtain time.

"I can always turn on the siren if push comes to shove," he joked.

"Don't you dare, cowboy. One of these days a cop is going to nail you."

He grinned and continued uptown toward the Theater District. They managed to get to within a block of the theater at seven-forty and Elizabeth convinced him to pull into a lot. He hated the idea of paying to park, but time was of the essence. They rapidly walked the short distance to the theater and were seated with five minutes to spare.

He smiled like a Cheshire cat.

"I'm impressed, fifth row center. You really do have connections. I guess the chief gets the first row!"

"I turned down the first row- too close. You wouldn't want old Ethel falling in your lap." They laughed softly as the orchestra played the opening medley and the curtain rose.

CHAPTER FIFTY SEVEN

"**A**mazing!" Elizabeth exclaimed as audience members leapt to their feet to give a standing ovation to Ethel Merman and her accompanying cast. "Really spectacular."

"I presume that you enjoyed the performance."

"I'd say so. And I'd say that you're in my good graces."

"Well, lady, the best is yet to come. I hope you're hungry."

"Starved!" Where are we going?"

"It's a surprise, but I know you'll approve. You'll also be the best-looking woman there," Geller complimented. "You really look beautiful."

"Well thank you," she replied, the tips of her ears reddening slightly beneath the wispy tendrils of hair.

They left the car and took a cab to the restaurant, the sight of which further brightened Elizabeth's face, if that were possible. At eleven-thirty, the place was hopping with the after-theater crowd.

They entered the exquisitely up-scale, beautifully appointed and furnished lobby, where they were greeted and shown into the dining room, decorated for the summer season. After being seated they started with perfectly chilled vodka martinis, a twist for him and an olive for her. Once comfortable and after a bit of preamble, Geller reached into the pocket of his jacket and pulled out her gift.

"I know this may seem a little forward, or even premature, as we barely know each other, but I want you to have this. No strings attached," he added quickly.

Her eyes glowed as she recognized the distinctive box. "May I open it now?"

"Certainly. "It's yours."

She gently pulled off the white ribbon and opened the pale blue box. "You have really outdone yourself," she gasped as she saw the delicate bracelet. Then, a bit meekly, she said. "May I put it on?"

"Please do."

She fastened the clasp, stretched out her arm to survey the bracelet, and then said, "Oh, I love it. It's absolutely beautiful. You're a wonderful man, and I thank you from the bottom of my heart."

"Not too premature?" Geller asked warily. "I saw it and knew it belonged on your wrist."

"You know, unlike that "tough cop" exterior so many of you police detectives assume, you're tremendously thoughtful and sensitive and really kind."

Now it was Geller's turn to redden a bit.

***

They dined slowly on chilled raw oysters served with a rice wine vinegar and shallot sauce, lobster crepes with grilled, buttered asparagus accompanied by a perfectly chilled California Chardonnay from the Napa Valley. An amazing crème brulee for dessert with coffee finished off a perfect meal.

They didn't leave the restaurant until two-fifteen and by the time they retrieved the car, it was almost three. But they didn't feel fatigued and chatted constantly on the drive back to Brooklyn. He parked opposite her building and walked her to the door. He didn't quite know what to do next as they reached the doorway, but Elizabeth relieved him of the responsibility by saying, "Come in, Larry. I know it's late, but you're not turning me down again."

"You're intimidating me, so I'll stay," he replied with a smile.

She sat him down on the sofa after putting a long-play record on the turntable, Frank Sinatra's, "In the Wee Small Hours of the Morning," and poured brandy into two squat snifters. She took off her shoes and sat on the couch next to him, one leg curled under her. She looked up at him with impish eyes and wiggled closer. He leaned down and softly kissed the top of her head. Her hair smelled like spring, and her perfume was intoxicating. She responded to his gentle caress by giving him a long, sensuous kiss. When they broke he lightly brushed his tongue along her lips until she opened her mouth, and they touched tongues. He moved his mouth to her neck and then her cleavage. She was breathing heavily now. They passionately kissed and rubbed each other with increasing urgency. He put his hand behind her back, gently tracing its curve with his fingertips. He slowly undid the zipper to her dress and slid his other hand to her neck and then slowly to her breast. She whispered, "Let's go into the bedroom."

He picked her up in his arms and carried her to the bedroom, gently lowering her onto the bed. He eased off her unzipped dress and she, with much less self-control, ripped off his tie and shirt. Their skin touched, and they kissed as he unhooked her bra with one hand and felt one of her firm breasts with the other. He kissed her breasts and licked her erect nipples. He could almost hear her heart pounding as he slid her slip completely off. She had just enough control to get up and remove her stockings and panties. She was magnificent in the shimmering moonlight streaming through the blinds. She got back into bed and pulled the covers over them as Geller removed the last of his clothes.

In bed body to warm body, they continued to kiss, caress, and explore. He felt her hand on his erection, slowly and rhythmically massaging. He, in turn, stroked the inside of her thighs and then slid a finger gently between the moist lips of her vagina- she moaned. The in-and-out movement of his finger made her back against him, sighing and breathing heavily. He removed his finger and began to kiss and lick her navel and lower abdomen, feeling the soft, downy hairs. In response, she arched her back as he moved downward and caressed her with his lips. He entered her with this tongue as she moaned. She was on the verge of orgasm, and he could think of nothing but to give her ultimate pleasure. He slowly licked the moist inside of her, and within seconds she had several violent spasms. She whimpered with pleasure and finally collapsed into the pillows. Still breathing heavily, she gasped, "Please come inside me."

"Let me put on a condom," he said as he groped for his wallet, where he had one that had been there for at least a year or two. He rapidly put it on and, then rolled between her legs, guiding himself gently into her. She was moist, warm, and very responsive, grinding her pelvis in rhythm with his thrusts. He was in paradise and moved more slowly and deliberately, but soon lost control and moved faster until he could no longer hold back. He came violently, again and again, and she could feel his penis throb inside of her. She responded with a deep, shuddering orgasm.

They lay entwined, holding onto the moment, lightly touching and caress-ing. Finally, Geller rolled alongside this perfect woman and looked into her eyes.

"Where have you been all my life?"

"Right here in Brooklyn just waiting for you."

CHAPTER FIFTY EIGHT

The movies ended around eleven and the kids were bushed. We all walked wearily back to the cabin, ready for a good night's sleep. Rummaging around for t-shirts and boxer shorts to sleep in apparently revived the boys, for when they were in bed they wanted to hear a scary story. I decided to finish the tale of the fishing boat that floated into the New England harbor with a dead captain and a missing crew.

"If you remember," I began, "the fishing boat floated into the fog-shrouded harbor, eerily quiet with no motor running. The captain was found dead, a knife in his heart, on top of a pile of ice-cold cod. The crew was nowhere to be found."

"It was a mystery to the townsfolk, as the vessel seemed undisturbed, with no sign of any sort of struggle. The captain's body had little blood around the knife, and there were no splatters or bloody footprints in the area. What had happened? The autopsy done the next day showed the expected; death by a penetrating wound into the heart, causing blood to accumulate into the pericardial sac around the heart and causing it to stop beating. There were no defensive injuries or signs of a struggle."

The kids looked a little scared, but they were all awake and wanted me to continue.

"The mystery was never solved, and the crew was never found. Oh, there were many theories, and everyone had an opinion. Some felt the crew killed the captain and abandoned ship to be picked up by Canadian, Japanese, or Russian fisherman, but why? Some thought that competing seamen killed the captain and set the crew adrift to die of thirst or drown. But if so, why didn't they take the catch or the boat?"

"But no matter what happened to the skipper and his crew, what no one could ever explain was how the vessel made it back to the harbor without power, considering the prevailing winds and strong riptides common in the area. And how did the boat find the harbor entrance along the irregular coastline?"

"Many thought there were supernatural powers at work, maybe ghosts of the past. All I know is that from that day forward no Massachusetts fisherman has ever worked the waters off the cape northwest of Nantucket without great fear."

"Whatever you think, I can tell you this; no one has ever been able to start the boat's motor again, and it stands forever in dry dock. Many say they hear strange sounds and see strange shadows in the area when the fog rolls in."

"What do you think, boys?"

There was no answer from any of the campers, just looks of uncertainty and, in some, fear.

"Sleep tight," I said and I turned off my flashlight.

CHAPTER FIFTY NINE

Sunday morning broke with sunshine pouring through the partially closed blinds, painting a slatted pattern on the bed. Geller rolled over, a little disoriented, until he saw Elizabeth sleeping soundly next to him. He studied her in the bright morning light, the curve of her neck, her disarranged hair fanned lazily over the pillow.

"How could a woman look so good, so tempting, this early in the morning?" he said to himself. He leaned over and gently kissed her forehead. She stirred and opened her eyes, gave him a sleepy smile, and then leaned over to give him a kiss of her own, light and soft.

"Stay in bed. I'll put some coffee on," said Geller.

"You're a wonderful man, but I'll do it. I don't want you ruining everything by serving me awful coffee."

"I take offense at that," he responded playfully. "You stay where you are, I'll have everything under control. You'll see."

He got up and suddenly noticed his nakedness. Embarrassed he reached for his underwear, strewn on the floor, as Elizabeth giggled.

He padded to the kitchen, where he took the coffee pot from the stove, rinsed it out, and filled it with water to the four-cup mark. He found the ground beans in the fridge and scooped the grounds into the container above the water, again enough for four cups. He put on the lid, which had a glass bulb that filled when the coffee percolated, and lit the gas burner. In short order, the aroma of fresh brewed coffee filled the air. He grabbed some sugar and a container of milk from the fridge. He put a tray on the kitchen table and loaded the sugar, milk, two cups and saucers, spoons, and napkins. When the coffee was done, he poured two cups and brought everything into the bedroom. They sipped in silence, grinning sheepishly at each other.

"This is good, not great, but good," Elizabeth admitted.

"I've made better, but it's OK," he answered modestly.

"Let's get showered and go for a bagel. I'm starved," said Elizabeth with a lean and hungry look.

"Sounds like an idea. I'm in."

She got out of bed and put on a robe. On her way to the bathroom, she stopped and turned. Poised in the bathroom doorway, smiling, she said, "How about joining me for a bath?"

"Wow, that's an offer that no red-blooded American male could turn down, least of all me."

"I'll start the water. Does a macho guy like you mind bath salts?"

"Sure. Bath salts, bath oil, bath beads, bath whatever is OK as long as you're in the tub with me. Truth is, though, I haven't taken a bath in years - um, let me rephrase that," he said, seeing she was about ready to make a remark about his hygiene. "I'm a shower kind of guy."

"Well, then this should be a nice change of pace," she said with a sly smile.

After a few minutes, he went into the bathroom and found her immersed in a tub full of frothy bubbles, the scent of gardenia filling the room. She slid forward and tilted her head toward him, indicating that he should slide in behind her. Taking her lead, he slid into the warm water and sat behind her. She nestled between his legs. She leaned back against his chest, squirmed a little to get comfortable, and sighed melodramatically,

"Nice, huh?"

"You're not kidding," he replied lazily.

They just luxuriated in the warmth of the water and the scent of the bath oil until he tilted his head downward and kissed the nape of her lovely neck. She moved forward and he took a soapy washcloth and started to wash her shoulders and back. He dropped the cloth and started to massage her soft shoulders and back with his soapy hands. He traced her spine with his fingertips, and she started to become aroused. He moved his hands around to her breasts and gently rubbed. The sensation of the slick soapiness heightened the pleasure and she started to breath heavily. Her nipples were erect as he stroked lightly. She could feel the hardness of his penis, and she reached down and began stroking, as he moved his hands to her soft, flat stomach and then to her groin. She was moaning now and awkwardly turned in the tub and mounted him. Sliding into her, it only took a few strokes before he came, and a few seconds later she shuddered with an orgasm of her own.

"I'm spent," he said wearily. "You're killing me."

"I am an animal, aren't I?" said replied. "I don't know what's gotten into me. I've never been this aggressive. You bring out the beast in me Geller."

***

They spent another half-hour lying against each other until the water become cold and they decided to get out. They toweled each other off, and Elizabeth went into the bedroom to dress while Geller shaved, brushed his teeth, and combed his hair. He used Elizabeth's razor, which was dull from shaving her legs, but he survived with only a few nicks. Luckily she had an extra toothbrush and comb. He felt refreshed and hungry. Sex always made him famished.

***

He dressed quickly while she used the bathroom, and they walked to a local deli that had bagels, cream cheese, lox, whitefish, and herring. Her eyes lit up as she perused the refrigerated glass showcase filled with all those delicious items. Geller was continually impressed with her appetite. She was slim and shapely and ate like a horse.

She ordered an onion bagel, toasted, with cream cheese and lox, an orange juice, a dish of fresh fruit with yogurt, and coffee. Geller had a toasted pumpernickel bagel with herring in sour cream and coffee.

"If it doesn't get too hot, could we go to the Brooklyn Botanical Garden? I just feel like strolling and then lying under beautiful trees and taking in the fragrant scent of flowers."

"Sure. Sounds like a great idea."

Their food arrived and as expected, Elizabeth attacked with gusto.

They ate and talked, joking like children. Actually she ate; he talked.

"We're a real fit," he thought. "There's definitely chemistry here," and he felt a surge of contentment run through him.

***

They spent the afternoon at the gardens, walking among the flowers and foliage, throwing pebbles into the ponds, and finishing in the lovely Japanese garden. It had been a wonderful day as they walked hand-in-hand to the car.

They were tired and hungry and hit a small, family-run Italian place close
to her apartment where they stuffed themselves on heavenly pasta and finished
the meal with cannoli and espresso.

They walked back to her apartment and talked for a few hours, keeping
their hands off each other, though with considerable difficulty. Geller kissed
her, held her hand, and said he had to go.

They walked to her front door and faced each other.

"You are the loveliest woman I've ever met, and I wish I didn't have to
leave, but I must."

"I had a very special weekend, Larry, and you're a very special guy."

"I'll call tomorrow. I can't wait to see you again."

"Goodnight." She stood on her toes and kissed him.

The magic of the weekend was over, and real life was intruding again. He
anticipated a busy Monday. He would see Peter Cartright for a little face-to-
face intimidation.

CHAPTER SIXTY

I awoke to another gorgeous morning, which was fortunate, as I had planned a day of boating and a cookout at the end of the lake with my cabin. Camp was winding down and I wanted to do something special for the boys. Nellie had planned to pack up hot dogs, hamburgers, and potato salad in a cooler with all the fixings. I had to check out the boathouse to make sure we had four canoes ready for the trip.

I quickly washed, dressed, and ran down the hill before the bugle sounded for breakfast. I readied the four canoes by the edge of the lake, along with paddles, and then went back to the boathouse to lock up.

As I was padlocking the door I heard a sound behind me. Before I could turn I was hit from behind on the nape of my neck. I stumbled forward and fell, rolling over on my back. I was groggy, and the pain in the back of my neck was intense and burning. As I tried to figure out what hit me, I received another blow, this time to my forehead.

"You little fucker, you told that cop to make my life miserable."

I looked up, my vision blurry, but acute enough to make out the hulking presence of Peter Cartright.

"What are you talking about, you prick?" I countered, my speech a little slurred.

"Fuck you, you little shit," barked Peter ferociously. "I'll rip you a new asshole with my bare hands. You had to mess with things, you and that little bitch with the dog. You had to put your nose where it didn't belong. Now that fucking cop is after me, all because of you." In spite of his bulk, he slugged me with his fist so quickly that I couldn't duck or roll away. His blow caught me on the forehead, and I could feel blood dripping down my face. I felt woozy, and that's the last thing I remembered before passing out.

***

When I awoke he was gone. I didn't know how long I'd been out, but I had a good-sized lump on my forehead and dried blood on my face.

"What the hell was that about?" I said to myself as I staggered to my feet.

I washed my face and forehead by the lake edge and then made my way, unsteadily, to the lodge, where I went immediately to the kitchen to get ice for my wound. I had decided not to tell anyone what had happened.

"What happened to you, Mr. Berman?" Nellie Flanders exclaimed upon seeing me. "Good Lord, you're a mess." She was obviously upset and clucking like a hen.

"I fell in the boathouse and hit my forehead. Pretty clumsy, huh?" I said lamely.

"Oh my," she clucked again. "Let me get some ice."

She returned within seconds with a small block of ice wrapped in a dishtowel. "Put this on your forehead, and keep it there for at least an hour."

"Thanks, Dr. Flanders," I kidded.

"It might be a good idea if you saw Nurse Sloan, just to be on the safe side," she added.

I got a junior counselor to supervise for breakfast, and I went back to the cabin to lie down. I would get checked out by Betty Sloan, but not right now.

***

I lay on my bunk trying to figure the whole thing out. What was Cartright talking about? I'd never mentioned his name to the police, although Geller had asked my take on him. Maybe the discovery at the end of the lake unnerved him.

The ice helped and the throbbing diminished. I wanted to go through with my plans for a leisurely lake canoe trip and cookout with the boys.

CHAPTER SIXTY ONE

Peter was coming apart. He was obviously panicked, but now he was becoming irrational. Nervous and sweaty, he started to pace, swearing and screaming. He wanted to hurt something or someone, even himself.

He went to the cellar door and descended the stairs, walking steadily toward Lester's gunroom. He knew where the key was now hidden, unbeknownst to Lester, who had moved it from the molding above the door to under a can of paint. He opened the door and took a shotgun from the weapons rack. He loaded it and sat down on the floor with his back to the wall, crying. Tentatively, he raised the rifle, his hands shaking, and put the barrel in his mouth. Seconds passed and sweat was pouring down his face, but he couldn't pull the trigger. He started to cry harder and lowered the shotgun. Convulsive sobs caused him to drop the weapon, which thankfully did not discharge. He lay there on the gunroom floor, shuddering and sobbing like a frightened lost soul.

CHAPTER SIXTY TWO

G eller had new-found energy. Up early he showered and dressed to go to the office and then to Lake Spotswood to "visit" Peter Cartright, unannounced. He was nervous and wary, but it was more nervous anticipation.

He grabbed a coffee on the way and called Elizabeth as soon as he hit the office, making a date for dinner and a movie on Wednesday. He made a few more calls pertaining to other cases, did some paperwork, and then left for Sussex County by eleven.

Traffic was light going out of the city, and he made good time. It was a beautiful clear day and the drive was almost pleasant. As he drove, he formulated a plan.

***

He hit Stillwater by one-fifteen and drove the few miles to the camp, and then proceeded down the dirt road past the lodge for about a quarter of a mile to the first driveway on the left. He parked on the dirt road and walked down the gravel drive toward the lake and the Cartright home, so he would not alarm Peter or Lester or give them the opportunity to run or maybe even arm themselves.

As he approached the house, Peter, who was in the kitchen, saw him coming. Panicked, he ran to the basement and locked himself in the gunroom, hiding behind a tall cabinet, shaking and hyperventilating. Maybe he would get tired of looking and leave.

Geller knocked on the front door and when no one answered, he tried the latch and found it unlocked. He walked in and yelled hello several times, and when he got no answer, he proceeded to look around the place. He looked through the living room, inspecting the few photographs on the end table, mentally noting how few there were. He moved on to the kitchen, where he found several plates, glasses, and silverware in the sink. With his handkerchief he picked up two forks and put them in his pocket. He would have his expert dust them for prints, which might come in handy in the future. He checked the upstairs, opening closet doors, checking under beds, and looking in the bathroom between the two bedrooms. He was always wary, with his right hand on his weapon in the shoulder holster. Once convinced that no one was upstairs, he started to look through chest of drawers, under mattresses, in the bathroom cabinet for anything incriminating, any piece of evidence linking Cartright to Lilly Miller, although he had no search warrant. In the back of the bottom drawer of a bureau in the second bedroom, he found an old cigar box. He carefully lifted it out, put it down, and gingerly opened the lid.

Inside he found a treasure trove of newspaper clippings. There were articles about Lilly Miller's disappearance and presumed drowning, but there were also articles about other disappearances of local children. Some were the same articles he had received from Bill Tracy at the "*Newton Chronicle*," though fragile-looking and yellowed with age. His heart began to beat faster with anticipation as he leafed through article after article. Peter had to be involved in the crimes; it was obvious to him. But proof, rather than supposition, was another matter. Hard evidence would be difficult to come by, but enough circumstantial stuff could lead to a confession, especially if he really unnerved Peter.

He replaced the cigar box and straightened the room before going downstairs. As he descended the stairs, he noticed the door that probably lead to the basement.

"What the hell," he thought, and he opened the door, turned on the light, and descended the squeaky wooden stairs. He found the bug collection, but nothing else of interest and was about to leave when he noticed a door in the far corner. Approaching it cautiously, he saw a sliver of light under the door and guessed that Peter might be hiding there. He unhooked the strap of his holster and withdrew his handgun, clicking off the safety. He tapped lightly on the door, and in a sing-song voice called. "Are you in there, Peter? I know you…"

Before he could finish the sentence there was an ear-splitting boom, and the door exploded, sending Geller spinning and crashing to the hard cement floor. He writhed in pain, and then all went black.

He was unconscious on the cold floor and no one knew he was there. He had never let the desk sergeant know where he was going in the motor-pool car, and he'd never contacted Elizabeth or anyone in the department. He lay there for minutes, barely breathing, until the blackness started to lift. His head ached, his ears were ringing unceasingly, and he couldn't move, but he was alive.

How much time had elapsed? How long had he been out? He didn't know or care, he was alive. He began to make out vague objects in grays and blacks, blurry, but definite shapes. He couldn't recall exactly what had happened, but he remembered a blast, and he knew he was injured.

Bits and pieces slowly began to come back to him. He had been shot; he was sure. Gingerly he tried to move his fingers, but he experienced a searing pain in his left arm and left chest that was unbearable. He knew he was in trouble.

He wiggled his feet - OK there. He had no pain in his legs. His right hand and arm surprisingly did not hurt and he was able to lift the extremity. With great effort he reached around with his right hand and felt the warm stickiness seeping from his left upper arm and soaking his sleeve and jacket. He was bleeding too much, and he was feeling lightheaded. The throbbing, searing pain was the only thing keeping him conscious. He had to do something soon or he would bleed to death.

Now he remembered. It was a shotgun blast for sure. Only a shotgun could have caused that noise and shattered the door.

He had to try to move. Unless someone heard the shotgun blast and came to his rescue, he would die. With incredible effort he was able to pull himself up against the wall into a sitting position. The pain was excruciating, and his arm was going numb, but he had to keep awake and he had to keep going.

He guessed that Peter was long gone, but just in case he wanted to find his firearm. Peter had turned off the cellar light, but there was some illumination from the light in the gunroom and a small window behind him.

He scanned the dimly lit room searching for the revolver that had been blown from his hand by the blast. It kept his mind off his arm. There it was, not more than a few yards from where he was propped against the wall. It could have been a mile.

He slid down until his back was on the concrete floor and, then rolled enough on his right side so that his body weight took him over onto his stomach. The process left him breathless with pain, but he managed to crawl one agonizing inch at a time toward the gun. He had gone only a few feet, but it felt like he had just finished a marathon. He was exhausted, felt faint, and was sweating profusely.

After what seemed like hours, but was probably ten minutes, he reached his Glock. He had to rest; he could go no farther.

***

The door had taken the brunt of the blast or he would have been killed instantly. That was a given. The shotgun pellets could not have severed a major artery or he would be dead by now, so he reasoned that the bleeding was venous and should slow with pressure.

He put his right hand over the painful area of his left upper arm and pressed as hard as he could tolerate. Knowing he couldn't go any farther and that getting out of the cellar by himself was out of the question, he would have to slow the bleeding down and wait for help.

It was incredible, but he felt calm. Maybe he was resigned to just waiting and praying. Damn what a stupid "cowboy" he had been! In his weakened state he started to doze off.

***

As he slept he drifted into a realm of the surreal. There in front of him was the slovenly Peter Cartright, wild-eyed and drooling, with a shotgun in his hand. He raised it and put the muzzle to Geller's forehead.

"Goodbye," he said and pulled the trigger.

Geller screamed and was instantly awake, panting and sweating.

Once more conscious he was immediately reminded of his predicament by his throbbing chest and arm. Hours had probably passed; he wasn't sure. He could still feel a radial pulse, although rapid and thready. His left hand was not cold, and he could wiggle his fingers. These were all good signs.

Lying in the basement he had no idea what time it was or whether it would be dark soon. His only hope, really, was Lester's return from work. Of course it could have been Lester and not Peter who shot him.

CHAPTER SIXTY THREE

Around four-thirty Jean took Max for a walk along the road near the Cartright homestead, intending to go about a mile or so. She noticed the car parked on the dirt road near their driveway but didn't give it a second thought. They continued down the road for about half a mile and then turned to walk back. Again she saw the car. "Why did such a non-descript auto look so familiar?" she thought. As she approached the vehicle the radio started to squawk, indecipherable police jargon. That made her think.

By this time Max had wandered off toward the Cartright home and was sniffing around a cellar window. He started pawing at the ground in front of the streaked glass and seemed agitated, as if he was trying to get at something inside. Jean, noticing Max's pacing, walked over to the window and looked through the grimy pane, seeing nothing but cellar floor, although the light was bad.

Maxie continued pacing and started barking. He was definitely beside himself, giving Jean pause. He definitely had sensed or smelled something in the basement, but Jean as not going near that house, especially since Bob had told her the Cartrights were up to no good.

Then it hit her; she recognized the car! It was the same car that the inspector from the NYPD had driven up to the camp when he'd questioned them about the body and when he returned to ask Bob more questions about the Cartrights. So that guy, the inspector, must be around. She checked the car and found the police on-duty visor as well as the staticky police radio. It had to be him. Was he in trouble? Did Max sense something? She ran back to camp with Max leading the way.

"Bob, I don't know if there's a problem, but I just saw a police car parked near the Cartright house. No one was in it, and there were no signs that anyone was around, but Max seemed upset about something near the cellar window. I think the car is the same one that belongs to that Geller guy."

"Holy shit. I think Geller wanted to question Lester and Peter. I wonder if things got ugly."

"Maybe someone should look around," said Jean.

"You may be right, but before anyone checks it out, I'm going to tell your father and have him call the police. It could be dangerous."

"Sounds like a good plan," Jean responded. "If Inspector Geller is in trouble and needs help, the police should be here."

***

Al told us that he would call the police, but he did not forbid us from investigating. I went back to the cabin and grabbed a flashlight. There were still about two hours of daylight left. Jean, Max, and I headed for the Cartright homestead.

***

Geller had been on the verge of unconsciousness, but he was sure that he had heard a dog near the cellar window.

"Please, please come back," he screamed. "Don't let me die." His words were raspy and not nearly loud enough for anyone to hear. Moments later he lapsed into a stupor.

He saw Elizabeth, that lovely face with shining eyes, and she was crying. She was calling his name, pleading for him to live.

"Don't die," she sobbed. "Please don't die. I love you."

He awoke with a start. A dog was barking. This time there was no mistake about it. He definitely heard a big dog.

"Please find me." A whisper was all he could muster in his weakened state.

He thought about firing his revolver but rejected the idea, thinking he might scare off whoever was out there. So he lay there summoning the strength to yell.

In his despair he looked above at the window and suddenly saw a light. The beam was weak, but it looked like someone was shining a flashlight. The narrow beam was tracing the floor several feet away, and he willed it to shine on him. Slowly the beam rose scanning more of the floor. Finally the faint light hit his arm, then his shoulder, and finally his face. Did they see him? He didn't know; the beam was so faint. His mouth was so dry and his body so weak that he couldn't even scream. Then the light was gone, and so were his hopes.

Outside I was straining to see into the basement.

"Jean, I think someone is in there lying on the floor, maybe hurt."

"Let's go back and wait for the police. I'm not going anywhere near that basement," added Jean.

We sprinted back to camp in a hurry to see Al. We found him on the phone in the lodge and he hung up as soon as he saw the worried look on his daughter's face.

"What's going on? Did you go back to the Cartright place?"

"We think someone is in the basement, possibly hurt. It could be Inspector Geller," I said.

Al was pissed. I had put his daughter at risk when I knew he was going to call the police.

"I've already called the police. They're on the way. We do nothing but wait. Do you understand?" said Al abruptly.

***

Ten minutes later we heard the squad car from Stillwater roaring up the dirt road and into the parking area by the lodge. Two officers hurried out of the car and up the stairs to the lodge, where Al, Jean, and I were waiting.

I filled them in on the details of what Jean and I had found.

"My partner and I will check things out. I want no one else there. Do you understand?" said the cop.

"Don't worry. No one will move from here," said Al, looking me square in the face.

The Stillwater cops got back in the squad car and drove the short distance to where the unmarked police car was parked. They drew their firearms and approached the house cautiously.

They entered through the porch and front door. A quick search of the first floor on their way to the cellar revealed nothing. They approached the cellar door cautiously, one officer putting his hand on the door knob while the other had his weapon pointed at the door. They opened it slowly and the hinges creaked.

Nothing - no sounds in the darkness. The cop felt for the light switch and flicked it on. They stood motionless for several seconds, waiting, before descending the stairs. Then they heard it, a low-pitched, labored groan. Someone was obviously hurt and in pain. They slowly descended the stairs until they reached the concrete floor. They strained to see in the dim light and saw a form on the floor. Another moan came from the body. They approached slowly, weapons raised, and then they saw him: a man was sitting on the floor, a pool of blood beside him, his left arm a bloody mess but he was alive. Next to him was a blown-out wooden door. In his right hand was a gun.

"Identify yourself and drop the gun," the younger cop yelled.

Geller let the gun slip from his right hand and struggled to talk. His mouth was incredibly dry, but he willed himself to say, "Geller, NPYD."

"Anyone else here?" said the other cop.

"No," Geller gasped.

More relaxed now, both cops approached to check his wounds, picking up his Glock in the process.

"Radio in for an ambulance ASAP. Tell them we have a gunshot victim. Now go," said the older cop.

The young cop ran up the stairs to radio dispatch while the older man attended to Geller.

"Hang in there. We'll have an ambulance on the way. You're not going to die," said the older cop.

Geller just groaned as talking was an effort.

The cop went into the gunroom, grabbed several blankets and shirts, and then returned to Geller. He pressed the shirts against the wound and placed Geller's right hand over the wound for pressure. Then he covered him with two blankets.

"I'm going to get you some water. Don't go away."

Geller smiled ever so slightly.

A few seconds later the man appeared with a glass of water and helped Geller take a few sips. He choked and coughed but did manage to get down a few sips. The cool water soothed his parched throat.

The young cop reappeared to help.

"Ambulance is on the way."

"Let's take a look at those wounds," said the older man, who the young man called Frank.

Frank got a hunting knife from the gunroom and cut away part of Geller's shirt, exposing his left shoulder and upper arm. It was a mess, chewed up flesh from a 12-gauge shotgun. The door had saved his life, but pieces of wood were embedded in the wounds. There didn't seem to be any severed arteries, but the area continued to actively ooze.

Jim, the younger cop, ran upstairs to get towels to pack against the wounds and fortunately found several rolls of adhesive tape, which they used to keep the towels in place. As they feverishly worked, they heard the sound of sirens. The cavalry had arrived.

Within seconds the medics and a nurse had loaded Geller onto a gurney, covered him with a blanket, and pushed the stretcher into the ambulance for the ride to the hospital in Newton. Just before they left, they started an IV drip and packed Geller's wounds.

Radioing ahead, they described the injuries and the victim's condition.

Geller was coherent enough to tell the medic, "Call Elizabeth Curry in Brooklyn. She's in the phonebook, Brooklyn Heights."

"I'll do it, buddy, but not until we get you to the hospital."

***

He had passed out during the ambulance ride and when he came to, all he could see was a light that was so bright that it was almost blinding. He squinted and tried to raise his right arm to shield his eyes. He was lying in a recovery area, and the bright light was a penlight the doctor was shining to check his pupils.

"You're a lucky man. Another hour or two of bleeding and you would have been a goner," the doctor stated with an encouraging smile.

Geller nodded slightly but couldn't speak. He felt doped up, and his mouth was incredibly dry.

"You just got back from the OR," the doctor continued. "We took you there to debride your wounds and stop the bleeding."

"Debride?" Geller mumbled, still feeling fuzzy.

"We removed splinters of wood and shotgun pellets and cut away some dead tissue. Fortunately there were no injuries to any vital nerves or arteries, and the orthopod made sure you had no fractures. Your chest wounds were fairly superficial considering the blast you took."

Geller was barely awake and could hardly understand the MD's jargon, but the doc persisted in describing the injuries in detail.

"No pneumothorax or air compressing your lung, just a few cracked ribs. All in all, for someone shot at such close range, you had miraculously little trauma. Actually you're lucky to be alive."

Geller was dozing, but the MD persisted.

"You should make a fairly rapid recovery, but you'll be real sore for a while. I'll check in on you again in a few hours."

***

Geller awakened enough to glance over at his left arm, which was wrapped from shoulder to wrist in gauze and stained with blood in several areas. His chest was wrapped in a strap-like manner that made it difficult for him to breathe, and he was packed in ice to limit the swelling and soreness. He had an IV running in his other arm and oxygen was being administered through a nasal catheter, the prongs irritating his nostrils. There were wires all over him, and they were connected to a machine that kept track of his heart rhythm and rate. He must have had a guardian angel looking over him.

After an hour in recovery the nurse told him that he was being moved to the ICU overnight just to be safe. He would be monitored more closely.

"Did you call Elizabeth?" a drowsy Geller slurred.

"I don't know what you're talking about," responded the nurse. "But I think that one of the ambulance guys called someone for you."

Once in the ICU he was given a shot of morphine and fell into a deep sleep.

CHAPTER SIXTY FOUR

Hours later he awoke to a tender touch on his forearm.

He opened his eyes and glanced down at his right hand. It was clasped by a soft delicate hand with beautiful slender fingers. The hand released and the fingers traced his palm, every ridge, line, and callus. Now a figure leaned over and kissed his hand and held it to her breast. It was Elizabeth.

Geller tried to smile and then talk, but both efforts failed. He was able to say everything with his eyes. They were pleading for her to hold him and comfort him.

As she read the longing in his eyes, she kissed him on the forehead. She then knelt and gingerly embraced him, careful not to put too much pressure on his ribcage. He took his right hand and stroked her cheek. A small tear rolled from her eye.

"Thank God you're alive," she stammered.

He tried to answer, but his throat was too dry and his tongue felt swollen and coated. He just lay there feeling her warmth, being infused with her strength and resolve. He knew he was going to be OK.

PART FOUR

"Mayhem"

CHAPTER SIXTY FIVE

Peter was manic and desperate, yet he knew where he was going to hide. He knew the forest from boyhood, and many areas were still remote enough that he could avoid detection for days or even weeks but not forever. He knew they would come, and they would be armed and have dogs. He knew they would track him down. After all he had tried to kill a cop, and he may have succeeded. He knew that they would never stop coming.

He was on the run, but he was well-armed and well-equipped, and he had nothing to lose. He would not go down without a fight, and he would be sure to take some of them down with him. He had killed before and he would again, but this was different. This was not to quell his urges. This was for survival.

Peter had numerous hiding places in the mountains of the Kittatinny range, places they would have trouble finding. He was an outdoorsman and had learned early how to blend in and camouflage himself. He knew how to cover his tracks and block his scent to keep the dogs away, and he knew how to live off the land, tame the elements, and disappear for weeks at a time.

"Fuck you, Geller," he hissed. "I hope I killed you, you son of a bitch."

***

By nightfall Cartright had covered about fifteen miles, moving toward the northwest corner of New Jersey, toward High Point, where New Jersey, New York, and Pennsylvania meet. If he made it over state lines, the New Jersey police would be less involved in their search. Still he'd have to do it on his own since he probably couldn't count on Lester for help. The police, no doubt, were watching his brother and would follow him if he tried to find Peter. No, he'd keep to the woods, stay hidden.

As the sun began to set and the woods became a pattern of dark shadows, he reached his first hideout, a copse of white pine alongside a small brook. He had shown incredible stamina for a morbidly obese, middle-aged man-child, operating on pure adrenaline, anger, and the fear of capture.

Authorities were always trying to tell him what to do, trying to punish him, telling him he was sick. Geller was like those asshole psychiatrists who thought they knew all the answers. They wanted to put him away to protect society.

Well no one was putting him away. He was free and intended to remain that way. They'd put him in a hospital once, for years, and that wasn't ever going to happen again. He had hated the place and all the crazies in group therapy. One of those guys kept confronting him, making threats to hurt him. When the guy wasn't hallucinating, he was busting Peter's ass. But Cartright taught him a lesson with a fork in the hand. It was worth the two days in a straightjacket. "Hell," he screamed in the empty woods, "I'll never go back to that shithole or prison. I'd rather get shot by the cops."

***

He made camp in the pines, putting his gear next to him for security. He had taken several handguns and ammo as well as a high-powered rifle with a scope. In the knapsack he also had a heavy jacket and some food. He knew that he was only several miles from a cave that he and his brother had discovered while hunting a few years back. It was cool and dry, and the entrance was well hidden. They had left supplies there - blankets, kerosene lanterns, mess kits, hatchet, and canned foods with an opener. He figured that it was three or four hours away, but he would have to wait until morning.

He couldn't risk a fire, so he put on the heavy jacket, as he knew it would cool during the night. The mosquitoes were swarming and would be a nuisance, so he hoped for cold or rain. He got his wish. It rained heavily and he was soaked, but the rain also wiped out his footprints and made his scent undetectable. He started to laugh at his good fortune. The rain was a good omen, and he was able to sleep.

He awoke before daybreak, wet and uncomfortable, but free. He gathered his belongings off the soggy ground and made his way to the brook to drink and fill his canteen. He longed for the cave and safety. The three or four hours would not go by fast enough, so he broke camp as soon as the first sliver of light came through the wood.

A few hours into the walk, he heard a sound in the distance, sort of a hum or a buzz. He stopped dead in his tracks, not daring to breathe. The sound got louder and he ducked down and hid behind a large oak, panting and starting to perspire. The sound got closer, and now he placed it - the whine of an engine. Now it was almost upon him and he cowered. The sound was above him now and he sneaked a quick peek. It was a small aircraft, single engine, and he was low, just over the tree-tops.

He was sure he wasn't seen, but the plane kept circling. Were they onto him? How could they be? They were just looking for a needle in a haystack, but he was still frightened and sweating.

He was about to bolt from behind the trees, when the plane changed direction and the engine noise lessened. Within seconds it was gone, and Peter took a deep breath. He was still safe.

Two hours later he reached his destination. Before entering the cave, he gathered small pieces of wood and brush for camouflage. He stacked the wood, changed into dry clothes, and then covered the small cave opening with the brush. It was still raining lightly, so there was no need to sweep away footprints. He spread a blanket, lit a candle, and went to sleep.

CHAPTER SIXTY SIX

G eller dozed off and on throughout the day, barely noticing Elizabeth's presence. He was being medicated with narcotics regularly, and finally the nurse told Elizabeth to go home.

"He won't even realize you've left, honey. Honestly he's not going to remember much of anything."

Reluctantly Elizabeth left the hospital, but decided to get a motel room and not face the long ride home. She would call the cemetery to explain why she needed several days off. They would understand. She went for a quick bite at a diner and then retired early. She tossed and turned throughout the night, preoccupied with Geller's brush with death. All she could see were heavy bandages, blood transfusion lines, and monitors beeping and buzzing.

***

She woke early and checked out of the motel, grabbing a cup of complimentary coffee in the lobby. When she reached the hospital she was surprised to see Geller wide awake and sitting up in bed, his heavily bandaged left arm in a sling across his chest. He still looked wan and drawn, but he was obviously better.

She walked the few paces to the side of his bed, took his right hand gently in hers, and kissed his hand. She then gently stroked the side of his cheek, bristly from a two-day growth.

"What happened, Larry? All I was told was that you were shot, and I just drove here like a madwoman."

He was so happy to see her, his dry lips forming a weak smile.

"All I remember is that I went to question Peter Cartright and found someone hiding in the cellar. When I approached with my gun drawn, he blew off the door with a shotgun. The rest is pretty much a blur."

"My God, you could have been killed. Why did you take such a crazy chance going after him alone in a dark cellar?" she said with an increasing sense of concern. "And why didn't you tell anyone where you were going?"

"I'm not in the mood to be chastised, Elizabeth. I know I made a mistake, but I didn't think anyone was going to try to kill me."

"That possibility hadn't occurred to you?" A note of hostility crept into her voice.

"I knew I had Peter a little rattled and that he's a bit unstable and unpredictable, but attempting to kill a cop? I really didn't think he'd go that far."

"Larry, for God's sake, you went there in the first place because you thought he killed that little girl and maybe others. Why should he stop just because you're a police officer? Hell, that might have given him even more reason to want you dead." She was becoming increasingly agitated.

"I know, I know," he sighed.

She sat silent for about a minute and then said, a bit more calmly, "Now maybe you won't go it alone. Maybe you'll let the duty officer know where you are and where you're going."

"Please don't lecture me, Elizabeth," he said wearily. "I'm not a kid, and I know I screwed up. Rule one - never underestimate the enemy."

"I was just so worried about you and now that you're safe, all my anxiety is coming out. Forgive me." Tears welled up in her eyes.

"I'm sorry. I truly am. I just didn't think," he said gently, squeezing her hand.

"I love you, you dope. I've waited years for someone like you, so don't go getting yourself killed," she said with a forced laugh.

***

A few minutes later the door opened and two men appeared, cop types. Geller introduced them to Elizabeth, who was self-consciously wiping away the tears. She extended her hand, said hello, and then quickly excused herself to put on makeup while they attended to police business. Before leaving she kissed Geller on the top of his head and whispered," I'll be back in a little while."

The two officers, Jack Vetti and Vince Cramer, had come to question Geller about the details of the shooting and also update him on the manhunt for Peter Cartright.

"There's a three-state APB out for Cartright and continuous surveillance on his brother. We obtained pictures of Peter Cartright for the newspapers, TV, and local post offices. The house is under constant stakeout, and the phone is tapped," said Vetti.

"Please, Jack. Try to take this guy alive. He has information on other abductions and killings, I'm sure. I need to talk with him," said a tired but concerned Geller.

"We'll try. Right now we just want to find the SOB. It's like he disappeared into thin air."

"He's an outdoorsman and probably knows the mountains like the back of his hand. Even though he's fat and out of shape and not the brightest, he will be hard to find," said Geller.

"You're right Larry. The Newton and Andover-Stillwater police have no leads, and the state boys in Pennsylvania, New York, and New Jersey have nada. The dogs have picked up no scent, and so far there have been no footprints to follow. Of course, the overnight rains didn't help," added Vetti.

Although tired and achy Geller kept up the discussion with Vetti and Cramer until Elizabeth returned, composed and carrying a package, and with a mischievous look on her face.

"You need a shave. So when you boys break it up, I'll go to work. It'll make you feel like a million bucks," said Elizabeth.

The two men remained standing and put away their notepads and then approached the bed, each giving Geller a clap on the shoulder and promising to return. They would keep him updated on the search.

✷✷✷

Elizabeth took a tray from his bedside stand and disappeared into the bathroom with her paper bag of "goodies." She soon emerged with the tray filled with a hot, wet towel, a razor, a mug of shaving soap and brush, a dry towel, and a cup of steaming hot coffee.

"What do you have there, you sadist?" Geller said.

"What do you mean? I'm just here to give you a much-needed shave. You'll probably feel better after this, and you'll definitely look better, I promise. I must admit that I'd really rather give you a bath," she said slyly, "but I don't think the nurses would go for it. I guess you'll have to wait until we get home." She grinned broadly.

CHAPTER SIXTY SEVEN

Al Simmons was worried sick. There was a known madman on the loose who had tried to kill a cop, and he was presumably in the woods not far from Camp Spenser. This presented a sizable risk to the campers and staff, and he had to make an important decision.

He called a meeting with the assistant director and the rest of his staff, and within minutes a unanimous consensus had been reached; camp must be closed as soon as possible. The kids and counselors would be terribly disappointed, but safety was the first concern. Closing early would, of course, create many logistical problems. All the parents would have to be notified and arrangements made to pick up their sons a week early. Some would not be home when calls were made, some would be on vacation, enjoying summer's end without children. So contingency plans would have to be devised. Money would have to be refunded, one-eighth of the total cost, yet the staff would have to be paid for the whole summer. Problems, problems, problems. Al was beginning to get a headache.

✳✳✳

I heard about the decision from Jean later in the day and had to let the boys know before lunch. I knew they'd be crushed, but they had to be informed as soon as possible as there would be a lot to do before the planned pickup tomorrow afternoon or the next day.

"Guys, I'm afraid I have some bad news. Mr. Simmons and the staff have decided to close camp a week early for all our safety. It's the wise thing to do, but I know you will be as upset as I am. I had some great things planned for the last week, but they'll just have to wait until next year. We have one day left, so let's pack and get everything ready. We're going to have a farewell campfire tonight." That appeased the boys for the moment, although there were looks of disappointment on all their faces and even tears in Danny's eyes.

As the boys started to pack I looked at each of them, realizing how far they had come in seven weeks. Little Danny Golden, despite his asthma and small stature, had become self-confident and popular, finding his niche on the ball field. Jeffrey Lebowitz, obese and ungainly on land had turned out to be a dolphin in the water. With every stroke he was building self-esteem and acceptance, and he was looking more fit. Tony La Rocca had learned that the tough-guy act was unnecessary to be admired and liked by his cabin mates. Bobby Moore, accomplished and mature, had learned how to be a leader, showing empathy and concern, especially for the smaller kids. Then there was Kenny Sawyer who had almost been killed by a freak fall, but had made it back to camp and secured a place in the hearts of the rest of the boys. And there was Paul O'Neill, smiling and happy, who had never wet his bed, not even once. Finally there were Steve Wilder and Mike Kennedy, my rocks, my veterans.

Eight boys had become young men over the course of a shortened summer camp experience. All were destined for great things, in my opinion. I couldn't help but feel pride in knowing that I had a part in their maturation process. I knew I would miss them, especially since I knew that my return next summer was not a given. Starting college was a big commitment, and I could not extrapolate a decision that was a year away. I might want a better paying summer job, or I might want to go out for a fall sport in my sophomore year and have to "sacrifice" the summer to training camp. If things really turned out poorly, God forbid, I might have to spend the summer retaking a failed course. I shivered, as that was unthinkable.

Then I thought about Jean and our premature departure from camp. We would lose our last week to be together. I was somewhat heartened by the fact that we lived only a few towns away from each other, but it wouldn't be the same. Summer romances were usually that, summer romances. Everyone promised to write, call, and see each other when home, but once school started and separation occurred, the budding relationships usually withered and died. In spite of my lack of experience and naiveté, I sensed this was true. I not only felt a physical desire for Jean, but also a real comfort and fondness when I was with her. But at age eighteen and going off to college, I realized the harsh reality that we would probably drift apart, as much as I didn't want that to be true. She would be seventeen and a senior, pretty and popular, and would, no doubt, be asked out on many dates. Did I really believe that she would want to wait around for the college man to come home every now and then? Was that even fair to wish for? I decided to just let things evolve- no sad farewells, no promises.

***

The boys were doing well organizing their things, joking around, and just acting goofy, so I decided to visit Jean before lunch. I reminded them to pick up their laundry, get their craft projects, and close out their canteen accounts. They would start before lunch.

I made my way up to the Simmons's cabin, petted Max on the porch for a minute, and then knocked on the screen door. Mrs. Simmons answered and invited me in.

"I was wondering if Jean was around. I want to talk to her, maybe go for a short walk."

"I'm sure she would love to go, but she went to help her father with some last-minute chores. I expect her any minute, so why don't you come in and sit down. I'll get you a Coke, and we can talk for a second. I have something that I want to ask you."

Kathy Simmons returned from the kitchen with a bottle of Coke and sat down on the sofa across from me, handing me the cold beverage. I took a big swig and waited for the axe to fall. Could she know about Jean and me – our make-out sessions?

"Bob," she began and I shuddered, "What do you know about this Peter Cartright? Or for that matter, his brother, Lester?"

I breathed a sigh of relief. "I know the police think that Peter might have been involved in the murder of the little girl in 1920, and he just tried to kill a policeman, if he was the one in the basement. He's a pretty desperate man I'd say, he will most likely be captured or killed. He's a weird guy, really. I heard he's nuts. I know that he's the one who hit Max, and I think he has been stalking Jean and me." I regretted the moment that the word "stalking" came out of my mouth. Kathy Simmons didn't flinch, although her voice became more edgy.

"Do you think he'll try to come back here or will he try to escape to New York or Pennsylvania?"

"Personally, I think he's long gone, but he may still try to contact Lester. He's limited mentally and I don't think he can go it alone. Even so I don't blame Mr. Simmons for ending the camp season early. It's too risky with Peter on the loose, in spite of the police presence. I know police are all over, and your husband has arranged for a protective perimeter, but it's not safe and there is too much liability. My uncle George, a lawyer in Philadelphia, represented a camp that was sued for a camper's injury, but they had to settle for almost fifty-thousand dollars to avoid court action. Insurance had only covered some of the costs, mainly legal fees, and the camp was forced to close.

"Do you think there is a connection between the happenings at camp and the body found near the lake?"

"Yes, I do. Now that Lilly Miller's body has been found, the police are sure that she was murdered, and Peter Cartright is the prime suspect. I think Lester is at least an accessory to the recent events because I don't think Peter has the smarts to plan all this by himself. Whether Lester is evil or just trying to help his brother, I don't know. But either way they both give me the creeps."

"Thanks, Bob. That gives me some insight. Jean is really upset and scared. You realize that, don't you?"

"Definitely, Mrs. Simmons. I'm well aware, and I'm not too comfortable either."

I was just getting up when Max started to bark. He rose with great effort as Jean bounded onto the porch.

"Hi. What are you doing here?"

"Came to take you and Max for a walk. Not outside the police perimeter, of course," I added while glancing at her mother. "I had a talk with your mom while I was waiting for you."

"Great. Let me get a sweatshirt, and then we're out of here."

***

Jean and I walked around camp, talking and holding hands with trusty Max at our side. We skirted around the real issues, just making small talk.

I put my arm around her, and she began to cry softly.

"Jean, why don't we see how we feel when we're apart? Maybe we will care enough about each other to make an effort to be together, even if it won't be as often as we'd like. Maybe it will be something we want."

"I feel like such an idiot, sobbing like a child, but I just feel an impending sense of loss."

"Look, let's not be so pessimistic. We'll know if it's right or not and if we have something, which I think we do."

"OK," she sniffled. I wiped away one of her tears with my thumb, and we hugged each other.

CHAPTER SIXTY EIGHT

Geller had been transferred to Mount Sinai Hospital in New York City because he was driving them crazy in Newton. By the time he left, he was a new man, no longer doped up, sitting up in bed and reading *"The New York Times"*. He'd become a pain in the ass, but he needed step-down care before being discharged and he wanted to be closer to home.

He was having a breakfast fit for a king: apple juice, diluted grape juice, and tea. As sick as he was of liquids only, he remembered how sick he became when Elizabeth smuggled in a sandwich and gave him a small piece. The Newton Hospital staff was really pissed. Now he knew he could handle regular food.

Elizabeth had left a message at the nurses' station that she would be over after work. She would take a bus or the subway, but it was much easier than when he was hospitalized in Newton. She would probably arrive around six or six-thirty, so he would call the precinct to arrange to have a cop drive her home, as it would be late after her visit.

***

He spent the day reading the paper and came across a small article tucked away on page ten about the manhunt for Peter Cartright, old news by now. He had heard several news clips about it on the radio and TV, but it was not big news in the city, although a cop from the NYPD had been shot. He was alive, so it was on page ten. If he had been killed it would have been on page one for about a week and then page two or beyond.

At any rate he was becoming restless and wanted to take an active part in the manhunt. He needed Peter to be apprehended alive, and he couldn't count on the police not to shoot and ask questions later.

***

He buzzed for the nurse and asked if it was possible to have a phone. Reluctantly she asked her supervisor, who consented, but only after imposing a strict time limit. After all he needed rest to regain his strength and vigor. Once the phone was hooked up to the wall jack, he called Elizabeth at work just to say hello and then called information to get the number for the *"Newton Chronicle."*

His arm was stiff, and it was fortunate that he was right-handed. With some effort, he dialed the number given by information.

After several rings, a young woman answered, "Newton Chronicle."

"Editor's desk, please," Geller asked.

He heard a brief click and then, "Bill Tracy here."

"Hi, Bill. It's Larry Geller. I'm calling to pick your brain."

"Christ, the dead has arisen. I heard you almost cooled it. Pissed Cartright off and he tried to blow you apart."

"Hey, I was able to dial the phone, wasn't I?"

They both laughed.

"Nothing's gonna keep you down, I guess. What's on your mind?"

"Remember those missing children cases? Well I need names, addresses, and telephone numbers of the surviving parents. Is that a problem? It would save me tons of time."

"I'll get the boys busy on it right away. It might take a little while, and the info may be outdated. Where can I reach you?"

"I'm at Mount Sinai Hospital in New York City, room 1015. I have a phone, but I think it's only temporary. Just call the main number and ask for the nurses' station.

"Will do. Speak to you soon." He hung up.

Geller ruminated, turning over facts and concentrating on the recent turn of events. Where was that asshole? Two and a half days and nothing. The bastard just up and disappeared. Geller bet big brother knew where he was. He just needed to be leaned on. Geller would make calls.

***

Elizabeth arrived at six-twenty looking tired, though she beamed when she saw him. She had a suspicious-looking large brown bag with her, and Geller noticed a grease stain on one side.

"OK, what do you have there?"

"Just a little something to build up your strength. I don't think tea and apple juice will do it."

"Out with it. What do you have?"

"Two hot corned-beef sandwiches, half sour pickles, potato salad, and Dr. Brown's celery tonic," she confessed.

She put the feast on Geller's rollaway tray along with plastic forks and napkins. "What do you think?" she asked, clearly proud of herself.

"All I can say is, wow!"

"I don't know about you, but I'm famished," said a salivating Elizabeth.

"What a surprise, you're hungry!"

"Well I'm starting, with or without you." She grabbed half of one of the huge sandwiches.

Mustering up all his strength, he grabbed the other half. He was starved, but feared the probable aftermath of nausea and the harangue of the nurses if they found out. He had not eaten anything for days, if you didn't count Jell-o or gingerale.

They ate ravenously, savoring every bite and thanking God that they lived in New York City, the Jewish deli capital of the world.

As Geller was taking his last bite, his nurse entered with a tray of broth, juice, and tea.

"What do you think you're doing?" the nurse shrieked. "You're on a clear liquid diet only."

"After all the work that the surgeons did in the OR on my chest and arm, I don't think they want me to die of starvation," countered Geller with a smile.

"The doctor did not want you to have solid food yet. He wanted the after-effects of the narcotics to wear off. You don't want to puke all night, do you?"

"They've worn off, believe me. I feel great, and you can tell the doctor that the sandwich was terrific. Just what I needed."

"Miss Curry, I hold you responsible. You're picking up his bad habits." Then she said with the slightest of smiles, "I'll call the doctor and have your diet changed to regular. We wouldn't want you to starve to death. It would be bad PR for the hospital."

"Any idea when I'll get sprung?" Geller asked just as the nurse got to the doorway.

"No idea at all. That's up to Dr. Grant, the vascular surgeon."

"Come on, give me a break. When you call Dr. Grant for orders let him know that I'm ready to go and that I'm driving the staff crazy. Besides you probably need the bed."

"That last part is true enough," she replied with a smile.

"I promise that I'll behave, and I'll even do rehab."

"That's not for our benefit, Mr. Geller, it's for yours," she said primly, although she smiled as she left the room.

An hour later Geller got the message that he would be discharged in the morning. He smiled and looked longingly at Elizabeth.

CHAPTER SIXTY NINE

The next day Dr. Grant appeared in the late morning and was in a snit. He had had a bad case in the OR and he was in no mood for Geller and his smart-ass commentary.

"I hear you want out, Mr. Geller."

"My pain is much less. I'm a little stiff, but I can rest at home. I'm working on a major homicide case, and I can't work from here."

"OK, buddy. I'm tired of looking at you anyway, so I'll sign you out before you leave AMA. But remember: no driving, lifting, or sex."

"Doc, my left arm is sore, I'm bandaged from wrist to shoulder, and my chest is wrapped so that I can barely breathe. I don't think I'll be able to do much."

"Don't con me, Mr. Geller. I've been doing this for a long time. But your pulses are full and bounding, your hand is warm to the touch, you don't have a fever, and your dye studies look good. All in all, you should consider yourself a very lucky man."

As they were talking Elizabeth arrived, and Dr. Grant gave her the quick once-over and then turned back to Geller. "Remember the restrictions: no driving, no lifting, and no sex." He tilted his head ever so slightly toward Elizabeth and threw Geller what almost looked like a leer."

"Dirty old letch," Geller thought.

Now he turned directly to Elizabeth. "Miss Curry, this man is going home, but he's going to need a lot of help and a lot of rest. It's clear that he's not going to pay attention to what I've said, so I need you to keep him from overtaxing himself. All kidding aside, it's important that he keep his activities to a minimum if he is going to heal properly."

"I'll take care of it, doctor. I took a week off from work just for that purpose."

Dr. Grant gave Geller specific instructions along with prescriptions for a pain-killer and an antibiotic and a follow-up appointment. Geller, in turn, promised to obey his commands.

***

Down at the hospital entrance the escort service helped Elizabeth load him into the car she had borrowed from the police pool.

"Your place or mine?" asked Elizabeth.

"If you don't mind the drive to Queens, I'd really like to check my mail, make some calls, and get into clean clothes."

"I don't mind, but do you have a bathtub?"

"Why do you ask, Miss Curry? What do you have in mind?" Geller asked with a grin on his face.

"Well mister, frankly you smell like you could use a bath and some clean clothes, and you can't take a shower until the dressings come off. Besides I know you'll enjoy the bath, but remember, no hanky-panky - doctor's orders."

"Tell you what, help me pack a bag with some fresh clothes and my mail, and we can drive back to Brooklyn. I know you have a tub."

Back at his apartment Geller packed his bag one-handed, enough clothes and toiletries for several days, but not a week. He didn't want to overstay his welcome. Elizabeth helped some but for the most part stayed out of his way. Before leaving he made several calls: to the precinct, the "*Newton Chronicle*," and Stella Williams. Nothing new. The mail was mainly advertisements and no bills.

"Let's go. I'm all set," said Geller.

When Elizabeth offered to help him down the front stairs of his building, he shot her a glance and she knew immediately not to coddle him.

***

They drove to Brooklyn just ahead of the late afternoon traffic and settled into her apartment well before dinnertime. He asked for a scotch on the rocks while sprawling on her comfortable couch and was disappointed when she emerged from the kitchen with two Cokes.

"No booze, you degenerate. How fast you forget the rules." She handed him the soda.

They sat for a few minutes sipping their drinks when Geller said, "How about that bath?"

"Boy, are we ever eager. Get undressed, and I'll start the water."

Geller walked into her bedroom and began to undress. Though his progress was impeded by his immobilized arm, he managed to strip down to his underwear. Then he suddenly felt self-conscious standing half-naked in her bedroom, like he was invading her space. Slightly embarrassed he walked into the bathroom where Elizabeth had begun drawing his bath. She had added oils and salts, and it smelled delightful. He awkwardly removed his shorts and eased into the warm water, keeping his left arm as dry as possible. He had unwrapped the bandage around his chest beforehand, and now he could see the extensive bruising, what Dr. Grant had called ecchymotic areas. He lay there totally relaxed, and for the first time in weeks, did not think of Peter Cartright. Elizabeth rubbed his neck and shoulders with a washcloth and the sensation was incredible. She moved from the back of the tub to the side and gently washed his bruised chest and stomach. He had lost weight, and his ribs were showing. It was a hell of a way to diet. He was so relaxed, yet at the same time he was becoming aroused by the gentle stroking of the lovely Miss Curry. He lazily noticed her beautiful hands, with their long, slender fingers and light touch. He had meant to ask her if she played the piano. She got up and briefly went to the living room to retrieve their Cokes. When she returned, Geller asked,

"Why don't you join me in here? The water is great, so soothing."

"Don't push it, Geller. Dr. Grant made it very clear that you're not to overexert yourself, so don't play dumb," she said in response to his come-hither glance. "You know what I mean. Now I'm going to get something together for dinner. I planned a quiet meal at home tonight, if that's all right?"

"Sounds good to me, but do you mind if I soak for a bit?"

"Just don't fall asleep. It'd be a pity to have cheated death only to drown in my bathtub."

"You're morbid."

She smiled warmly. "I'll be back in a few minutes to help you towel off."

***

Elizabeth prepared some greens, put them in a colander and laid a damp cloth over them to keep the leaves cool and crisp. She then sliced some beautiful ripe beefsteak tomatoes and red onion and whipped up a quick vinaigrette with olive oil, vinegar, mustard, salt, and pepper, adding minced fresh garlic and chopped fresh basil. It smelled divine.

Next she took two thick New York strips from the fridge to season them with salt and pepper and let them get to room temperature. "God, they'd better be good," she thought. She had spent a small fortune on them. Finally she sliced fresh button mushrooms, which she would sauté with herbs while the steaks broiled.

When all was in order she returned to the bathroom to attend to the now waterlogged Lawrence Geller. She tousled his hair as she dried him and then said, "Why don't you take a nap? I'll wake you when dinner's ready in about an hour or so."

"That would be great. I didn't realize how sleepy I would get from the bath."

"Clearly you need rest. So don't fight it and just lie down." She turned down the bed and helped him in. She kissed him and told him to just sleep. Within seconds he was fast asleep and dreaming of her pianist's fingers.

***

She woke him at six-thirty with a gentle kiss to his forehead. His eyes blinked open, and he tried to focus and orient himself to where he was. Immediately he realized how remarkably refreshed he felt after the short nap. Obviously he had been quite tired. He stroked her arm while she sat next to him on the bed and kissed him tenderly on the lips. He responded with firm pressure, and the kiss became more passionate. Before things got out of hand, however, she pushed away and rose from the bed saying,

"I have to get dinner ready. How does a nice juicy New York strip with sautéed mushrooms sound? Unfortunately the decent French Bordeaux will have to wait for another night when you may have alcohol."

"Why don't you get up and put on a robe and watch me cook."

"That's a deal, but let me set the table. I do have one good arm, you know."

***

She sure knew her way around the kitchen, and Geller was impressed. She quickly sautéed the mushrooms in butter and garlic, adding fresh chopped rosemary and thyme. Next she tossed the salad greens with the vinaigrette and put them on a platter to be covered with sliced tomatoes and red onion, more dressing, and then fresh ground pepper. She lit the broiler and started the steaks.

She refilled his glass of Coke, and out of the blue, he said.

"How come you're still single?"

"I like it that way. I was married once, and I didn't like it. Never got around to trying it again. Never met the right guy, I suppose," she said with a hint of sadness in her voice.

"Seriously, you're bright, attractive, and articulate. You can cook, and you're great company, so I can't believe that some red-blooded American man didn't gobble you up."

"Well one did. It lasted two years. We were both young, right out of college, and he would be going to medical school at Downstate. We met in college, dated for two years, and married. I worked in the city while he went to school. Within a short period of time, it became obvious that he didn't want a wife but just someone to take care of him as well as support him. Don't get me wrong. I was not blind to the demands of medical school, especially the first two years, but Jim did nothing in the marriage. He wouldn't even make the bed or think of picking up a dust cloth. God forbid if I didn't pack his lunch the night before. It really became intolerable, as I was working ten hour days and taking two courses at NYU toward a master's."

"Jim came from a wealthy family and grew up as a privileged child in Greenwich, Connecticut, doted on by his mother and treated as someone special because of his academic achievements. He was taught that he didn't have to lift a finger to help, and I wouldn't have put it past his mother to tell him not to do anything to risk injury to his golden hands."

She paused and took a sip of soda. "I know I sound bitter, and I probably am. In our senior year at Cornell, he took me home to meet his folks, and they obviously did not approve of his choice. I was pretty enough and bright enough, but my background left a lot to be desired. My father owned a grocery store in Syracuse, and my mother was a secretary in a law office. Not exactly what they wanted for their golden boy who deserved a Southern Connecticut or Westchester County debutante. I was not from the country club set, and I was on scholarship due to need.

"Despite his parents' objections, we married one month after college graduation. Not a lavish affair, just a small gathering of about a hundred at daddy's country club. We probably would have had more people, but I don't think Jim's mother wanted her socialite friends to meet any more of my family. After a honeymoon in Jamaica, we moved to the city. Jim started school in late August while I worked at Saks and took master's courses in art history."

She abruptly stopped the narrative to check the steaks. Geller sensed that she needed a short break. After turning the steaks she continued.

"Jim didn't even work over the summer, as he was preparing himself mentally for school. He really didn't have to work, as his parents paid his tuition and helped me with our apartment rent and incidentals. I suppose that most people would have envied us or thought that I had it made, but this was not how I had pictured married life. Things started to come apart, as I knew they would and as his mother hoped for, when I realized that we had two separate lives and, now that I think about it, very little in common. After two years we called it quits. We just needed to go our separate ways, and I was tired of being a mother rather than a wife. We just stopped loving each other, if we ever did, and I realized, with a great deal of soul-searching, that our relationship was doomed from the beginning, as we never talked, never touched, and never felt. I guess that it was a union lacking intimacy from the start, and I needed more."

"Any regrets now?" Geller asked.

"No, not really. I don't think we ever had a future together. That was eight years ago. Jim is an internist in southern Connecticut, after finishing his residency last year. We occasionally talk and exchange Christmas cards, but that's it. Kind of a sad commentary on what might have been. Anyway I've dated off and on since, no one special. I did, however, finish my master's program, and I've interviewed at several small museums in the city, but the real plum is the Metropolitan Museum of Art. They need someone to manage their impressionist collection, my true love. Keep your fingers crossed. I've interviewed twice, as I already told you, and I should hear within a week or so. I'm a nervous wreck."

She stopped abruptly, stood, and said, "I'm such a babbler, and this is so maudlin," and then she checked the steaks.

"I remember when I was a child, my mother had a reproduction of a Renoir hanging in the living room. It was your standard copy but nicely framed, and I was fascinated by the beautiful young girl in the picture. Even now I think about that painting often, the softness of the colors and the innocent beauty of that face caught by the master. I would just stare at it for hours," he said. "I have complete faith that you'll get that position. They would be crazy not to take you. I'm sure they saw that sparkle in your eyes and your passion for great art."

"Geller, you never cease to amaze me."

She took out the steaks to rest. Then predictably, she asked the dreaded question.

"Now that I've bared my soul, Larry, tell me about yourself. I mean everything."

"Not much to tell, really," Geller lied. "Grew up in the NYC area, the son and grandson of cops. I guess my future was already decided, but I must say that my dad never pushed me into police work and seemed delighted when I went off to college to get a bachelor's degree. I know my mother, a schoolteacher, wanted me to be a doctor or a lawyer, and she was so proud when I graduated with a BA in psychology from NYU. My plans for graduate work were changed by Pearl Harbor, and I spent two years in Europe with the infantry after being trained as an officer. After two years of combat, I was stationed stateside until discharge.

"I'm going to put things together for dinner, but go on with your story, and don't change the mood."

Geller took a deep breath and then continued. "Coming home, I felt different, a sort of isolation and a lack of direction. I didn't know where to pick up the pieces; I had been away for so long. Eventually I decided to use my psychology background and become a cop. Not just any cop but an expert on the criminal mind. Using the GI bill, I graduated the academy and gravitated toward homicide and forensic work. I got lucky on a few high-profile cases and voila, my career took off. A few books, some lecturing, teaching, and clinics, and there you have it, a modicum of fame."

"All very cut and dry, but what about your love life?"

"I was married and it even lasted a few years. It ended about seven years ago, although Pat, my ex, would say it ended years before. I could give you a lot of excuses, but the truth is, I never really had time for her and never really tried. My job always came first. Unlike your situation, we didn't split on good terms, and we don't exchange Christmas cards. Luckily we had no kids.

"Let's take a break. Dinner is ready, but you're not off the hook yet," Elizabeth said.

The steaks were ready, oozing reddish juices, rare to medium-rare. She quickly reheated the mushrooms and then put the platter on the table with the salad and tomatoes. It looked and smelled incredible.

***

Like an emotional weight being lifted, the meal provided a break from the unpleasant memories. Elizabeth portioned out the salad and gave him a steak, helping him cut the meat and tomatoes while he voiced his objections. The meat was his first good meal (except the hot corned-beef sandwiches) in days. Light banter continued throughout the meal; the heavy stuff would wait.

Lingering over coffee, but no dessert, they sat in the kitchen talking while the candle on the table flickered.

Elizabeth could see that he was becoming tired, so she got up to straighten up a little and soak the dishes until morning.

"Larry, you look exhausted. Let me get you settled in bed. You can bare your soul tomorrow."

He did not object as she puffed the pillows and helped him lie down. His chest and arm ached, and she got him a pain pill and some water. Within minutes he was fast asleep.

***

She went back into the kitchen, wrapped the leftovers, and put them in the fridge. She quickly washed and dried the dishes and put them away and then cleaned the table and stove. She put the broiler pan in the sink and covered it with soap and water to soak overnight. Once done she turned off the lights and used the bathroom. As she brushed her teeth, she looked in the mirror at her reflection and thought how lucky she was to find this man.

She snuggled in beside him, putting her hand inside his robe and rubbing his muscles and bruised chest, which he had not rewrapped in bandages. Geller had just the right amount of musculature and hair, with perfect skin, smooth but tough. They lay close to each other until she, too, fell asleep. Exhausted, they slept deeply, never dreaming of the events ahead.

CHAPTER SEVENTY

Peter Cartright was getting impatient. He was almost out of food, and he'd been hiding for over two days. He was considering abandoning the cave and heading farther into the woods. Anger and boredom were replacing reason, and he would not stay put.

Although Peter was limited he did know that he had three choices: continue to hide, run farther away, or circle back to Spotswood and create some mayhem. Desperate and with little to lose, he made the decision that would probably cause his death. He decided to double back and return to Camp Spenser.

He gathered the essentials he would need in a knapsack, mainly ammunition, a handgun, and a hunting knife. He picked up his powerful rifle, equipped with a night scope, and toted it jauntily on his shoulder. He almost seemed happy as he broke camp.

As he made his way through the woods he listened for dogs and the rustle of a search party. He was driven by anger and desperation, but was enough in control to cover his trail and walk in streams where possible to eliminate his scent. He had to avoid capture before he reached Spotswood. He needed one more shot at the cop, if he was still alive, and that prick counselor and his girlfriend. He didn't care what happened, he just wanted to take them out. He would get to the camp and wait for his chance. It would be easy to get the boy and girl, as he knew the camp and woods well, so a sniper shot from the trees would be a piece of cake.

Geller would be a different problem. He would not be at the camp unless there was violence, like a shooting. That would cause him to return, and that would be grand. Create chaos and get the cop. Peter was starting to get excited.

***

Lester was worried about his brother, so sick, so demented. He had taken care of him, and in return Peter had done the dirty work, a sick symbiotic relationship. Peter, of course, was now out of control and would have to be "sacrificed" in the end, but by that time Camp Spenser and the summer residents would be a thing of the past. Peter did the terrorizing, and for that, Lester would let him have his little "fun" and relieve his sadistic urges.

Lester knew where Peter would be hiding, and he knew the police would have a difficult time finding him. But he also knew that Peter would not stay put. He would get anxious and restless, and he would move.

CHAPTER SEVENTY ONE

I had spent the day getting the boys ready to go home. I was not happy with the decision to close camp early, but I realized that we were all in danger with Peter Cartright on the loose and it had to be done. If he was crazy enough to try to blow away Inspector Geller, who knew what he would do if he got his hands on a camper. The local and state police had set up a perimeter around the camp and patrolled regularly so I was a little less worried, but knowing that nothing was a hundred percent, I kept alert and wary.

I tried to keep busy and keep my mind occupied, but I kept having this uneasy feeling that Peter was near and after me, a palpable cloud of dread that I couldn't shake. In an effort to clear my mind I suggested that we all sit in the cabin before dinner to tell each other what we got out of our camp experience. What we learned, how we grew, our thoughts about the summer, and our new friendships.

Danny wanted to speak first, seemingly ready to burst with all that was on his mind.

"I hate to say this, but I was really scared when I first got here; scared that I would be teased and not liked, scared that I would not be able to keep up and that I would be called a sissy. Well I don't feel that way at all anymore. I feel like you like me. I really like you guys, and I can't wait until next year." Tears of joy welled up and Danny hugged each of his new-found friends. And so it went, each boy expressing similar feelings of growth, acceptance, self-reliance, and camaraderie.

When they all had said their peace I "took the floor."

"Boys, I feel blessed and honored to have been your counselor. You gave me a great summer, and I've come to feel really close to each and every one of you. I'll be off to college with some fantastic memories of a special bunch of young men. You all have bright futures, your potential is limitless, and always say you can do it. Have fun at home over the remaining weeks of the summer, and I look forward to seeing all of you next year."

After hugging my charges we headed up the hill for dinner. After dinner we would have the spectacular closing campfire. Tomorrow, sadly, the boys would leave.

***

Hidden in the woods about three miles from camp was the hulking figure of Peter Cartright, hugging his rifle and practicing looking through the night scope.

CHAPTER SEVENTY TWO

Elizabeth awoke feeling surprisingly well-rested in spite of the heavy meal. She got up and went to the bathroom.

Geller awoke soon after and could hear water running in the tub. He tied his robe, walked to the bathroom, and knocked on the door.

"Come in," said Elizabeth.

He walked in to find her wrapped in a large, fluffy bath towel next to the almost-filled tub.

"I started a tub. It'll relax you, and you'll smell good. I'll step out for a sec while you disrobe and use the facilities," she giggled.

He took off his robe and urinated before his bladder would burst, and then he slid into the hot, aromatic water. Elizabeth reappeared and massaged his neck and right shoulder and then washed his hair and rinsed it with warm water from the sink.

She stood, let the towel fall, and eased into the tub facing him. He rubbed her feet and when she lifted her leg, he kissed her toes, the nails painted red like her fingernails. They just sat like that for almost an hour, day- dreaming until their skin looked like dried prunes.

"I have to do some work today," Geller said.

"Well, I'm off. Mind if I tag along to keep you company and make sure you don't overdo?" Elizabeth answered.

"Sure, I'd love the company. Have to drive to Newton to talk with the editor of the paper and the town clerk and check with the state police on the manhunt. I also want to set up interviews with the family members of the kids who disappeared over the last twenty years in the Sussex county area."

"Just promise that you won't overdo it. I don't think Dr. Grant would approve of the drive to Newton. So why don't you take it easy, and I'll drive?"

Geller nodded his approval.

"Let's get dressed and I'll make breakfast."

"Sounds great."

"I cleaned up last night while you slept, so you escaped doing the dishes, you lucky man."

"Tell you what. I'll shave while you dress, and I'll take you out for breakfast."

"A deal!"

***

The day was mild and sunny, not humid or oppressive and they walked to a local greasy spoon for the special - a Greek omelet loaded with feta and fresh oregano served with home fries, toast, and coffee, which they devoured without preamble.

"I made some calls before we left the apartment while you did your hair and put on some makeup, and we have an appointment with Bill Tracy at the *"Chronicle"* and Stella Williams at the town hall. I was also able to contact a few of the families that lost children, but we can't do it all in one day. So my proposal is to pack an overnight bag and work today, stay overnight in a guesthouse, and finish up tomorrow. I'll spring for the room and meals.

"How can a woman pass that up, especially when it's free? I'll just have to sacrifice."

CHAPTER SEVENTY THREE

They arrived at *"The Chronicle"* at one and got an update on the other missing children.

Bill Tracy, in editorial fashion, reviewed the disappearances of the children, adding details not in all the newspaper articles and important facts and high points in the cases plus the rest of the needed phone numbers and addresses of the families of the murdered girls. Geller thanked him and asked to use his phone to make appointments. He promised the editor that he would keep in touch. He then left with Elizabeth for the town hall to meet Stella.

Stella had the information that Geller had requested and provided some much-needed details. However, she was not happy when Geller showed up with Elizabeth, who appeared to be someone special to him and also was extremely attractive and ten to fifteen years her junior.

She practically ignored Elizabeth while talking to Geller and turned her back on her at any opportunity.

When they left the town hall Elizabeth had had it. She stopped abruptly on the sidewalk, and with hands on hips said,

"What a bitch. What was that all about? Do you believe her? What gall."

"What are you talking about?" said Geller with a blank look on his face.

"Couldn't you see it, you dolt? For an investigator, a hotshot cop, you know nothing. You didn't notice how rude she was to me and how she sucked up to you?"

"No, I didn't."

"Come on, you idiot. She treated me like I wasn't there while stroking your ego, fawning over your injury, talking about your hero status. Give me a break."

"I don't know why you're so angry. I think you're over-reacting."

"No, I'm not. But I'll drop it for now for the sake of the investigation. I'll be gracious. I'll be a big person."

***

They decided to skip the state barracks for now and headed off to nearby Andover to visit with the family of a little girl, age eleven, who had disappeared twenty-seven years ago and was never found. Her name was Susan Ross, and she had disappeared from a schoolyard in broad daylight. No signs of a struggle, no witnesses. She simply vanished into thin air. She was small, frail, and blonde, and it had been raining all day when she did not come home.

Finding the tree-lined street they parked in front and approached the house, an orderly ranch on a pretty wooded lot. A woman answered the door when they knocked, probably in her early sixties, but looking ten years older, probably from the grief she'd suffered with the loss of her only child.

She introduced herself as Martha Ross, and Geller introduced Elizabeth and himself, showing his badge. Mrs. Ross showed them into her home, sitting them and herself in the living room. Déjà vu from his trip to the Berman home.

"How may I help you, Mr. Geller? It's been so long, and I know so little about Susan's disappearance."

"I'd like to ask you some questions that may help me give you some closure. I will probably open old wounds, as my questions may cause thoughts to surface that you have tried to bury for years. For this I apologize. If I go too far, just tell me. I know this will be painful, but I know it will help in the long run.

"I don't know what I can tell you that the police don't already know."

"Let me be the judge of that. I think you will be able to help."

"OK, I'll try to cooperate."

"Where did your daughter disappear?"

"She disappeared after school before dark. She left school and never made it home."

"She wasn't with any friends?"

"She started to walk home with friends but stopped halfway, remembering that she had forgotten a book. She told her friends to go on without her and not wait, as it was raining. After all the school is only about six blocks from home.

"What happened after that?"

"Nothing. She was never seen again. Vanished!"

"When did you call the authorities?" Geller asked.

"Once it started to get dark my husband and I became worried."

"He went out in the car looking for her while I called all her friends. No one had seen her. The school was locked up tight and all the lights were off. Susan would never be late and not call. We were panicked, and my husband drove to the police station and reported her missing. They searched for days with dogs, volunteers, and local and state police. Practically the whole town turned out looking for her. Her picture was posted all over the county, and the radio stations described her looks and what she was wearing when she had disappeared. Nothing turned up. No clues, no ransom note, no calls from a kidnapper. She was never found. That was twenty-seven years ago; she would have been thirty-eight now."

Martha Ross started to cry, and Elizabeth got up and sat beside her. Geller offered her his handkerchief as she tried to compose herself.

"Why don't we take a short break," Geller suggested.

"No, Mr. Geller, I want to go on."

"Did the police have any suspects or any leads?"

"Not that they shared with us. I know they suspected a child predator and I don't think they suspected a local."

"Tell me, do you remember any adult male who befriended your daughter, someone who was not a family friend?"

"No, absolutely not."

"Anyone at school who showed her extra attention?"

"Not that I can recall."

"Was there anyone you ever saw around your daughter at school who would have been in his mid to late twenties, fat, and with thick glasses?"

She was rapt in thought, trying to remember details of a crime that had happened almost thirty years ago. Suddenly there was a look of recognition on her tired, drawn face.

"What is it? Do you remember something?"

"Yes, yes, I do. I can't believe I never thought of it before. There was a custodian at the school who would have fit that description. I remember because Susan liked him even though the other kids didn't. They thought he was odd, and they teased him endlessly. I think he was retarded, quite harmless."

"When did you see him last?"

"I don't know. I think he left about a month or two after Susan disappeared, but I'm not certain. I really took little interest in him."

"Do you remember his name?"

"No."

"Does the name Peter mean anything to you?"

"No."

"Did the police ever question him?"

"I don't know. I think so, but I'm not certain."

Geller's thoughts were racing. Stella Williams had given him Peter's employment and health records. They only went back so far, but he had been employed by the Andover-Stillwater school system as a janitor during that time frame. It didn't list the specific school, but this was good enough.

Thanking Martha Ross, Geller thought that he should tell her some of what he knew. With all the conviction and empathy he could muster, he said.

"I'm hoping that I may be able to bring closure after all these years. I have a suspect, and if I get a confession, I'm hopeful that he will tell me where Susan is. I promise that I will do everything possible to bring her remains home for a proper burial and punish the person responsible."

Martha Ross wept. He kissed her on the cheek and said good-bye.

CHAPTER SEVENTY FOUR

The drive to the secluded lake took about an hour, but the lovely inn, overlooking the shimmering water, made the effort rewarding. The late afternoon was warm, but there was a light breeze, and the building had an inviting screened-in porch running its whole length, a perfect place to enjoy a glass of wine while sitting on antique rocking chairs. The chirping birds attacking the feeders on the lawn, the sounds of late afternoon insects and fish breaking the water's surface, and the perfumed aromas of pine and the herbs in the inn's garden added to the incredible scene.

Elizabeth held his arm and stood on tip-toe to kiss him.

"This is just a perfect setting. It doesn't look real."

***

The wine was well-chilled and crisp, a very good Californian chenin blanc. Elizabeth's hand was cold from the glass, but he took it and kissed her palm and fingers. His warm breath was comforting. As they sat on the porch a soft breeze came off the lake, heightening the sense of peace and tranquility. Tomorrow would be more interviews and more pain, but tonight they were in paradise.

They dined later that evening after showering and dressing. They ate slowly and talked idly, all in the glow of candlelight. Lake trout sautéed in butter, parsley potatoes, and broccoli from the garden, accompanied with a chilled Beringer chardonnay, was the perfect meal. Imbued with romance and flushed by the wine, they lingered over coffee, enjoying looking at each other and holding hands. Elizabeth traced the veins of his right hand and then turned the palm up, tracing his lifeline, which was good and long. Oh how she loved this man, this kind and gentle cop, not yet warped by the sickness and depravity of the killers he dealt with daily.

They declined dessert and Geller signed the check.

***

The inn had six rooms, all decorated with colonial furnishings and hand-made quilts for chilly nights. They were able to get the last room, which had doors that opened onto the screened porch. They sat on rockers with the remains of their glasses of wine and just lulled to the rhythm of the noisy crickets and cicadas until fatigue overtook them.

"What time do we have to get up?" queried Elizabeth.

"Around seven, if that's OK. We can take a walk by the lake and then shower and have breakfast. If we check out by around nine we should get to Branchville by ten. Our interview is at ten-fifteen. We have a second meeting in Blairstown at twelve-fifteen."

"Sounds like a plan," she said as she arose to go to bed. Although it was only nine PM, they were tired. She took his hand, gave a gentle tug, and led him into the bedroom. As she turned down the bed, she said,

"I have big plans for you tonight. You don't think the bed squeaks, do you? I mean, they won't hear us next door, will they?"

"Don't know, but I think I'll risk it. Dr. Grant, eat your heart out!"

They made slow, passionate love, and then finally fell asleep in each other's arms at eleven. His arm and chest would be sore in the morning.

***

Waking at six-thirty with a dry mouth and headache from too much wine, Geller looked over at Elizabeth, lying peacefully like a cherub. Did he detect a slight smile on her face, or was it wishful thinking? He resisted the urge to kiss her and instead let her sleep for a few more minutes. He quietly slid out of bed, put on jeans, and went downstairs where he found an urn of fresh coffee, cups, sugar, and cream. He readied two cups and put them on a small tray, noting the familiar odor of bacon and something else. Yes, there was another aroma wafting from the kitchen -cinnamon. They were baking fresh cinnamon buns.

He started to salivate and couldn't wait to tell Elizabeth. How he loved country inns. He could not understand why people went to motels.

Upstairs he gently woke the beautiful Miss Curry with a light kiss and scored major points when he handed her the cup of coffee.

"Wait 'til you see breakfast. Or should I say, wait 'til you smell it."

"That good?"

"If you like bacon and cinnamon buns and lord knows what else."

She shot out of bed and donned shorts, a sweatshirt, and sneakers in record time.

"You don't think they'll run out of anything while we're walking, do you?"

"Elizabeth, it's not even seven. I think they'll have a few items left."

"Well the faster we take our walk, the sooner we eat. Let's go."

The grass was wet with dew, and a mist rose from the lake as the cool morning air touched the warm water. Life was beautiful. Peace and serenity ruled here.

***

Once back in the room they ran water in the antique claw-footed tub while they brushed their teeth and stripped naked. They sat opposite each other in the warm water scented with bath beads and played with each other's toes.

"Don't start any hanky-panky, mister. Let's just get clean and dress. I'm famished, and I don't want to miss anything at breakfast."

Dressed in slacks and tennis shirts, they descended the stairs into the dining room to partake of the anticipated treasures. Even in their wildest dreams they could not have imagined this breakfast.

The table was set with linen and Lenox china. In the middle was a basket filled with hot cinnamon buns and covered with a linen napkin. The innkeeper rushed over to help Elizabeth to her seat and with great flair shook her linen napkin and put it on her lap.

"Would you like some orange juice and coffee before we start?"

Before Geller could open his mouth, Elizabeth blurted,

"We'll have both."

He disappeared into the kitchen, and Elizabeth, not able to contain herself, lifted the napkin on the buns and took a deep whiff.

"Unbelievable. This place is great."

Not waiting for Geller or the coffee or juice, she reached over and helped herself to the steamy sweet roll. On her small plate, she pulled the roll in half and swathed both pieces in sweet butter.

As she took the first bite, the innkeeper and his wife reappeared with a pitcher of fresh-squeezed orange juice and a pot of coffee. They seemed pleased to see her eating.

They poured the beverages and announced the menu - eggs, bacon, home fries, grilled tomatoes, and toast. If that didn't interest them, they could whip up some French toast with warm syrup and fresh strawberries.

Geller sensed that Elizabeth would order everything, so he kicked her under the table and gave her a look that said, "Behave yourself."

Elizabeth took the hint and said that eggs and the other accompaniments would be fine. There was no need to make French toast, but she made him promise that he would make it for her when she returned for another visit. He beamed and said it would be a pleasure.

Two other tables were occupied, but the rest of the guests seemed to be sleeping late. That was OK with Elizabeth.

The innkeeper looked at Elizabeth and said,

"Miss, you look awfully thin, so I'm going into the kitchen with the missus to whip up a nice cheese and herb omelet with all the fixings."

"That's so kind of you."

"Did she really bat her eyes?" Geller thought.

"What about you, sir? We don't want you going away hungry."

"Not a chance here. I think I'll take two eggs over easy."

The innkeeper seemed satisfied and disappeared into the kitchen while his wife took orders from the other tables. He obviously wanted to please Elizabeth, Geller thought.

"Are you on a diet or something?" asked Elizabeth.

"Why would I be on a diet?"

"Two fried eggs over easy? That's it?"

"Well it comes with a lot of stuff."

"You're a big disappointment, Geller. I thought you were an eater. You haven't even tasted the cinnamon buns," she said as she reached for her second.

Out from the kitchen in short order came a young girl, probably eighteen or nineteen, carrying the plates piled high with food, so hot that she carried them with oven mitts on. Elizabeth's plate had an omelet of at least three or four eggs, oozing cheese and the smell of thyme and sage. Next to this perfect egg dish were slabs of bacon, ham, and home fries, all garnished with grilled tomatoes. Elizabeth looked like a kid in a candy store with a dollar in her pocket.

Geller's dish was impressive, but looked paltry next to hers.

As if this were not enough the young girl came back with a basket of hot buttered toast made from home-made bread, home-made preserves, and more soft butter. She poured more coffee before she curtsied and left.

"Dig in, woman. You haven't eaten a decent meal since last night and those buns just won't cut it."

Elizabeth ate everything except the tablecloth. Making love gave her a voracious appetite.

***

After checking out and thanking the couple who owned the inn profusely, Elizabeth embarrassed Geller by accepting a basket of fresh-baked cookies for the car ride. Yes, they obviously liked Miss Curry.

"Did you taste those preserves? Incredible."

"I never had the chance."

"Don't get huffy with me. You're just jealous because at your age you have to be careful and watch your waistline. I just can't seem to put on weight as hard as I try." She giggled.

CHAPTER SEVENTY FIVE

They arrived in Branchville at nine-fifty-five and found the Lawrence home after ten minutes of searching. They were greeted by Bob and Carol Lawrence, the parents of an eleven-year-old daughter who disappeared in 1942.

After introducing themselves they all settled down in the comfortable den of their split-level. Everywhere there were photos, family pictures with many children. The room was tastefully furnished and had a warm, lived-in feel.

Rather abruptly, Geller asked,

"Tell me about your daughter and that awful day in 1942."

"I've told the police all that I knew, many times, many years ago." Mrs. Lawrence responded a little taken aback.

"I know that, but just be patient with me. I have some new information and I think some new avenues to explore."

"My daughter, Joanna, disappeared from a girl scout outing. The police questioned the troop leader and all the children and parents who chaperoned. Nothing. That was seventeen years ago. In an instant she was gone and never found."

"I'm going to ask you one question, and I want you to think carefully before answering."

"OK," said Carol Lawrence as her husband nodded.

"Did your daughter know a young man, say around age thirty-five, very fat, thick glasses, mentally slow?"

"No, she never mentioned anyone of that description."

Geller just sat and said, "Take your time."

After what seemed an eternity, Carol Lawrence said,

"That's strange because I remember someone like that who picked up our garbage on Mondays, I think. Even after all these years I remember him. He worked for the town refuse department, and I remember him because we had words over his habit of leaving some of the garbage by the curb and the cans thrown on the lawn."

"What do you mean you "had words?""

"I remember yelling at him and calling his boss at the telephone number that was on the side of the truck. I never saw him again; I guess he was fired. Sorry, Mr. Geller, but that's it. I don't know of anything more I can add."

"You've been a great help, and I will keep in touch. If you think of anything more, here's my card."

"You said you have some new avenues to explore," interjected Bob Lawrence.

"That's right. It's a little too early to know if we have anything concrete, but I will keep you informed. You want answers, and you need closure. That's what I want and I will not stop until I find out what happened to your little girl."

In Blairstown they heard more of the same, and on the ride back to New York, Geller revealed more details that made a case against Peter Cartright. According to Stella Williams' information, Peter had worked at one time for a waste management company. Things were coming together.

"Where were the police? How could they not have questioned Cartright more intensively or linked him to any of the disappearances?" questioned Elizabeth.

"You have to remember, the disappearances occurred many years apart, and no one noticed a pattern. There were no clues and no real suspects. I guess they wanted to believe it was not a local who was involved. They never connected the dots."

Reaching Brooklyn before dark, an exhausted Geller told Elizabeth that he had to call the state police in Newton to check on the manhunt for Peter Cartright.

"We'll try to take him alive, but at this point we have no idea where he is. He just vanished in the woods," said the state cop.

CHAPTER SEVENTY SIX

Peter Cartright was at Camp Spenser, hiding in the woods and unseen by anyone, armed and dangerous. From his vantage point, he saw that things were closing up. It was too early for camp to end. However, there it was, numerous battered bags and trunks up on the lodge porch with kids milling around and carrying laundry bags, fishing poles, bats and balls, and all kinds of paraphernalia.

He would have to act fast. The police, state cops, and maybe even the national guard would never have expected him to circle back to the camp. Most of the men would be combing the dense woods miles away. He decided to wait until late afternoon to make his move. He heard no dogs, so he knew he was safe where he was.

***

Lester Cartright had no idea where his brother was at this minute. He figured that he had made it to the cave, but he knew Peter would not stay there. He also knew that little brother was a dead man. After all he had tried to kill a cop.

Lester had hated his parents for what they had done to Peter. He would have eliminated them earlier, but it took a lot of time to plan a fool-proof scheme to murder them without being suspected. He had been cool, controlled, and calculating, and there had been no investigation.

What a lovely, dysfunctional family. Now everything was starting to come apart. Peter would have to be killed by the police.

CHAPTER SEVENTY SEVEN

That afternoon I said a final good-bye to my boys, hugging each one and helping them carry the last of the knapsacks, sleeping bags, fishing gear, and craft projects to the lodge to await their parents. They didn't have too long to wait, as families started to arrive at one.

Obnoxious Dr. Golden and the missus were actually low-keyed and even seemed grateful for the transition in Danny. The great man, believe it or not, shook my hand and even slipped me a tip. No compliment, just cash.

"Dr. Golden, I have nothing but admiration for your son. He's a terrific kid, and I think he had a great summer. He looks and feels healthy with no asthmatic attacks since the hospital stay."

"He told us about the chess match and was quite proud of that, you know. I think it's fair to say that my wife and I are grateful for what you have done for our son. He's already talking about next year."

That was a major compliment, and I almost fainted from the praise. As I gloated, he abruptly left with his family.

I had nice chats with many of the parents, who appreciated my leadership and rewarded me with a major haul of tips – forty dollars. By late afternoon, thank God, everyone was gone and I took a quick half-hour jog with Jim. I wanted to spend the evening with Jean, as by this time tomorrow I would be packed and on my way home.

Sweaty and smelly, I went back to the cabin to grab a towel and a change of clothes, and then trotted off to the washroom for a lukewarm shower. The water was warmer than usual and it felt good, helping me to relax and calm my psyche. My muscles were sore from carrying trunks and going up and down the hill to the lodge.

I lathered up and shampooed my hair, letting the now hot water rinse off the soap. As I reached for the faucet to make the water a little cooler, I heard a crack and felt a sharp, searing pain on the side of my right thigh. In an instant the shower stall shattered.

"What the fuck is going on?" I screamed. The pain in my thigh was intense and hot, and as I looked down I saw bloody water swirling down the drain. I reached down and felt a fleshy wound, warm and sticky.

"Holy shit, I've been shot," I yelled into the empty washroom. I dove to the floor a second before another bullet shattered the wooden frame of the shower and the stall behind it. I was sure my life was over. Scenes of my childhood did not flash before me, only the thought of dying at age eighteen.

I could not have moved even if I had wanted to, and I didn't want to. Someone was out there trying to kill me, and I was terrified. Blood continued to fill the drain. My thigh was becoming numb, and I was starting to feel lightheaded. I knew that I couldn't stay put much longer, but what options did I have?

"I'm going to bleed to death," I screamed.

I must have passed out, for when I awoke I was being carried out by police and placed on a gurney. I was naked, but I didn't care, as I was hustled to the infirmary past a worried-looking Al Simmons.

***

Betty Sloan soon was standing over me with a bright light behind her. It made me squint. Someone had covered me with a blanket.

"You're a lucky young man, Bob. The bullet just grazed you, and the second one missed. No major vessel or bone damage that I can see, so I'm going to clean this up a bit and put on a good pressure dressing, give you a tetanus shot, and have the police take you to the hospital for a complete evaluation and X-rays. They may want to take you to the OR for a better look under anesthesia."

I was feeling lightheaded, but I was coherent enough to ask, "Can I have something for pain?"

"Sure, Bob," and she gave me a shot.

***

Al Simmons was screaming at the police, accusing them of sloppy protection and incompetence.

"That crazy out there is armed and dangerous, and you can't even protect this camp. Thank God the boys are gone, but my staff and family need to feel safe and secure. How the hell did he get through the perimeter?"

"Calm down, Al," said Parker from the state police.

"Now we know what we're up against. He's here and we'll get him." Parker was thinking of Geller's call to try to take Cartright alive. At this point he would take him any way, preferably dead.

"I'll have a mix of state and local law enforcement in the camp. I'll even call the governor for the National Guard if I have to. We'll comb the woods, and trust me, he won't get away again."

***

Peter was pissed. He had missed a golden opportunity to take out the little prick, Berman. He wasn't sure how badly he was hurt, but he knew it was not a good hit. A rustle in the woods had distracted him slightly as he pulled the trigger, probably a squirrel or a chipmunk. By the time he shot again the fucker had fallen to the ground.

After the shooting he ran deeper into the woods, past the rifle range to another hideout, a dugout prepared years before. Peter and Lester had numerous hiding places in the woods. This blind was well hidden, with a wood roof covered with foliage for camouflage, which opened like a trap door and could not be seen or easily detected unless you knew it was there. It was now time to hide.

CHAPTER SEVENTY EIGHT

I was being probed and poked while lying on the exam table with several surgeons peering down, mumbling about my wound. Then I was informed that I would be going to the OR. That was OK with me as long as I would be asleep. I seemed to remember that they said my parents were on the way.

As I learned later they had waited for my parents to arrive so they could sign for my surgery. It was not an emergency, and since I was a "minor" under the effects of a narcotic, they preferred that I not sign the OR permit for myself. Thank God I was dozing because my mother must have freaked out.

I awoke in the recovery room to see my parents hovering over me, blurry, but definitely mom and dad. I guess they had pulled strings to get into the recovery area. Mom looked overly worried, but I didn't think I was going to die.

"Hi son," my dad said. "I know you're drowsy, but give us a sign that you're OK, a thumbs-up or something."

I raised my right thumb, which I guess made them both relax, although I could hear mom sobbing. Knowing the police, they had probably called my parents and told them I had been shot, with no further explanation. Probably never told them that it was only a superficial wound. Undoubtedly the drive from Millburn to Newton must have been the longest drive of their lives. Now they knew I would live.

***

Once I was able to ambulate, urinate, and drink clear liquids without vomiting, I was allowed to leave the hospital to recuperate at home. I begged my parents to allow me to return to camp to get my gear and say my good-byes.

255

"The place is crawling with police, so I know I will be safe," I begged.

"Forget it, Bob. You are going nowhere near that place, so stop the protest. Jim Butler can drop off your clothes and you can call Jean Simmons from home," said my dad with a look that said, "Don't argue."

"Mom, tell dad to be reasonable. I'll have a policeman with me at all times. There will be no risk."

"Forget the arguing, Bob. It's a done deal. Camp is over," they both said.

"You were supposedly safe before you were shot. Obviously you weren't. Don't tempt fate," Mom added with a certain finality.

CHAPTER SEVENTY NINE

Geller told Elizabeth that he had to go to Camp Spenser at the crack of dawn. Peter Cartright had shot Bob Berman and then disappeared into the woods without a trace. They searched for him for hours and now it was dark and they had found nothing. He had to supervise the search in the morning.

"I'll go with you to keep your company, if that's OK," said Elizabeth.

"I'd love the company and your opinions, but you have to stay where I tell you, and you have to stay under police guard. The situation is dangerous."

Elizabeth agreed, and they drove to Sussex Country for the umpteenth time.

Upon their arrival he spoke to state trooper Parker, the man in charge of the search.

"Where the hell is he? He just can't vanish into thin air."

"Well that's exactly what he did. Don't ask me how, but he's gone. Shot the kid and just disappeared. We have been combing the woods since yesterday afternoon and even the dogs can't find him. He must have hiding places or he's Houdini."

"Come on, Parker. You have a veritable army here. It's not exactly like looking for a needle in a haystack. He's a big, fat guy with little gray matter - not much of a challenge."

"Why don't you give us some suggestions and maybe we'll find him," Parker said sarcastically and with an element of disdain for Geller. "We'll have to be careful because this dumb guy was almost able to kill a cop."

Geller just glared.

"First of all I would try to find the firing spot where he shot the Berman kid. I'm sure he picked up the shell casings, but he might have left some footprints or broken branches. It shouldn't be hard since you know where Berman was standing when he was hit."

"What do you think, that I'm an idiot? This was exactly what we did and we found absolutely nothing."

"Come on, Parker. He's got to be out there. There's no place for him to go. He has no transportation and his brother is under constant surveillance, or at least I presume so," said Geller with a smirk.

"Believe it or not, big, dumb Cartright is gone, and we've checked everywhere."

Geller had heard enough, and he asked Parker to assemble some local police and state troopers to retrace Peter's probable escape route with him.

***

While Parker picked his men, Geller checked on Elizabeth, who was having coffee in the lodge with Al Simmons and his daughter, Jean. She was well guarded but he still worried.

When they started out he carefully inspected the foliage. He was accompanied by a police dog, a sleek black Doberman with rust-colored underbelly. The dog was purported to be a great tracker and had been given the scent earlier when he sniffed a shirt and pants that the police had confiscated from Peter's closet. He walked alongside Geller, sniffing and tracking, getting a little more excited. After fifteen minutes he started to sneeze, became distracted, and seemed to lose the scent. He began scratching his snout vigorously as if it were itchy. Geller had seen this before when a perp spread pepper or used pepper spray on a dog. Geller's pulse quickened - Peter was here, but where? The woods seemed empty. Then the thought hit him. He must be in a concealed dugout; it had to be.

Carefully going over the ground, he could see it; a trapdoor camouflaged with foliage. He motioned to Parker's boys and the police. Parker leaned near Geller, who said,

"He's in there," pointing to the ground. "Don't let anyone near that hiding place. Get a bullhorn and tell him he's surrounded. And Parker, don't let anyone fire unless fired upon. I want him alive."

***

Parker had unbelievable firepower that he positioned around the bunker. He did instruct them to hold fire unless fired upon. He then raised the bullhorn.

"Cartright, we know you're in there and you're surrounded. You have no chance of escape, so give yourself up before more people get hurt. We won't try to kill you."

An interminable silence followed, and all that could be heard were the forest sounds: chipmunks scurrying, birds chirping, leaves blowing in the light breeze, all of which sounded louder due to the dreadful quiet from the blind. Parker raised the bullhorn again, but before he could repeat his pronouncement, the trapdoor flew open with blinding speed, and a crazed, wild-eyed Peter Cartright emerged holding two handguns.

Stunned by the suddenness, the police were slow to react and Cartright got off four shots, wild ones that hit no one. But all hell broke loose. Everyone started firing, and Peter fell, along with a local cop. Parker had dropped his megaphone and had joined in the melee, firing at will.

Geller was screaming, "Hold your fire," but it was too late. Peter lay badly wounded, face down in a puddle of blood, bleeding profusely from his left upper arm and wrist. Geller grabbed a walkie-talkie and called for an ambulance and an emergency medical team while he kicked away Cartright's weapons.

They rolled him over, and he was still conscious. While Parker applied a tourniquet to Peter's arm, several cops stood over the scene with guns at the ready. The local cop who went down was just grazed and needed little attention.

The bleeding slowed considerably, and Geller quickly assessed his other wounds. There were no obvious head or neck injuries, but there was a bad-looking chest wound, an entrance wound in the right thigh, and his left hand had been almost blown away, leaving a disgusting bloody stump. His breathing was labored, and Geller could hear gurgling sounds, but he was not coughing up blood, and his heart was still beating.

Geller leaned over the stricken man and whispered,

"Stay alive, you son of a bitch. I need to talk to you."

Cartright could barely speak but grunted what sounded like, "fuck you."

***

As they raised Peter onto a litter from the infirmary and started carrying him toward the lodge, they heard the faint wail of a siren.

In short order medics arrived, jumping from the ambulance to unload a stretcher and supplies. They transferred Peter from the litter to the stretcher and assessed his injuries quickly, rapidly started an IV with a large needle, and slapped on an oxygen mask. A heavy, patch-like bandage was put over the chest wound, which seemed to be sucking air. The medics then reapplied the tourniquet and put a pressure dressing and wrap on his mangled left hand. The stretcher and supplies were loaded onto the ambulance and the team yelled, "Let's go." Two cops jumped into the ambulance with the medics, and one joined the driver. With their siren blaring they high-tailed it down the dirt road from the lodge with a police escort until they reached the camp entrance and turned onto the paved road for the ride to Newton.

An OR team would again be awaiting their arrival. The trauma from Camp Spenser had exceeded, in one month, anything they had seen over many years.

***

When the ambulance hit the ER bay, Cartright was quickly unloaded and wheeled to a large surgical area, where a team of doctors and nurses took over. Except for two armed police, the remainder of the contingent was told to leave.

Back in the ER, a second IV was started in his neck, a skillful surgeon cannulating his jugular vein. Blood was sent for a stat CBC and type and cross match. Vital signs were unstable, his blood pressure falling and his pulse rising. The surgeons, ER docs, and nurses seemed cool and methodical although they had little experience with gunshot wounds. They had the occasional hunting accident, but this was not an inner-city ER.

A portable chest X-ray revealed a bullet lodged near a posterior rib and a left pneumothorax, with a partially collapsed left lung. The general surgeon rapidly inserted a chest tube to try to remove air and blood between the lung and chest wall to help the lung expand. He replaced the pressure bandage over the sucking wound. Next a catheter was placed in his bladder to monitor urinary output and also to make sure there was no blood in his urine - there was none. Blood gases were drawn, and an X-ray of the abdomen showed no free air under the diaphragm, a good sign.

Someone shouted, "BP- ninety over sixty; pulse- one- twenty."

"Call the blood bank. Get four units of Oneg if they don't have the type & cross match done and get the hemoglobin and hematocrit results.

A nurse ran to the phone and within seconds yelled, "Hemoglobin's eight."

"Keep those fluids running. Hang two units when the blood arrives, yelled the surgeon in charge. Cartright looked terrible; pale, sweaty, and gasping for air in spite of the oxygen, but he was stabilizing.

"BP- one-ten over sixty, Pulse one-oh-two," came the cry.

"Once we get the blood, we'll move him to the OR to fix the damage."

CHAPTER EIGHTY

Under anesthesia the tourniquet, which had been released and tightened every five minutes, was removed and the arm and hand were prepped by a circulating nurse with a liquid soap and sterile water and then an antiseptic solution. Blood was running in both IV's. The surgical team: a general surgeon, an orthopedist, and a gynecologist acting as an assistant, draped the arm and hand and began the exploration and repair. Meanwhile the anesthesiologist got another portable chest film, which showed that the pneumothorax had improved, and ventilating the patient became easier. The chest tube, bubbling below water level in a pail, was no longer draining blood.

A severed artery was found in the upper arm and was bleeding actively with the tourniquet off. Clamps were applied, and the vessel was tied off with sutures. The surrounding muscle and soft tissue were lacerated and contused, but there appeared to be no nerve damage. The wound was packed with medicated gauze, and X-rays were taken of the entire arm, which showed a shattered humerus near the elbow.

"You're on, Jerry," the general surgeon said to the orthopedist.

"I'll see what I can do, but let's look at the hand first," replied the orthopedist. After a quick assessment he decided to attack the arm first. He would amputate the mangled hand later.

He said to the scrub and circulating nurses, "I'll need an ortho tray and the usual rods and plates." The ortho tray contained the usual assortment of sterile "carpentry" tools like drills, saws, screwdrivers, and gruesome-looking retractors.

The right thigh was debrided by the general surgeon and the bullet removed, and X-rays surprisingly showed an intact femur.

"What a fucking mess, but it could have been a lot worse," said the gynecologist, now embarrassed by his language in front of the nurses.

"How are his vitals?"

"BP- one-twenty over seventy-eight, pulse- ninety-two. Blood gases are good, and he's easy to ventilate now. We're OK," said the voice behind the ether screen at the head of the OR table.

The orthopedist did his best to remove bone fragments and stabilize the lower end of the humerus. After an hour he seemed satisfied. The amputation took another hour or so.

"Let's get out of here. It's been a long day, and I'm sick of the mayhem at Camp Spenser. I've never seen so much trauma in my whole career," said the exhausted surgeon.

The wounds were dressed with sterile pads and gauge wraps and the left arm immobilized. After three and a half hours Peter Cartright was still alive, and he was transferred to the recovery room, still intubated and attached to a respirator. He was heavily sedated so he would not pull out the endotracheal tube, and he would be carefully monitored for an hour or two before being moved to the ICU. Two cops, in scrubs, sat in the recovery area and would follow to the intensive care area when Peter was moved. He would be watched by the police around the clock. His condition was listed as critical but stable. The press would want to know. It would become a media circus.

***

Geller was beside himself, pacing and cursing. Elizabeth tried to calm him, but to no avail. If Cartright died, all hopes of finding the missing children would die with him. He didn't know whether Cartright was conscious, but he had to question him.

After seven hours of waiting, a cop reported that Cartright was alive and in the ICU. He was not conscious and had a tube in his throat.

"You tell me the minute he wakes up and when he can talk."

"He can't talk with that tube, and the doctors didn't say when they would take it out. Besides who cares whether he lives or dies?"

"I do," said Geller.

Geller gave the cop his card and told him to call any of the numbers. He had included his home phone, Elizabeth's phone, and the precinct number.

***

They decided to stay in a motel overnight, as it was late and he couldn't face the ride back to NYC. He called the hospital with the number of the motor inn.

He tossed and turned while Elizabeth, as usual, slept like a baby. He tried a hot shower, but still he lay awake, dozing only occasionally, and when sunlight broke through the blinds of the motel room, he was exhausted.

Breakfast didn't help. He couldn't eat and drank cup after cup of black coffee as he watched the unflappable Miss Curry down pancakes and bacon as if she didn't have a care in the world. The coffee frayed his nerves even more, and he became jumpy and irritable. Finally she finished, and they left for the hospital.

***

"Good news for you," said the cop at the entrance to the ICU. He's conscious, and the doc just took out his tube. I tried calling you at the motel, but you had checked out."

As Geller was led in and approached Cartright's cubicle, he was intercepted by two nurses, one short and fat and one tall and thin, but both hostile and impervious.

"And where do you think you're going?" said "shorty."

"To question the scumbag in that bed," retorted Geller.

"Oh no, you don't. He's a sick man and he's still critical," said the tall nurse.

"Do you know what this guy did?"

"I don't care. He's our patient, and in here we rule."

"I'm going in there to question him and if you try to stop me, I'll book you on obstruction of justice." They left in a huff and went to the nearest phone, probably to call the doctor or nursing supervisor.

Geller approached Cartright's bed, leaned over, and whispered in his ear,

"Hello, Peter. I'm back."

Cartright looked up, glassy-eyed and confused, but showed some recognition and mouthed, "Fuck you."

"Look you prick, you're dead meat. Every cop in New Jersey and New York is ready to lynch your ass."

No response.

"I can save your ass from the mob, but I need some answers, so listen up."

Geller saw a slight reaction, so he persisted.

"We have you dead to rights in the Lilly Miller killing and the attempts on me and the Berman kid, so you have no future. But I think we can arrange a trade. We know you were involved in the disappearances of at least four other children who were never found. I want to know where you put them and if there were any others. If you help, I'll save your ass."

Peter could not answer, but he shook his head - no.

"You don't have a choice, fucker. You tell me what I want to know, or I feed you to the wolves. They would love to see you fry."

As if on cue the medical staff arrived, the surgeon in change and the two nurse henchmen.

"What the hell do you think you're doing?"

"I'm questioning your patient. The guy tried to kill me and one of the camp counselors."

"Bullshit you are," said the irate, red-faced surgeon.

"Don't worry, doc. I won't screw up your handiwork. All I'm going to do is ask him some questions. I'll be sure not to tire him out or overtax him."

"Geller, you have ten minutes max, and then you're out of here. No matter what this man is accused of, he has been seriously injured and needs rest. Once he's out of the ICU, he's all yours."

"When do you think that'll be, doc?"

"If he gets by the next twenty-six to thirty-six hours without complications, I'll transfer him to the floor."

"Good. I'll try not to kill him before." Geller went back to Cartright's bed.

This time Geller noticed a difference in Peter's eyes; he noticed fear.

"Before you shot me, I was looking around your cellar. You have quite a collection of insects, especially the butterflies. Truly beautiful."

Peter looked up at Geller, wary, but he didn't say anything.

"It would be a shame if I got pissed and wrecked all that beautiful work, tore it to pieces." He had Peter's attention.

"Think it over, shithead. I'll be back when they move you out of here. I'd sure hate to ruin all that work."

With that Geller turned and walked out, nodding to the cop sitting just outside the cubicle.

He had him. He was sure.

***

He picked up Elizabeth and they made their way toward the hospital entrance.

"Oh, shit. Let's go back. The press is here," he said to Elizabeth.

At the front entrance were dozens of reporters and newsmen. A TV station was setting up shop in the front lobby, and Geller wanted no part of it. He wanted to sneak out to see Bill Tracy to give him all the inside info, so he would have a lead on the other papers. Unfortunately he saw Parker already holding court with some newsmen.

"Out the ER entrance, and we'll walk to the "*Newton Chronicle*," he said to Elizabeth as he hustled her to the stairwell.

They made it out unscathed and walked to the editor's office, where Geller filled him in on everything, much of which he already knew, but he was thankful for the scoop.

***

With nothing left to do in Newton and with Elizabeth due back at work tomorrow, they decided to grab a quick lunch and drive back to New York.

They checked out a local luncheonette, and luckily the press had not yet arrived, so they sat in a booth and perused the menu.

"What do you think it will take to get him to talk?" asked Elizabeth.

"I think I have the leverage."

"You're the psychologist, the expert on human behavior. I'm sure you have ways," said Miss Curry.

"Yeah, I told the son-of-a bitch that I would destroy his precious insect collection. I think that might do it."

"You're a genius. Let's have lunch."

She had a club sandwich with fries and a chocolate shake. He had tuna on rye with lettuce and tomato and a Coke.

"I hope you become a pudgeball someday."

"You're just jealous," she laughed.

They walked the five blocks to the car, enjoying the late summer day. There was a faint hint of crispness in the air, a prelude of the fall weather to come.

Even though he was tired, he got behind the wheel rather than ask Elizabeth to drive. His arm had mended well and it wouldn't be a bad trip as it was mid-afternoon and any traffic would be coming out of the city.

About an hour outside of Newton they were cruising on Route 46, going about sixty toward a downgrade. He was behind a truck and starting to close fast, as the semi was doing about fifty. He went to pull into the left lane but caught a glimpse of a car in his blind spot and swerved back to the right, causing Elizabeth to look up.

Taking his foot off the accelerator, he tapped the brake pedal. Nothing happened and he kept approaching the truck. He pressed harder on the brake and again no response. The steep grade of the road caused him to gain speed even with is foot off the gas pedal.

He swerved left just missing the back of the truck, making the driver of the car on his left slam on his brakes and veer to the island in the middle of the road. No sound of metal hitting metal, just the blare of the scared driver's horn. In his rear-view mirror he could see the guy giving him the finger.

Swerving back and forth and downshifting with some difficulty, he tried to slow the vehicle while screaming for Elizabeth to climb into the back and lie on the floor.

"We don't have any brakes," yelled Geller.

She did as he said while he tried to maneuver out of trouble. The road started to level out, and the car slowed noticeably. They had a chance. Sweating profusely, he worked the wheel with one good arm and one still healing. They were definitely slowing, so he jerked to the right so the tires would catch in the gravel of the soft shoulder. Finally after half a mile, they came to a halt.

"Are you all right back there?"

"I think so," she said in a shaky voice.

He went around to the back seat and embraced her. She was trembling, and he pressed her to his sore chest.

"It's OK. We'll be fine."

Geller radioed for help, and several minutes later a cruiser, with siren blaring, approached from the opposite direction, swung around into the eastbound lane, and pulled up behind them. With blue and red lights flashing, the state trooper got out of his car as Geller was opening his door.

"Inspector Geller, are you and the passenger all right? Do we need an ambulance?"

"Lost my brakes and nearly crashed. But we're OK. Miss Curry is a little shaken, but we don't need medical help. Thanks for responding so fast."

"Let me take a look." The trooper walked around the car several times and then crouched down to look under the chassis. He saw brake fluid leaking onto the gravel.

"I'd better call for a tow truck. You can't drive this vehicle."

"What'd you find back there?"

"Brake fluid all over the road."

Geller went back to the car. Elizabeth had calmed herself.

"He's going to tow the car. It's not safe to drive. They'll get us home ASAP."

"Whatever you say, Larry. I'm just thankful that we're safe."

"Someone tried to kill us today," he said abruptly and without emotion.

"What are you talking about? The brakes just failed. It was an accident."

"Elizabeth, I just had the car completely serviced at the department and the brakes were fine."

CHAPTER EIGHTY ONE

The weather fit my mood, damp and gray. It had been a day since I had been released from the hospital, and I had spoken to Jean many times to assure her that I was well. She was really freaked.

Jean assured me that she and her family were safe "with that madman wounded and under twenty-four hour police guard."

I told her to be careful and that I wanted to see her once my leg was healed. She seemed to like that.

"Say good-bye to your folks, and tell your father that he did a great job handling a very difficult situation."

"I will. Call me anytime. We will be in West Orange tomorrow." She hung up.

The doctor told me that my leg would hurt for two to three weeks and he had given me some pills for pain. I was not allowed to drive for at least a week.

Jim arrived in the late morning, and he and my dad carried in all my gear.

"Hi Mrs. B. How's the patient?"

"Difficult to keep him still, but I think he'll live. How about a soda or sandwich?"

"I would if I could, but I promised my folks that I would drop off the bags and be on my way. I'll take a rain check," he said.

"I'll hold you to that," Mom said.

Jim bent over and kissed my mom good-bye. He shook hands with Dad and gave me a guy-type hug.

"Best of luck in school, Jim." Mom said.

"Thanks, and I'll keep in touch. Don't forget to send my best to your daughter."

The guy never stopped trying.

I walked him to the door, hobbling on crutches. He stopped and faced me.

"Bob, take care of yourself. Knock 'em dead at Lafayette. You're a great kid with a great future."

***

Now that I was officially back, my belongings home, Mom started hovering and became preoccupied with my injury. She insisted that I take a warm bath so Dad could remove the packing and change the dressing. My achiness had returned as the pain pill wore off, and I didn't argue.

Mom smiled and delightedly disappeared into the bathroom to draw the tub water. Dad gave me a shrug and a wink and left me so that I could undress in my room in private.

As I undressed I looked in the mirror. I was lean and healthy, tan and well-muscled after two months of work and recreation in the outdoors. I liked what I saw. I was in prime shape.

I limped into the bathroom in my underpants. Mom poured some Epsom salts into the tub and then left.

"Call if you have any trouble getting in or out, Bob."

"I will, Mom, but I think I can manage."

I must admit, Mom was right. The bath was warm and very relaxing, and I began to loosen up, physically but not mentally. I couldn't help but think how close I had come to leaving this earth. I could have been killed, or worse, seriously wounded or paralyzed if the bullet had hit my spine. That son of a bitch was a maniac. Thank God the police had him. I thought back to the day that I broke into the Cartright home and was almost caught by Peter. I shuddered and thanked my lucky stars that I got out of there alive.

CHAPTER EIGHTY TWO

Geller was at a loss. Someone had released brake fluid, but who? Peter Cartright was out of commission under police guard in the hospital and Lester, supposedly, was under constant surveillance. It was possible that he could have slipped out and done the job, knowing how poor the police work had been thus far. He certainly had motive, but did he have opportunity? Once Peter was captured, the watch on Lester had most likely become less intense, even casual, and he could have slipped out. But how did he know where I had parked?

The police had gone over the car, dusting the undercarriage, tire hubs, brakes, and cables, and found numerous sets of prints. They would have to be compared to those of the police mechanics, and they needed a set of Lester's prints for comparison. He had no police record and had not been in the service since the early part of World War II. So they needed fresh prints. Geller would gladly get them. He would get a search warrant and dust Lester's house.

He was now starting to worry about Elizabeth's exposure. Being with him was a risk, a liability. He was concerned about her when she was with him, but also when she was alone. Someone may use her to get to him or punish him.

He decided to have her watched twenty-four hours a day and have her apartment under surveillance, at least for the present.

That night, tired from the afternoon's ordeal, they decided to go to a local place for Chinese. Geller had told Elizabeth that Lester was now back under close police watch and was at home reading. This seemed to mollify Miss Curry, and she was now ready to eat.

Arriving at the China Dragon they sat at the bar for a drink while the owner prepared a table at the busy eatery. While he settled for a much needed double scotch on the rocks, Johnny Walker Red, she had a mai-tai.

Moving to the dining room they ordered the standard fare of egg roll, pork fried rice, and lobster Cantonese, washed down with Chinese beer. As per usual Elizabeth did most of the eating and talking, and Geller drank most of the beer. Pineapple chunks and fortune cookies completed the pig-out.

Elizabeth played with her fortune cookie, eventually cracking it open and taking out the strip of paper, which she scanned and smiled.

"You have sought love and found it," she announced with a sly, provocative look. Very apropos.

Geller's split cookie revealed a strip of paper with red lettering. It simply said, "Always look over your shoulder." He paled.

They stayed in the restaurant talking and holding hands, sipping beer, until the waiter started to look impatient and pointed to the bill in a leather holder at the end of the table. Geller took the hint and paid while Elizabeth used the restroom.

It was a little before nine, so they decided to hit a movie. *"The Bridges at Toko-Ri"* was playing in a neighborhood theater that showed old movies for half price. They held hands, and Elizabeth cried at the sad parts. Geller was too preoccupied to get into it, even with Grace Kelly on the screen.

"Wasn't it wonderful?" Elizabeth gushed. Geller nodded and tried to look interested as they strolled toward her apartment.

It was eleven-thirty by the time they got to her street. Geller noticed a non-descript gray sedan by the curb across from her apartment and about one hundred feet down the road. His boys were there, watching. He felt relieved.

***

They took a long bath together, sipping wine and trying not to drown. Geller always felt it was dangerous to drink alcohol in a bathtub, but he doubted that both of them would fall asleep or pass out at the same time. He enjoyed looking at Elizabeth's body and her lovely face. She saw him staring and became self-conscious, covering herself with her arms.

He wasn't too bad either for his age. Elizabeth loved the small cleft in his chin; he hated it because it was a pain shaving. His arm and chest injuries were healing well and were causing minimal discomfort and the bruises had turned a pale yellow.

Once the water started to get cold, they got out, toweled off, and got into bed naked. They kissed, exploring each other's mouths with their tongues. Geller was aroused, and Elizabeth fondled his erect penis with those soft, delicate fingers. He moved his face to her breasts and kissed her erect nipples. He gently licked, and she let out a soft moan. He moved down and kissed her flat stomach, rubbing his lips against the soft, downy hairs while he stroked the inside of her thighs. He moved down and spread her legs gently as her moans increased, and he licked and caressed the lips of her vagina and clitoris. She was incredibility moist and panting rapidly, on the verge of orgasm. Within seconds she arched her back and head in violent spasms. Instead of mounting him, she took his penis in her mouth, moving up and down. Within seconds he came and she kept him in her mouth until he became flaccid. She stopped and got up to use the bathroom.

***

He awoke at three and went to urinate. When he got back in bed, Elizabeth stirred, opening her eyes and reaching for him. She was aroused and this time wanted him inside her.

"I love you, you big clunk."

Geller just smiled and nodded. "Same here."

She was moist to his touch and almost immediately was on the verge of orgasm. She was a woman of incredible appetites.

She rolled over onto her stomach and got into knee-chest position, guiding Geller into her. He reached in front and fondled her breasts, which seemed fuller in this position, as he slowly moved in and out. She was breathing heavily, and he moved his hand down to rub her clitoris. She came within seconds and had multiple orgasms, as she moved frantically with him inside her. She moaned, panted, and almost screamed as he ejaculated. She was almost out of control and would not let him withdraw. She wanted him inside her until he became soft. Finally spent, sweaty, and exhausted, they stopped the lovemaking.

She was in love with him and couldn't get enough of him. It wasn't just a sex thing, although the sex was great. It was a oneness she felt with him, the want and need to be with him and be a part of his life.

Geller had the same feelings, wanting to engulf this lovely creature.

They slept soundly until eight.

CHAPTER EIGHTY THREE

Dad pulled the wet packing from my thigh and said, "Looks good, nice and clean and granulating in." That seemed to please him.

I was feeling better, but the thigh still ached. No more searing pain, but rather a dull discomfort like a toothache. I was anxious to start moving and get rid of the crutches. I had to start walking and then eventually light jogging and calisthenics. College was only one week away, and I had to rehab.

Now that I was almost fully recovered, my mother turned her attention to finding out about her sister's murder and Peter Cartright. Although I tried to avoid the subject, she had other ideas and prodded, coaxed, and coerced me into describing him. She wanted to know why he'd killed Lilly. What in his demented mind made him commit such a heinous crime?

"That man killed my sister and sucked the life out of your grandparents. They thought Lilly had drowned, and they never got over the tragedy. I just thank God that they never knew that their daughter was murdered. And now he tried to kill you, my son. I can't bear it."

She seemed to be talking as if I were not there, and just as I thought I could sneak off, she said,

"Bob, we have to bury Lilly in Brooklyn next to your grandparents."

"I agree. It is the appropriate final resting place for her."

"Do you think the police will release her remains?" my mother asked.

"Yes. I would think they are done with their investigation. I'll call Inspector Geller to see if he'll pull some strings."

"That would be nice, Bob. It's the right thing to do."

"That's the least I can do for her."

"Do you believe in fate, Bob?"

"I don't know, Mom. I guess I believe in coincidence."

"Well of all the camps that you could have gone to, you ended up on Lake Spotswood. Was that a coincidence? I visited many times during your camp years, but never knew that it was the lake where we spent the summer of 1920. And then you found Lilly. Just like that, after thirty-nine years, you found her. You know what that means?"

"It was just blind luck, Mom."

"No, Bob. It was fate. You were destined to find her for us, for George and for me. Lilly called you; she sent you a signal."

"Mom, this is freaky, and you're scaring me. This was not some type of psychic experience."

At this she just smiled gently, and a single tear fell from her eye and rolled down her cheek.

CHAPTER EIGHTY FOUR

They showered, dressed, and walked to a nearby café for breakfast.

"What's on the agenda today?" Elizabeth inquired between bites.

"I have to make some calls and check what they found on the car and get a status report on Peter."

"I have to go to the Met for a conference at two-thirty. Keep your fingers crossed. If all works out, I could get the full-time position today. If not, I'll be out on the street."

"I feel terrible that I haven't even inquired about your job. You must be nervous, and I never even asked. I'm sorry."

"You're sweet. I think I'll keep you around awhile." She kissed him gently.

"I won't even cross my fingers because I know they are going to take you. What more could they want?"

Geller walked her back and then left for the office. She would change later and splurge for a cab to the museum. They would meet for dinner.

Geller called Newton to check on Cartright's status and then called Parker to check on Lester Cartright.

"Parker, we have to question Lester. I'm sure that son of a bitch fixed my brakes. Who else had the motive and opportunity?"

"I heard about your near accident; glad you survived," said an unconvincing Parker. "I don't see how he did it since he is being constantly watched."

"Maybe you should watch him more closely," said Geller as he hung up.

CHAPTER EIGHTY FIVE

Elizabeth was excited. Things went well and she got the job. To celebrate they went to the Oyster Bar at Grand Central Station. It was noisy and crowded, but they had excellent oysters and fresh seafood, good service, and a real New York chic. They dined on chilled oysters with perfect vodka martinis followed by red snapper stuffed with fresh crabmeat and herbs, small sautéed potatoes in butter, and grilled eggplant. A shared raspberry tart finished a superb dining experience. They stayed for another hour, talking over snifters of Courvoisier VSOP. No one seemed to mind, as the crowds were thinning and there were empty tables.

"Have you cracked the case yet?"

"No. I need one more session with Peter. He'll confess, but I also need the details and burial sites of the other victims. I plan to see him tomorrow. I also want Lester. He's up to his eyeballs in trouble. I'm convinced he knows about Peter's kills and is protecting him, and I know he tried to kill us."

"So you think he tampered with our brakes?"

"Who else could have done it and who else would have a motive? Proving it will be tough."

He paid the bill and they strolled back to the car. It was a lovely, late summer evening with a star-filled sky.

PART FIVE

Terror and Violence

CHAPTER EIGHTY SIX

Lester was in a quandary and decisions had to be made. He knew Peter would crack under pressure. Really what could Peter tell them? A far-fetched story of how Lester killed their parents. Who would believe it, and who could prove it?

But then again, if Peter admitted to the murders of children, he would be implicated as an accessory or be charged with obstruction of justice. No, Peter would have to be eliminated. He was a loose cannon, and there was too much at stake.

How would he do it? That question kept Lester up most of the night. The police were guarding the house, and Peter was under constant surveillance at the hospital, with cops outside and inside his room. He would have to visit Peter as a concerned brother and check out the hospital, the security routine, and adjacent buildings. He would check how and when Peter got his meals, medications, and water. What was checked and what wasn't. There were so many possibilities, but so many chances for failure. Would it be poison, a bomb, air in his IV, a bolus of IV potassium or insulin, a fire, or a sniper's bullet? The thrill of the hunt and out-foxing the police and Geller almost made him cry. He would plan and re-plan; it had to be perfect. "Good-bye, little brother. It's time for you to go. Big brother has big plans, and you have become expendable."

CHAPTER EIGHTY SEVEN

Geller couldn't wait to get to Newton. Peter was stable, fully conscious, and almost ready to be transferred from the ICU to a medical-surgical floor. The doctors would have no reason to keep him from seeing Peter.

"It's beyond my better judgment to let you go in. Just keep the visit short," said the doc.

"He's a piece of shit, doc. You're wasting your time and talent on him, so don't worry about me overtaxing him. Maybe he'll do the state a favor by confessing to his crimes and giving me all the details before dropping dead."

"Geller, I'm warning you. Fifteen minutes max."

Geller went into the ICU cubicle, where a police officer was seated across from Cartright's bed. He asked him to stay as a witness as he set up a tape recorder and microphone. He took it slow, as he knew Peter was watching his every move. Geller had dealt with this type of killer for years, and he would get results.

"Hello, Peter. I understand you're recovering quite well."

Peter just stared with his rheumy eyes, a blank expression on his face.

"I have nothing to say to you."

"Bullshit. I'm getting tired of you, you fat prick. You're in a lot of trouble, so don't jerk me around. You talk to me, or I'll wreck every fucking collection of bugs you have. You'll have nothing left. All that work - poof, up in smoke."

"You wouldn't. You're just trying to scare me."

"The hell I wouldn't. I'm tired of you, so let's end this shit. You tried to kill me and the Berman kid. That alone would be life, but you killed Lilly Miller and others. They'll fry you for that."

"Bullshit. I just tried to scare you and that little counselor shit. I don't know a Lilly Miller."

"Well, Peter, let me refresh your memory. I'm going to take you back almost forty years, when you were a fucked-up teenager. You beat a little girl to death, crushed her skull, and buried her by the lake where you live."

Peter seemed unmoved, showing no emotion, but Geller knew he was scared. He would crack.

"You crushed her skull with a shovel. You kept beating that little girl, that poor, defenseless child. Why, Peter? Did she make fun of you? What sick urge caused you to do this?"

Peter remained silent, but he was losing control.

"What about the others, Peter? The little girl in Branchville, the girl in Andover, the child in Blairstown, and probably others? You just couldn't help yourself, could you? The urges were just too overwhelming. They needed relief. I understand, Peter. I understand you perfectly."

No reaction, no comment. But his hands were balled up in tight fists.

"Don't make this hard. Don't make me trash your basement. I can save your specimens and maybe cut you a deal with the police."

A faint glimmer of hope crossed Cartright's eyes, and Geller did not miss it.

"I know about your urges, but the police don't care. They want you in the electric chair. It's a terrible way to die. You bite your tongue, foam at the mouth, have convulsions, and shit in your pants while all those people watch you die and laugh. I can save you from that."

The hate was gone in his eyes, replaced by a distant, almost lost, faraway look.

"You give me a little, and I can bargain for your life. No death penalty. I need to know where you buried them, all of them."

His tightened fists opened.

"I didn't want to kill Lilly. I thought she was my friend, but she made fun of me. I had to do it, don't you see?"

Geller nodded. "Tell me everything."

Peter proceeded to describe the murder and aftermath in great detail, as if it had happened yesterday. When he was finished he went on to tell Geller about the other abductions and murders and where the bodies were buried. Some details were hazy, but Geller had enough to start the search for the remains. He would come back for more details if needed. He shut off the tape recorder and left the room. He thought he would vomit.

***

He left the hospital and went to see Parker at the state police barracks.

"What do you have on Lester?" Geller blurted out before even shaking hands.

"Nothing yet. He's stayed pretty much at home and out of sight. Can't understand why he hasn't visited Peter yet."

"He's too busy fucking with my brakes."

"Don't worry, Geller. We'll get him. He'll make a mistake."

"I know he's involved in this. It's just not a matter of protecting Peter."

"Jesus, Geller, where do you come up with this shit?"

"Well Peter's too dumb to pull off all this shit. I think he just likes to kill animals and little girls. But Lester is another story. He has a mission, a reason to want all this mayhem, and he is capable of planning."

CHAPTER EIGHTY EIGHT

The next morning Lester called the police to see if he could visit his brother. The OK was given, but with certain restrictions. He had to be accompanied by a cop at all times, and the visit would be limited to fifteen minutes. Lester amiably agreed to the terms and later in the day arrived at the hospital.

Outside Peter's room Lester was frisked and made to empty his pockets. He was then accompanied into the room, where another officer was stationed near Peter's bed. Lester saw a nervous, sweaty, disheveled, and drawn Peter.

"How are you, little brother? You look tired." Lester said in an almost mocking tone.

"I'm OK, but keep that Geller away from me."

"Does he worry you?"

"He's always prying, asking me questions about missing children."

"Just don't answer him. Tell him to fuck off."

"I told him about the children."

"You're a fool. Just shut up."

Peter was worried, but after looking into his brother's eyes, he felt true fear. Lester's eyes were hard and cold. At that moment, Peter knew his big brother wanted him dead.

Lester quickly cased the room, casually eyeing the equipment, placement of windows, location of the bathroom, and proximity to the nurses' station. He would later find out that Peter had three meals delivered a day from the cafeteria, all checked by the police. His mediations were dispensed only by nurses and not aides. The police had a man stationed outside the room by the door and a man inside 24/7, both equipped with walkie-talkies and well-armed. This would not be easy.

On the ride back to his home on the lake, Lester started to formulate his plan. He had two choices, a long-range or short-range approach. Pros and cons would be considered. He would sleep on it.

CHAPTER EIGHTY NINE

I started to prepare for college. The summer was winding down, and I had about four days before orientation and a week before the start of the fall semester. I needed to buy some school supplies and start packing. A couple of loads of laundry were also a good idea, as I was down to my last pair of underpants. With some unsolicited help from my mother, I did several loads in her new washing machine, a Westinghouse, with all the bells and whistles. We didn't have a dryer, so we hung the clothes outside. Mom had a contraption in the backyard that looked like a huge umbrella and held much more than a clothesline.

"I know it's a lot of work, but everything smells so much better when clothes dry outside in the warm air," said Mom, rationalizing against a dryer.

After hanging everything I owned outside, praying it wouldn't rain, I went back inside to beg dad to use the car.

It was true that I needed school supplies, but the real motive for a trip into town was the car, a new red Pontiac Bonneville convertible. Dad picked the car and Mom the color, and I approved of their choices.

"Dad, I just have to run into town for some school supplies, sneakers, and t-shirts. Could I borrow the car? Pretty please."

"What about your leg, Bob?"

"It's fine, practically back to normal. You know I wouldn't ask for the car if I knew it was unsafe."

"I've heard bull like that before, but I think I'll trust you this time. Just make sure you're home for dinner." He threw me the keys.

As soon as I cleared the garage, I loosened the clips to the top above both front seat window visors and pressed the button that said "top." Automatically the canvas top lifted and started to fold backward into the recessed area behind the backseat. This accomplished, I was ready 'to cruise." While negotiating the driveway, I turned on the radio with my right hand, moving the knob until I heard Paul Anka singing "Diana." I cranked up the volume. Does it get any better than this?

In spite of my cool image, at least in my mind, I did drive slowly and carefully into the center of town and parked on the main drag near the drugstore at the corner of Main Street and Millburn Avenue. After picking up notebooks, pens and pencils, a pocket dictionary, and a thesaurus, I ran into two of my high school buddies, Dan Rosen and Lou Fried. After shaking hands and exchanging backslaps, we walked back toward my parking space.

"Nice car, Bobby boy. You must have made a bundle at camp," Dan chuckled.

"Kind of sporty for your dad, don't you think?" added Louie.

"Dad wanted black, Mom red. You see who has the last say in our house," I quipped. "Hey guys, if you're not in a hurry, how about a sloppy joe at the deli, and then I'll take you for a ride?"

It didn't take much coaxing, and we crossed the street to the Millburn Deli, the home of the best sloppy joe in New Jersey. It was not that chopped meat mixture on a hamburger bun, but a delicious triple-decker. We ordered three with Cokes to go. The sandwich was made with three thinly sliced large pieces of rye bread. The bottom piece was covered with Russian dressing, thin sliced boiled ham, thin sliced Swiss, and coleslaw. The next piece of bread was put on top, and the process was repeated. With a huge carving knife, the sandwich was cut into three sections and wrapped in wax paper.

Drooling, we took our stash to Taylor Park, just down the block. We sat on the lawn near the pond, eating and reminiscing. We talked about our summer and plans for the fall. Louie would be off to Cornell to study engineering and Dan to the U of Penn for pre-law. His dad was an attorney and would have liked nothing better than to have his son join the firm.

We just ate, talked, and soaked in the rays. We knew, regretfully, that we probably wouldn't see each other until Thanksgiving.

We walked back to the car, and true to form, Louie plopped himself into the backseat, lounging sideways as Danny, by default, inherited the shotgun seat. We made a beeline for Short Hills, the wealthy part of town.

Short Hills was very exclusive and was purported to be a restricted community, although it was never said. We all knew that Jews and Negroes were not welcome. The area was loaded with gorgeous, sprawling homes with lush lawns and manicured landscaping on old tree-lined streets with no sidewalks. It was an ideal enclave for the privileged and wealthy, with good schools, good real estate values, and proximity to New York City. The train station, across from the exclusive Racquets Club, was on a direct line to the city, less than a one-hour straight shot. Perfect for the Wall Street types and their wives, who could shop at Bergdorf Goodman, Saks, and Tiffany's on Fifth Avenue and then lunch at the Plaza or the St. Regis.

My parents were comfortable, but nowhere near this class. We were perfectly happy in Millburn.

***

We looked around the old parts of the "hills" near Christ Church and then headed into the reservation, hundreds of acres of preserved land between Millburn-Short Hills and the towns of South Orange and West Orange. It was a great place for picnics, ball-games, and fishing in the reservoir. There was even an area where kids could hand-feed deer. At night it was "the place" to park and make out, although the cops were cracking down and starting to spoil the fun.

On an elevated area overlooking the town of South Orange was a place called "Grunings," a hangout with unbelievable ice cream, sundaes, shakes, and floats. They had hand-packed ice cream in pint, quart, and half-gallon containers, creamy and rich, scooped out in gobs right in front of you, not like the store-bought stuff. The coffee ice cream was the best, no argument.

We couldn't resist, so we stopped for cones. I had a double dip on a sugar cone, one scoop of coffee and one of maple walnut.

"No way you guys are eating this in the car. My dad would kill me if we stained the upholstery. That's probably too kind. He would tar and feather me and then kill me." They chuckled, but I was serious.

It was great seeing my friends. Being away all summer and knowing that college was around the corner made this time together more special. I had known Danny and Louie since kindergarten, and we had gone to grade school, junior high, and high school together. There was real history here. We had played ball together, walked to school together, watched TV at each other's houses, and just hung out together.

We eventually finished our cones and had to call it quits. I drove the guys home, and we said a tearful good-bye, promising to keep in touch and see each other on holidays and school vacations.

***

I carefully eased the car into the garage, unscathed, thank God. Going up the cellar stairs, I heard my mom yell, "You had a phone call from Inspector Geller." She opened the door at the top of the stairs and added, "He won't be available today, but he wants you to call him in the morning. I have his number."

"What does he want?" I thought. I was getting paranoid, jumping at the mention of his name and frankly, I was tired of the Cartrights and the investigation. I wanted to see it all end.

"Mom, how much time 'til dinner?"

"About two hours. Why?"

"Thought I might do a light jog. The leg feels great and I need to exercise."

"Are you sure, honey? Don't push yourself. You're just starting to heal."

"I'm OK, Mom, really. I won't overdo it, but I need to work -up a good sweat."

CHAPTER NINETY

I put on a pair of shorts and t-shirt and headed for the high school, a half mile away. It had a quarter-mile cinder track, and I was able to do eight laps pretty easily. I toweled off and decided not to overdo it. My thigh was a little tight, so I started to walk home rather than jog.

About a block or two from home, a car approached from behind me, slowly as if on the prowl. I glanced subtly over my left shoulder and started to walk faster. The car sped up. I went into a jog, and the car kept pace. My pulse quickened, and I started to sweat. God, was it happening again? Was someone after me?

Making a snap decision I darted to the right and hurdled a hedge, sprawling on the guy's lawn. The car roared by with its horn blaring and a bunch of kids yelling, "Jock," while throwing an empty six pack of beer at me. I just lay there, shaking. I was becoming a basket case and this had to stop.

***

I pulled myself together enough to shower and dress for dinner. Mom had made a roast with mashed potatoes and gravy and green beans. She wasn't a gourmet cook, but she made "substantial" meals, which in my family meant it tasted good and there was plenty of it. You never left the table hungry.

Dad was the gourmet cook, but he never had the time to do more than dabble in the kitchen. He had great skills with a knife and an artistic flare. He loved to dine in gourmet spots and had tried a good many in the city. His food fetish extended to reading numerous cookbooks and experimenting on the stove. Mom was good, but I loved it when he cooked.

As we ate, mom said,

"I talked with George today, and he agrees with a memorial service for Lilly, low-keyed and just for the immediate family. The rabbi is willing to say prayers even though a burial almost forty years after a death is a bit irregular and probably violates Jewish law."

"That's big of him," I added sarcastically. The rabbi had officiated when I "became a man," and that counted for something, especially when you considered the distractions I had in 1954. That was the year my New York Giants made their run for the world championship of professional baseball. That year my team won the National League pennant with the likes of my heroes: Wes Westrum, Whitey Lockman, Alvin Dark, Monte Irvin, Bobbie Thompson (the hero of 1951 with "the shot heard round the world"), and the greatest player in the game, Willie Mays. Yankee fans always felt that Mickey Mantle was the best, but everyone else knew it was Mays.

They would have their hands full with the mighty Cleveland Indians, the winners of a record one-hundred-eleven games during the season, and arguably the best pitching staff in baseball with likes of Bob Feller, Bob Lemon, and Mike Garcia. They also had a couple of superstars in Vic Wertz and matinee-idol Rocky Colavito. The Giants were big underdogs, but what did those asshole baseball writers know?

My birthday was on October first, so it became painfully obvious that the World Series would be played around the time of my bar mitzvah, which was not a good thing.

I was too preoccupied to prepare my haftorah, which was my reading from the "great book." I had to prepare mentally for the series, and even school would interfere. My poor preparation, of course, was readily noticed by my Hebrew school teacher and the rabbi and those turncoats notified my parents, making my mother quite apprehensive. After all I would be reciting in front of hundreds of family and friends, and a poor performance would be a major embarrassment. My mother was a wreck, but I assured her that I would be ready (a big lie) and that I would pull it off.

"I won't blow it. I'll make you and dad proud, I promise."

"I just don't understand how you can be so blasé. Don't you care about your religion?"

"I care, Mom, but I'm just not a Hebrew student. I'm not motivated, but I'll do enough to get us through this. You'll see."

The Giants were sensational, sweeping the Indians in four straight, thanks to Willie Mays. He had made "The Catch," and the Giants never looked back. That catch, in game one, was one of the greatest happenings in my young life, second only to the greatest homerun ever hit, Bobbie Thompson's four-bagger off Ralph Branca of the Dodgers that won the pennant for the Giants in 1951. They had come back from 13.5 games down in September to win in a playoff and earn the right to play the Yankees in the series.

"The catch" changed my life and helped to make a success of 1954, still a hallmark year to this day. Mr. Willie Mays, with his back to home plate, raced full tilt to the deepest part of straightaway centerfield in the Polo Grounds and caught a towering drive off the bat of Vic Wertz that traveled almost five-hundred feet. He caught it over his shoulder without looking back. That was the greatest catch that I had ever seen made by the greatest player I had ever seen. That one play broke the hearts and spirit of Cleveland, and I was on cloud nine, but my haftorah was in the toilet.

I did, I am happy to say, get through my bar mitzvah, although my recitation from the Torah was a bit short. Thankfully few of my relatives noticed. All my aunts and uncles thought I was cute and had performed admirably. They stuffed my pockets with envelopes containing cash, and my aunts gave me wet kisses.

Unlike the lavish affairs of the nouveau riche, my parents had a simple Kiddush at the temple after the service, during which a blessing was made over the "wine," which was really Concord grape juice, and the bread. My father said the blessing over the bread and cut the challah into many small chunks to be eaten plain or with some pickled herring. My uncle George followed with the honor of blessing the ersatz wine, and I was welcomed into the congregation as an adult. The party broke up early and we all walked back to our house, only a block or two away, for the "reception." While the adults talked and noshed on various hors d' oeuvres and had real alcoholic drinks throughout the afternoon, I had a party with all my friends in our finished basement. We drank Cokes, ate chips, and danced to records on a jukebox that my dad had gotten second-hand.

When dinner was ready, my mother called us upstairs to join the adults for a buffet cooked almost entirely by my folks: brisket, noodle kugel, potato kugel, salad, sides of pickles and sour tomatoes, herring, smoked fish, and rolls.

The food was great, and everyone stuffed themselves, to the delight of my beaming mother. To top things off, Mom had a large birthday cake for dessert, chocolate with vanilla icing, ordered from a great local bakery.

During the cutting of the cake, I gave a short speech thanking all of my relatives and friends for my success and praising my parents for providing me with excellent values, love and encouragement, and making this a very special day. I was serious, but my friends giggled and thought I was sucking up. But it had been a wonderful day, a treasured memory.

At the end of the evening and when the table was cleared, my mother had everyone sign the tablecloth with a ballpoint pen. At first I didn't know why, and I wouldn't for many months to come.

My relatives and friends said their good-byes and wished me prosperity and good health. "Mazel tov," they said. Mom and dad were so proud; it had been such a memorable day and night.

A husband-and-wife team had come in to help with the serving, cleaning, and washing of the dishes, glasses, and silverware. Before leaving, they washed the kitchen floor, vacuumed the dining room and living room rugs, and put out the garbage. Dad thanked them for the help and wrote a check with a sizable tip. We were now alone, just the four of us.

"Mom, great party. I love you all." I thanked them profusely, kissed them all goodnight, and disappeared into my room to count the loot.

I threw all the envelopes on my bed, about twenty to thirty, and all I could think about was buying a baseball mitt at Modell's and a Giant's bat. What I didn't want to think about was writing dozens of thank you notes.

Months later I found out that my mother had hand-embroidered each signature of our guests and had the tablecloth dry-cleaned and pressed, and she has it to this day.

***

I batted my eyes and came out of my reverie.

"I spoke with the funeral parlor, and the director is going to contact the police in New York City, but I was hoping you would speak with Inspector Geller about it. You have to call him anyway."

"I'll ask, Mom. You can count on it. Can't see any reason that they would not release her remains."

"I want her buried with her parents in Brooklyn, as I told you."

"Do you have a plot?" I asked.

"Oh yes. Grandpa Miller had bought five plots in 1918 at a bargain price. He had such foresight."

This ended the rather maudlin discussion, and we went on to talk about college, which invariably led to the guilt trip about grades, my future, and not disappointing the family.

Mom was going down the path of the tradition of higher learning in our family. Everyone was a doctor or a lawyer or had a profession and not just a job.

"You would be wasting yourself and your education if you didn't become a doctor like your father."

"Mom, I'm planning on being pre-med, but there are many talented and educated people in this world who are not MD's."

"College tuition is a sacrifice for your father, so I just don't want you to fritter away your time at frat parties, playing poker, or shooting pool."

She was really laying on the guilt, but at least she didn't mention carousing with loose women.

The roast was fabulous, and I was stuffed. My sister and I cleared the table for dessert, maple walnut and black raspberry ice cream. I couldn't resist.

CHAPTER NINETY ONE

After dinner, I decided to call Jean, just two towns away in West Orange, but it already felt different away from the atmosphere of camp. Maybe a movie or a drive or vice versa, but I really wanted to see her. I dialed, and after twelve unanswered rings, I realized she wasn't home. I would try again, but maybe this was an omen. As it turned out, Dad had to make a house call and needed the car.

About ten minutes later the phone rang, and it was Jim Butler.

"How about a flick and a slice of pizza, Bobby-boy?"

"Have to check with mom. Hold on a sec."

"Mom, OK if I go to a movie with Jim? I won't be home late."

"Just make sure he drives carefully. You know how I worry about cars and speeding," she said.

"Great. Sorry to leave you, but I'll help with the dishes until he gets here" I responded.

"Jim, it's a go, thanks."

"See you in twenty minutes," he said, and hung up.

***

I loved going to the movies, and I always enjoyed Jim's company. We hit an avant-garde theater in Montclair where we saw a movie starring Brigitte Bardot, the French actress and the sex symbol of the fifties. Actually she could act and the movie was quite good, although I hate subtitles. We hit a pizza joint for a slice and I was home before eleven-thirty.

***

The next morning I reluctantly called Geller, who surprisingly was very pleasant and not the least bit intimidating. He actually wanted my help.

"Bob, I need to talk to you about Lester Cartright, not Peter. I think you might have some insight in an area that I have questions about. When would be a good time to meet? I'll come to you."

"Anytime, really. I have three days off before leaving for college orientation, so you name it."

"How about tomorrow at noon? I'll pick you up, and we'll go for lunch and a chat."

"That sounds fine."

"Good. See you at noon."

Just as Geller was about to hang up, I remembered my mom's request.

"Mr. Geller, I almost forgot. My mother wants a proper burial for her sister, and I'm checking to see if the police would release her remains to the funeral director."

"I don't see why not, but I'll check. I'll pull some strings and call your mother."

He hung up, and I ruminated. "What does he want to know about Lester Cartright?"

CHAPTER NINETY TWO

That night my sister joined us, and we all went out as a family to one of my favorites, "The Star," an Italian place in the Vailsburg section of Newark, the Little Italy of North Jersey. They had great Italian food, but their pizzas were to die for. Great crust and cheese that stretched" two feet" when you bit into the pizza. The pies were cooked in brick ovens with coal fires like in New York City and came out bubbling with perfect crust, black on the bottom. We ordered one large pie with extra cheese, sausage, and black olives. A family salad with an Italian dressing, olives, peppers, anchovies, and chunks of provolone completed the feast.

When the food arrived we attacked like starved savages. It was so good seeing my mother smile, my dad enjoy a night out without a call from the hospital, and my sister indulging in calories. I knew I would miss this in the weeks ahead, but I kept this thought to myself.

***

For the first time in two days my leg started to hurt, sort of a throbbing ache. Dad said it was healing well, but now I had some doubts. I excused myself to go to the bathroom, where I lowered my jeans and peeked under the dressing. The wound looked red and angry, a little tender to touch, but it didn't smell, and I didn't see any pus. I would have dad look at it later.

I washed my hands and pulled up my jeans, returning to the table as the waiter was packaging up the leftovers in a pizza box. Everyone looked stuffed, but dad managed a spumoni and coffee while mom finished off her tea. My sister and I clicked glasses and drained our Cokes.

***

We got home around nine, and Dad removed my dressing and checked the wound. It was swollen with red borders and had a sticky material in the center. There was a slight odor.

"Bob, I think it's infected, so I'm going to give you a shot and start you on an oral antibiotic. I have oral and injectible penicillin in my bag. Take a hot bath, and after, I'll redress it."

I did as he said and felt better. He took my temp - no fever. He gave me the shot of penicillin.

"I'm fine, Dad. Really I am."

"OK, but I want to look at it again in the morning."

"I'm not tired, I said, "so how about checking on the Yankee game?"

Dad was dozing by the time Mel Allen and Red Barker were recapping the seventh inning. I turned the TV off and woke Dad so he could go to bed.

"Goodnight, son. I'll see you in the morning."

In my room I decided to read until I felt exhausted. I propped up my leg on several pillows, and there was less pain and I tried to finish Salinger's *"Catcher in the Rye."* After an hour I turned off the light, but blissful sleep did not come and I tossed and turned. When I did finally fall asleep, I dreamed.

The dream sequences were so real and disturbing - vivid pictures of a young girl with blonde curls, her face bloodied and her eyes blank, lying in a shallow grave with me standing over her, weeping uncontrollably. And then everything turned dark with the figures becoming unrecognizable. Then I saw a hulking shadow, and the darkness lightened. Peter Cartright, eyes aflame and with saliva drooling from his mouth, was standing there with a bloody shovel in his right hand.

I was suddenly awake. I lay there for minutes, shaking until I got the energy to get to the bathroom. I urinated and then just sat on the toilet until I calmed. I took my temperature with the oral thermometer, still no fever. I washed my face with cold water and returned to bed, fearing sleep.

CHAPTER NINETY THREE

Lester Cartright made a call.

"We have to get Peter out of the picture. He's unraveling and has confessed to all the murders of the children. Eventually Geller will find out more, and Peter knows too much."

"Relax. Peter's an imbecile. All Geller cares about is the Lilly Miller case and the other abductions. He knows nothing of our dealings and could care less about your parents."

"I've been giving a lot of thought to this. I think the best approach is the IV, either potassium or insulin."

"Forget it. He's watched night and day. When one cop takes a leak or a break, the other takes his place in the room. He's never alone."

"Do you have any suggestions?" said Cartright.

"Yes, a bullet in the head from long range or poison in his food."

"Well I've checked out the room, the windows, and the surrounding area, and there is no place for a long-range shot."

"So the best bet is to get at his food or drink," said the voice at the other end.

"I'll check out the possibilities. I'll need something that's tasteless and odorless and not too fast-acting. Something that's hard to detect and readily accessible. Then I have to figure out how to get it in his food," said Lester.

"Getting it in his food is the easy part. I'll check his food tray each meal as a matter of security, and voila. No sweat." Lester's contact hung up. He knew that the tap on the phone had been removed after Peter's capture, but he still felt uneasy talking on an open line.

CHAPTER NINETY FOUR

Geller arrived at the Berman house a bit before noon. He was speaking with Mom and having a cup of coffee in the kitchen when I limped in.

"Hi Bob. Good to see you up and about. Thought we could go out for lunch and a chart."

"OK by me, but I don't know what I can tell you about Lester Cartright that you don't already know."

You'd be surprised at what people are able to offer when you ask the right questions."

Geller turned to Mrs. Berman and said,

"I called the medical examiner's office, and your sister's remains will be released to the funeral home tomorrow."

"Thank you, inspector. You have just made me very happy and have given me and my brother closure. I will let George and the rabbi know so we are able to plan the memorial service. We would be honored to have you attend."

After a few more minutes of chit-chat with Mom, we left for lunch and the interrogation, heading for Don's Drive-In, a great hamburger joint and hangout between Short Hills and Livingston, famous for its pizza burgers.

Over burgers, fries, and chocolate shakes, we talked.

"Bob, a while ago you told me about your suspicions of Lester Cartright and the strange happenings at camp. Let's take it one step further."

"What do you mean, one step further?"

"Well it's no secret that Peter is of limited intelligence, and although I think he is solely responsible for the murder of your aunt, I'm sure that Lester is involved in some way with some of the other disappearances and the mayhem at the camp, and I think you may be able to help me in that regard."

"How so?" I said. "I don't know anything more than what I told you before."

"Well I did some checking, and it seems that Lester has access to highway planning throughout the northwest corridor of New Jersey."

"I still don't see where I come in."

"Did you ever hear anyone mention Route Eighty?"

"Nope, I never heard of it."

"The word is that this highway will run from the Jersey side of the Hudson in Bergen County to the Delaware River near Stroudsburg, Pennsylvania. An east-west highway that would run right through northwestern New Jersey. Big bucks to the right people, I figure."

"You know, I remember my dad mentioned something about this. I think he even considered an investment near Lake Hopatcong, but for some reason it never happened."

"We'll come back to this, Bob, but first I want to know if you ever witnessed any hostility between Lester and Al Simmons?"

"No. Actually I thought they were kind of friendly. Lester did odd jobs for Al, and they seemed to get along.'

"What about Peter? Did he ever show up at camp with Lester?"

"No. I never saw him except at his house."

I took a bite of burger, the juices dripping down the sides of my mouth. I wiped with my paper napkin and took a gulp of shake. God it was good.

"Did you ever see Lester fix his truck or a car?"

"Yeah. I used to see him work on the truck a lot, and I know he changed the oil and fixed some problems on Al's car."

"What kind of problems?"

"Something was wrong with the brakes, and Lester was able to fix it. He's real good with his hands, a real good mechanic."

"See kid, you are a great help and you don't even know it," thought Geller.

I took another bite of burger and gulp of shake. What was Geller talking about? It helped him to know that Lester was good with cars?

"One last question, and then we'll concentrate on eating."

"Shoot!"

"Did you ever see Lester show violence or become uncontrollably angry?"

"Well I never saw him lose it, but he once caught me going through the cab of his truck one night, and his eyes were stone cold. He didn't lose his cool, but that stare was menacing."

"Thanks, Bob. You were a great help. Now let's eat; this place is great."

CHAPTER NINETY FIVE

"That Mr. Geller is such a nice man and I'm so grateful for what he did for Lilly and our family," Mom gushed.

"What did he do that was so great?' I said.

"He pulled strings to get her remains released to the funeral home. Now we can bury her, and she'll be at peace."

"Mom, she's been at peace for almost forty years."

"Stop it. Stop that kind of talk right now. You know very well what I mean, so don't be smart."

"Sorry, but you're so touchy."

"When you're ready to talk to me without some wise-guy remark, I'll go over the plans."

"I'm ready to listen. Honest," I said.

"I called the rabbi about the graveside service and burial. It will be in Brooklyn this Sunday," Mom said.

"That's a long trip from here. Maybe we should consider another cemetery."

"Don't ever let me hear you say that. We are not looking for convenience. She will be buried next to her parents."

I did not argue any further. When mom made up her mind, that was it. Case closed.

CHAPTER NINETY SIX

Geller made it to Queens by three-thirty, beating the traffic. Pouring himself a beer, he leafed through his mail. Elizabeth was working at the museum until six, so he had time before meeting her for dinner in the city. Something Italian would be nice. He'd call the "Grotta Azzurra" on Mulberry for a table. "Seven would be perfect."

The lukewarm shower eased his muscles, but his mind was going full tilt - the evil Cartrights, the missing children, the lure of big money. His neck muscles were still tense, and he tried to relax, rubbing his temples and closing his eyes, breathing slowly and deeply. His ex was right; he breathed cop and couldn't leave it at the office. Only Elizabeth gave him time away, and only she could pry his mind away from the next homicide.

He dressed in off-white linen slacks, loafers without socks (very Italian), and a teal Izod tennis shirt, carrying a blue blazer. At precisely six he pulled into the fire lane in front of the museum and awaited the lovely Miss Curry. He didn't have long to wait, but he did have to pull his badge as a patrolman tried to make him pull away from the curb. Before an argument could get started, Elizabeth arrived and winked at the patrolman, as she opened the car door and hopped in.

"Hi sweetie!" She leaned over and gave him a kiss on the cheek.

The patrolman reluctantly closed the door, and Geller pulled out onto Fifth Avenue to the blare of horns.

***

She was wearing a light blue sundress and white sandals without stockings, and she smelled great.

"How was your day?"

"Boy, that's real original," said Elizabeth.

"I meant to say, I was looking forward to dinner with you and hoped you were in a good mood and not too tired or out of sorts."

She smiled. "I'm feeling great, and I'm starved."

They drove to Little Italy, across Canal Street from Chinatown, and parked in a lot off Mulberry. It killed Geller to pay for parking and she knew it and had a silent laugh.

The "Grotta Azzurra" was an old standby, Italian-American with a flare. Two good glasses of a Barolo, and they perused the menu with no chit-chat, a concession to Elizabeth, who was all business. Finally Geller broke the silence but Elizabeth read on, almost salivating over the descriptions of fresh mozzarella, bubbling marinara, succulent chops, home-made pastas, and sweet clams.

"How's the job? Interesting or do you just dust old paintings all day?"

"Funny, Geller! Interesting day but I spent a lot of time just being oriented and learning the basic floor plan, which I thought I knew by heart. The place is huge, and the number of artifacts, sculptures, paintings, tapestries, costumes, weapons, and antiquities, is mind-boggling. I tried to sort and catalogue the inventory in my head."

"I thought you were just a maven on the impressionists."

"That's my interest, my narrow focus of expertise, but my department head insists that I have a feel for the whole museum. She assured me that after my week of orientation, I would spend most of my time with the likes of Monet, Renoir, Van Gogh, and the boys."

"And what were you up to all day?" she asked Geller

"Routine. Drove to Millburn to talk to the Berman kid. He told me that Lester had quite a way with cars, especially brakes."

Elizabeth paled. "You don't say."

The waiter arrived with bread and olives and looked Elizabeth up and down. He enthusiastically named and described a few additions to the menu, but Elizabeth had obviously made up her mind beforehand. Food was all she thought about, it seemed, and she appeared annoyed when Geller asked the waiter for a few more minutes.

"What's your problem, Larry? You've been looking at that menu for ten minutes. Do you need help?"

He acquiesced and motioned for the waiter who seemed relieved at the prospect of taking their order.

"I'll have the clams oreganata and the fresh grilled pompano puttanesca," said Elizabeth in her heavenly "I'm starved" voice.

"I'll have the grilled calamari and the shrimp scampi."

The waiter seemed to approve of the choices and started to leave.

"Oh, we'll take a bottle of a good soave, very cold and as soon as you place the order."

He cleared the glasses from the Barolo, put out white wine goblets before heading for the kitchen.

Minutes later he arrived with the bottle and proudly showed the label to Geller, who nodded his approval. He carefully uncorked the wine, wiped the lip of the bottle with a cloth, and poured a small amount for Geller to taste. Geller slowly swirled the wine by the stem of the glass, being sure not to hold the goblet part in his warm hand. He held the glass to the light, seemed satisfied, and then sniffed and took a slow sip - very good and perfectly chilled. He nodded and the waiter excitedly filled both glasses, noting Elizabeth's cleavage in the process. He set the bottle in a bucket of ice alongside Geller, covered part with a napkin, and departed for the kitchen and his other guests.

They sipped the smooth, dry, but fragrant wine and continued to talk. In short order the appetizers arrived and Elizabeth attacked, as predicted, like she hadn't eaten in a week.

"Don't you eat all day?"

"I try to but I don't always have time."

Geller just shrugged.

The calamari were delicious, grilled whole and served with lemon wedges and a garlic aioli with tarragon. He offered none to Elizabeth who was busy working on her clams, with no intention of giving him a taste. They were small, sweet cherrystones covered with breadcrumbs, garlic, and oregano and drizzled with butter and olive oil and then put under the broiler and served bubbling hot. A great beginning.

Geller was already feeling full and regretting the pizza burger and shake he'd had earlier. She didn't seem to notice his struggles, as she was busy sopping up the garlic butter from the clams with a chunk of good Hoboken Italian bread.

Finally she looked up and noticed his half-empty plate and said,

"You don't seem very hungry. What did you have for lunch, a monster corned beef sandwich or a huge burger and fries? Come on, "fess up."

"Why do I need an appetite? You're inhaling the entire table on your own."

"Don't change the subject. What did you have for lunch?"

"Just a small burger and a few fries. Nothing big."

She was ready to lovingly scold him about his eating habits when the waiter arrived to clear the dishes. He poured more wine and smiled approvingly at Elizabeth's cleaned plate.

"She like," he said to Geller. Geller just nodded, and a grin came across his face. He had a theory about women. Those who ate heartily with a wide range of tastes were often good in bed. They had an appetite for pleasure. Woman who picked at their food and ate little, in his opinion, did not like sex and were not adventurous in bed. Elizabeth proved his point.

The waiter scraped the tablecloth of crumbs, put out new silverware, and handed Elizabeth a fresh napkin.

"Any chance of you coming by the museum this week? We just obtained some Degas', on loan from the Louvre, and maybe you'll be inspired enough to contact your "agent" for tickets to the ballet."

"I'll think about it and let you know by the end of dinner."

The main courses arrived, smelling divine. The fish looked wonderful, and Elizabeth beamed. It was cooked to perfection, covered with a light sauce of tomatoes, garlic, capers, and black olives, and served with roasted potatoes and sautéed spinach.

The scampi were huge, grilled and served in a sauce of butter, garlic, lemon, and white wine over angel-hair pasta. The waiter came by with fresh ground pepper.

Geller just picked. It was delicious, but he had no appetite. Elizabeth, on the other hand, was having no trouble and was even eyeing his scampi.

"You go near this plate, and I'll put a fork through your lovely hand. I'm taking this home."

"Calm down. Don't be so touchy. I was just looking, and you're obviously not hungry. Besides if you take this home, everything in your apartment will smell of garlic." She smiled slyly over the rim of her wine glass.

CHAPTER NINETY SEVEN

The man sat at his desk and thought over what Lester Cartright had said. Things could be salvaged, but Peter had to be eliminated. There was a lot of money at stake here, and Peter also knew about the circumstances of his parents' deaths. Things could become unraveled, and the thought of prison for obstruction of justice, abetting a felony, and other charges did not appeal to him. Cops weren't treated well in prison. He and Lester had been friends since childhood and now were partners in crime, but no one had made the connection. He guessed that Geller had come close, but never put two and two together when he most likely looked at the photos in Lester's house. That one picture of him with Lester and Peter – he should have removed it when he had the chance. OK, he was fifty pounds lighter and had more hair, but the face was the same if you were looking. Geller had been too preoccupied with Peter and if he did see the photo, he didn't make the connection.

CHAPTER NINETY EIGHT

Lester racked his brain for an answer, the perfect poison. That was the decision he had made, poison Peter. He couldn't buy it or make it. That would leave a trail. He had to decide on the substance and then steal it. After all there were plenty of poisons and chemicals lying around the storage sheds and garages at work.

"Let me just think," he said to himself.

It came to him several minutes later - warfarin. The stuff they used to kill rats. They used to spread it in the warehouses and truck hangars. The rodents ate the shit, and it made them bleed internally. He also remembered that it didn't smell and he would try just a speck to see if it had a foul taste.

It was perfect. If it worked on Peter, the docs would think he was having complications from his wounds and surgery. Death would take time, and they would never connect it to him.

Once Peter died, case closed. No more surveillance, no more nosey cops. The camp may or may not open in 1960, but if it did, the intimidation would restart, and eventually Al Simmons would close up shop. The property would have to be sold, and he would wait for Route 80.

CHAPTER NINETY NINE

Several days later Geller wanted to wrap things up on the case against Peter Cartright. He had his confession and information on body locations, although he wasn't sure Peter remembered or told him everything. He had contacted the powers that be to start the legal proceedings to have Cartright committed for life to a facility for the criminally insane. At the same time the authorities were turning up some skeletal remains, but not all.

It was hot for early September, and there was major traffic in and out of the city. Because he had been uptown working a new case, he took the George Washington Bridge and inched his way, bumper to bumper, toward the Jersey side.

What the hell was going on? Didn't people go from Jersey to work in New York and not the other way around. His only solace was that the traffic was even worse going into the city.

He was sweating profusely, his underarms wet and his shirt sticking to him and the back of his seat. Patience was running thin. After an hour and barely off the bridge, he was in a pissed off mood. To make matters worse he now saw police cars up ahead with red-and-blue lights flashing.

"Fuck, an accident," he shouted. He beat on the steering wheel and then started to nervously strum his fingers while shouting obscenities.

He turned on the radio in time to hear the traffic report, an update on an accident on the Jersey side of the GW Bridge. "No shit," he yelled. "I'm living it."

Tempted to turn on his siren, he thought better of it and sat and waited. After all, sitting in a hot car in traffic wasn't any worse than seeing Peter Cartright.

***

Finally cars started to move, and he could see the tow trucks pulling two badly damaged autos away. Luckily there seemed to be no need for an ambulance.

Eventually hitting Route 46, it was smooth sailing and at sixty the breeze through the windows felt great. When he arrived in Newton he was a new man, ready to work and no longer pissed off.

When he got to Peter's room, there was chaos. Blood was everywhere. Peter was bleeding profusely from his nose and his Foley catheter, and he was vomiting.

"What the fuck is going on?" Geller screamed. "Did someone shoot the son of a bitch?"

"We don't know what happened. All of a sudden he started to bleed from everywhere," a cop yelled.

The doctors were working furiously, frantic to stop the bleeding while not knowing what caused it.

"Did the blood clot?" yelled one of the docs, a professional-looking, reed-thin man in a white lab coat.

"No. It's been almost ten minutes," said another physician, holding a test tube of blood.

"Call the lab for the protime results and get as much fibrinogen and blood up as we have in the blood bank."

They looked worried, as Peter's vital signs were unstable with a rapid, thready pulse and a low blood pressure.

"Don't waste your time and effort on this scum. Someone else may need the blood," yelled Geller. He had gotten most of the information from Peter, so if he died, no big deal.

The doctors gave him a dirty look and then ignored him and continued to work. The blood arrived and they hung two units, one in each arm. They asked the cops to wait outside.

"Protime is four times normal. What the hell is going on?"

"I don't know. He has a clotting problem, but why? Let's just continue the blood and give him fibrinogen and see what happens," said the doctor in charge.

Their efforts were rewarded, as Peter started to respond. First his nose-bleed lessened and his blood pressure started to rise and stabilize. His pulse slowed. It was still above one hundred but was fuller. He still looked gray and was sweating profusely, but his doctors now seemed optimistic. A stat hemo-globin and hematocrit were drawn.

Geller opened the door slightly and watched. Peter sure looked like shit - pale as a ghost and breathing hard, but looking better than when Geller first came in.

When a cop was within earshot, Geller asked, "Did they leave him alone any time over the last few days?"

"Not that I know of. He's been constantly watched day and night."

"Was anyone near him besides the cops guarding him?"

"No. Just the guard at the door and the cop inside. Several nurses checked him and also Parker stopped by numerous times and checked his security, food, and all that shit."

"Parker? What the fuck was he authorized to do?"

"I don't know. You'll have to ask him, but we weren't about to stop a state trooper."

"I'll just do that," responded Geller. "One last question. Was Parker ever alone with Cartright?"

"I don't know. Maybe our inside man went out to take a leak with a state cop there, or maybe Parker told him to take a break. It's possible, but I really don't know."

Geller ruminated. Parker visited several times in the last few days, and Cartright mysteriously started to bleed. He didn't believe in coincidences.

***

Geller stayed put as Peter started to respond. The nosebleed stopped com-pletely, and he was being given oxygen by mask. After another hour the exhausted medical staff looked satisfied, as Peter was stable. His hematocrit was twenty-four, his blood was clotting, and his vital signs were OK. Geller watched as the physician team wrote orders for the nurses and left. Then he moved in.

"Someone tried to kill you today, so listen up. Who wants you dead?"

"I don't want to die," Peter cried. "Help me."

He was pathetic, sobbing like a baby. "Peter, I have to know where the last body was hidden even if it takes all day. The search teams have turned up the remains of all but one child. Try to help me with the little girl from Hopatcong. Do you remember where you put her body? What you told me before was not correct." He added. "If you tell me the true story, I will protect you from harm."

It took less than thirty minutes to coax out all the details of the abduction, murder, and burial and Geller relayed the information to the police.

Peter was tiring but Geller persisted and asked: "Who tried to kill you; was it Lester?"

Peter just stared into space and didn't answer.

"Your brother knew about those kids you murdered, didn't he?"

"Some of them. I'm not talking anymore."

"And he protected you all these years?"

"I'm not saying anymore."

It took all of Geller's self-control not to pull out his weapon and put a bullet through the fucker's forehead. He turned off the small tape- recorder in his pocket. "I'll be back. You can bet on it. And just remember, someone tried to off you today. Think about it. Who would do that?"

CHAPTER ONE HUNDRED

The state police barracks loomed ahead, an ugly gray building on an equally ugly piece of land just outside of Newton. Geller hoped to confront Parker and parked in a slot that had "visitor" stenciled on the asphalt. He entered the building and was in luck. Parker was there.

"What can I do for you, inspector?" Parker said. Parker loved to call him inspector, especially in his condescending tone, just to be a pain in the ass.

"Heard you saw Peter Cartright today. How'd he look to you?"

"Looked OK to me. Why?"

"He almost died this afternoon. Some kind of bleeding problem."

"Is that so? What a pity. I thought the docs said he was all right, out of the woods."

"That was yesterday. Today he almost cooled it."

"No shit. Well, no big loss."

"What were you doing in his room? There was no reason for you to be there."

"Just wanted to check on his protection and condition. Why?"

Parker was very good. Cool as a cucumber.

"Just wanted to know why a state cop took such an interest in Peter's condition."

Before he could answer Geller said, "What's your take on Lester?" He wanted to see Parker's reaction to the question.

"Like what?" Parker responded.

"Like could Lester have been involved in Lilly Miller's murder or the other disappearances? Did he help Peter, or is he knowingly protecting him, an obstruction of justice?"

"How the hell would I know? You'd have to ask him yourself."

"That's what I intend to do."

***

After Geller left, Parker went out and drove to a gas station with a payphone outside. He dialed a number. It was answered on the second ring.

"Yeah, what can I do for you?"

"Get lost. Pronto."

Parker left the phone booth and got into his cruiser while Geller watched from across the street, unnoticed. "Bingo," Geller said to himself.

Once the state trooper's car was out of sight, Geller swung a U-turn and high-tailed it for Lake Spotswood, where the police presence was now absent. He stopped in Stillwater to talk to a few cops. Everything had been quiet.

"I need one of you to accompany me to Lester Cartright's place, to keep watch outside."

A young blond guy, eager to make points, immediately volunteered, and they headed down the road to the camp and Lester's house.

***

Geller knocked - no answer. He knocked again and again and still no answer. This time he yelled, "Lester." No response.

"I thought he is under surveillance. Can he just come and go as he pleases?" asked Geller.

"Can't say for sure. He's not under house arrest, but if he tries to leave we put a tail on him. We let up a little after his brother was captured," said the Stillwater cop.

"He could be home and is choosing not to answer but I think he's gone. I want to go in and search the place; I have a warrant. I need you to stand guard.

It was obvious early on that Lester had left undetected, but Geller still wanted to continue his search. He started in the shabby sitting room where his eyes were drawn to the black and white photographs. He looked at them again, a little more closely.

The photo of thin Lester and fat Peter in a rowboat piqued his interest. He saw something that he had barely made notice of before. There was a third boy, standing by the shore with a camera around his neck. He looked to be around Lester's age, and he looked familiar. Geller took the picture and held it up to the window for better light. The boy had a familiar appearance, but the distance from the camera and the fading of the photo over time made an ID impossible. He took the photo out of the frame and put it in his pocket to look at later with better light and a magnifying glass.

He decided to go back upstairs to look around Lester's room and go through his memorabilia in the cigar box in more detail. He went through all the newspaper articles and pictures again and found nothing new. As he returned the box to the bureau drawer, he noticed a book under some clothes. It appeared to be a yearbook. He pulled it out and perused the cover. It was dark blue with a white strip and had a tiger logo on it. The date was 1922. He opened the book, and there on the inside of the cover was a sticker that read:

"Lester Cartright – graduation -Newton High School - 1922."

Geller decided to look through some of the pictures. It was a small graduating class, so it wouldn't take much time. Under the C's, he found Lester's picture with the descriptive bio below it. "A real outdoorsman with great hands and can fix anything."

He continued to thumb through the book: pictures of the debating club, the French club, the basketball and football teams. More pictures and bios followed, and he was about ready to close the yearbook. As he turned the next page, his eyes inadvertently focused on a photo. He scanned the three by three picture and the name below it - Charles Parker, in bold black print. The face was now unmistakable, a young version of the handsome state cop. The bio said it all. "Great with rifles and pistols, an A-1 shot. Tough as nails whether playing football or wrestling."

Geller excitedly searched through the book until he found the pictures of the football and wrestling teams. There were Lester, the punter, and Parker, the linebacker featured under the composite of the team. Parker, it read, was all-county.

The wrestling team consisted of eight boys and the coach and student manager. Smiling in the front row were Cartright and Parker in wrestling singlets.

Geller closed the book with a faint sense of satisfaction. He knew Parker had called Cartright to warn him, and now he knew why. They had graduated high school together and had probably been friends for years. Could it be that they were partners in this scheme? They obviously were hiding their relationship, as they had acted like they didn't know one another during the investigation.

Geller reached into his pocket and pulled out the old photo. Now he knew the depth of what he was up against. The boy in the picture, the boy with the camera around his neck, was Parker.

He put back the yearbook where he had found it, and soon left the gloomy house with the young cop. He had a long drive back to Manhattan, but this would give him time to think.

CHAPTER ONE HUNDRED ONE

He called Elizabeth from his precinct desk while going through his memos and files. She was finishing up at work.

"I'll pick you up in forty-five minutes. How does dinner at my place sound? I'll cook."

"What are you planning to feed me?"

"Why? You'll turn me down if you don't like the menu?"

"No, but I want to know if I should eat the Milky Way in my pocketbook while I wait for you. I haven't eaten all day."

"Don't eat anything. We'll have pasta with a great meat sauce, and I'll improvise on dessert. We'll just have to stop on the way home for supplies. You'll meet my friends at my favorite Italian grocery. They'll love you."

"A deal, but what's the catch? It sounds too good to be true."

"After dinner you have to listen to my case and some interesting new developments. Wait 'til you hear the latest."

***

Geller picked her up at five forty-five, the traffic interminable. They crept toward Queens and finally reached the Italian specialty grocery he knew so well at six forty-five. Luckily he knew they were open until eight during the summer and early fall. He parked and they entered.

Elizabeth was beside herself as she took in the sights and smells of the cheeses, salamis, and olives. She could barely control herself as she looked in the case of prepared items: fresh artichokes baked with breadcrumbs, garlic, and olive oil, eggplant parmesan, homemade meatballs, mushrooms marinated in olive oil with fresh herbs, and many other delights for the senses and the taste buds. Geller seemed to know his way around and had headed immediately to the fresh meat counter. Elizabeth made a beeline to the cheeses and salami.

"Hey, Salvatore. How's it going?"

"Hey, lieutenant. Good to see you. It's been a while."

"Too long, Sal. I miss this place. I brought a special lady with me, but it looks like she's already making herself at home." They could both see Elizabeth at the cheese counter tasting multiple samples offered by an admiring counterman. They both laughed.

"I'll introduce her in a minute, but in the meantime I need a half pound of ground hot Italian sausage and a half pound combo of ground beef, pork, and veal."

"No problem. The sausage you'll love. It's my best. The other meat I just ground this afternoon."

While Sal was filling the order, Geller snagged a box of rigatoni, a large can of good Italian plum tomatoes, fresh basil, a head of Boston lettuce, a jar of dry red pepper flakes, a head of garlic, and a red onion and put them in his small cart.

"How's the cheese?" said Geller as he tapped a mesmerized Elizabeth on the shoulder.

"This place is unbelievable. How'd you find it?"

"We cops have our ways."

"The parmesan and provolone are incredible," she said as she offered him a small piece.

She was right; the small, nutty chunk of hard parmesan was incredible.

"Frankie, this is a special lady."

He introduced him to Elizabeth and then ordered a small wedge of a good gorgonzola and a chunk of grana padano. As he was turning to leave, he remembered the ricotta.

"Frankie, do you have any fresh ricotta?"

"Is the pope Catholic?" he said, and he disappeared into the back, returning with a stainless steel container filled with the rich, white, milky cheese.

"Fresh today, lieutenant." He took a scoop with a slotted spoon and let it drain."

"Enough or do you need more?"

"That looks good, Frankie."

The counterman put it into a small plastic container and then into a plastic bag before handing it to Geller.

"Don't be a stranger."

"Thanks, Frankie."

"Goodbye, miss. We expect you back even if he doesn't come," Frankie said to Elizabeth with a wink.

"I just have to get a bottle of wine," he said to Elizabeth, who was now sniffing porcini mushrooms. Sal had a small collection, but good stuff. He went into a small alcove in the store where the Italian wines were stored: barolos, chiantis, pinot grigios, valpolicellas, and soaves. He picked a medium-priced valpolicella and joined Elizabeth to pay for the haul.

Sal scurried around to the register and checked them out, bagging all the groceries himself, while Geller introduced him to Elizabeth.

"Delighted to meet you. Come back again any time. I'll have something special for you, maybe a little homemade Italian wedding soup." He winked at Geller.

***

Back at his apartment Elizabeth started to giggle.

"Did you hear Sal? Italian wedding soup!"

"Yeah, he thinks you're cute. Doesn't really know the real you."

"And what is the real me?"

"An absolute pig with an insatiable appetite. He thought you were cute, and all you cared about were the olives, artichokes, cheese, and mushrooms. When you see food, men don't matter."

"Is that so? Well even with a plate of eggplant parmesan and garlic bread in front of me, I would still look at you."

"I'll let Sal know."

He opened the bottle of wine and poured two glasses.

"You sit and watch. The maestro is about to perform."

He rolled up his sleeves and took out a large frying pan to brown the meat mixture. He heated some olive oil and added a clove of chopped garlic, red pepper flakes, and oregano, and then added the meat mixture that he broke up with a slotted spoon. Once the meat browned, he turned down the heat and added the can of tomatoes, breaking the large chunks with his hands, a pinch of salt and several grinds of pepper, and a little red wine. He turned the knob on the stove to simmer and partially covered the sauce with a lid. He then took a bow; Miss Curry seemed impressed.

"It needs about an hour. I'll throw a salad together, and then we'll sit."

"OK, but let me set the table."

"A deal."

While Miss Curry set the table, he cleaned and dried the lettuce and put the leaves in a large bowl. He added thinly sliced red onion, Tuscan peppers, black olives, and chunks of the incredible gorgonzola. He would add olive oil and red wine vinegar just before serving. He put the bowl in the fridge until dinner. His last chore was to fill a large pot with cold water for the pasta, adding a liberal amount of salt.

"Done. Let's sit."

"One last thing," said Elizabeth. "I'll grate that wonderful cheese," which she did.

***

They moved to the small living room and Geller turned on some soft music and lit a candle on the coffee table.

Elizabeth shook off her shoes, and he sat on the sofa next to her and poured more wine.

"Just take a deep breath and relax. Then tell me you're impressed."

"Geller, you never cease to amaze me. You're not only good-looking and good in bed, but you can cook!"

"Years of having to fend for myself."

She took a sip of the deep red wine and said,

"So tell me about the case."

"Well Peter, as you know, officially confessed to the murders of Lilly Miller and the other missing children. As we speak, the police are searching for the remains of one more child. This is no surprise, but what happened next is a stunner. Someone tried to kill Peter with a blood thinner and I think it was Parker from the state police."

"You're kidding."

"No, I'm dead serious. He had access to Peter's food and made several unauthorized visits to his room. Then I caught him calling Lester to warn him that I was on his trail. But best of all I found out that old Lester and Charlie Parker were good buddies and graduated high school together. How about that."

Elizabeth looked stunned, but managed to say, "Tell me more. This is exciting."

"Wait a sec. I have to check on the meat sauce."

Geller got up and went into the kitchen while Elizabeth perused his record collection. As she thumbed through his Sinatra, Tony Bennett, and Mario Lanza albums, he yelled from the kitchen, "Looks and smells great."

He stirred the simmering sauce and replaced the top, leaving a large slit to let off the steam. He turned on the flame under the pasta water and returned to the living room.

"Of course I have no proof. But I know that son of a bitch Parker's involved, and I'd stake my life on the hunch that he and Lester probably fixed our brakes."

"Why do you think they tried to kill Peter Cartright?"

"He was losing it and probably knew a lot about the dealings of Parker and his brother. Also, the doctors seemed stunned by Peter's sudden hemorrhaging and did not think it was a complication of his injuries or surgery."

***

They moved to the kitchen and he added the rigatoni to the now boiling water. "Ten minutes and we eat," he said as he added more wine to Elizabeth's glass.

He uncovered the meat sauce, removed the excess grease, and added two globs of ricotta. The fresh cheese instantly melted and thickened the sauce, giving it a smoother texture. He tasted it, added a pinch of salt, and announced, "Perfect."

He whipped up a quick vinaigrette, adding it to the salad and tossing. The pasta was now done, and he drained it in a colander and put it in a large bowl. He now added a large amount of the meat sauce.

"Let me help you," said Geller as he portioned a large scoop of pasta and meat sauce on her plate. He added the fresh grated cheese and a good portion of salad. She was salivating.

"More wine? He said.

"Please. But make yourself a plate, and let's eat. I can't wait."

And wait she didn't. She dove right in.

"This is fabulous. I mean really excellent."

"I can't take such adulation, just eat." He said, and she did.

CHAPTER ONE HUNDRED TWO

S he couldn't stay the night, as she had an important conference in the morning and needed to change clothes. On the drive back to Brooklyn they made plans for the weekend.

"How about a show and dinner on Friday? We'll stay overnight in the city, and if it's nice, we can drive down to the Jersey shore on Saturday. Pack for a couple of days and bring a bathing suit."

"How can I say no?"

Once at her apartment he parked, and they walked across the street, saying good night on the front steps. He waited until he saw the lights go on in her apartment and then went back to his car. As he drove off, a shadowy figure appeared in an alley-way, lit a cigarette, and looked up at Elizabeth's apartment window. He waited until the lights went out before he put out his cigarette and made his way across the street, careful to keep in the dark shadows to avoid the line of sight of the surveillance team he had easily spotted down the street.

The man moved like a cat and easily made it to the side of her building, where he cut the wires to the security system and picked the lock to the back entrance. Once in the building he stealthily made his way up the stairs to the third floor. He was breathing hard, partly from climbing three flights, but mostly from the excitement of the hunt. He would rough up the girl and terrorize her to send a message to Geller to back off.

He slipped a ski mask over his head and put on gloves before working on the lock to her front door - double-bolted and a chain. No sweat. Within fifteen seconds, he was in. Everything was dark and quiet.

***

Elizabeth was reading in bed and thought she had heard a slight click. She sat up and listened. Nothing. She turned off the light and lay down to try to sleep. A minute or two later she heard it, a definite movement in the hall. Panicked she quickly slipped out of bed and, with her hand shaking, locked the bedroom door. She then propped a chair under the knob and ran to the phone.

As she dialed, the door burst open with an ear-shattering crack. That's all she remembered. In a flash she felt an intense pain on the side of her head, and everything went black.

CHAPTER ONE HUNDRED THREE

She awoke groggy and disoriented, gasping for breath, frightened but alive. She started to cry, uncontrollable gasps at first and then sobs and whimpers. Her head ached, but she was too frightened to think about it. She looked up at the clock on her night table. She had been out for almost an hour.

She tried to get to her feet, but she was too unsteady. Fear gripped her again as she realized that her attacker could still be in the apartment. She crawled to the nightstand and pulled the phone to the floor. She got a dial tone. Thank God he had not cut the phone line.

"Operator, this is an emergency. I've been attacked, and the man may be in my apartment. Send the police, please. Please send the police. "Hurry," she cried.

"Give me your address and try to say it clearly."

Elizabeth told her the street and apartment number in between sobs. She was almost incoherent, but she was certain the operator got the message.

"You start to scream; wake your neighbors. I'll call this right in." said the operator.

"Please call Lawrence Geller of the NYPD," and she gave the operator the number.

"Don't panic. I'll take care of it."

She did not scream, but crawled to the bathroom and locked herself in. She would wait for the police there.

"Please, please don't come back. Leave me alone," she cried. She started to bang on the floor, but she was overcome with exhaustion and just lay there.

She rested for a few minutes and then tried to pull herself to her feet. She was able to hold onto the sink and groggily rose. She splashed cold water on her face and noted that the medicine cabinet door was open. She reached to close it, as she had to look at herself in the mirror to assess the damage.

As she closed the mirrored door, her heart missed a beat and she felt an intense wave of nausea. There on the glass, written in lipstick, was a message:

"Next time you're dead."

***

Geller arrived about a half hour after the Brooklyn Heights police. The place was crawling with cops and gawking neighbors. Numerous squad cars were on the street with blue and red lights flashing. The building was being cordoned off and neighbors were told to return to their apartments; they would be questioned later.

Inside the apartment, the police were managing the crime scene. Geller pushed his way into the foyer, flashing his badge, and reached Elizabeth, who was trembling on the sofa. He grabbed her in his arms and pressed her to his chest, stroking her hair and back to comfort her. She sobbed and he whispered softly in her ear to try to make her feel secure. She soon quieted, and he got her some water. He would stay with her for the night and then ream out the surveillance guys in the morning. He sat with her and held her hand while the police took evidence samples, dusted for prints, and checked the picked lock and broken chain. Once they had finished and completed their reports, he turned to her and in a calm, soothing voice asked, "Did you get a look at him?"

"No. He had on a mask."

"How about his height, weight, skin color?"

"It happened so fast, Larry. I couldn't tell you anything except he was big."

"Let's go to sleep. You need rest and not a lot of questions. We'll talk more tomorrow, but I promise, you will never be alone again."

The medics had arrived and checked Elizabeth's injuries, which appeared minor. They dressed her head wound and instructed Geller. She would be rechecked in the morning.

***

The big man removed his mask as he drove and threw it onto the highway. He had a long drive home, pleased with his night's work. Geller would get the message.

How wrong he would be.

CHAPTER ONE HUNDRED FOUR

Geller arose early and showered and dressed while Elizabeth slept fitfully. He saw the mirror in the bathroom and seethed. He vowed that he would get the SOB, no matter what. He knew he would also turn his anger on the surveillance team. They blew it.

He was sitting in the small kitchen, sipping the strong coffee, when a heavy-eyed Elizabeth staggered in.

"It smells good. May I have a cup?"

"Here, sit. I'll pour you some." Geller stood and helped her to the chair.

"Do you want to talk?" He said.

"All I know I told you last night." He wrapped his arms around her and tried to comfort her.

"I'm so sorry. I'm risking your life, and I put you in this position. I won't let you be unprotected again."

"Larry, I love you and want to be with you. You have become my life, but I'm scared."

"You know I'll do anything to keep you safe. As of today, I'm off the case. No more talk of the Cartrights, Camp Spenser, or missing children. I don't want to lose you."

"I'm terrified, but I don't want you to quit the case. You're a cop. It's your life and it's in your blood, and I don't want to force you to change on my account. Just protect us. We are too out in the open and vulnerable," she said.

"I'll get dressed. I want to go to work. It'll be good for me, and I don't think he'll risk an attack in the Museum of Art," she added.

"I was going to call your boss to get you excused from your conference, but if you want to go to work, it's OK with me. I will have a cop keep an eye on you at work, and I want a doctor to check you out after you're done."

"I can deal with that," she replied.

"Go get ready. I'll drive you to the museum, and we'll talk more. This was too close."

Elizabeth was right. He couldn't throw in the towel, and he couldn't be intimidated by felons. But he had to give her better protection.

CHAPTER ONE HUNDRED FIVE

"Hello. Town clerk's office."

"Hello, Stella. This is Larry Geller. It's been a while since we talked, and I wanted to thank you for all your help."

Her mood brightened as she heard his voice, and she sat up straight at her desk and primped her hair. "And what can I do for you on this gorgeous day?"

"I need a small favor, some information that I'm sure you will be able to supply, but I hate to bother you again.

"Oh, it's no bother. It's been quiet in these parts since Peter Cartright was captured, and a little help on police matters will be a welcome diversion from my routine tasks."

"I wondered if you could check realty records to see if either Lester Cartright or a Charles Parker purchased any properties away from Spotswood over the last five years. I'm especially interested in purchases as far away as Lake Hopatcong."

"I'll do my best. I'll start on it right away. When do you need the information?"

"I don't know. I'll be up in a few days. Maybe forty-eight to seventy-two hours, if that's OK."

At this thought, Stella brightened.

"One other thing. The purchases may have been made under a company name or even an alias. Just see if there's a pattern. Properties don't seem to move much in this area."

"Got it."

"Great Stella. I owe you lunch." He hung up.

His next call was to the hospital. He told the nurse on the floor who he was and that he had to speak with one of Peter Cartright's physicians, either the internist or the surgeon. She paged both.

Within a minute Dr. Brady, the head physician on the case, came to the phone.

"Dr. Brady, this is Inspector Geller from the NYPD. We've met before, but now I need you to answer some questions about Peter Cartright."

"Mr. Geller, you know I may not divulge confidential information about my patient, even to the police."

"This is not confidential information that I need. I just have questions that are medical in nature, generic-type questions. I'll only take a few minutes of your time. I know you are very busy."

"I'll come right to the point," said Geller. "Could Peter Cartright's bleeding episode that nearly killed him have been caused by some sort of medicine, chemical, or poison?"

"Yes," said Brady guardedly. "Why do you ask?"

"I have reason to believe that someone wants him dead, and your medical team seemed stunned by the unexpected bleeding."

"Well any blood thinner would cause this- heparin or Coumadin. Heparin has to be given IV or by subcutaneous injection, and Mr. Cartright was watched constantly by the police. Coumadin, on the other hand, is given orally, but a layperson would have no access to it except by prescription unless it was stolen from a pharmacy or hospital."

"Why does the name coumadin ring a bell?" Geller queried.

"It is also known commercially as warfarin, a common poison for rats and mice."

"Bingo!" Geller said to himself. He remembered the super at his apartment building using it and asking him if he had a dog or cat. He didn't want any pets in the basement to be poisoned. He only wanted to kill mice.

"Doc, could someone have put warfarin in his food or drink? Would he taste it or know it was there?"

"Probably wouldn't taste it, but it would depend on the food or drink and the amount of the dose. If the food had a sauce or was spicy or aromatic, the chances are he would not taste or smell it. But it would take a large dose over time to cause this as he's a big man."

"How would you know if it was warfarin that caused the bleeding?"

"It would cause a marked elevation in a blood test called the prothrombin time. Other clotting parameters would be unaffected."

"Was Cartright's prothrombin time elevated?"

"Yes, it was. It was three to four times normal, but luckily we were able to reverse it.

Tell me, is warfarin readily available? I mean, you don't need a prescription to use it on rats, do you? I'm talking about the raw products and not a pill.'

"Sure. Any garden and lawn place, nursery, barn, water and sewer department, highway maintenance department, or food warehouse would have it readily available. Any place with a rat or mouse problem."

"Thanks, doc. You've been most helpful. I appreciate it."

***

Stella Williams hit pay dirt almost immediately. It seemed Cartright and Parker had been very busy over the last five years. They bought eight properties at bargain basement prices in Sussex County in almost a straight line from east to west. Interestingly all the purchases were handled by one realty company: "Properties Unlimited." It was not difficult to find out about "Properties Unlimited." It was a legitimate company that filed taxes yearly and was owned by LC and CP Real Estate. This meant little to Stella Williams, but it would mean a lot to Lawrence Geller. She would relay the info.

CHAPTER ONE HUNDRED SIX

In his apartment Geller showered and was sitting having a beer, looking through his mail, when the phone rang. He picked up on the second ring.

"Inspector, Stella Williams. I have some things of interest. Our boys have been quite busy." She relayed the info on Properties Unlimited.

Geller was beside himself - LC and CP. Lester Cartright and Charlie Parker. How perfect.

Before he could remove his hand from the receiver, the phone rang again.

"Hi, hon. How's your day?" said a calmer Elizabeth.

"So-so, but I'm making progress on nailing Lester and Parker."

"I have to get to a meeting, but could we go to Little Italy tonight. They're having a street festival, and I'm dying to go."

"I'll pick you up at seven."

"See ya." The phone went dead.

***

Geller parked across from Elizabeth's building and got out of the car, but before he could cross the street, Elizabeth came bounding out the front door. They met in the middle of the street and kissed lightly. Then holding hands, they went back to his car. As he was helping her into the passenger's front seat, he noticed the inconspicuous car down the street pulling away from the curb. Something about the car didn't seem right. It was moving too fast. As he took her arm, he glanced over his shoulder and noticed a glint of light. In an instant he made out the form of a gun barrel protruding from the driver's window.

He grabbed Elizabeth and dove to the sidewalk. Two shots cracked on the concrete. He felt shards hit his face and forehead, but no pain. Elizabeth didn't have time to react and was lying under him unhurt. He heard the screech of tires and saw the non-descript gray sedan hurtle down the street.

The next thing they heard were two plainclothes cops running toward them, panting, with panicked looks on their faces. Before they could speak, Geller yelled,

"Call it in right now- a late-model gray Chevy, four-door, with Jersey plates. Single occupant: male, Caucasian. Close the bridges. Go, go."

He turned back to Elizabeth, who was shaken but now standing near the car. She seemed unhurt except for some scrapes on her arms from the fall. Thank God, no bullet wounds. Fear and bewilderment were in her eyes.

"Come on. Let me take you upstairs," he said as he watched the two cops calling in the APB.

Upstairs he sat Elizabeth on the couch and went to the cabinet in the living room to pour her a small brandy. She took the glass and stared at the shimmering liquid and took a small sip, wincing as she swallowed the bitter, acrid liquid.

Geller kissed her gently and then went to the bathroom to get some antiseptic and cotton to clean her scrapes.

"It's my fault. I've put you in harm's way again, and this is going to end tonight. We'll get this guy."

"Larry," she said, "I'm scared to death."

"I know, baby, and I have to find a fool-proof way to protect you until we get all the bad guys. We will get this guy tonight, I promise."

After cleaning her scrapes he called headquarters and spoke to the dispatcher for an update on the car. "Nothing yet," said the dispatcher.

"They blocked the Brooklyn Bridge and have a net at the Manhattan and Williamsburg Bridges, and they're patrolling all exit routes and tunnels."

"Keep looking. Block every road out of Brooklyn, and call me if you get anything." He gave him Elizabeth's number.

***

Geller stroked Elizabeth's hair and held her hands. She seemed more startled than scared.

The phone suddenly rang, surprising both of them, and she almost flew off the couch. He quickly grabbed it.

"Geller here."

"They found the car, no perp. He must have had a getaway plan or another car."

"What about the car? Rental or stolen? Any registration?"

"Stolen. Reported missing by the owner three hours ago. It's being dusted for prints as we speak."

"He too smart to leave prints. In the meantime call the Andover-Stillwater police and the state police in Newton to check on the whereabouts of Lester Cartright and State Trooper Charles Parker. Get people out to the Cartright house and the state trooper barracks. See if anyone is missing. If they return find out where they were, and check odometers. My bet is on Charlie Parker."

"It's good as done," said the dispatcher.

"Put out a description of Parker: six feet two inches, blond, in his mid-fifties but well-built and fit. He is armed and dangerous."

"Got it." He hung up.

***

Geller went into the kitchen to make a pot of coffee. It was going to be a long night. In the morning he would look for the slugs and any other evidence.

He looked in from the kitchen and found that Elizabeth was starting to doze off.

He needed coffee even though he was jacked up, his nerve endings raw. As he was pouring, the phone rang and Elizabeth was startled awake.

Geller ran into the living room and grabbed the phone on its second ring.

"We may have him," the dispatcher screamed almost uncontrollably. "A cop saw this guy running toward a car parked near the bridge. He followed him and ran the plates. Guess what? The owner is a state cop, Charles Parker."

"Get him." Geller screamed.

"We're after him as we speak, and we have four squad cars closing in from all sides."

"Don't lose him and take him dead or alive. If you have to, shoot the fucker in the balls." Geller hung up.

CHAPTER ONE HUNDRED SEVEN

With sirens blaring, the four police cars were closing in on Parker. He made a sharp turn away from the bridge, tires squealing, and headed northeast toward Queens. The chase headed up the Brooklyn-Queens Expressway toward La Guardia Airport at eighty miles per hour. Parker really had no place to go. He figured he had three choices: keep going and hope for a miracle, surrender, or stop and shoot it out. He instinctively put the pedal to the floor. He was going out in a blaze of glory. Hell, he was now wanted for two attempted murders.

He was barreling ass now, missing cars by inches, his horn blowing. What a wild scene this was. He was screaming obscenities, totally out of control but loving it. As he approached Queens Boulevard, he lost it, and the car went out of control and hit an overpass concrete column at ninety miles per hour. The car virtually disintegrated and Parker was thrown through the windshield, probably already dead before he hit the pavement one-hundred-fifty feet ahead. The scene was horrific.

By the time the squad cars arrived with lights flashing, flames and the odor of gasoline and smoke were everywhere.

Several cops cordoned off the area with police tape, while another cop called for an ambulance and fire truck. The others ran to look for what was left of Charles Parker.

Homicide arrived as the gawkers were appearing from the side streets, bars, and alleys. Everyone likes gore, and this was one hell of a scene. Debris, blood, glass, fire, and flesh were everywhere.

What was left of Parker was covered with a sheet. The fire truck arrived and started to douse the car, creating more acrid smoke. On-lookers and cops started to cough and choke as the fumes reached their lungs. But no one left. Then there was more action, as radio and TV vans started to arrive at the scene.

"How do they find out so soon?" one cop said to the other as they saw the media arrive.

"Beats me, but they always get here first, sometimes before us."

"Must listen in on our police band," said the first cop.

***

Geller was pacing when the call arrived.

"The perp's in pieces on Queens Boulevard. Hit an abutment at ninety miles per hour."

"I want a full briefing from homicide when they're finished at the site plus a positive ID."

He wanted to be there, but there was no way he would leave Elizabeth.

"Sweetheart, the guy who shot at us is dead. He was probably the one who attacked you. He will never bother or intimidate you again. Do you understand me?"

She seemed in a trance, and he just put his arms around her and let her cry on his shoulder.

CHAPTER ONE HUNDRED EIGHT

Lester was in the Newton area, but undetected. He was sure no one had followed him. He was holed up in a small motel on the highway, his truck parked out of sight in the back, waiting for Parker. He was two hours late for their meet that night to discuss Peter. Parker had seemed preoccupied that afternoon and said he had to attend to some business. It was now two in the morning and it was not like Charlie to be late. He decided to wait a few more hours and if he didn't show he would go down Route 46 to an all-night diner for breakfast and then sleep in the truck.

Bored, he turned on the TV. At this hour most of the stations were off the air, leaving either a "snow screen" or the channel test pattern. However, channel eleven had some local news from the tri-state area, as the Yankee game from the west coast must have recently ended. He listened inattentively, his mind wandering, when he heard the late-breaking bulletin.

"A police chase in Queens ended in tragedy this morning as a devastating crash lead to the death of one man," stated the reporter in a monotone.

The camera panned in on the horrific scene. The reporter stood with a microphone in hand, while in the background a smoldering car could be seen, or what was left of it. The police could be seen carrying a body wrapped in a sheet stained with what was probably blood.

The reporter went on to say, "There are few details at this time, but the station has a reliable source who stated that the deceased was a state trooper from New Jersey, a Charles Parker. This is unconfirmed as the police are withholding information until notification of next of kin."

Lester froze. He gazed at the screen of the small TV in disbelief.

The reporter continued, "A reliable police source stated that the deceased had tried to shoot Lawrence Geller of the NYPD and his companion, Elizabeth

Curry, just hours before. We have no further details, and the reason for the attack on Geller and Curry is unknown."

"You crazy mother-fucker asshole," he yelled at the TV. "Why did you do it, you dumb prick? Terrorizing Curry with the break-in was enough. Why did you have to go off half-cocked to try to kill Geller? Well you paid the price, didn't you."

Lester slammed the off button. Parker was expendable. It just meant dealing with Peter alone.

***

Before Elizabeth arose, Geller spoke with the precinct dispatcher, who confirmed that Parker was the perp. He then called Newton Hospital to check on Peter's condition.

"Alive and breathing, unfortunately," came the reply from one of the cops guarding the room.

"Any word on Lester's whereabouts?"

"Still missing, but a team is looking. He can't get very far, and he'll never get near this room."

"Keep your eyes and ears open. He may still make a move to eliminate Peter. If he's behind all this, he may get more desperate."

CHAPTER ONE HUNDRED NINE

In spite of his troubles, Lester slept fitfully in the cheap motel and awoke early with a clear mind. He had already formulated a plan.

He left the motel at seven and headed for a diner for breakfast. Seeing a local police car in the lot, he decided not to risk it and continued further down Route 46. The day was overcast, and it was already warm and humid. About two miles down the highway he spotted a pancake house and pulled off the road. He parked in the back so that his truck could not be seen.

At the counter he had a full stack of buttermilk pancakes, bacon, and hot black coffee. He slathered the pancakes with soft butter and maple syrup. Not only was he awake and alert, but his senses were keen and his appetite voracious. His plans for the day exited him.

***

Stuffed, he paid the bill and got coffee and a donut to go. Back in the truck he re-evaluated the plan in his mind and smiled, he liked it. In the glove box was a .38 revolver, stolen from a gun shop several years ago and untraceable to him. It was clean, oiled, and loaded, with an extra box of ammo next to it.

By nine AM he reached Newton Hospital, parking several blocks away on a side street. He put on a baseball cap and pulled it down to partially obscure his face, affording some protection from recognition as he walked slowly toward the hospital.

He clutched the handgun as he entered through the ER, not risking the main entrance, and walked to the stairwell. He went down two flights to the basement, being careful to avoid hospital personnel. If stopped he would act the part of a lost visitor.

He finally found what he was looking for, a storage area for emergency vehicles. It was loaded with gas cans, rags, and oil containers, all against fire code. The area was empty, and he slipped in quietly. He worked quickly gathering rags, soaking them with gasoline, and scattering them near a wooden desk loaded with papers. He poured more gasoline over the floor and on an emergency vehicle. He recapped the gasoline cans, put them back in their original locations, and then surveyed his work. He was satisfied.

As he turned to leave, he casually struck a match and threw it into the room. The inferno was something to behold.

Wasting no time, Lester quickly ran to the stairway and headed to the main floor. He went to the gift shop and purchased a small vase of flowers and a newspaper, making him look like an ordinary visitor. He made his way to the second floor, sat in the reception area, and waited.

He tried to look inconspicuous, reading his paper, but his heart was going a mile a minute. Soon all hell would break loose.

***

Within minutes, as if willed by Lester, fire alarms started to blare. This caused an immediate response and fire doors were shut, elevators evacuated, and the fire department automatically called. The nurses' station became animated as they followed procedure and started the evacuation of patients, the elderly and seriously ill first.

Lester could now smell smoke and hear the distant sound of sirens. He had to move fast and time was of the essence.

The hospital had four stories above the basement. The top three floors housed patients, and the staff started moving them in response to the emergency. Orderliness deteriorated to chaos as people saw and smelled smoke and panicked. Screams and cries rang out, and ambulatory patients and visitors ran toward the stairwells, trampling all in their way, in spite of the appeals for order from the staff.

On the second floor Lester stayed in the recesses of the waiting area as nurses, aides, and orderlies rushed from room to room. Sooner or later the cops would emerge from Peter's room to help, and Lester would be ready.

As if on cue, the door to Peter's room opened, and the two cops on guard ran to the nurses' station to check out the situation. Lester would have only minutes before they would return to move Peter. He acted rapidly and slipped into the room. He moved to the hospital bed and looked into Peter's eyes. With a sardonic smile, he said, "Good-bye, little brother."

He raised his .38 and slowly aimed between his brother's eyes. Peter was sobbing but made no effort to move. Lester slowly started to squeeze the trigger.

"Hold it, asshole. Put down the gun, slowly, or you're a dead man."

Lester turned and saw a cop with his police revolver in hand, pointed straight at his head.

"It's a Mexican stand-off. What do you think we should do, copper?"

"I think you're fucked. Just put down the gun."

"No. If you shoot, Peter's dead."

"No. If I pull the trigger," the cop said, "you're dead, and if Peter gets it, who cares?"

"Geller will care. He wants to keep my brother alive. He loves to hear his sordid stories of murder."

"I don't give a shit about Geller. I'm giving you five seconds to put that gun down or I shoot." "One, two, three."

As he was about to reach four, Lester started to lower his weapon, and the cop relaxed for an instant, a big mistake. Lester suddenly turned and fired from his waist, two quick shots tearing through the cop's skull just above the ear and his neck, severing the carotid artery and jugular vein. He fell and was dead within seconds of hitting the floor. Before Lester could pivot and fire on Peter, now hiding under the bed covers, two cops came in firing. Lester was hit in the left ear, throat, back, and right arm. His body went into a spasm, creating a jig-like dance, before hitting the floor. The spasms continued, and he lost control of his bladder and bowels. In a final gasp he coughed up blood and then fell silent. A pool of sticky blood formed around his body. The two cops knelt down and felt for a pulse. There was none.

Peter was hysterical, trembling and babbling like a frightened toad. He had survived a murder attempt, and now he watched in horror as his brother lay dead on the floor.

CHAPTER ONE HUNDRED TEN

Geller couldn't believe the phone call. Lester was dead trying to kill Peter. He wanted to get to Newton, pronto. He had to check out the carnage in person.

When he reached the hospital fire trucks and ambulances were everywhere. The smell of smoke was strong in the air, and everything was covered with soot. Some semblance of order was being restored by the hospital staff as patients were being ministered to on the lawn and fire-fighters worked to limit water damage and evacuate the smoke.

Geller walked rapidly to the second floor, where police were swarming like flies. Peter's room had been cordoned off, but Geller stooped under the tape and entered the room. Blood was everywhere; it looked like a grenade had gone off. Lester's body, riddled with bullets, was being removed to the morgue while the forensic team was examining and photographing everything.

"Are you guys done?" Geller asked.

"Just about, Larry," said one of the cops from Geller's team.

"I just want to talk with Peter for a few minutes."

"The doc checked him out and he has no injuries from the attack, but he's pretty shaken up."

Peter had been moved to an adjoining room and was in bed, clutching a sheet and rocking mindlessly. He was a basket case.

"Hello Peter. I guess you saw what your brother thought of you. He tried to off you, for Christ's sake."

No response.

"Why did your brother and Parker try to kill you? What did you know that they were afraid of?"

"They killed my parents. The suicide stuff was bullshit."

This revelation was not unexpected.

"Why did they kill your parents?"

"They were bad people and deserved to die. They beat me and put me in the basement, and called me sick and stupid. And my father was a drunk."

"Why didn't you kill them? Why did Lester and Parker do it?"

"I wanted them to love me, but Lester hated them and didn't want them to live."

"Why did Parker help?" asked Geller.

"He was Lester's best friend, and he liked hurting people."

"What about Lester's scheme with Parker to buy up property near the lake?"

"I don't know too much about it. I really didn't understand what they were doing, but Lester wanted everyone to leave the lake. He wanted to get rid of them all. He scared the boys at Camp Spenser and let me have fun with that little prick counselor and his girlfriend."

"Tell me more about why he and Parker bought the land."

"All I know is that they knew that a big road was coming and he would get offered a lot of money for the land."

"Did Lester and Parker plan to kill any of the campers?"

"I think so. I really don't know for sure, but I think so."

Geller breathed a sigh of relief. At least the boys from Spenser were home, safe and sound.

Geller stood and turned off the recorder that was previously set up. "I'll be back soon and we'll talk more. You'll be safe now."

CHAPTER ONE HUNDRED ELEVEN

He called Elizabeth to tell her the news. He would be home in a few hours. As he drove toward the city a wave of exhaustion covered him like a very heavy cloud. He had not slept well in days, and the frustration and tedium of extracting the details from Peter was tiresome and sad. All he wanted now was a shower and change of clothes, as if trying to wash off the blight of the Cartrights.

He reached the tunnel by five, and although most of the traffic was going the other way, he still found the going slow. He went straight to headquarters rather than his apartment. He kept a change of clothes there, and he could shower and shave in the locker room. Elizabeth was in a conference, but he left a message that he would pick her up at the Fifth Avenue entrance at six forty-five.

***

Elizabeth was waiting for him as he pulled up. As usual she was a picture of loveliness. She hopped in and gave him a peck on the cheek, which temporarily elevated his mood.

"Rough day? You look bushed, but you smell nice," she said.

"Just the usual. I spent the day looking at a bloody murder scene and listening to a sicko. I need a drink and a good meal."

"That should be no problem."

"On a good note, the case is just about wrapped up. I have all the details of the killings, and Parker and Lester are dead. I just have to get Peter committed for life."

CHAPTER ONE HUNDRED TWELVE

They settled on a great Greek place in midtown and had moussaka and lemon chicken with salads loaded with Greek olives, onions, feta, and oregano. They had a nice chilled white wine and finished the meal with bitter coffee and retsina. Elizabeth was mellow and satisfied, and Geller felt renewed.

"How about a walk? It's a beautiful night."

"I could use it. I've been driving all day," he said.

Geller paid the bill and they left, arm in arm.

***

Once they were back in her place, they took a long bath and then got into bed and just cuddled. He fell asleep in Elizabeth's arms, absolutely spent.

***

Meetings with the state attorney general lead to a grand jury indictment, and Peter was eventually committed for life to a maximum security institution for the criminally insane. The remains of all the murdered children had been found and they all had received proper burial. It was over.

CHAPTER ONE HUNDRED THIRTEEN

The service for my aunt had been touching and simple, and my mother found solace in knowing what had happened to her sister and that she would rest in peace next to her parents. The rabbi, my father, Uncle George, and I said prayers for the dead. Aside from the immediate family, Mr. Geller and Miss Curry attended, which touched my mother deeply.

"Thank you so much for coming today, Mr. Geller, Miss Curry. I also want to thank you for your efforts to bring my sister home. My family will be forever grateful."

"You should thank your son. He helped us a great deal."

"Bob is a good boy. I'm very proud, as you can imagine."

Surprisingly my mother did not mention the Cartrights and did not seem bitter or angry. She seemed at peace.

Epilogue

My freshman year did not start out memorably. Against my parents' advice, I rushed a fraternity and got in with a group of card-playing, pool-shooting, beer-drinking juniors and seniors. Luckily, freshmen could not live at the frat house, and I had to stay in a freshman dorm, which, in retrospect, probably saved my first semester.

I spent as much free time as possible at "the house" but at least spent some time studying at night, though not enough. My grades suffered, prompting a visit from mom and dad after mid-terms.

"Buckle down and study or no more fraternity." said my unsmiling dad.

"Dad, I barely started school. I'm on top of things."

"Bob, if you felt it was so important to pledge this fraternity, then make dean's list or you're out."

I knew he meant it. I would try to clean up my act.

Jean came up for homecoming, but our hearts weren't in it, and when I took her to the bus station for her ride home, we knew it was over. She had her life as a senior in high school, and I was moving on. It was different, we weren't at camp.

"I had a great time, Bob. Your friends are sweet. It makes me look forward to college."

"Glad you had fun."

"Have a great year, and enjoy your new life. I'll always remember you as my first love."

"Jean, I don't know what to say."

"You don't have to say anything. We both know it's over, and that's OK. We are too far apart, and we're in different places in our lives.

***

Later that week I received a letter. I didn't recognize the return address, but the handwriting was that of a young person and looked familiar. I tore the envelope open with a feeling of anticipation.

My heart rose. It was from Danny Golden, and as I opened the letter, a photograph fell out. It was Danny holding a huge large-mouth bass.

Dear counselor Bob,

Well I'm back at school and loving it. I feel like a new person. I feel so confident. I'm even popular. And I haven't had an asthma attack since I left camp.

My family and I want to thank you for giving me such a wonderful summer. I was a little scared when I got there, but you made all the difference. You are the best counselor, and you made me feel important, even special.

I will always remember you, and I hope we will meet again. I know you're in college and may not come back to camp next summer, but you will always be with me in spirit.

I sent the snapshot from our fishing trip. I hope you like it.

Love,

Danny

I couldn't hold back the tears. That little guy, that bright and sensitive kid, loved me. He felt I had influenced his life, and that truly touched me.

***

My mother mailed me a news clipping with a note later that week.

"I thought you'd be pleased to see the enclosed. I came across it by accident when I read the Sunday "*New York Times*.""

The article had a picture of Lawrence Geller and Elizabeth Curry. God she was a knockout.

"Prominent New York detective to wed art historian."

"Elizabeth Curry, an expert in the Impressionist Movement and a member of the staff at the Metropolitan Museum of Art will wed Lawrence Geller, a rising star in the NYPD.

The couple plans to wed in June and honeymoon in Italy."

I read the entire blurb and felt good. Mr. Geller had given my mother peace, and I knew she was fond of him.

Funny how things work out. I just couldn't get over the series of events that lead to finding Lilly. Maybe Mom was right. Maybe it was fate. Maybe I ended up at Camp Spenser to find her sister.

About the Author

B ruce Brodkin is an obstetrician living in Wellington, Florida with his wife, two dogs, and three cats. He has been practicing medicine for over four decades and now devotes himself to helping indigent, inner-city women. He is an avid reader and passionate about writing. "I have always been fascinated by the art of conveying thoughts, descriptions, and emotions through the written word." Aside from reading novels and historical fiction, Dr. Brodkin is "addicted" to crossword puzzles and word games, loves reading and analyzing bridge columns, plays some tennis and poker, and is a serious cook. He recently purchased a motor home for numerous RV trips in Florida. He hopes you enjoy this book-it was a labor of love.

16448978R00205

Made in the USA
Middletown, DE
15 December 2014